Praise for Jane Lark

"Jane Lark has proved what a writing talent she really is. This is an engrossing and telling read.… Be prepared to have your heart squeezed!"

BestChicklit.com

"An amazing book. It is dark and edgy yet flirtatious and even made me laugh. It's such a combination that made me not want to put my kindle down at all."

After the Final Chapters

"Dark, gritty and wholly mesmerizing, I Found You is a haunting and compelling read you will not easily forget!"

Bookish Jottings

"Emotional, romantic, and heartbreaking."

Imagine a World

JANE LARK

I love writing authentic, passionate and emotional love stories. I began my first novel, a historical, when I was sixteen, but life derailed me a bit when I started suffering with Ankylosing Spondylitis, so I didn't complete a novel until after I was thirty when I put it on my to do before I'm forty list. Now I love getting caught up in the lives and traumas of my characters, and I'm so thrilled to be giving my characters life in others' imaginations, especially when readers tell me they've read the characters just as I've tried to portray them.

You can follow me on Twitter @JaneLark.

I Need You

JANE LARK

Harper*Impulse* an imprint of
HarperCollins*Publishers* Ltd
77–85 Fulham Palace Road
Hammersmith, London W6 8JB

www.harpercollins.co.uk

A Paperback Original 2014

First published in Great Britain in ebook format by Harper*Impulse* 2014

A catalogue record for this book is
available from the British Library

ISBN: 9780008119058

Automatically produced by Atomik ePublisher from Easypress

I Need You

Guilt can eat away at you, but love can cut like a knife...

Wanting his best friend's girlfriend is a cliché Billy knows well – it's the tightrope he's walked for years.

But now Jason and Lindy have broken up and Billy can't help but be there for the girl he's loved from afar for so long. She's hurting. Fighting to find a road to the future, Lindy's heart hurts. She's trying to escape the truth, but Billy keeps making her face it – and it's ugly. How can she keep living when it feels like everything around her is made of glass and it could shatter at any moment? Her one constant is Billy. Only, rebound isn't his style and when Lindy starts to see him in a different light, he just can't trust her. He's no one's second best.

Chapter One

Billy

Jason's hand gripped my shoulder as we walked. "I'm glad you agreed to this. It's cool we're talking again."

Glancing sideways, I smiled. I felt good. We'd had a few beers, talked and the world seemed a lot better. We hadn't talked for months but he'd texted earlier and said, "Rach had the baby. A boy. We're calling him Saint. And, Billy, I need someone to go wet his head with… I want it to be you."

I'd wanted things to be right for half the months we hadn't talked; I was glad he'd made a move to fix it.

Stars pin-pricked the black sky above. But the street lamps lit the ground white and smothered the true splendor of the night sky. Out at the lake you could see millions, not thousands, of stars. They were up there, just hidden by the brighter, closer, streetlamps, and yet if you were in space, each star was a sun, and it would be loads brighter.

Jason swayed and his fingers gripped my shoulder firmer for a moment, before falling away.

We weren't that drunk, although I was drunk enough to be into philosophy—and I'd definitely had too many to drive, so we were walking home, and laughing like we hadn't laughed since we were kids.

"The store." Jason pointed over the road, like he announced *The White House*, on some tour bus journey.

I laughed. *The store* was his dad's. Nope. Jason's now. His dad had signed the business over. He'd been telling me all that shit earlier.

"Hey, why don't we go in and steal the spray paint, like we did when we were kids." Jason's words slurred together a little.

"'Cause you'd be stealing from yourself and we aren't kids."

He laughed. "I'll never forget Mr. Dent's red face when he charged out of his house…"

"And you had to do it to your dad's neighbor. The guy knew us, there was no getting away."

Jason grinned. "That guy shouldn't have taken my ball hostage."

"You're an idiot." A surge of the camaraderie we'd shared for years hit me as I looked over at the store.

A figure, a woman, sat slumped forward a little on the steps. "Shit! Jason! There's someone over there!" I looked left and right, checking the street was clear, then crossed.

"Shit." Jason ran past me. "It's Lindy!" His ex-fiancée, my ex one-night-stand, and the reason we'd not spoken for months.

Her head came up and her body swayed. She looked sick.

Pity, need and anger kicked my gut. I loved and hated her.

The bracelet on my wrist felt like it tightened, like a rope pulling me in her direction, with an urgency that pissed me off. I'd done enough chasing, but my stupid fucked-up heart refused to let her go.

Jason squatted down next to her, his hand on her shoulder. "Lind, are you okay?"

She wasn't. She was wasted. She'd had more to drink than either of us. Her head rolled on her shoulders.

She turned away from Jason, gripped the step with her hands, and threw up.

Attractive.

She and I had fallen out partly 'cause of her drinking. She'd stopped being herself.

She retched. Jason rubbed her back.

I stood there with my hands in my pockets, watching, like I'd always done. The leopard I'd had inked on my chest sank its claws of jealousy into my skin.

I still craved her. I hadn't spoken to her in months, but I still craved her. My best friend's girl had been my secret addiction for years.

"Lind, is someone coming to meet you? Have you got a ride home?"

When she stopped retching, she took a breath, wiped her mouth on her sleeve then glared at Jason. "Just fucking leave me alone! Don't touch me!" That was the other reason she and I had parted ways, as friends. We'd never really been anything else, but finally I'd given up on even that option—because when Jason had finished with her, he'd opened up her vicious streak. It could hit at anyone, anytime.

Jason lifted his hands, stood up and stepped back. "Okay. I'm not touching you. But you need to get home, and you're in no state to get there."

I stepped forward, my hands slipping out of my pockets. "Lindy, it's Billy…" I touched her shoulder, but her arm swiped out to knock me away. "Get off me, you're no better. Just leave me alone!" That wasn't an option.

I squatted down.

"I'll call her dad," Jason pulled his cell out of his pocket.

Great, her dad; a cop was not gonna be thrilled. This didn't look good.

"We're gonna help you. Jason's calling your dad."

Her gaze turned to me but she was too drunk to focus. "Don't call him."

I saw the cogs of thought shifting in her eyes as she realized I was with Jason. "We haven't got a choice, we've been drinking, we can't take you home."

Her face screwed up. "Why?" She pointed at Jason, who talked into his cell a few feet away.

"Yeah, Mr. Martin, we just found her, she's down at the store. She's drunk."

She was probably so drunk she'd need her stomach pumped. I'd never seen Lindy this bad. "Lind, how did you get down here?"

She mumbled something but I didn't understand it.

Jason came back over. "Your dad's on his way."

"Go away, Jason! Just fuck off and leave me alone!" Last time I'd seen her she'd been drunk and swearing at Jason.

She tried to stand.

She'd have fallen and smashed her head if I hadn't caught her. It was no state for a girl to be in. Hell, it was no state for anyone to be in.

She pushed me away and turned to be sick again. Jason came close to help her instead. But she shoved him away too. "You don't care! Just go away!"

But he did care, and I cared.

We looked at each other.

I felt like shit. The girl was beyond helping; she'd got hurt and broken, and it was like she was unfixable.

"Lindy, I never meant to hurt you. I'm sorry I did…" Jason tried to help her again.

She curled up on the steps, lying on them, her face buried in her crossed arms, looking isolated, even though we stood there.

It cut at me.

Jason straightened up and his hands slipped into his pockets.

I squatted back down. "Lind, it's okay. Your dad's coming. You're gonna be okay."

She didn't look like she'd ever be okay, though.

I rested a hand on her back. Her body jerked like she sobbed her heart out, but she wasn't making a sound.

I looked up at Jason. He pulled his cell out of his pocket. "I'm gonna call Mom, she or Dad can come and pick us up. Rach will get worried if I'm any later."

His wife had bipolar disorder and I'd never seen a guy as protective of anyone as he was of Rachel. I couldn't imagine what that must make Lindy feel. She'd been engaged to him until a little over six months ago—then he'd met Rachel.

The guy had back-pedaled at ninety miles an hour. Within two months he'd dumped Lindy, got married to Rachel, and she'd had a kid on the way. That was the baby's head we'd just been wetting.

Shit. Guilt punched my chest. Maybe I'd been disloyal. My fingers brushed back Lindy's hair.

She was too difficult, too angry, too judgmental, too everything. That was why I'd given up on her. But she'd been dating Jason for years, and in all those years we'd been friends too. We'd gone to college together.

Jason talked on his cell, walking a few feet away. I guess he'd told Rachel we'd found Lindy.

Tonight had been about a new start, drawing a line on the past, so Jason and I could move on, but we couldn't when Lindy was like this.

A siren screamed in the distance. It got closer. Shit. I stood up. Jason looked at me and said something to end his call, then slipped his cell back in his pocket.

The cop car sped up Main Street. Its wheels screeched when it pulled up on the parking lot.

Great. Her dad was angry.

The driver's door opened and Mr. Martin stepped out.

"What's been going on, boys?"

Jason answered, "We were walking home, Dwayne, and Billy spotted her on the steps—"

"You don't know what she drank?" Mr. Martin walked over.

I moved out of the way.

Lindy's parents had used to be really social; we lived in a small town, everyone knew everyone, but I hadn't seen them for months,

Jason looked down, his gaze scanning the parking lot near Lindy. "There's nothing around to say she's drunk anything."

Her dad squatted down and touched her shoulder. "Lindy?" I'd thought the way he'd pulled up, he'd be shouting at her, but his voice was more concern than frustration.

Jason and I had encountered his temper as kids, the day we'd stolen that spray can. It wasn't fun.

"Lindy?" he said more strongly when she didn't answer, or move. He straightened, then bent over her, turning her head. There was absolutely no sign she even knew he was there. He lifted one of her closed eyelids.

All there was beneath it was the white of her eye.

Shit. She was in a hell of a mess.

Mr. Martin sighed like he had the weight of the world on his shoulders as he straightened up and his hand reached to the breast pocket of his shirt. He pulled out a cell, turned his back on us and walked a few feet away.

I looked at Jason. He looked at me. I was sure he felt like I did. Neither of us could move on with Lindy like this.

"Miriam, I've got Lindy down here at the Macinlays' store… Yeah. Don't worry I'll sort it. You don't need to fret, it's not good for you, but just tell me what time she left home?"

I probably hadn't seen her mom for more than a year, let alone months.

"Okay. Go check her room would you, she's been drinking, or taken something, I wanna know which and what…"

There were a few minutes of silence.

"It's empty?"

"How many were in there, do you know?"

"Okay, I'll get her some help and call you. Don't worry, honey. It won't do you any good to worry, you know that, you have enough going on. She'll be okay." He sighed when he ended the call. He didn't look at Jason or me, just stared into the distance for a moment, then took a deep breath, like he was drawing on some reservoir of strength and patience.

He probably needed it for Lindy, if she'd been this messed-up for six months. No wonder her parents had gone into hiding.

Jason and I looked at each other, waiting on the verdict.

With his back to us, he lifted another cell from a clip on his pants pocket.

"Hi, I'm at the Macinlay store, in Main Street, I need an ambulance, quick time. It's an emergency. An overdose." He sighed again. "It's my girl…" There was so much pain in his voice it hit me hard, and I could see it hit Jason too.

We'd been celebrating a new life in the world… and Lindy… was so unhappy she'd tried to check out. Shit.

"What did she take?" Jason said, when Mr. Martin turned around, clipping the cell back onto his pocket.

He didn't answer straight off. Lindy probably wouldn't want Jason to know.

But she'd come down to his store… Fuck. Why?

"She's taken all the anti-depressant meds she's been prescribed." He walked back over to Lindy, and as he moved I caught something glinting in the light by the lamppost behind him. I walked over to get it as he bent over Lindy again.

"And this," I held it up. "A quarter bottle of vodka to wash them down with."

"Is she going to be okay?" Jason said, watching Mr. Martin slap her face as he braced it with the other hand…

"Those pills will make her dopey; they shouldn't kill her." He looked back at Jason. "But I'm no medic."

"She's been sick. It was like her stomach was empty."

"Yeah, well she took them three hours ago at least, that's when she left home."

Her dad sounded defeated. I'd never heard him talk like that. She had fucked up her parents not just herself.

"Lindy! Lindy, honey! Come on, you got to wake up!" He slapped her face and shook her.

Her hand swung out to stop him slapping her, but so weakly it was pathetic.

She'd been the center of attention at school, the leader of the girls, the one every guy wanted… Now she lay in a wasted heap. She'd hit a self-destruct button.

Lindy what the hell did you do to yourself?

Problem was Jason and I had both played our part in her destruction.

My heart ached and my lungs were too tight to get any air into.

Her dad kept talking to her and smacking her face. She mumbled something back at him, annoyed.

Jason's dad pulled up. He got out of his truck, then came over. "I've come to pick the boys up, Dwayne. How is she?"

Mr. Martin looked back at him. "Darren. I'd appreciate it, if you, and you boys…" He looked at us with a meaningful gaze, "say nothing to anyone about this."

I nodded, as Jason did. But I doubted Lindy would want us to be the keepers of her murky secret. She couldn't trust either of us.

The ambulance came along the street, siren screaming.

At least the street was lined with stores so no one peered around their curtains, watching.

Mr. Martin stood up as the medics got out. He told them in a low voice what she'd taken.

In minutes she was strapped on a gurney, then rolled into the ambulance. He didn't go with her. He said he had to get the car back to the station and find someone to cover his absence. He said he'd meet them at the hospital.

I wanted to go. But, it wasn't my place—she and I hadn't spoken for months so I could hardly force myself on her in an ambulance when she couldn't say, *fuck you, you bastard.*

My gaze and my heart followed the ambulance as it pulled away.

"Will you let me know how she is, Dwayne?" Jason said, before Mr. Martin got back in his car.

He stared at Jason for a moment, then nodded. "Thanks for trying to help her, and for calling me."

It didn't seem like he blamed Jason for Lindy falling apart.

I wondered if he knew about my part—if he blamed me. I blamed me. I owed her bad.

Jason's dad climbed back into the driver's seat of his truck. Jason stood beside it holding the passenger door. "You coming?"

"No. I'll walk. Clear my head."

Jason gave me a concerned look, then he let go of the door, walked over, held me and then smacked my shoulder. "It was good catching up. We'll do it again? We've made up now, right?"

"Right," I answered, fist bumping his hand. But my voice was subdued. Our reunion had been ruined.

Lindy

Had I hit my head? God, the pain was crazy. I opened my eyes. Where the hell was I? The walls in the room were white, the bed I was in metal, and the pillow like a pack of cement, and a smell of disinfectant hung in the air. I was in a hospital.

Oh my God, I'd taken the pills and survived and now I had to face everyone…

Shit. Guilt and embarrassment washed in with the force of a tsunami. I'd let Mom down. Dad would be heartbroken and disappointed. I'd hurt them.

I'd been wrapped up in pain last night, trapped in it, in the darkness, in chains of self-pity, I knew that, I could see the external perspective others saw—but *they* weren't in my head, in the dark.

It had stopped being just emotions months ago, maybe years ago, and become a jail cell. I couldn't see any end to this life sentence.

Everything had become scary. Others lived but I couldn't.

Then there had been Jason's news, everywhere—on Facebook, Twitter, Tumblr and Instagram. The baby had been born. The pictures were circulating like crazy.

Everyone we'd been at school with had shared them.

They'd called the kid, Saint. It was a crappy name.

People said he'd picked a name for the kid to grow into.

I rolled on to my side, tears running onto my cheeks and curled up hugging the cement-like pillow. A year ago, he'd been with me. I'd been engaged. I'd had a future, something to look to, now there was nothing.

I gave up my job, because I'd worked at the store with his dad.

His new girl, *his wife*, worked there now.

Life sucked. I hated fate. Why did it have to pick people out for bad things when they'd done nothing wrong? I'd given up believing in God or Karma or anything. Except angels… I hoped people came back after they died and watched over you.

I wiped the tears away.

There weren't any monitors in the room, so I couldn't have been so sick but I should probably buzz for a nurse and tell them I'd woken up.

I couldn't. Embarrassment hit too hard. Maybe fate had been kind to me in that, keeping me alive, but now I felt stupid for taking an overdose… I didn't know how I'd face Mom.

Billy

My thumb hovered over the send icon for the twentieth time today. Jason had texted yesterday to say he'd heard from Mr. Martin. Lindy was okay, just sleeping the drugs off in the hospital. He'd said she'd be out of action for a while.

I wanted to text her. But cowardice had a grip on my hand.

I switched the cell off, put it back in my pocket then got in the SUV to go to my next client.

I didn't think of her while I worked. I had to watch my client, to make sure he did the exercises right and didn't strain anything, and to count his repetitions.

But as soon as I left the guy my mind was back on Lindy.

Was she still in hospital?

Would she want me to text?

Did she know we'd been there?

Why the hell had she taken an overdose? Was it just a cry for help or had she really meant to end it?

How did she feel now?

The only way I was gonna get any answers was to text her. I took my cell out of the pocket of my sweat pants as I threw my backpack on the back seat of the SUV.

I got in with it gripped in my hand and sat there for a minute, looking at her picture. I'd taken it last year, after Jason had left for New York, when she and I had been hanging out a lot more, alone for the first time.

'Hey, Lindy, sorry I haven't been in touch. I should've been. How are you?' My thumb hovered over 'send', my heart pounding out a bass beat. I had to do this. She was never gonna break the ice between us and I couldn't stand feeling guilty anymore.

I didn't expect an immediate reply. But relief hit me just because I'd done the deed.

I threw my cell on the passenger seat, slipped the gear shift into drive and pulled my seatbelt on, then pressed my foot on the gas.

My cell rang ten minutes later. I was on the road into town. Flicking the indicator on, I pulled into the side and parked on the dirt on the edge.

I picked my cell up. She'd called.

My hand shaking like a douche, I called her back. The leather bracelet I had on my wrist declared its presence as it slid a little up my arm.

"Hi—"

"Hey, Lindy, you called me. How are you?"

"Are you driving?" Her voice was quiet and weak—it still cut through me like a blade.

"I've pulled over. You can talk if you want to talk. Why did you do it, Lind?"

"Because I feel like shit."

"Lind—"

"You don't need to tell me it was foolish, I know. And selfish, and pathetic, and… terrible… I… I'm sorry you saw me. Thank you for helping me. I think I'm gonna have a lot of apologizing to do." She took a breath. "Say sorry to Jason too." She hung up.

Shit, I smacked the wheel with the heel of my palm. Why did she have to be so frickin' hard? Why did she have to hurt me so much? Why the fuck did I have to care about her? I wished my asshole of a heart would fall for someone else.

Dammit.

I called her back. "Don't hang up on me. Are you still in the hospital?"

"Yeah."

"How long for?"

"They're going to let me go soon, but I've got to see a psychiatrist first."

"Well that sounds like a good idea. Look, I'm here for you. I know I've been a shit friend for the last few months, but, forget that, forgive me, and let's make up and be friends again."

She didn't say anything. I didn't push it. She had a lot to forgive me for.

"Why did you do it, Lind?"

"It was stupid, I—"

"This is me you're talking to, be honest. Why did you do it?"

She sighed. I imagined the air leaving her lips. I'd watched her sigh so many times in the last year or so.

"Because Jason had the baby and he's so happy, and his life is perfect and my life…" she started crying. We were back to what Lindy and I had always been—I was her confidante, her life coach, her safety net, her servant, her punch-bag… God the list went on. I was everything, without getting anything I wanted. *Her fucking fool.*

She took a breath. "I hear myself, and I hate me. I know why you and Jason and everyone else dislikes me because—"

"Everyone doesn't dislike you, Lind—" *and I love you..*

"It's okay if you do dislike me. I understand…"

"Well I don't, Lindy. I feel like I've let you down. I should've been around for you."

"My mess isn't your fault, Billy. You can't do a thing to change it."

I could. "I want to help you."

"You can't."

"Let me be your friend again, Lindy. Let me make things up to you."

"Billy, honestly, you have nothing to make up."

"Well, I can't stand seeing you like I did last night."

"Sorry."

I took a breath. "Do you want me to come and get you from the hospital later?"

"No, Dad'll come."

"Well then, text me when you get home and we'll organize something. I'll come over and see you."

"Okay." I could imagine her nodding, but I heard uncertainty in her voice.

"Lindy, you need a friend. That's all I'm offering, I promise. No expectations. No pressure." She didn't have anyone else. She'd dumped all her girlfriends when we'd gone to college. She'd been one hundred percent full-on all over Jason since we'd left school. She'd isolated herself and that's why we'd spent so much time together when he'd gone to New York. I was the only friend she had left. And that was torture.

"Okay, maybe. It depends how I feel."

I couldn't ask her for more.

"Don't do it again, Lind. And if you're tempted, call me…" But then I remembered the one night she had called me when it was late… Crap, I was not the one she'd pick to call.

"Bye." The word ran through me. It sounded final. I couldn't have stood it if anything had actually happened… if she'd succeeded and killed herself.

"Take care of yourself."

"Thanks, Billy. And you will say thank you to Jason? I know he didn't have to help me." She hung up.

But why wouldn't he have helped her? He'd just fallen in love with someone else; he didn't want to see her dead.

When we'd been at school she'd been full of vitality—energy—she'd always been smiling. When we hit college she's started changing.

Well, whatever, there was nothing I could do right now.

I slipped the SUV back into drive, looked in the side mirror, to check nothing was coming, waited until a vehicle passed, then pulled out and drove home.

Lindy

My finger kept hovering over Billy's name in the contacts list on my cell. I'd seen the psychiatrist and she'd told me I had to start seeing her regularly, to talk out all the stuff going on in my life—and in my head. Then I'd come home and all the stuff going on in my life had hit me in the face. There was an atmosphere in the house. Fear. Loneliness. Pain. Because Mom was sick—she couldn't help being sick—but I had to watch her wither away. It was too hard—I didn't want to let her go.

My head, belly and heart ached. Life had been hard and cruel for too long. That's why I'd tried to end it—I'd just been selfish for a moment. I'd tried to escape everything; Mom and Jason. His baby had been the thing that slid me over the Niagara Falls of despair, though.

But I wouldn't do it again. I'd learned my lesson. Guilt was heavy. Mom had looked hurt and disappointed and Dad hadn't been able to hide how bad he'd have felt if I'd succeeded.

If I was meant to die I'd have died. I was meant to face up to all this bullshit and keep going.

And Mom…

Now I could see all the stuff I'd been blind to.

I felt lousy, not because I'd swallowed a massive dose of happy pills, but because I'd hurt my parents.

Mom had every reason to bow out, and she didn't—I'd tried.

I needed someone to hold me. I felt sore inside.

I touched the screen. Billy's picture and details came up. He smiled at me out of the cell, with those warm dark-blue eyes of his. My thumb hovered over his number.

We hadn't spoken since just after New Year, until I'd called him the other day. But I had no one else. He'd been the closest person to me other than Jason for years.

I wished what had happened, hadn't…

I shut my eyes—I wish, I wish, I wish. If I had shiny red shoes on and clicked my heels, I wondered if I could go back in time, to when everything was right, then I could make sure everything stayed right.

That's what my life had become—wishes that things had not happened, wishes that they wouldn't, wishes that people would stay in my life.

I'd lost my friends. I'd given them up in favor of Jason, and look how that had ended. He'd moved on and left me behind. The only friend I'd had left was his best friend, until I'd messed that up too.

I was super-good at messing things up.

I sighed. Courage. I wasn't going to fix things with the only possible friend I had left unless I made the move. He'd taken the first step the other day when he'd texted me—now it was my turn. I just had to do it.

I tapped the icon.

"Hi." He answered, right off. My heart pounded.

"Billy?"

"You. Okay?"

"Yeah. I'm at home now. Dad picked me up at seven last night and brought me back. I appreciate you helping me out. I'm sorry you had to see me like that. I'm—"

"It's okay, Lind. I'm glad you're home. How did you get on with the shrink?"

When Jason had gone to New York, Billy had become my best friend, as well as Jason's. But then he'd ended up in the middle of everything when Jason had deserted me.

"Okay, I have to see someone regularly."

"Well that's probably a good thing isn't it?"

"Yeah."

"How are you today?"

"Down." I sighed. The psychiatrist had told me to be honest rather than keep things trapped inside. "Jason having the baby makes me feel like crap still. Is that a bad thing to admit? Only the woman at the hospital told me I should admit how I feel."

"Lind, if it's how you feel, it's how you feel, it just is. I know all this stuff is hard on you. I'm not judging you. Like I said the other day, I feel like I've let you down... Do you want me come around so we can talk?"

"Yeah." God the thought of having someone to talk to outside of my house, and everything weighing down the atmosphere in here, was wonderful. Like an oasis in a desert.

"I'll come over now then, yeah?"

"Yeah. You're not working?"

"I've got a gap between clients. I'll come over."

"Don't knock. Call me when you get here."

"Okay, I'll be there soon."

"Okay. Bye."

"Bye, Lind. See you in a while."

"Yeah."

I fell back on my bed, lying on my back, with my cell still in my hand and stared up at the ceiling. Tears blurred the white fluffy clouds Dad had painted against the blue sky when I'd been a kid. The tears wouldn't stop. I'd cried loads since I'd woken up in the hospital.

It was twenty minutes after I'd spoken to Billy that I got the second call.

"Hi, I'm parked outside your house. Do you want me to knock?"

"No, stay there, I'll come out." I ended the call, wiped my eyes, and stood, then glanced in the mirror. I looked like a ghost, pale and pasty. I hadn't gone out of my room yet. I sat down to put some makeup on to hide the sorry-looking state of my face. I hated looking at myself in mirrors but I had to face that ugly girl to put on the mask I hid her behind.

Mom was in her chair in the living room. "I'm going outside." Guilt made me feel I had to tell her everything so she didn't worry I was doing something stupid.

"Why?"

"Billy's outside, I'm just going to sit in his car and talk to him."

"Lindy, love, you can bring him in…" She felt guilty too. Mom didn't really want anyone in the house, she'd said so, anyone who saw her would know she was sick, and she didn't want anyone to know—but after what I'd done, she was worried about it hurting me. It made me feel worse.

"It's okay, I'd rather speak to him outside. We won't go anywhere."

"Darling—"

"Sorry. I just need to talk to him, then I'll be back in." I knew what she wanted to say, I didn't have to explain myself—but then I knew she was afraid I'd try to kill myself again. "You can look out the window if you want."

"Lindy…" My name was said on a sad, weak, sigh. She needed to know I was okay, but she didn't want to have to know.

I'd messed everything up by taking an overdose. I don't even really know why I'd done it. It's just, that night, everything had seemed too much, and I'd had a drink, and escape and relief had opened up like a window I could jump through. I'd seen freedom from the pain ripping my soul apart, and I'd taken the chance.

But if I'd succeeded it wouldn't have been an end to anything; it would have just made things worse for the people I'd left behind.

Fate had saved me from doing that.

But now I had no choice. I had to cope.

I turned, opened the door and went out.

Billy's SUV was parked on the other side of the road. Nothing was coming up the street. I crossed over and went around to the passenger door, my heart racing as if someone was beating a crazy drum solo on it. "Hi." I climbed up into the passenger seat.

"Lindy…" He'd freed his seatbelt already, and now he twisted sideways. He had long, loose shorts on.

We hadn't spoken properly for so long—I didn't really know what to say.

I pulled the door shut, anxious and nervous, and stared ahead, avoiding looking at him.

"You okay? Do you want me to drive somewhere?"

"No."

"Do you want to talk?"

Yeah. So much. Tears gathered in the back of my throat, hurting. I didn't look at him. I'd cry.

My hands were in my lap. He leaned over and gripped one of them. "Lindy, I'm here."

Oh Lord, the tears tumbled, rolling down my cheeks, and I was sobbing as his grip on my hand pulled me over, and he moved forward. Then his arms came around me, holding me tight.

"I'm sorry… I didn't realize how bad you felt. I wish… God, I wish I'd handled things better. I let you down."

I shook my head and looked at him. "It's okay. It's not your fault. It's nothing to do with you." I had a lot of people to apologize to. Surviving had made me see two things; I had to change and I was meant to accept things and just get on with it—like Mom did. But doing that wasn't easy.

"I don't know what to say." His dark-blue eyes were warm and deep with feeling.

I sighed. I didn't know what to say either. All I knew was that I hurt too much, and I didn't know how to escape it.

"Do you want to get away?"

"What?"

"I could drive you out to the coast somewhere, once I've had time to book something, and you've had time to pack…"

I wanted to hug him back like he'd just hugged me—hard and

tight—with gratitude and relief.

"We could run away together for a couple of weeks and not tell anyone where we're going. No Jason. No baby. And no expectations from me, I swear. We'll just be friends. I want you to be happy."

I took a breath. I didn't know what to say. What about Mom? And then there was my psychiatrist. And… "I don't know."

His hand gripped mine hard; the emotion in his eyes shining bright. "Lindy, let me make this up to you. I've been a shit friend for the last six months, and you need a friend—"

I did… "But you were with Jason." My pitch came out as an accusation; any thought of Jason still raised a bitter taste in my mouth.

"You remember?" Guilt passed over his face.

"Why were you with him?"

His skin reddened, like he was going to confess something awful. "He'd called me that day. The day Rach had the baby."

The day I'd overdosed.

"He asked me to wet the baby's head with him and put everything behind us…" Billy's eyes looked into mine as if he tried to judge my thoughts. "We've made up, Lind… and then we saw you and I knew I could never move on until you did too."

All the pain trapped inside me raced to the surface. I couldn't. That wasn't a choice I had.

Tears rolled down my cheeks.

I wish…

Billy leaned over and his arms came around me. I rested my head on his shoulder, my arms about his neck. I needed someone to hug.

Billy's arms and shoulders were really muscular. His body mass was double the size of Jason's. He'd played football at school and college, and he'd studied sports and become a personal trainer. All that strength and solidity was reassuring.

But that's what had got me into all the bullshit I'd fallen into back in the fall.

But I didn't want to think of that. I just let him hold me while I reveled in the comfort and security.

Billy gave good hugs.

This was worth so much more than any conversation on a psychiatrist's couch, or medication. Relief bloomed inside me, aching.

I'd needed to be held by someone outside my family.

His fingers combed through my hair. "Did you mean to end it, or were you crying out for help?"

I didn't lift my head and didn't answer. The ache of comfort was gone and instead the forest fire of guilt flared. I wouldn't admit the truth; the truth was too awful. I didn't have a good reason to give in.

The psychiatrist had told me, "Everyone has burdens to carry, and you shouldn't feel guilty." She'd said, "It's stopped being about choice, the chemicals in your body are all muddled up so you can't think straight." I was on happy pills, and counseling now, and she'd promised me I'd feel better and I'd get out the other side.

I didn't want to.

"Why did you go to Jason's store…?" Billy's fingers ran through my hair. I felt like a kid being comforted. It took me back years; to the years I'd been happy.

Why? I didn't answer. He probably thought it was for revenge. It wasn't. My life had been there, I'd worked there for years, been Jason's second half for years.

Who was I now? What was there to do?

"I'm sorry, Lindy. If you let me help, I'll make everything up to you."

He had nothing to make up, not really, everything that had gone wrong between him and me was my fault.

"Do you want to get away for a while? Just for a couple of weeks even? I swear to God, there'll be nothing in it. No expectation on my part at all."

I needed help. I needed to escape. Just until I could get back on track. "Yeah."

His hands gripped my shoulders and moved me back. He looked like he didn't believe what I'd said. "Yeah?" His voice questioned.

"Yeah." I nodded, my vision clouding with tears. I needed to go somewhere and pretend my life wasn't what it was—for a short vacation. "I'll have to speak to the psychiatrist, though. When do you want to go?"

He smiled. Billy was so nice, his heart shone right out of his eyes along with his smile. He hurt for me. We'd been close, before everything went wrong. This was him trying to put it right again. But nothing could ever be right.

Tears rolled onto my cheeks as the flames of guilt flickered. Mom…

Billy held me against his chest. His big, solid arms fencing me in and holding the world out.

I felt better, like I had in the fall… *And look where that had got us.*

I pulled away, looking at the house. Mom must be at the window. This wasn't her fault.

"What about Saturday, two weeks' time?" Billy's voice came out husky. "I'll cancel my client appointments. You get everything agreed with the hospital and your Mom and Dad, and we'll just get out of here for a bit, so you can escape all this shit?"

"Thank you, Billy. You're a good guy, you know that?"

He gave me an apologetic smile. "We both know that's not true. But I will be now. I swear, Lind, just friends…"

"I better go back in." I wiped my face on my sleeve, trying to wipe off the tracks of tears so Mom wouldn't see them, but it wiped my foundation off too. I hoped my mascara hadn't run. "Text me."

"I'll let you know what time I'll pick you up."

"Okay." I tried to smile, then turned away, opened the door and slipped out of his SUV. I didn't look back as I crossed the road and ran up to the house.

When I let myself in, Mom stood by the window. I knew she'd been watching.

"You okay?" she asked.

I nodded, "Yeah." But I didn't stay in the living room. I walked on to my room, threw myself face-down on the bed and sobbed some more.

I was so messed-up and selfish.

Billy didn't need the burden of a broken girl, I shouldn't have said yes. He'd been ready to move on.

The forest fire of guilt flared and consumed everything else.

Billy

I slipped the SUV into drive and pulled away, my heart a boulder in my chest.

What that girl did to me! If Jason knew half the things I'd imagined over the last five years he wouldn't have called me to meet up and wet his kid's head.

Fuck.

Jason and I had messed her up.

This was a pile of shit.

When I walked in the door back home a lot later than I'd usually come in, my kid sister, Eva, called, "Hey, Billy!"

"Hey, Eva." I lifted a hand.

"Where have you been?" Mom asked as I walked through the living room.

"At the gym."

"You work out all day. You can't have spent that long at the gym. You're hiding something! I bet you've got a girl!" Eva's passion in life was teasing me. But underneath it she loved having a much older brother to flaunt before her friends, and catch rides off of. She always gloated when I drove her to her friends' parties. But she wasn't a kid anymore, she was fifteen. "Don't tell me you've finally given up on winning Lindy?"

I made a face at her. My family knew my trouble. In a bad moment I'd said something to Dad a couple of years ago and from then on my whole family had been a part of my secret Lindy addiction. "Nope, I saw her today."

"Billy! I thought you'd stopped that."

"I'm taking her away for a couple of weeks."

"OMG!" Eva screamed.

"Is that a good thing?" Mom stood up.

"When you and that girl get together, it always ends badly, Billy." Dad threw in his cent without moving from his armchair.

"Thanks for the enthusiasm." I shrugged and turned away, but Eva grabbed my arm and then hugged me.

"I hope things work out. I'll be glad for you if they do." I gave her a squeeze then let her slip away.

"As will I," Mom said, smiling at me.

My gaze shifted around them all. "Except this isn't like that. It's just as friends…"

Eva rolled her eyes. "Lindy is so blind."

Mom kept smiling.

I turned away and headed for my room.

I scanned through my calendar and called clients to tell them something personal had come up; the stretched and worn leather band on my wrist sliding up and down.

I always wondered what the hell I'd do if it broke. It was my talisman.

The fingers of my other hand span it around my wrist a couple of times as I waited while a call rang.

I knew where I was gonna take her. To the place I'd run to every summer for years. It had started the summer we'd left high school.

There was no answer. I ended the call, but then my cell vibrated.

"Lindy's back home." The message was from Jason.

"I know, I went 'round to see her."

"She okay?"

"Nope, quiet and crying."

"Tell her sorry. And tell her Rach and me are thinking of her. We didn't want her to get hurt."

"She said to tell you sorry too. She's sorry we saw her like that.

She said she felt guilty about getting us caught up in it."

He didn't answer for a minute, but then came back and said. "Tell her it's okay. I get it. I know I messed her around. But tell her I hope she can be happy."

I sighed. So did I. "I'll tell her. Do you still want to go out for a drink again next week?"

"Shit, yeah, I need another night out to get over that one. When?"

"Thursday?"

"Okay."

The place I was gonna take Lindy to was beautiful. You could stay right on the beach in an apartment, listen the ocean and watch the waves roll up on the sand. It was the sort of escapism Lindy needed to put her vibes right.

I looked at my cell, and my thumb instinctively slid up Lindy's image. "Hey. I'm gonna take you to a place I know on the coast. It's perfect for chilling out. You'll get caught up in the awesomeness of the universe and forget about yourself."

While I waited for a reply I booked the accommodation. I'd cancel the rest of my appointments later. I booked adjacent apartments.

"That sounds amazing."

"Cool."

":-) Shall I transfer my share of the money to you?'

"Lind you're not paying. I asked you. I owe you."

"You don't owe me anything. But thanks if you'll pay. I'm not earning."

'I know. Maybe when we're out there we can start working on what new job you feel like doing."

":/ When I feel better, Billy."

"Yeah. Sorry I'm pushing. Too much. Too soon. One step, Lind. By the way, Jason said he's sorry too, and that he and Rachel wish you well. He wants you to be happy. That's what we all want."

"Thanks."

The thanks seemed final and I didn't know what to say next. My fingers tapped the desk, beating out a rhythm.

I wanted to call. I had a feeling she was crying. I shouldn't have mentioned Jason. I didn't call though 'cause I'd grown a coward's streak since the fall. I didn't want to hear her tell me how she missed him and how much she still loved him.

Guilt curled up in a hard ball in my belly.

Why the fuck was she speaking to me? She shouldn't be.

Why the frick was she going away with me?

The girl was crazy.

This could be the stupidest idea, I'd ever had.

Chapter Two

Billy

"You're sure everything is squared off with the hospital, Lind. You've got your meds…"

She nodded, but she was scaring me, her hands trembled as I took her case and put it in the back of the SUV, next to my surfboard.

Her dad stood on their porch, in his uniform; it meant he'd ducked off work to come back and say goodbye to her. He watched us, like he didn't want her to go.

He certainly wouldn't want her to go if he knew the truth. But he didn't. No one did except me and Lindy.

I hadn't seen her Mom. That was weird because she didn't work. I'd have thought she'd have come outside to say a final goodbye to Lindy.

"Is that everything?" I asked. Lindy nodded, her blue eyes glittering with tears.

"No, I forgot my purse." She turned away and ran back up the path into the house.

This was weird.

I slipped my hands into my pants pockets as Mr. Martin came down.

"If she wants to come home, you'll bring her back right away?"

"Yeah." Of course I would.

"Well, you look out for her. She's my girl, and she's all I've got."

"Yeah, Mr. Martin." He knew I'd been hanging around her a lot last fall; he knew we'd been friends for years. I bet he wondered why I'd stopped hanging around and why we hadn't spoken for months. I was glad he didn't know.

Lindy came hurrying back out of the house, her purse swinging in her hand.

"Did you say good-bye to Mom?" Her dad asked.

"Yeah." She hugged him, firmly. He kissed her hair.

The guy had scared the hell out of me when I was kid, but now all his scariness looked hollow. Lindy had hurt him when she'd chosen to press the eject button. He looked in pain. That was a new look for Mr. Martin.

"You'll call me if anything happens, Dad, won't you? Don't wait. I'd hate not to get back…"

What was it with getting back? We hadn't even gone yet. I suppose her family must be cautious now, though. Maybe they didn't trust her not to try it again. I'd have to watch her when we were away.

Her dad nodded. Tears shining in his eyes. Hell, I'd never thought I'd see that.

I turned away and got in the SUV. I didn't think he'd welcome me watching him, but in the side mirror, I saw him give her a kiss on the cheek. Then he walked her to the passenger door, opened it and held it while she climbed in.

He shut it only after she'd settled and pulled her seatbelt over.

I pushed the button so the window went down and they could talk.

My abs gripped tight with nerves and my belly rumbled. I hadn't eaten this morning. I was too nervous about how this was gonna go down. My forearm rested on the wheel, the leather braid hanging loose on my wrist. That thing was so much a part of who I was.

My fingers started tapping on the dashboard.

"Ready?" she asked.

I looked over at her. Her dad stepped back from the window as she looked at me.

Shit, she probably thought me tapping the dashboard had been telling her dad to hurry up. It wasn't. It was just a habit.

My other hand gripped the gear shift.

I was ready, though. I wanted to get away from her house. There was a ton of bad energy coming from it. I could feel it everywhere in the air around her.

I smiled and slipped my arm off the wheel. "Yeah. Mr. Martin."

She looked at him. "I'll call you when we get there and I'll call you every night. I promise. Don't worry about me. You'll make me feel guilty if you do. And tell Mom I love her… I'm really sorry."

"Honey…" He came forward again and leaned in through the window to grip her hand. "Your mother understands. She's not angry, or hurt, or anything. She just wants you to be okay."

Lindy nodded, tears rolling down her cheeks.

No matter how nervous I was. Or how awkward it felt. This was right. She needed to get out of here for a while.

"I'll be okay," she whispered. "But I feel selfish. Good-bye." She leaned and kissed his cheek. Then her dad stepped back and finally we could go.

My heart started pumping on hyper-drive, as I slid the gear shift down and pulled away, super- cautious not to over rev the engine with her dad watching.

I glanced at her as I drove up the street. "Did you eat or are we stopping for breakfast?"

She looked at me, a broken heart in her eyes, tears tracking down her cheeks. She wiped them away with a sniff. "Sorry, I'm going to try and not be bad company. But I don't want to eat. I'm not hungry. How long is it gonna take to get there?"

"A couple of hours." I looked back at the road. "We can settle in, then get lunch."

She laughed, a low half-choking sound that was almost a sob.

"I forgot how hungry you get. You can stop for breakfast if you want…"

I threw her a smile. "Sorry, you'll have to accommodate my appetite. I don't eat like a bird like you do, but I can wait 'til lunch."

She'd fed me and Jason through most of our college years. In the shared apartment we'd had. The couple and the spare-part best friend—three had definitely been a crowd. But I'd still hung around them. I bet people had thought it weird.

I was weird.

Fucking crazy!

I'd always wondered if Jason knew. But he hadn't said anything the other night when we'd got everything out in the open. I figured he'd have said something then if he'd known.

"I can't believe you still wear that thing." She leaned over and flicked the leather bracelet as my hand gripped the wheel.

How the hell did she not know?

I glanced at her, giving her a twisted, guilty smile, as something hard grabbed my heart. "Yeah."

"I made you that years ago."

"I'm just lazy, I can't be bothered to cut it off." I let a fake sound of amusement slip from my throat, acting as if it was nothing—like I had every other time she'd mentioned it.

She'd made it at high school. It had been the thing all the girls were doing at the time, braiding these silly leather bracelets and threading beads into them. It was before she'd been seeing Jason. We'd been fifteen.

Yeah, I had been wearing it that long. Pining over a girl that wasn't mine.

But shit I can still remember the feel of her gentle fingers touching me as she'd tied it off, and it had done stuff to my cock. I'd liked her before, but that was the day she'd got me. It was like her fingers had touched my heart too. I'd had this burning need for her ever since.

I should cut the thing off.

I glanced over at her. Her hands were in her lap and she stared ahead. I didn't know what to say to her. I was too anxious to hold a meaningless conversation and I didn't want to quiz her, 'cause I was taking her away to forget all the stuff that made her feel bad.

I said a few things and she answered, but then I couldn't think of anything to add. She said some things and I nodded, not knowing what to say back.

In the end we were quiet most of the drive.

I was relieved when I finally pulled up in the apartments' parking lot on the coast.

"Wow, this is nice."

The ocean rolled up onto the miles of beach before the parking lot. This place just calmed me. I'd come here the summer we'd left high school and it had been the best therapy. This beach and the ocean was my psychiatrist. I'd come back every summer since.

I hoped it was gonna work for her too.

I freed the door and as it opened the sound of the ocean swept into the SUV.

I looked at Lindy.

She was wide-eyed, watching the beach.

"Let's go get our keys. I'll get our stuff later."

She looked at me, uncertainty creeping into her eyes, but she nodded.

I wanted to grip her hand as we walked across the parking lot. There was a whole minefield of protective energy bubbling around inside me. But it had blown up in my face before. I was steering clear of too much touching.

The thing with Lindy was she was so tiny it made me want to just put my arms around her and wrap her up. She was like a precious, breakable doll, five-two, to my six-one.

I glanced over at her. The ocean breeze flicked her wavy blonde hair against the curve of her cheek.

Her fingers tucked her hair behind her ear.

I'd wanted to do that for her. There was a hard need to touch her in my belly. But I'd spent years ignoring that instinct. That was nothing new.

She didn't look at me. She looked ahead at the apartment block.

She'd won beauty pageants as a kid. Her Mom had been into all that shit, driving her to loads of contests and Lindy did have the look for that sort of thing, perfect symmetry.

At high school she'd been full of confidence. At college that had died for some reason.

She glanced at me, her blue eyes seeming bluer under the clear sky.

"I've ordered adjacent places, is that okay? I can ask them to change them if you want?"

"No, that's okay." She nodded.

The apartments were stacked and set out in rows spread along the edge of the beach. The guy at the desk said ours were on the top floor. The place was something between a hotel, a motel and cabins, and the rooms 'slash' apartments were accessed via a long hallway, with stairs at either end of the block.

When we got up there, I slid the card key through the lock, then stepped back and shoved the door open for her to go in. "You can have this one."

It had a small kitchen and a sofa that turned into a bed. But most importantly, at the end of the room was a big window that looked out on the ocean. It had a balcony too.

"I'll go get your stuff." I left her in her room. But before I went back down to the SUV, I went into mine.

Shit. I combed a hand through my hair, then realized I'd fucked it up, and rubbed it so it spiked again.

It was going to be a hell of a couple of weeks.

I walked over and slid the glass door to the balcony back, letting in the soothing sound of the ocean. It pulled me outside.

Lindy stood out there, on her balcony, gripping the wooden rail and looking at the ocean. I turned my back on it and rested my butt against the rail. "You okay?"

"Yeah, just taking in the air."

"Look, Lind—"

"I'm not in the mood to talk."

Well, there was probably nothing I could say that would make anything better anyway. "I'll go get our things."

I dumped mine in my room, then went round to her door and knocked. She opened it, but stood there, stopping me from going in.

"Here you are." I dropped her case and backpack just inside the door. "Are you ready for something to eat? We could walk downtown and then walk along the beach if you want?" I leaned against the door jamb, watching her, waiting on her answer.

I'd spent hours in this position, on the border to Lindy's and Jason's bedroom at college, talking to one or the other.

"Yeah, I can unpack later." She turned away, knocking the door open wider, before walking back into her room.

I stayed where I was. "Did you call your dad to say we got here okay?"

"Yeah."

"He's okay with it?"

She turned, her eyes flashing impatience, a little of the real Lindy shining through the dark clouds hanging over her. Like a beam of intense sunlight catching me off-guard and blinding me.

"He may be a cop, but he doesn't order me about. I'm twenty-two. I can do whatever."

Yep, she could. When she was herself, she always did whatever she wanted, with a just-deal-with-it attitude. That attitude had made Jason go silent. He'd always let her have her way.

I lifted my weight off the door frame.

"You ready to go then?"

"Yeah."

When she came out of the room, my hand hovered behind her. I had no need to touch her; it would have been strange to do it and yet it felt strange walking down the hall not touching her.

Lindy barely came to my shoulder.

I'd picked her up once or twice, messing around, and she was as light as anything. So frickin' tiny.

Her thick blond hair flowed in waves about her shoulders as she moved. My hand itched to touch that. Literally.

Crap.

I lifted my hand to touch her shoulder. I didn't. Instead I slipped my hands into the back pockets of my pants to keep them tamed.

The way out from our apartments was a wide wooden staircase, leading down from the third floor.

The view was amazing, the beach and ocean stretching into the distance. I breathed the salt air in. It felt good. Like it healed.

"Wow." She smiled at me.

I hoped the healing would work for her. "Just being by the coast always makes me feel different, better somehow, lifts the weight off my shoulders—"

"What weight have you got on your shoulders?" Yep, the old snappy Lindy was coming back.

I didn't answer, and that killed the conversation.

But, it wasn't really the old Lindy. It was just the pre-overdose Lindy. College Lindy. That wasn't the girl I'd fallen for originally. She'd been pushy and self-confident at high school… but not snappy and not the bitch she could be at times. Those elements had slipped in while we were at college.

We didn't talk much the rest of the way into town, but we'd been friends long enough that our friendship could take silence.

When we got there, though, we wasted half an hour arguing over which restaurant to stop in.

She wasn't hungry. I was ravenous.

In the end we chose a place that did the salad she wanted and a huge portion of fried chicken that would do me.

She was quiet again when we sat down.

"What do you wanna do this afternoon?"

Her head came up. She'd been looking at her food, but not

eating much of it. Her gaze hit mine. "You said we'd go for a walk along the beach."

"Well, I just wanted to check that's what you want, Lind. You haven't said much; you might've just wanted to go back and be on your own."

"I didn't come here to be on my own, did I? I could be on my own at home." There was sore-headed Lind again. The bitch.

I took a breath, to call her out—

"So you and Jason have patched everything up. Are you buddies again?"

That's why she'd been quiet. She'd been spinning that around in her head.

I wondered how it made her feel. Betrayed by him? And then betrayed by me? But I was friends with Jason again, and I wanted to be his friend. I wasn't gonna change that even if she asked me to. "Yes." I lifted an eyebrow, waiting on her judgment.

"So everything's forgotten?"

Not everything. "Lind, don't. I like him. He's been like a brother most of my life. I want him around." A brother whose girl I've wanted to fuck for years, but hey.

Her lips compressed as anger flashed in her eyes, but she didn't vent it at me.

Looking down at her salad, she stabbed a piece of chicken with her fork. Maybe she imagined it as part of Jason's anatomy—or mine.

"Have you seen it?"

"It?"

"The baby?"

"*The baby* is called Saint, and, yeah, I went 'round to Jason's parents' one night this week, before we went for a drink, and saw Rach and the kid."

"Saint's a stupid name." She stabbed a piece of tomato.

Annoyance and exasperation rippled inside me as I took a bite out of a piece of fried chicken.

This is what I needed to fix for her. I hadn't only brought her here to get her away. I wanted to smash open this fucking ball of anger she wrapped herself up in. It had been there for years, but not when we were kids. It wasn't who she was, it was what she'd become. The only way she'd be happy was to be who she'd been at high school. I had no idea why she'd changed.

I leaned back, watching her. "The baby isn't going anywhere when we go back, you know. It's you who has to learn to live with Rach and Saint in the town, and Jason being with them. Not the other way around."

She glared at me, standing up and dropping her fork on the tray. Then without a word she turned and walked out.

Cool, we'd been here a couple of hours and we'd clashed already. I pulled some dollar bills out of my pocket and left them on the table to get the check, then followed her.

She'd headed toward the beach. I ran to catch up with her and grabbed her feeble little bicep to stop her. Then made her turn and look at me.

"I said I'd get you away, give you chance to breathe out here. But I'm not gonna lie to you, Lind, or put up with your bad moods. I'm not Jason. Don't expect me to just let you bite. I'll bite back."

I wasn't telling her anything she didn't know. At college we'd had some really loud arguments. The neighbors had bashed on the wall a few times to shut us up. I'd never put up with her shit like Jason did, and she knew it. We were both fire and we'd flare quick and fast at each other.

Jason—he was calm, cooling water.

But we'd always been okay when the air cleared, and if she'd had problems and needed to talk, or just moan and shout, she'd always come to me, not him… Cause Jason would either have a solution or walk away from an argument and sometimes people like us just needed to shout.

I sighed, letting her go. My fingers lifted and ran through my hair. Shit. I ruffled it when I remembered I'd knocked it flat.

Her coming to me had been the beginning of how everything had got messed up between us. A year ago, when Jason had gone to New York to live and left her behind... It had been the first time he'd stood up to her and not just done what she wanted. She'd hated that. So who had she come to, to moan and shout about it? Me.

She turned away and started walking again, her movement stiff with anger.

"You're gonna have to get over him!" I called after her, following.

She headed on down to the beach. I followed a dozen steps behind her, my fingers now in my front pockets.

Maybe this had been a stupid idea...

I held back a bit more, to give her some space, and let her go on ahead alone and storm her anger out. She'd calm down soon.

When I sauntered onto the beach a while after I'd seen her walk down there, I spotted her about two hundred yards on. She'd taken her shoes off and held them in her hand, and she was heading toward the ocean.

The sand worked its way into my sneakers. I stopped and toed them off, then carried on, holding them in my hand. My feet sank in the warm sand. The air was way cooler than the sand. But the sun's heat seeped into the ground while the breeze from the cold ocean stopped the air feeling so warm.

Lindy was a silhouette in the distance, outlined by the waves rolling in.

I hit the compact, flat, wet sand. It oozed under my feet. The tide was out, so I was still a long way off where she stood.

When I caught her up, she was looking at the last ripples of the waves wash over her bare feet.

She stepped back a couple of paces with a little run, dodging a higher one as I got near her.

"Hey."

She walked into the ripples of a different low wave, ignoring me.

She didn't look angry anymore, just thoughtful, like not only had she walked away, but her mind had left me behind.

That was my problem. She was on my mind constantly and I think I was hardly ever on hers. "Lind?"

She glanced at me, her eyes really blue out here where the sky and ocean reflected in them.

I gripped her arm gently, so she couldn't run away from this again. "I'm sorry, but that's it now. He's never gonna come back to you. He's got a new life. You've got to move on too." I was glad she didn't try to pull loose or look away. "I've got you away from there. You've got two weeks. But in these two weeks, Lind, you've got to let him go. For your sake, not his, or anyone else's. Because you need to start your life over without Jason."

She didn't answer.

Shit. A wave rolled in, a lot bigger than the last. It washed right at us, sweeping up and swilling about our legs, over our jeans, coming over my knees and even higher. The water was freezing, like bathing in firckin' ice.

Lindy screamed, trying to rush backwards, but stumbling, just as I felt the ocean dragging the sand out from beneath my feet, sucking it away as the wave headed back out.

With my shoes gripped in one hand, I only had the other to save her. I caught her arm but she'd lost balance. She went down, tumbling into the water as it pulled away, dragging the wet sand from all around her, pulling it down the beach and out toward the ocean.

She laughed and grabbed my arm, then pulled on me to get up. But I was off-balance too, as the sand got dragged out from under my feet...

"Shit."

I landed on my hip, on the far side of her, my legs all tangled up with hers as the water swilled away, leaving us there like a couple of fish flapping on the sand.

She still laughed, her head on the ground, her hair in the sand. It was a laugh-or-cry moment for her. I was glad she'd chosen laughter. I hadn't heard her laugh for months.

As much as we'd used to shout at each other in college we'd used to laugh a lot too. We always used to piss Jason off when we'd be arguing one minute and then laughing the next. This was us. This was how we were.

The girl was meant for me.

Why the fuck had she never been able to see it?

She needed my fire, like I needed hers.

She looked at me, her head turning as she stopped laughing.

I smiled when her blue eyes looked right into me and my fingers stroked her sticky, salty, damp hair from her forehead. "Two weeks, Lind. Promise me? Two weeks to mourn him, then let him go, and go back and make a life for yourself without him." I didn't expect her to pick me instead. We'd travelled that road and it hadn't worked out...

If she was ever gonna be into me, she'd have known it by now. But I was into her and I couldn't bear to see her hurting. It had to end, and if I could do nothing else for her, then I'd get her over it and help her start again.

But fuck, it was going to hurt me once she'd pulled herself together and moved on to someone else.

I sat up. "Damned sneaker waves!"

"If that was a sneaker it was a wimp..." She laughed as she sat up too.

"I'm not on about that one..." There was another one coming in, a huge one.

"Ahh," she screamed, but she laughed as she struggled to get up.

It rolled in at a fast pace, foaming and frothing, we were on our feet, but it crashed into us, coming up to my waist.

I caught her up off her feet, gripping her in one arm, and stepping off the shifting sand as it tried to drag us with it, while holding my sneakers up above the water.

When the wave swept back out, I got us away from the water and set her on her feet.

"Oh my God." Her laughter turned to horror as she caught her breath, looking at me, her shoes lifting to point at me. "You look a mess—"

"So do you." I lifted one brow at her.

"Oh my God, my hair…" Her hand touched it. "We better go back."

Our jeans clung like a second skin and the white sleeveless tee Lindy had on beneath her open sweater had me swallowing. Every contour of her stomach and chest was visible through the translucent cotton, as well as the pale-pink lacy bra her nipples showed through. She'd be freezing when the shock wore off.

Shit. I looked up, then laughed. Her hair was matted with salt and sand, and stuck to her head in rats' tails.

Her shoes hit my shoulder. "Don't laugh at me!"

I still laughed. "Come on. You need a shower. You're all sandy."

"You douche," she said as she turned away.

Lindy

"Two weeks to mourn him, then let him go, and go back and make a life for yourself."

I sighed, Billy was right. I knew that.

I let the water run over my head as I rinsed my hair under the shower.

Forget him.

I wish I could.

I wish my heart wasn't empty. I wish my soul didn't feel like I was dead and in Hell. I longed to let Jason go, because then maybe I could feel like a whole person again, not like someone with an arm cut off. Not like discarded trash.

But forgetting Jason was hard when I hurt so much and I'd needed someone. He was meant to be here. To help me.

My tears mingled with the water from the shower. I'd cried every day for months. I wanted to stop crying. But how could I get over him? How could I work out what to do without him?

We lived in a small town. I walked past his shop all the time and saw the girl he'd dumped me for with him, standing where I used to. A constant reminder that I wasn't good enough.

Leaning back against the tiles, I let the tears come and the water wash them away. Then I slid down to the floor, sitting with my knees bent, my hands gripping in my hair, as hurt roared through me.

Why was life so unfair? Why did all this have to happen to us? Why had Jason let me down when I'd needed him?

I needed him…

I wish someone would take this pain away.

That was why I'd taken the pills. Because the pain in my head was too much.

But that had been unfair—selfish and mean. I hadn't been thinking properly.

Mom.

I was a coward. She wasn't. She was brave and I loved her so much.

My cell rang. I'd heard a couple of texts arrive earlier.

I didn't know how long I'd been in the shower.

Whoever was calling hung up.

But a moment later my cell started ringing again.

I got up, not hurrying, and turned off the shower. By the time I'd wrapped a towel around me, to hide my body so I didn't have to see it in the mirror as I passed it, my cell rang for the fourth time. I caught up another towel and wrapped it around my hair.

Something thumped the door of my room. I'd guess the side of Billy's fist.

"Lindy! Are you in there! Answer! You're scaring the fuck out of me! How long does it take to have a fricking shower! Lind! Lind! Are you okay?"

I hurried across the apartment and shouted through the door, "I'm just putting on my makeup, give me a minute."

"I'll wait!"

I hurried back into the bathroom, unzipped my makeup purse and began applying foundation.

"Lind, come on!" Billy shouted after a while.

I stroked the mascara brush up my eyelashes one last time.

"Lind!" He bashed the door again as I pulled out my lip gloss.

"Wait!" My hand shook as I painted the lipgloss on.

When I opened the door he was just about to bash it again, and the side of his fist came flying at me, I fell back, leaning out of the way. Instead of hitting me, his hand grabbed my arm.

"You okay?" His eyes and his voice were loaded with concern.

He smelt good. He had on a clean white tee, that stretched tight across his chest, hugging all his muscular contours.

Billy always looked good, even on the beach earlier, when he'd been covered in sand and salt.

"Lind, I thought… I'm not saying what I thought…" I knew what he'd thought; he didn't have to say it. He'd thought I'd taken an overdose.

"I was just having a shower."

My new guilt complex poked a finger in my ribs. We were good friends. I'd loved him like a brother for years, and I guess he felt the same about me. I lifted up onto my toes and hugged him. The guy had taken two weeks off to bring me here, and paid, and planned it all. Tears slipped out.

Billy stood outside my room, so technically I was in the hall, in a towel sobbing, with my arms wrapped around his neck.

He lifted me up, like I was nothing. His massive biceps like bars around me, and carried me into the room three paces before shutting the door with his heel.

He put me down then, his big hands bracing my head, and then he kissed my temple. It was a protective gesture. I'd scared him.

His fingers splayed on my cheeks as he looked into my eyes.

I liked his eyes. They were always warm, they were dark blue, but there was heat in them. The guy had always been the complete opposite of Jason.

"I'm allowing this," he said, "because this is your mourning time, but you're gonna have to stop crying in seven days, and you are definitely gonna have to carry your cell at all times. You scared the crap out of me."

I knew. He'd hugged me back fiercely.

His hands dropped. "Do you want me to get lost until you're dressed?"

"No, stay. I'll get my stuff and change in the bathroom. You can talk to me around the door." I didn't want to be alone.

I valued his friendship. I'd lost touch with all my girlfriends the summer we'd left high school because everything in my life had changed and I'd turned to Jason. I'd spent every moment with him, and Billy had become mine and Jason's shared possession. He could be relied on for anything.

I grabbed my clothes up from the bed I'd pulled out from the sofa.

He hadn't answered.

I glanced back.

An odd expression twisted his lips, but he smiled. "Okay. I'll wait out here." He turned away and headed toward the balcony. "What do you want to do once you're ready?"

"I'd like to go back to the beach!" I headed into the bathroom. "The air down by the ocean felt good. There was so much energy in it. We can paddle now you've got your cargo shorts on."

"I'd have thought you'd have had enough of the ocean?"

I pushed the bathroom door up so there was only a narrow crack we could talk around.

"I don't mind splashing around in the shallows! I hate swimming in the ocean, though! It scares me! You never know what's beneath the water and if the seaweed wraps around my legs I think it's something horrible!"

"Then I guess you're not gonna want to go surfing with me? I was gonna take you out on my board."

"Since when did you learn to surf?" I looked up, avoiding the reflection of my ass in the mirror as I slipped my panties on, without taking the towel off. My heart pounded. I hated seeing myself in mirrors. Scratch that. I just hated myself. I hated my face and I detested my body.

"I learned here, the summer we left high school. I've come out here every year since. Believe me, it's awesome. Just sitting out there letting the waves swill under you, until the right one comes along, and then you fly…"

I hadn't even known he'd been out here. But the summer we'd left high school, I'd had other things on my mind. Like Mom. And last summer Jason had decided that what he really wanted to do was leave me behind and go fulfill some dream I'd never heard of before.

"Don't worry, we'll go paddling and jump the waves like little kids."

I faced the mirror once my body was hidden under my clothes. The makeup mask I'd painted on my face looked back at me. I looked okay. I think I'd managed to hide the fact I'd been crying but I was overly pale. . My skin could do with some sunshine. I'd hardly gone out of the house for months.

"What's taking you so long?"

"I've got to dry my hair."

"Lind, you're going down by the ocean, it's salty and damp. Forget your hair."

"No way! I am not looking ugly just 'cause I'm gonna be walking on a beach."

"Believe me, you did not look ugly in that towel combo…"

I laughed, though the sound only came from my throat not my soul. Billy was vibrant, full of talk, and a *just-do-it* attitude… I really did like all those things about him. Jason had always been more silent, thoughtful and hesitant. I really did need Billy's company to get me out of my shell and over Jason.

He didn't say anything else as I finished getting ready, and if he had said anything when I turned on the hairdryer I wouldn't have heard.

When I came out of the bathroom, he still stood out on the balcony.

"Hey."

He turned and his gaze dropped to my bare feet, then ran up my legs, over my mini-skirt and up to my face. "Sorry."

I frowned. What did he have to be sorry for?

He stepped forward. "Come on, then, let's go jump some little bitty waves." His hand lifted.

I held it for a moment, but then let go. "Is there a pool some-where outdoors?"

"Yeah, there's a pool."

"Cool, I'll swim when we go to the pool. I like swimming outdoors, but in a place where there's no seaweed and fish."

"Wimp," he said, as I slipped my sandals on. "Swimming in the ocean is exhilarating… You could swim in a pool back home." There was a breathless sound of excitement in his voice. Billy was all about energy rushes, exercising, discovering, danger—full-on intensity no matter what he did. When we were at college just watching him wore me out.

"You okay?"

I smiled. "Yeah."

"Come on, then."

Billy

My chest was hollow. There was no fucking air in the room. Lindy had on a little denim mini skirt that was frayed at the hem, and the flowery camisole thing she wore with it had tiny little straps that could be slipped off her shoulders so easily, and it hung loose over her breasts, just begging me to do that.

She'd called me a douche on the beach; I was a douche. I was so sickeningly hungry for a girl I couldn't have.

It looked like she was wearing a pale-peach bikini top under-neath the camisole, and I imagined my hand slipping inside that to cup her soft breast.

You are sick, Billy.

She picked up a sweater with a zipper and turned to go ahead of me out of the room. My gaze dropped to her legs. She had good legs. She was short but perfectly proportioned, like a little blonde Barbie doll.

Hunger gripped hard in my gut.

Great. It was going to be a long painful, pitiful two weeks.

Her fingers shook as she unlocked the catch on the door. That had my lust subsiding and love and friendship taking over. I just wanted to protect her… and that included from me.

I got the door and held it open as she walked out. Then, like before, I walked along beside her, with my hands in my pockets to keep them off of her. But this time we did talk.

She asked me about work, about my clients, and then asked me who I kept in contact with from college, that led to us reminiscing as we walked along the shore, while the ocean waves rolled up, rippling over our bare feet, as we carried our shoes.

It was nice… But it felt false, because the guilt inside me kept burning. Lindy looked vulnerable and heartbroken, walking next to me, swilling her feet in the frothing water, and brushing her toes through the shifting sand, her head down and her voice quiet.

She was sad. But at least now she was trying not to be trapped in it.

We'd walked the whole length of the beach when I looked at my watch and saw it was gone six. I suggested we walked back up to the town and looked for somewhere to eat. She looked at me for the first time in hours and nodded.

We found a seafood restaurant and sat inside out of the breeze to eat.

The conversation lapsed into silence a couple of times, but it was an easier silence.

My guilt kept poking me, though, like someone jabbing a finger.

When we'd finished eating, I said, "Shall we order another drink and go and sit outside? Then we can watch the sunset.”

She nodded at me. Her eyes looked a little glassy from the drink. She’d had two large glasses of wine, and now she’d moved on to a cocktail.

“Come on, then.” We got a table right at the edge of the terrace. No one was sitting around us, as the ocean breeze was cold.

She pulled her sweater around her a bit more. “I know what you thought this afternoon.”

I looked at her, my grip tightening on the beer bottle. We’d been avoiding serious subjects, dancing around them, but I was taking my lead from her. If she wanted to talk serious things that was okay. I lifted an eyebrow at her.

“You thought I’d taken an overdose again or done something else when I was in the shower.”

I let go of my beer, reached over and embraced her small hand, that lay on the table.

Her blue eyes looked into mine.

“I’m not going to do it again, Billy. It was a mistake. A moment of weakness. I hurt people. I am not going to hurt them again. You don’t need to worry. I’m just sorry you got mixed up in it. Sorry I scared you.”

“You already said sorry…” My fingers squeezed hers as my guilt punched at me rather than poked. It was me who needed to apologize. “Lind…” This was touching an untouchable subject, but I couldn’t spend two weeks with her and not say it. “I…” God I needed to get a pair of balls. “What happened in the fall—”

Her hand pulled free from mine and she leaned back in her chair, taking her drink with her, her big eyes staring at me.

I took a breath. “It’s me who owes you an apology. I know you didn’t want it to happen.” Her forehead screwed up. She didn’t want to talk about it, but we had to. “All you wanted was someone to hold you and I took it too far.”

Dual tears rolled down her cheeks and she sipped her drink, her gaze dropping to the table. She shut her eyes, like she could just make me disappear and not listen.

But I carried on. I had to say this. I needed to get it out. "I'm sorry. I feel like… I forced you into it."

Her eyes opened and she leaned forward, setting her drink down. "Do we have to talk about this?" She still wasn't looking at me.

"Yeah. I'm living with it and I can't stand it. I want to put things straight. I'm sorry. Now I've thought about it, I feel like I raped you."

She glanced up at me, pain in her eyes. Now I couldn't look at her. My head dropped and I sipped my beer, shame slashing a knife at my chest.

I'd had a drink that night, we both had. Jason had gone to New York a couple of months before. She'd gone out with me, to talk, and we'd *been* talking but I drove her out to the lake and parked up, to keep talking before I took her home. She'd got upset and turned to hug me, her arms hanging around my neck.

She'd wanted comfort, that's all, but I'd had a drink and I'd read it wrong, and my form of comfort had been to kiss her.

She'd answered it, she'd been in a mess over Jason, she'd been hurting, she'd needed someone, and she'd accepted me.

She'd had on a short loose skirt and my hand had roamed where it shouldn't have gone, sliding up her thigh, then I'd I gripped her shoulders and tipped her backwards so we were both lying down… I'd taken it way too far. She hadn't stopped me. I wish she had stopped me. She just hadn't said anything, and let me do it.

With my beer-fogged head, I'd carried on…

The look in her eyes had haunted me for all the months we hadn't been talking. She'd stared at me, just lying there, waiting for me to finish.

I'd been an ass. She hadn't said no, but she hadn't said yes either.

When we'd finished, or when I had finished—she hadn't taken any part in it. She'd sat up, with tears running down her cheeks. When I drove her home, she'd cried all the way back into town.

Then she'd jumped out the SUV as fast as she could, and run into her house.

When I'd seen her the next time, neither of us had acknowledged what happened. We had never spoken about it. Not that night and not since. We'd just carried on pretending it hadn't happened.

But it had happened.

The only time it had been mentioned was when Jason threw it at her that he knew. Apparently she'd talked to his cousin about it, and his cousin had told Rachel. Ever since then I'd been wondering what she'd told his cousin. The more I'd thought about that night, since then, the guiltier I'd got. Why hadn't she said no? She hadn't enjoyed it; she hadn't wanted to do it…

"You didn't," Lindy whispered.

I looked up.

The onyx centers at the heart of her blue eyes were huge. She shook her head, disgust gripping her expression.

I didn't blame her. I was disgusted with myself. But I was facing up to this. I leaned forward, resting my elbows on the table. "I am sorry, and I told Jason the other night that it was all me. You weren't unfaithful to him, you were just looking for someone to hold you and I took it too far…"

More tears rolled onto her cheeks as her gaze fell. She wiped them away as her eyes shut. But then they opened and her head came up, anger burned there, accusing me. "Why the hell did you tell him? It's none of his business! Why did you talk about it?"

"I…" *Because that was what I thought you'd want—for Jason to know the truth.*

"You shouldn't have said anything to him!"

She stood up, drank the last of her cocktail and thrust the empty glass down on the table, then turned away. "I'm going down to the beach."

Shit.

I left my beer and headed inside to settle the check so I could follow.

Chapter Three

Lindy

I sat on the dry sand, hugging my knees, looking out at the ocean. The sky was painted red by the setting sun.

Tears rolled down my cheeks. What was worse, that he thought doing it with me was like rape? Or that he'd actually told my ex that?

Humiliation swept through me like a rippling wave and nausea gripped at my belly.

Oh my God, Billy! I hate you right now!

Sand kicked up against my thigh.

He'd followed. He dropped down next to me, copying my posture, leaning forward and gripping his knees.

I wiped the tears off my cheeks.

His big arm came around me.

I turned into him and then both his arms were around me. This was where it had begun in the fall.

He'd held me, then I'd lifted my head and he'd kissed me. I hadn't really kissed him back but I hadn't stopped him. I'd felt so broken, I hadn't cared, and he'd made me feel wanted. When I'd felt unwanted and lonely for weeks.

Frick, if I'd been lonely then, what about now? Jason hadn't just moved away, he'd dumped me… He had left me alone.

"I'm sorry, Lind."

No, I wasn't alone. I had Billy… and Dad…

My counselor told me—when you think negative, change it to positive… There were hardly any positives…

I pulled free of Billy's hold and turned, looking at the ocean and hugging my knees.

One of his hands fell to the sand. He picked some up, then let it run through his fingers, like an hour glass—a life glass—time just ran away.

His other arm settled on his bent-up knees.

He hadn't raped me. I had let it happen and regretted it after, and never spoken about it with him. "It wasn't rape, Billy."

How did I tell a guy all the mixed-up shit I had in my head. I didn't understand anything myself, so how could I expect anyone else to. Jason hadn't.

Billy watched the last of the sand slip through his fingers, then he looked at me.

"I didn't stop you, because I wanted it too…" At the time, it had been comforting, in a stupid way.

"But not with me, Lind, admit it. I was just a Jason-replacement."

That part was true. "Is that what you told him?"

"Yeah, because I didn't want him to keep thinking you'd betrayed him."

Bitterness thrust a knife into my belly. "Or keep thinking *you had*, 'cause you wanted to make up and get your best friend back…"

His Adam's apple shifted as he took a breath. "I did betray him. I betrayed you both… But… Look… Just say you forgive me and we'll move on from it."

"I don't need to forgive you. It happened. That's all. At the time I needed it." Despair crashed into me, like another sneaker wave hit us, ripping into me and trying to drag me out into the ocean.

Frigid. That's what Jason's new girlfriend had called me. She'd said he'd told her I was no better than sleeping with stone, and now Billy thought doing it with me was like rape.

My forehead dropped onto my knees as I let the wave of pain

wash away, and the tears came again... I just wanted everything to be normal. I wanted to turn back time and make sure none of this had happened. But it was happening, and I couldn't change it.

Think positive—I'd got to twenty-two and had years of happiness to remember and hold on to, and Dad and I could make loads more happy memories.

Tears rolled down my cheeks as I lifted my head and looked at Billy. I couldn't fix other things, but I could fix this... "Why did you think I didn't want to?"

"Why?" The surprise in his voice was matched by his eyebrows lifting. He thought it was obvious.

He dropped his second handful of sand, rubbed his palms on his shorts, then rested his forearms on his bent knees. "You hardly moved." A sigh left his lips. "I was going to stop, but I didn't know which was worse, to stop and pretend it hadn't gone too far or... Well..." He looked at me. "Sorry."

My forehead dropped on to my knees, so I could hide. I was *that* bad.

The weight of his palm settled on my shoulder, then rubbed a little before tugging me against him.

I fell into him, sobbing, still hugging my knees, not holding him, but he held me. "Lindy. I really am sorry."

"I'm shit," I said against his shoulder. "I'm crap in bed." I'd never felt comfortable with sex, probably because I'd never felt comfortable with myself. I didn't like sex. It just made me aware of all the bits of my body I hated and didn't want to think about. Sex had always been awkward.

A laugh rumbled in his chest.

I pulled away and smacked his shoulder. "It's not funny."

Jason had left me because of it. He was all over Rachel, touching and kissing her. I'd even seen them full-on kissing in the store.

He'd never kissed me like that. Our sex had been crap, and it had not been his fault because he didn't seem to have a problem with Rachel.

It had been my fault and he'd been mean enough to tell his new girlfriend and she'd fucking cruelly told me.

Billy's palm lifted, calling truce. "Okay, it's not funny. It's just the way you said it."

Awesome. He'd gone from an apology to laughing at me, humor hovered in his eyes.

I pushed myself up and headed toward the ocean. The sun was a giant-red ball dipping its toes.

"Lindy! I didn't mean to upset you!"

I slipped my sandals off, bent and picked them up, while he caught up with me.

"Honest, I'm sorry I didn't mean to laugh."

I looked at him, my eyes accusing. "You're getting good at saying sorry, Billy."

His lips twisted in a dismissing smirk, but his eyes questioned me.

I poked my tongue out at him then turned toward the ocean again. I could just keep walking. Walk into the waves and let them take away the turmoil in my head. But shame and guilt wouldn't let me do it now I'd seen how much it would hurt Mom and Dad… and anyway, I was afraid of the ocean and everything beneath it.

I turned to walk parallel to the waves. His arm came around me. The weight of his hand on my shoulder. Frickin' tears started falling again. He pulled me against him as we walked. The world span.

I needed to be held and loved. The feeling rippled through my nerves. It was that feeling that had made me let him do it in the SUV. Jason had been miles away in New York.

I pulled free of Billy and moved away, walking along in the last ripples of the waves. The water was freezing, numbing my feet. Like life had numbed my soul.

My belly did a queasy turn as I looked down at the water. The sky had turned a deeper, darker blue. It was getting dark. The sun had nearly disappeared. I felt a bit drunk now.

"Why am I so bad at doing it?" I looked over at Billy.

The douche laughed again.

I lifted my hand to hit him with my sandals, but he grabbed my wrist, meeting my glare with a look that said, *no way*.

"Lashing out is a habit you need to get out of, Lind."

Maybe it was, but it was a good way to vent everything I felt. I growled at him, snarling.

He laughed openly, but then he bent and—

Frick! The guy picked me up like a fireman, so I dangled over his massive shoulder. My belly revolted. "Billy! Billy!"

He started walking back up the beach, in the direction of our apartments.

"Billy!"

Nausea rolling through me, I smacked his ass with my sandals. "Billy put me down, I feel sick!"

He still didn't.

"Billy!"

He just kept walking, laughter rumbling in his chest. "I'm sorting you out once and for all girl."

A guy we passed gave me an odd look. Billy was flashing my panties at the other people on the beach.

"Put me down! I'm gonna be sick, Billy!" I screamed this time. He didn't stop. My belly lurched. "If you don't, I'm gonna be sick all down your back!" I was desperate now.

He stopped. I think he'd got the message.

He slid me off his shoulder, lowering me carefully.

I didn't stop to rant. I was going to be sick. Oh, I felt bad.

I turned and ran. My head pounded out a message that I'd drunk too much.

I really was gonna be sick.

When I got to my apartment, I swiped my key, shoved the door open and ran for the bathroom.

When Billy came in, I was on my knees leaning over the toilet bowl. Happy pills, cocktails and being tipped upside down really didn't mix.

"You okay? Dumb question, you're obviously not. Shit." He turned, filling a glass with water as I kept retching.

His hand settled on my back when I finished. Then there was a tumbler of water in my hand. I didn't drink it. I was sweating and shivery and I felt awful. He took it back out my hand and put it on the floor. Then as I just collapsed over the toilet bowl, he sat on the bathroom floor across the room, with his back against the tiles.

"Lindy?"

I shook my head. I didn't want to talk.

"Are those your pills?" He was looking up at a shelf over the sink.

I grunted and was sick again.

He got up, picked them up looked at how many were there and then read the packet. "You're not meant to drink alcohol with these..."

Yeah, I knew that. My head had a hammer in it reminding me, and I was throwing up in the pan.

When I finished this time, there was a cold washcloth pressed into my hand. "I'll stay in your room tonight. Make sure you're okay."

I didn't say anything. I felt too sick to care.

Lindy

When I woke the sunlight in the room hurt my eyes and I blinked a dozen times. Billy had picked me up in the bathroom and carried me to bed last night. I must have fallen asleep leaning on the toilet.

He came into focus. He sat on the bed, wearing the same cargo shorts and t-shirt.

"Can I have a glass of water?"

"Here." There was one beside the bed. He just reached for it and handed it to me as I sat up.

I sipped it, watching him.

"You talk in your sleep."

"Great. What did I say?"

Not answering, he got up and pulled his cell out of his back pocket, looking at something on it, as his thumb moved the screen and kept tapping it.

"Billy, what are you doing?"

"Give me a minute." He didn't look at me.

I sat up properly, sipping the water again. He still didn't look at me. "What, Billy?"

"I said give me a minute…"

A smile touched my lips. We could argue, and we had argued, but there had never been anything underlying or hidden between us, well not until we'd done it in his SUV. But even then, he'd still met up with me a couple of days later, and we'd still got on okay. With Billy you got what you saw.

Since Jason had dumped me, I'd spent hours wondering how long he'd wanted to dump me. He'd gone to New York to get away from me. But he hadn't had the balls to tell me… Last night Billy had come right out and told me how he'd been feeling—

"Here." He threw his cell on the bed and pointed at it. "I'm gonna go down to the gym. You take a look at that." His cheeks were scored with pink, like he was embarrassed.

"Billy?"

"You've been moaning half the night about how bad sex is. That's your answer."

"What?"

"I looked up a website for you. How to jerk yourself off. You don't need a guy, Lind. Learn to do it yourself."

Oh my God. "Billy!" That was crazy. Now my cheeks burned. I put the water down. "What did Jason tell you?!"

"Jason didn't tell me anything. You said it all in your sleep, and last night."

"Liar. He told you I'd never had one didn't he?" There was a mirror on the wall across the room. I caught sight of my face. My makeup had run. I looked awful. I hated seeing myself in mirrors.

"Jason didn't say anything! I told him you hadn't wanted to do it with me, you'd been thinking of him. That's all."

Frick… could he make me more embarrassed? It was like being whipped. "And Jason, said!"

Billy bent down his hands settling on the mattress either side of me, his dark-blue gaze striking mine. "I swear, he never said anything. But his eyebrows lifted. So after your night's babbling I guess it wasn't much better with him…"

I was gonna slap him, but he caught my wrist. "Lind, leave off the slapping or I'll tip you over my shoulder again and this time I'll just throw you in the shower to cool your temper down."

But I had good reason to be angry. "I can't believe you two were talking about me!" I tried to yank my arm free but he wouldn't let go. "Billy!"

I pulled again and nearly fell back when he let go. He caught my arm again. "Lindy. I looked it up so you don't have to. I didn't want you to come across anything you wouldn't want to see—"

"And how do you even know where to find shit like that?"

"I'm a guy. We pretty much covered every type of porn on our cells at high school."

"I'm a guy…" I mocked.

He let my arm go. "Whatever, Lind. You can look at it or not. I'm going down to the gym. Then I'll have a shower and knock for you, okay?" As he turned away, his fingers ran through his hair, then immediately ruffled it to re-spike it. That stupid leather bracelet I'd made at high school shifted on his wrist.

Was he implying I did it now?

"I'll see you later." He said from the door, glancing back.

This was too weird.

The door shut.

I got up, running away from his cell, that lay on the bed.

Why did he think I'd do that?

When I faced the bathroom mirror, it wasn't me I looked at. My makeup had smeared around my eyes.

I shut them.

What the frick must Billy think? In 24 hours he'd seen me

soaked in salt and sand, throwing up and then like this…

I turned away from the image, stripped off and got in the shower.

The water was warm and it teemed down over my head, washing all my pain away for a few moments.

Truth hurt.

What Jason had told Rachel was true.

I'd never had any pleasure from sex. We'd just done it. Or rather I'd let Jason do it. Boys wanted to do that stuff. It had always just felt uncomfortable to me. Lying there and trying to feel things that I really didn't. I'd thought it was like that for everyone—*until I'd seen him with Rachel.*

The guy who was supposed to be mine… my support… my defender… my hero… Had humiliated me and told his new girl I was bad in bed.

But since I'd talked to the counselor I'd realized I'd been piling all my anger on Jason, when most of it was nothing to do with him. It was only fate and I'd pushed him away, probably, because I'd been too busy fighting all the insecurity and pain I was at war with. I knew that—when I was honest with myself.

I'd been relying on him for everything, and not let him rely on me.

I toppled back against the tiles. Tears came again and anger gripped at me. I'd spent so many months wrapped up in anger. I wanted to smash the room up; smash the world up. Because the world was cruel.

I switched the shower off and wrapped myself in the towels. Then went back into the bedroom and threw myself down on the bed.

Billy's cell stared at me.

I ignored it for ages. But it started shouting at me to just pick it up.

I did.

When I tapped the screen, it opened on the website he'd looked up.

Trying not to think, or judge, or fear this, I scrolled through what it said.

The demonstrations made my skin crawl; that was why teenage boys looked this shit up. Heat burned in my skin as I watched, trying not to overthink.

Oh my God.

Chapter Four

Billy

Lindy's eyes sparkled in the white light when she walked into the gym.

I pressed the weights back up, the bite gripping in my arms and chest. I'd taken my tee off because I'd got hot. I'd turned the air con up too.

Her eyes dropped to my tattoo. She'd never seen my leopard.

"I didn't know you had that."

I set the bar back onto the brackets, then slid out from underneath it and sat up, breathing hard. I picked up my tee and wiped the sweat off my brow, then my chest. Lindy's gaze followed the movement of the cloth.

"I had it done here, last summer, when we left college."

"It's beautiful. I like it."

My lips twisted in a bitter smile. I'd had the thing done out of anger. It was a little like self-harm. The leopard looked like it climbed one side of my chest, scratching my shoulder, leaving scores of blood. Another claw cut into my belly and the other on my side, while its tail flicked up and curled around to my back. It was in memory of a girl, without having her name as a giveaway mark. The girl was Lindy.

I'd been angry with her. No, that was a lie. I'd been angry with myself for not being able to stop wanting her.

Her gaze followed the path of the leopard, dropping down to my abs. Then she looked up at my face.

"Your cell rang." She held it out.

"Who?"

"Jason."

Shit. Well she looked like she'd been playing with herself and that must have brought her down to earth with a bump.

I took it from her hand, then pulled up the missed calls. Sure enough Jason's number was there. I called the messages.

"Hey, Billy. You've disappeared, I was gonna ask you to go out for a drink again but your mom said you'd gone out of town. Everything okay?" I deleted the message. I didn't call back. I'd catch up with him when Lindy and I got back.

"How are you?" I asked her.

"Okay. Have you finished?"

"If you want me to be finished?"

She'd showered, blow-dried her hair and put her makeup straight. The white sleeveless tee she had on was a little sheer. I could see the green halter-neck bikini top she had on underneath it through the cotton and she was wearing shorts that showed every curve of her legs off. I did like her legs.

"What do you want to do?"

Her arms had crossed since she'd handed me the cell, and now she shrugged.

"We can go down to the beach and lie in the sun, or go down to the pool and swim…"

"I liked the beach yesterday. Let's go back down to the beach."

"Well, you're gonna have to give me time to shower."

"Are you going back up to your room?"

"Yeah, I need clean clothes as well as a shower, unless you want a companion who stinks."

She smiled with a sudden look of warmth catching in her eyes, the Lindy of happiness and high school shining through; the one who had somehow got lost in the last couple of years.

I stood up, wiping my face with my tee again. Then met her gaze. "So did you?"

That question had been tumbling around in my head for an hour and more. Asking it kicked me in the belly and sent a jolt of lust to my cock.

I'd been exercising with an uncomfortable condition, thinking about her—up in her room… Imagining. I shook my head, I probably shouldn't have asked.

She didn't answer anyway.

She turned away, acting like I hadn't asked the question, but as she did, her skin turned red.

I'd lay a bet she had. And that made my condition worse; blood pulsed into my cock.

But she could just be embarrassed I'd mentioned it. That would be like Lindy too.

My fingers combed through my hair. Then I caught my image in the mirror and ruffled my hair so it spiked again.

A part of me wondered if I'd brought her here not to make amends but to try and win her. Maybe I had been kidding myself that I was able to just let her go at last.

Whatever, I was still turned on, even though she wasn't turned on by me. Well that was the suicide sentence I'd been living for years—watching her with Jason.

I followed her upstairs, but she didn't talk until she got to her room. "I'll see you soon."

"Yeah." I nodded at her before going into mine.

I sorted myself out in the shower, jerking off as the water streamed over me, and ah, shit, the images playing through my head were her, lying on her bed and doing the same, holding my cell.

When I got dressed, I pulled my cut-offs on over my swim shorts, rubbed my hair with a towel to dry it a little, then slicked it up with styling wax, before pulling on a dark-blue tee. I locked my cell and wallet in the room safe, grabbed a zip sweat top and threw it on as I left the room.

When I knocked Lindy's door, it opened straight away. "You took your time."

I grinned at her, heat burning in my cheeks. My turn to be embarrassed. "You ready?"

She blushed too then. "Yeah, I'll get my backpack."

This was gonna be one long day of awkward. My hands slid into the front pockets of my cut-offs. I had a rolled blanket under my arm that I'd got out of the SUV for us to sit on.

We didn't talk walking down to the beach. My brain couldn't come up with any right stuff to say and she didn't have anything to say. But then there was the whole choosing where we sat: dry sand that was uneven, or on the flat wet sand. The breeze rolled in with the ocean whipping up a mini sandstorm.

We picked dry sand.

"I've got more blankets in the SUV and tent poles. Why don't I make a den? We can pen ourselves in, out of the breeze, if we're gonna sit."

"Okay."

I handed her the blanket. "I'll be back in a minute."

She was standing in the same place when I got back. Just staring out at the ocean, looking uncomfortable.

"I'm cold." She looked at me, hugging the blanket to her chest.

"It'll be warm inside our den. It's like a cocoon." When I smiled, she smiled back at me. "Go on, throw the blanket out and I'll build the den around you."

I positioned the tent poles in a square around the blanket she sat on and taped four blankets on them, with duct tape, making a little wall around us that would keep the breeze and sand out. I'd been to California once, with my family, years ago, beaches were warm there… Not here…

She laughed at me, "You're crazy. Have you done this before?"

"Not four-sided, but yes I've built them before for myself if the wind's whipping sand at you."

"Did you and Jason build dens when you were kids?"

I smiled at her as I taped the last blanket up. "Yeah."

She laughed again.

There were only a few people about on the beach. Some flying kites and playing ball.

Climbing into our new den, I grinned as I dropped to sit on the blanket next to her.

She slid her backpack off her shoulder. Then her knees bent up as she leaned forward and gripped her ankles. "You're right, it's warm down here out of the breeze."

"I'm always right."

She glanced at me, turned pink and then looked away.

I undid the button on my fly.

Lind caught the movement and blushed *again…*

Yep, today was going to be a whole ton of awkward.

I smiled to dismiss her insecurity as I stood up to unzip my cut-offs. When I let them drop, she looked away.

"If I'm here to get some sun, I'm getting some sun." I stripped off my sweat top.

She looked at me again. "It's still cold, even in here."

"Don't be feeble." I gripped the hem of my tee and pulled it up and off.

She was bright red as she turned to her backpack and started delving in it.

I lay down on my belly next to her.

"Do you want screen." She held out a tube of sun screen.

"Trust you to come with protection."

Another blush.

She so had.

Shit, my cock twitched, right at the moment her cold hand touched my back.

She hadn't waited on my agreement. But I wasn't complaining. Her touch was gentle and careful.

When she'd finished, she threw the screen on top of her backpack and lay down next to me, still fully clothed.

I turned my head to look at her, resting my cheek on my crossed arms. She was on her back and she'd shut her eyes. "Aren't you gonna strip down to your bikini?"

Her head turned. "No, it's cold, and I don't like to strip off."

"You're weird. Nearly every girl I know would freeze to get a tan."

"Yeah, well I'm not *every girl*."

Yeah, I did know that, but she *was* weird sometimes. "Get your shorts off, get your top off, and get some sun on your skin. It'll make you feel better."

She rolled onto her belly, mirroring my posture, with her arms folded and her cheek on the back of her hands as she looked at me. "No."

I frowned at her. "Come on, take your stuff off."

"No, I really don't want to."

"Why?"

"Billy, don't push me."

"No, the more you refuse, the more you make me think there's something wrong. What's wrong with taking your stuff off."

"I hate my stomach!" she growled at me, rolling onto her back and then sitting up.

Frick. I laughed.

The flat of her fist hit my shoulder.

"I thought we'd covered stopping the violence last night…"

She poked her tongue out at me, but there really was anger in her eyes.

I turned my head to rest my forehead on my crossed arms. "Lind, your stomach is fine."

"I don't feel comfortable." Her pitch rang with annoyance.

I looked at her again. There was nothing wrong with her! "Lind. Take your fucking stuff off. You've got a gorgeous body." Perhaps I shouldn't be admitting I thought that, but whatever. "Just take it off. You look thinner than 90 percent of the women in this town!"

"Billy!" That was a reprimand to keep my voice down.

"Just take your stuff off and lie down!"

She'd turned bright red and my guess was it was through anger as much as embarrassment. Glaring at me she gripped the hem of her sweat top, and as it turned out her sleeveless tee, 'cause when she pulled it up, she pulled both off and threw them on top of my head. So I couldn't see her.

When I moved them off, she'd lain down again, and her shorts weren't off but she must have undone them, because they were pushed down to where her bikini bottoms were. I could see the emerald-green line.

Cock twitch.

She was not overweight. "There's nothing wrong with how you look."

Her head turned, her cheek resting on her folded arms, as her blue eyes stared at me.

"Like yourself," I whispered. "That's half your trouble, you don't."

Tears glittered in her eyes. She shut them.

"Shall I rub some screen into your back?"

She nodded without opening her eyes.

I smiled as I got up to get the screen. She didn't move.

I grabbed the tube and straddled her thighs.

"Billy!" she squealed as I squirted the cold cream on her back.

"Just lie still and shut up." I laughed.

"That's so cold," she breathed.

"Now you know how I felt." She didn't really, 'cause I'd been aroused. Something she hadn't ever been around me.

I pulled her bikini top loose at the back so the strap wasn't in the way. Then I rubbed the cream in with both hands, sliding my palms up the gorgeous curve of her back and then over her shoulders, and along her arms to her elbows, before running them all the way down to start again as her soft skin absorbed the cream.

She jumped a little as my hands started running upward again.

Her backside wobbled against my groin. I loved it. Cause I loved her. The girl was mad thinking she didn't have a good figure.

I tied her bikini top up again and smacked the first curve of her ass, before I climbed off of her. She squealed again. "Billy!"

"Lindy!" I mocked, rolling onto my side, leaning up on my elbow to watch her and talk. Her head turned to me, her cheek resting on her crossed arms.

Halleluiah, the girl actually had a shallow smile on her lips.

"You do look good, you know. I'm not just saying it, and I'm not kidding. Didn't Jason ever say how hot you look."

Her smile fell and her head turned away.

"Didn't he?"

"He dumped me for Rachel. You've seen how skinny she is. So whatever he did say wasn't true, was it?"

"Yeah, but it doesn't mean there's anything wrong with you, and he was with you for years… He loved you, Lind. The thing with him and Rachel isn't about looks; it's just chemistry."

Her head turned to me again. But she didn't say anything.

"So did you?" I whispered to try and break her bad mood.

"Billy," she hissed at me, but she said it with another smile, before looking away.

I grinned. I was sure she had.

I turned onto my back. "Put some sun screen on my chest."

She looked back and didn't move for a moment, but then sat up, and now I could see her body better. Her breasts swayed in the halter-neck bikini top and her nipples had come up in peaks under the cloth. There was nothing about her that turned me off.

She squirted the cold cream on my belly. "Ah" My body jolted and I laughed.

"You could do this yourself, you know."

"I know, but it's so much more fun when you do it."

There was a twisted smile on her lips, that she hid by looking down to watch her hands move over my skin.

"How many hours do you work out?"

"Why?"

"Cause you are one big ball of muscle, Billy."

"I'm a personal trainer. I spend all day working out, Lind." I watched her face, hidden beneath a curtain of blonde hair, as her fingers ran down to my belly, exploring my abs.

"And this little cut above your hips, how do you get that?"

I laughed. "A guy's secret."

Her fingers ran right up and over my shoulders then down my arms, like I'd done to her. "Your biceps are huge."

I shut my eyes and chuckled, just reveling in her touch. "Nice to know you're impressed with my guns."

"Only a little." Her hands left me, and the sun-screen tube hit my belly.

I laughed, turning to my side as she lay on her back next to me.

My gaze skimmed down her body. "Well, if you measure that by how I feel about your belly, you can shut up complaining about being overweight."

She thumped my shoulder, but she was smiling and laughing, a little.

Lindy

Billy's long black eyelashes framed the gleam in his eyes. Emotion gripped in my chest as my gaze caught the dark blue.

He'd always been good at making me laugh. Always.

I smiled at him, shaking my head, then rolled on to my belly and rested my head on my folded arms. He settled in the same position beside me, looking toward me as I looked at him.

"So what have you been doing in the weeks we've not been talking? Have you been looking for a new job?" He changed the subject.

"A bit…" I took a breath. Images of home spun around in my head; the emotion piling in too. Sadness hung-out in every corner in that house… I'd escaped it for a while, but I couldn't escape it forever and it was strangling me. Pain pierced through my heart …

"But Mom's at home—and I've just not been in the mood for job-hunting. I should go into Portland, but I don't want to be that far away from home."

"It's not that far. Most of my clients are in Portland. It doesn't take that long to do the drive—"

"I know… but it's too far for me!"

His eyes looked his questions. If I'd have snapped like that at Jason, he would've just shut up and turned away, but Billy never accepted anything at face value, he always questioned why. His eyebrows lifted.

I couldn't answer why…

He didn't ask it, though. Perhaps he realized my soul was too sore.

"So, did you?" That question was spoken in a deep husky whisper, followed by a smile.

I smiled, too, I couldn't help it. He'd said it to break the ice that had settled over me. I shook my head at him, then turned the other way. But he had me grinning again and wanting to laugh, even though a moment ago I'd felt like the world ripped me apart.

It had felt awkward when he'd said it earlier, but now the glint of amusement in his eyes just made it a joke. That look in his eyes hovered in my head as I shut mine, listening to him chuckle.

"What music have you been listening to lately?" Another sudden change of subject.

I didn't look back at him, just talked with my eyes shut, feeling the sunshine warm my back, now he'd blocked out the wind.

It felt like the two of us were in a cocoon, the world beyond our den didn't exist. We talked about everything and nothing. TV shows, films, Vine and YouTube clips, it went everywhere, and we were talking for ages. I was so relaxed. I felt normal, when I hadn't felt normal for months—years.

Then all of a sudden he got up. "I'm going into the ocean for a bit. You coming?"

"Our stuff?"

"I left my wallet and cell in my room, did you bring yours?"

"No, but people don't know that, they'll take my backpack."

"Worry wart. There's a woman over there with four kids, she'll mind it; she looks trust- worthy."

"Billy! My clothes!" How could he see everything so black and white?

"Put them back on. It's freezing down there." He bent down and grabbed up his tee and top and pulled them on while I got dressed too. Then he leaned down and picked up my backpack.

He climbed over a blanket to get out, and when I stood up he was walking back up the beach toward this woman.

The woman blushed as he approached her.

When I climbed out, pulling on my sleeveless tee and my sweater, it felt scary. That was stupid. But I'd been safe in our little cocoon, and now the world could get at me.

"Sorted," he said, as he came back, grinning at me. A grin that said "victory".

My arms gripped over my chest as insecurity crowded in. "I bet she thinks you're really cheeky."

"Nah, she's just thinking she wished her husband still looked as hot as me." His smile split his face. "Come on." His eyes glowed reassurance.

Billy. My heart said his name in an odd way.

When we'd shared the apartment at college, Billy had always been easy company. Whenever Jason had gone into one of his quiet, thoughtful moods, Billy had always been there to shout at, *with*, to debate with, and laugh with…

I started walking beside him, my arms still gripped over my chest.

He looked sideways at me. "So, go on then, tell me, did you?"

He'd sensed my awkwardness. Amusement caught up in my throat, mixing with the feelings of despair that had started surrounding me again. It came out as a choked laugh and my lips twisted in a bitter smile. But it was a smile. I wanted to hug him.

I knew he didn't expect an answer. He was purely joking. To make me laugh.

My arms dropped to hang at my sides. What would I have done without Billy when Jason went to New York? I had missed Billy loads for weeks. I felt a lot better now he'd come back to me.

I poked my tongue out at him, wondering what the hell he'd say, or do, if I answered, *yes*.

That made me smile properly, a full-on smile like I hadn't done for months.

Shit, I'd had my first-ever orgasm this morning, barely hours ago. My hand clutching his cell and I'd thought of him, 'cause I could hardly think of Jason. That would have felt wrong on every level. I'd thought of Billy's muscular hips and thighs moving between my parted legs—of his weight pressing down onto me and into me, and the pressure of his movement inside me…

That would freak him out.

When I'd finished, I'd lain there breathing heavily and absorbing all the weird sensations humming and playing through my nerves—then Billy's cell rang out *Clarity by Foxes* and Jason's image had appeared on it.

I'd dropped the cell. It had felt like cheating on Jason, as all the feelings I'd had for him flooded to the surface, like it was only yesterday he'd finished with me.

My heart, and my head, still believed I was his.

But I wasn't.

They had to learn.

But Billy had said I could mourn this week, so I'd cried, letting the tears fall again before I went down to the gym. I'd only gone down there because I hadn't wanted to be alone anymore.

But, I'd had an orgasm… My first ever!

"Come on, you're so slow." He caught hold of my hand and pulled me into a run.

"Billy!" He didn't cease pulling as I stumbled along in a run beside him.

I'd tried to run with Jason once, but he could run real fast. I couldn't keep up with him; I hadn't even tried after that one time, I'd have just held him back.

But it was like he used to run to get away from me anyway. It was something he did alone. Spirit and soul, leaving me behind.

When everything had got messed up, I'd tried to make him stop, because I knew it separated him from me. I'd already begun to feel him slipping through my fingers, but he wouldn't give up. Running had been more important to him than us—*me*.

Rachel ran with him.

My toes caught in the dried sand and I nearly fell. Billy yanked me up.

"Come on! I want to get in the water."

"God, you're no better than a kid!"

That deep chuckle rumbled in his chest.

I was so glad I'd come here with him. I was really starting to feel better; as if I'd escaped. But that thought brought the guilt rolling back in, like a wave sweeping in off the ocean.

We were running over wet sand now, leaving the impressions of our footprints behind, footprints that the tide would wash away, when it came in.

When we reached the water, he didn't stop but carried on running into the shallow waves.

"Ahh, Billy, it's freezing!" The sudden cold numbed my bare feet.

"I didn't have you down for a coward, Lind." He pulled me on.

"Ahh," I shivered as the cold water swilled about my shins. I gritted my teeth. My toes were buried in the moving sand.

It was easier being with Jason. Jason never used to press against my boundaries. But Billy had never been like this at college. Well, he had been full of energy like a coiled spring all the time about to burst, but he had never dragged me into any of his wildness like this. I had only ever been his spectator.

I pulled back against his hold as he got deeper. I wasn't cool with this, the water was freezing, and—

"Frick, Lind, are you gonna be a chicken?"

I squealed when his hand left mine, but then instead, one arm caught about my waist and the other beneath my legs and he lifted me. "Billy!" I gripped his shoulders as he walked deeper, and the waves of freezing water swilled up at us.

I'd had a family vacation in Florida, the water there had been as warm as a bath; it was wonderful. Mom had been in the water with me, holding my hand, and we'd jumped the shallow waves together… I hadn't felt scared with her.

I clung to Billy, turning my head into his shoulder as the ocean washed up at us and hit his thighs, sending up spray as it also swilled up about his legs. The wave washed on past him, the water level dropping back down to his knees. I watched it travel up the beach over his shoulder and saw it swallow our footprints.

Would memories disappear as easily—washed away by time? I didn't want to forget anything.

"Have you ever been out in the water up to your middle?"

For years the water had been over my head, but only figuratively, not literally. I had never gone deeper than my thighs because I was too scared of the huge ocean and all the things I couldn't see. It should have been the future I was afraid of, and what was hidden by time…

Another wave broke onto his thighs, the white foam frothing about us.

"Have you?" he asked again. Then he clarified. "I don't mean that, I mean have you been into the ocean deeper than your middle?"

"No."

"Come on, then." He began walking forward.

"You'll get hypothermia!"

"I'll run when we get out, that'll warm me up."

My teeth were chattering, even just being in his arms, as the cold spray got me wet.

I gripped his shoulders tighter and he lifted me a little higher.

My gaze caught his. He smiled, then a glint caught in the onyx heart of his eyes. "No!" My fingers clawed. "Don't you dare drop me!"

"Would I?"

"You were thinking about it."

"I was letting you think I was thinking about it."

"You're nuts, Billy."

"And going deeper…"

He walked forward. I was laughing, properly laughing, I could feel it in my stomach, and the muscles I hadn't used for months were aching in my face. It felt so good to laugh. "Ahh, I turned into him, lifting my leg into his chest as a bigger wave rolled in." I was getting used to being held by him. I was completely sure he wouldn't drop me. His huge arms were firm and solid and strong. He wouldn't let me fall.

When the next wave crashed into us it was stronger and swilled right up to my hips. His top got wet and the spray dampened my bottom. Exhilaration washed through my nerves like the ocean swirling around him, and the scent of the salt water filled my nostrils.

He went in deeper still. I clutched his shoulders harder, but turned my head to watch the next wave roll in. It was bigger, but then he was further out.

"It's coming, Lind," he teased. I gripped his neck with both arms, and turned my head into his chest.

"Argh!" I cried as it hit us hard, swilling against my back, a rush of fizzing salty water tumbling over me like rapids and soaking my clothes, but it felt good. I was a part of nature; of a world I hadn't been part of for a very long time.

I laughed, lifting my head and clinging a little less.

Something glinted in his eyes and he took me even deeper.

"Billy!" I screamed as the next wave broke right before us, crashing open and starting to roar in a rush of white water that washed right into me, soaking me completely as I clung to Billy…

It was freezing.

My arms clung tight about his neck and I shivered like crazy as the wave rolled on past us.

"Billy what if there's a sneaker wave. I'm cold. Take me back!"

Insecurity, fear, pain, all flooded back. My teeth chattered and I was really shivering. "Billy, take me back."

His grip firmed on my thigh and shoulder, his fingers pressing into my flesh.

I couldn't breathe. I couldn't breathe!

"It's okay. I've got you."

I gripped his neck, shivering violently as he carried me out of the water and back up the beach.

I was crying. Stupid fears. Stupid head. Stupid life.

"I wouldn't have let you go, Lind." He didn't put me down, even when we reached the sand. He might think my fear was crazy, but he was still kind.

I liked the challenge in Billy, because he was right, I could face demons with him, and know he would keep me safe and get me out the other side, and if he could help me get out of the self-inflicted prison sentence I'd been serving, then I'd let him push me…

This was my week to mourn. Then I was going to let it go and try to learn to live again.

I'd had my first orgasm this morning because of Billy…

I'd gone into the ocean…

What else could I achieve with him?

When Billy set me down by our den, I was still shivering. He bent and grabbed up the blanket, wrapped it around me, then rubbed my shoulders.

His black eyelashes were all stuck together by the salty ocean water, and his hair clung to his head.

A wave had crashed into his back when he'd walked out of the water.

"Sorry, I took you too deep."

"No, you didn't." My teeth still chattered. "I enjoyed it for a while."

"But now we'd better get you in a shower. I'll leave the den here and come back."

"Aren't you cold too?"

"I'm a bit tougher than you, Lind. I'll go get your backpack."

He turned away. I picked up his shorts, my sandals and his sneakers from inside our den and followed him up the beach. Heat seeped back into my legs, and then they burned.

He walked with purpose. His swim shorts stuck on his tight buttocks as he moved. The same tight buttocks I had been imagining moving up and down between my thighs earlier. The dark hairs on his thighs and calves were stuck to his skin too.

The woman gave him my backpack and he talked to her for a moment, saying thank you, I guessed. Then he walked toward me as I walked up the beach, clutching the blanket around me.

"So did you?" He said with a grin, when I reached him.

I shook my head at him, smiling, as I walked past him. I was warming up, but I still wanted to go back to my room and shower.

When I stood in the shower, washing the salt out of my hair, feeling the water pouring over my head and body, I smiled, as I remembered the waves crashing into us, and Billy's strong arms hanging on to me.

So, did you?

The words he'd been asking me all day echoed in my head and heat burned across my skin.

Chapter Five

Billy

Looking at my reflection in the mirror, I splashed aftershave on my skin. I'd gone for a dark-blue shirt and black pants, but I'd kept my comfortable sneakers on.

The plan was to walk down to the Italian restaurant we'd seen.

I rubbed some styling wax on my hands and combed my fingers through my wet hair to spike it a little.

Taking one last look in the mirror, I told myself, silently, to get my shit together, then turned away.

Lindy and I had done a lot of laughing today, in the end, but I knew she was still unhappy underneath, and I still felt partly responsible, no matter what she'd said last night—and guilty.

I picked my wallet up and slid that, then my iPhone, into my pockets. Jason had tried calling twice while we'd been down at the beach. I'd sent him a text saying 'All's good. I'm just busy. I'll catch up when I get home.'

I left the room, going to knock on Lindy's door.

"Hey." She opened it smiling, wearing a skimpy cotton summer dress. It was held up by thin straps on her shoulders and from there the material just floated over her breasts and her belly, falling to the middle of her thighs. She looked good. Her eye shadow was a soft blue and her lip gloss a pale pink. They suited her. She looked more like the old Lindy. "I'll get my purse and my jacket, then I'm ready." She threw me a smile before turning away.

She came back in a moment, wearing a loose black jacket over the top of the dress, and a small pink purse, with a long strap, over her shoulder. It matched the flat sandals she had on.

"Have you spoken to your Mom and Dad?" I asked, as she shut her door behind her.

She glanced at me, with an odd expression. I guess she didn't want to be reminded of home. But she answered.

"Yeah."

"They happy you're okay?" No way did I want to end up on the wrong side of her dad.

"Yeah." She looked away again, but the happier mood I'd sensed when she'd come out of her room had subsided.

"Do you remember…" I started reflecting on funny stuff that had happened when we were kids. Then when we got to the restaurant, I began telling her what everyone I still knew was up to.

She didn't know anything about anyone. She'd not kept in touch with any of the girls and her eyebrows kept going up when I told her various bits of gossip as she laughed or oh'd and ah'd.

Once the waitress had taken away our dinner plates, I leaned over and said, "So why did you ditch all the girls when we went to college?"

Lindy
"So why did you ditch all the girls when we went to college."
The question hit me like a slap. He implied I'd done it deliberately, cruelly. I poked my tongue out at him, for being mean, before answering. "Cause I was with Jason. I spent all my time with him, *and you—*"

"So every other friend was tossed out the door, 'cause you didn't need them when you had what you wanted. Jason."

That sounded vicious, as if he had a problem with it.

But it hadn't been like that. That was the summer everything had changed, when Mom had found out she was sick and my mind had been too full of all the shit going on at home. I'd been scared and lonely, and… I couldn't take part in light, chatty, stupid conversations with girls who knew nothing about anything.

I glared at him as the waitress handed me a dessert menu.

I couldn't explain to him.

I'd promised.

He could think what he liked.

When the waitress walked away, I answered, "I just had nothing to say to them…" That was the truth.

"So you threw them all off."

Great. He really did have a problem. I didn't see that it made any difference to him. It wasn't him left with no friends after Jason dumped me.

I dropped the menu on the table. "I don't want anything. Can we go somewhere else?"

"Well I guess I was the lucky one, then, 'cause I was kept in your buddy group of two. Come on." He dropped his menu too, stood up, then went over to the counter.

I followed, but as he got his wallet out, I covered his hand. "You're not paying again, it's my turn!" When he was being antagonistic the last thing I wanted to do was let him pay. I didn't want to owe him too much—if we fell out again.

He held up his hands, palm out. "Okay, no need to get aggressive over it. I'm not fighting you for the check."

"You can be a real douchebag, when you want to be." Not looking at him, I opened my purse and paid.

"Lindy…" He said as I walked out ahead of him.

Fuck him. I glanced back and flipped him off.

He gave me a questioning look, his lips twisting. "Lind? What's up?"

I held the restaurant door for him to follow me out.

He and I were good at laughing together, and we'd done a lot of that today. But we were just as good at fighting…

"What are you, the social police?"

He didn't answer.

"Let's go to a bar."

"If you are gonna stay off the alcohol. I don't want a repeat of last night."

"And now you're trying to be my dad!"

He glared. "No, Lind. I am just trying to look out for you!"

"I didn't ask you to! I don't need you to look out for me!"

"If I can be a douche, you can be a bitch…" He said that in a low voice, like it was to himself.

I flipped him off again and turned into the bar that was next to the restaurant. When I got to the counter he gripped my elbow. "I am paying. You aren't working. And seriously, no alcohol, Lind."

I poked my tongue out at him, but actually, being honest, I liked his bossy side. Billy didn't take any crap. Jason would have just let me rant, stayed quiet and stayed out of it, but to do a bit of shouting felt good, like letting the cork out of a bottle of champagne, it released a little of the pressure in me.

"I could try a beer, it was probably because I drank a cocktail last night—"

"Or 'cause your meds say no alcohol," he mocked, in a low gravelly, bitter voice, as he pulled his wallet out of the back pocket of his pants.

I shrugged, screwing my face up at him, to say fuck off.

"Shall we go outside and watch the sunset again?"

"If you won't be too cold." He glanced down at my legs, then his gaze came back up as the barman came over.

"I'll be okay,"

"A beer and a soda and lime…"

He remembered what I used to drink in our college apartment.

I turned away and left him to handle the drinks. Outside I found a table right at the edge of the terrace and sat facing out to sea, but Billy was right, it was cold. I crossed my legs and wrapped my arms about my chest.

When he set down his beer and my drink, he said, "The guy behind the bar stared at you as you walked out, his tongue was fricking hanging out. I don't know why the hell you think you don't have a good figure, I see guys doing it all the time around you." His pitch had turned to my defender now, our argument forgotten.

This was the Billy I liked the most—my one true friend. The guy who would do anything for me.

He dropped into the seat next to me, then leaned over. "You okay?"

I met his gaze. "Yeah." Protective Billy made me think of this morning and the way he'd been all day on the beach, making me laugh, making me face my fear of the ocean.

Heat clasped in my chest as the image of him nearly naked on the blanket surged into my head, and a memory of all that muscle carrying me out into the ocean.

I looked at the waves rolling up onto the beach and drank my soda, letting the sound roll over me like the motion of the waves.

I loved it here.

The cold breeze sweeping in with the water blew my hair back from my face, brushing my shoulders like fingers.

Billy watched me, not the water.

I turned to look at him. "You know what you said last night?"

"About what?"

"About when we did it in the SUV." His eyebrows lifted. I guess he thought I wouldn't go back to that subject. "That wasn't about you…"

"Uhh…"

"I mean, when I did it with Jason we did it like that… That's how sex is for me."

His eyes narrowed and he stared at me. Like I was crazy. Then like I was someone to be pitied.

I'd got that look all the time from people over Christmas, when Jason had dumped me for prettier-sexier Rachel. Poor-sad-passed-over-not-good-enough Lindy.

I hated it.

It was obvious why Jason had left me—everyone had worked it out. He was getting better sex.

Standing up, I said, "I'm gonna go down to walk on the beach." I left my barely touched drink on the table.

Billy rubbed a hand over his hair, like I'd shocked him and made him feel awkward, then realized he'd flattened it and spread his fingers, mussing it up to spike it again.

"Are you coming?"

He nodded, drank his beer and then left the bottle on the table before standing.

Things were brewing up in me. I wanted to ask him something… But I didn't know how… But if I didn't do this with Billy, I wouldn't be able to do it with anyone. And I did like him. We got on, and even though he'd laughed at me last night, I trusted him—he'd messed around with me today, made me happy and had me laughing and forgetting everything else. Protective Billy wouldn't let me get hurt.

And we'd done it once before.

And if anyone was gonna teach me…

When we got down on the beach I slipped my sandals off. All the feelings that had crowded in on me this morning, when I'd touched myself and thought of him, were there, within me, brewing and bubbling up.

We were halfway down to the water when I looked over at him. He was walking about a yard away from me, hands in his pockets.

"Billy…" His gaze lifted to me and I forced the words out. "I want to do it with you." I sucked a breath back in and held it as the words hit him.

"Lindy…" He sounded in pain, and his hand lifted, along with his eyebrows. It ran over his hair again, then ruffled it to spike it.

"You don't want to?" I stopped. "Am I really that bad, Billy?"

He stopped too. I tried to catch every little gesture of his body language.

His hand fell and hung by his side. "Lind. It's not that. It's just…"
His eyes begged me not to ask… like he was in agony. "You don't
really want to… I know… We had this conversation last night."

"But I don't want to be on my own forever, and I want to—"

"Lind, you're beautiful, you aren't gonna end up alone." His
hand came up then and reached out toward me, and he stepped
forward but then it dropped, like he thought better of the idea.
It wasn't comforting.

I didn't let him see how much that hurt, but it made my voice
bitter. "You didn't let me finish—I want to enjoy sex. I want you
to show me how."

He just stared at me for a moment. Then he said, "Look, Lind,
I don't know what to say to you but I know damn well you didn't
enjoy sex with me, and I am not stepping into that minefield again.
I showed you how to get yourself off this morning."

He turned away and started walking parallel to the ocean, his
profile lit up orange by the setting sun.

Great. Like that was the answer. That wasn't.

I followed him, my sandals swinging in one hand as I hurried
to keep up with his longer strides. "I want what Jason and Rachel
have… and I want to know why he wasn't like that with me, and
you are the only one I trust."

His head spun and he glared at me, his eyes angry and accusing,
but he didn't stop walking. "My point exactly. You don't want to
do it with me. I'm just convenient, so maybe that's what it was
for you back in the fall, and I can stop feeling guilty. But if we
did it, you'd be thinking of him. I don't feel like having three in
the bed, especially when the other guy's my best friend."

"You did it before! When I was with him!" He couldn't go all
judgmental. He'd started it then, and he'd known I'd loved Jason.

He stopped and glared at me. "Yeah, and you thought of him
when you did it with me! And you regretted it! I've said sorry
now. I don't make the same mistake twice!"

His hand swept through his hair. This time he didn't ruffle it, to put it right again, but left some of it flattened, turned around and walked on even faster.

On the horizon, the sun began to disappear into the ocean. The shadows around us were becoming more dark blue.

"Ask me the question you've been asking all day!"

He stopped dead and turned back. "What?"

"Ask me the question you've been asking all day," I urged him to do it.

He didn't answer for a minute. But then he sighed out a breath before sucking it back in and said, "So, did you?"

Billy

I didn't know why the fuck Lindy wanted me to ask her this again. What difference did it make—whatever she answered? So she'd done it. So what? It didn't mean I was gonna give in and go along with what she wanted. It was stupid. She was still completely wrapped up in Jason. This wasn't about me.

Her eyebrows lifted and her gaze didn't move from mine. The first throws of moonlight caught her blue eyes. "Yeah."

Great. So what?

"And I thought about you…"

Frickin' shit, what was this girl trying to do to me? I was doing right by her and she was busy putting crazy images in my head.

I turned away, my hand running through my hair. I didn't want her to know my reaction—I was turned on—but I fought it.

I shut my eyes, but that just made the mental image more vivid. Fuck.

My fingers clasped in my hair as I opened my eyes, then I ruffled it, 'cause I was fucking it up, and my hand fell. I didn't look at her but turned and started walking again. She copied, walking beside me.

"Why?" My tone was bitter. Like she had no right to think about me.

"'Cause I was thinking about when we did it in your SUV—"

"You were stiff as a board when we did it in the SUV, and you were busy blotting out my face and imaging Jason's." I glanced at her. "Don't deny it. 'Cause I'm not dumb. I know."

She didn't answer. I looked ahead and carried on walking. "I knew you weren't enjoying it, and I don't want to repeat that. It was horrible… It fucking haunts me."

I heard her swallow, as if she was gonna start crying. "But that's not 'cause of you…"

When I did it with Jason, we did it like that… That's what she'd said back at the bar; she hadn't just been talking about the position. Shit. Everything about her body said that she'd had sex as bad as that with Jason. She was stiff and defensive. They'd been together years! But I'd shared an apartment with them and I'd never heard any noise. They'd also never been touchy-feely, like he was with Rachel. His hands were always all over Rachel.

He hadn't been like that with Lindy, and they'd never disappeared into their room in the day…

The weight of my cell hung in the back pocket of my pants. I wanted to call Jason and ask. *What the fuck were you and Lindy doing when you were together?*

I wouldn't, though. That would be off the scale of wrong.

My fingers slipped through my hair again, and then I ruffled it to spike it once more.

As my arm dropped, the leather bracelet tied around my wrist spoke its silent call of ownership. I belonged to her, whether I liked it or not.

I sighed as my hand dropped. "Lind, whatever. We're not going there."

She turned away, to walk toward the ocean, but I caught her wrist. "Wait."

Her lips twisted in a "why" look. She was angry but she hurt more.

Great.

"Can't we just cut this conversation? I know I brought it up last night. But I am not your answer."

Her arm tugged against my grip. I let her go, and she turned and started walking down to the ocean.

I'd fucked this up.

"Lind!"

Stupid thing was, I had been dreaming about this—her saying she wanted me—for years. But the key word was want. Not make do! That did not entice.

And make do, and thinking about Jason while she did it. That was a completely shit idea.

And I thought about you…

When she'd said that she'd had my temperature rocketing, and my cock twitching, but then she'd added, '*cause I was thinking about when we did it in the SUV.*

Shit, that had been nothing to think about it. She could not have been getting off on me.

She was a dark silhouette in the moonlight, her hair brushing over her shoulders and her back. I pictured my fingers settling in the hollow at the back of her neck. Then she bent suddenly, picking something up, flashing a long length of the back of her thighs. The cold breeze blowing up from the ocean swept her dress against her lower body, making the fabric cling to her curves.

I wanted her. I did. There was no denying it. I had for years. Thing was, she didn't want me. No matter what she said.

My hands back in my pockets I walked up to her. She looked at whatever she'd picked up.

"What have you got?"

She glanced at me, sensing my peace offering. "A shell." Her pitch was curt, but quiet. "I like shells, I like how smooth they are. This one has a metallic glow in the moonlight." Her fingers rubbed across it. "I like all the different colors that come through in them in the sunshine, but I have never seen one in the moonlight before. It's different now… Look, it glitters." She looked at me. "It looked like a fallen star, lying on the beach."

I couldn't work out how the confident, assertive, competitive, yet fun, warm-hearted Lindy I'd grown up with could be this uncertain-angry-self-condemning girl.

But then if her whole thing with Jason had been so badly flawed… It must have been making her question herself for years.

My cell felt heavy again as we turned back toward the apartments and walked on. I wanted to call Jason. He was the only one I could talk this stuff out with. Did he never really like her or what?

It couldn't be his sex drive. I mean everything about him and Rachel suggested they were at it like rabbits.

I was getting myself caught up in a frickin' whole pile of bullshit here.

When we got back to the apartments it was still pretty early, but she didn't ask me if I wanted to do anything, she just said, "Goodnight," slotting her door key into the lock.

"Night."

She glanced back at me before going in, then that was it.

Great.

I hovered outside her door for a moment, but what was I gonna say or do?

Sighing, I headed for my room and then threw myself down on the bed with a grunt of frustration. I was making a mess of this. I'd brought her out here to make her feel better and me less guilty, and things were worse on both counts.

Then I heard her crying through the wall.

Awesome.

I got back up, went out and knocked on her door. "Lind?" No answer. But she stopped sobbing. "Lind? Let me in!"

A couple of minutes passed. I leaned against the wall by the door. "I'm not going away! I know you're crying. I heard you. Open the door."

"I'm not going to do anything!" She shouted back.

"I know that. But I want to be able to comfort you."

"You were the one who upset me!"

"I know! Let me come in and say sorry."

There was no sound, but then the door opened. She didn't say anything; just walked away again.

I went in and shut the door, my heart hitting in my chest like my fingers were beating out a drum beat. Fuck. I wanted her. "Look, okay. We'll just take this slow."

She sat down on the bed, her eyes red-rimmed and mascara smudged, and her hands tucked beneath her thighs. "What's this?"

"Whatever this is." I guessed neither of us really knew. "Look tonight just let me hold you. If it goes further, it does, but I'm not gonna force it."

She looked up at me, eyes wide, but she didn't look pleased, she looked terrified.

"Do you want me to sleep in here?"

She sighed. "Yeah."

"Well then get ready for bed, and we'll snuggle up and put a film on the TV or something." She nodded. But she still didn't look happy.

I sat on her bed as she went into the bathroom, my elbows on my knees, and my head in my hands. I ran both hands over my hair, messing it up totally.

When she came out the bathroom, she'd refreshed her makeup, not taken it off, and was wearing satin pajama bottoms with a little sleeveless tee. She had no bra on and I could see every detail of her breasts through the cotton. She was gorgeous, fucking edible, literally.

I got up. "I'm gonna, go clean my teeth, I'll be back."

I used the bathroom in my room, did my teeth, and put on some more deodorant. Then went back to knock on her door. She'd turned the lights out apart from one lamp beside her bed.

"You okay with this?" I checked as I slipped my cell and wallet out of my pocket and she slid under the covers, then shifted across the bed.

"I invited you."

She had, but my plan right now wasn't about sex.

I undid a couple of buttons on my shirt, then pulled it off over my head, throwing it onto a low table across the room. She watched, but when I started unbuttoning my pants she looked away, rolling on to her side, with her back to me. Well, then, that said it all.

I slipped my pants and sneakers off and dumped them over by the table. Then I got into bed next to her wearing only my boxers. She didn't move and didn't turn.

"Do you want to put the TV on?"

"No, the anti-depressants make me tired."

Her whole body was stiff, and it screamed uncomfortable. "Turn the light out then slide back against me and let me hold you."

She reached out and clicked the light off, then shifted back and spooned with me.

I slid her hair off her cheek and kissed her behind the ear. Her whole body jolted, every muscle locking.

She didn't want to—really didn't want to.

Slipping my arm about her belly, I just held her, and eventually I felt her muscles relax as she fell asleep.

It took me longer.

Chapter Six

Billy

When I opened my eyes in the morning, Lindy lay on her side, facing me, looking right into my eyes, her breath brushing my skin. I had a hard-on.

"Morning," she whispered.

It was light outside.

"Morning."

"Do you want to?"

Shit, my sleep-fogged brain was not up to leading conversations. I guessed she'd misjudged my need for a piss as unconscious interest.

"I need the toilet, Lind." Rolling away from her, I threw the covers off and went into the bathroom. As I used the toilet, I caught my reflection in the mirror, my jaw was dark with stubble, and my hair riotous, spiked in every direction; a great just-woken-up look.

The image of Lindy's eyes looking into mine appeared in my drowsy brain. She'd had eye shadow and mascara on, and her lips had been tinted by whatever lip gloss she'd had on them last night. Oh, yeah, she'd got into bed wearing all her makeup.

I'd never seen her without makeup.

Had Jason ever seen her without makeup?

After I washed my hands, I threw some water on my face, to

wake up. Then I wiped my face on her towel. It smelt of perfume.

In the apartment, I went over to get a bottle of water, then glanced back over my shoulder. "Do you want a drink?"

She was still in the bed, under the covers. Her blonde hair spread out over the pillow.

She shook her head. "Are you gonna get back in bed?"

I took a couple of gulps of the water, screwed the lid back on the bottle, and turned around, smiling, but not pleasantly I was sure. My head dodged around all sorts of ideas and my heart played through a dozen emotions. Want. Anger. Pain. Annoyance… The list went on. There was a tornado of stuff going on inside me. "Why?"

"'Cause I want another cuddle. Get back in bed."

She turned to her side, looking at me, her legs curling up under the comforter.

I guess cuddling wouldn't harm, and the truth was my former piss-proud hard-on was dangerously close to being a real hard-on, as I imagined her nude under there. She wasn't nude, though.

I left the water on the side, walked over and got back in next to her. Immediately she turned around to snuggle against me, her arms slipping around my neck, as mine burrowed around her middle.

Lindy was tiny; she was like a little doll with her makeup on.

Her forehead pressed into my shoulder, her hair getting caught on my stubble.

But that didn't seem to bother her. She pressed in closer, her legs together next to mine and her warm, soft breasts brushing against my chest, through the cotton of her top.

Then she kissed my neck.

My whole body stiffened as a shockwave ran straight to the tip of my cock.

She carried on kissing, sucking and nipping at my neck.

My groin got heavy, flooding with lust. My brain knew better, but my body didn't.

I brushed her hair back from my chin and her face, running my fingers through it over and over as she carried on, and then started kissing the stubble on my jaw.

Something painful and desperate gripped hard in my belly.

There was no doubting I wanted her, and when her lips touched mine, I rolled her back onto the bed, taking over the kiss and slipping my tongue in her mouth.

Her tongue moved against mine, but there was hesitation in the movement and she did not press her tongue back into my mouth when I tried to lead her into doing it...

I broke the kiss, my forearm beneath her head as I leaned up on that elbow. My other palm rested on her hip over the satin of her pajama bottoms. "Lindy if you want this, honey, you're gonna have to take off your pj bottoms." It was a test. I wanted to know if she was really up for this, 'cause I still wasn't convinced.

She bit her lip looking up at me, then she said in a quiet voice. "Okay."

She looked scared, though. I wasn't sure. I got out of the bed, another test, and stripped off my boxers. My interest was plain. This hard-on was absolutely down to her and it bounced a little as I peeled my boxers off my feet.

She shimmied off her bottoms, still buried under the covers.

I got back in the bed, turning to her as she dropped her bottoms on the floor on the other side. My palm settled on her naked hip, touching flesh that felt smoother than the fabric she'd taken off.

She wasn't overweight at all. I could feel her hip bone through her flesh. She had broad hips, that was all.

I leaned to kiss her and pressed my tongue into her mouth. She answered it, her tongue moving around mine and her arms coming about my neck.

My erection brushed against her hip as she lay on her back, while my hand slipped up under the cotton of her sleeveless t-shirt. I didn't know why she hadn't just taken her top off too, but I wasn't going to stop again.

Kneading her small breast, I brushed my fingertips over her nipple. It peaked proudly for me. A sharp breath left her throat, leaking into my mouth, but her body didn't move. She was still lying flat, her arms about my neck and legs together. I kissed her harder, seeking more response, seeking something that would tell me this was about me, and nothing else… But her body didn't move much, just a little.

I slid my hand from her breast down her body to sweep through her pubic hair, but there was none there. Her body jolted and she gasped.

Was that good or bad? She was so like stone I couldn't read her.

She was just doing this. Not following instinct, and definitely not burning up with need for me.

I ran my fingers down the seam between her closed thighs.

She didn't part them.

She didn't want this!

I rolled to my back, sighing, one arm still beneath her, as my other lifted from under the covers, and my hand ran over my hair.

Fuck.

"Billy?" She rolled onto her side, leaning up on her elbow.

I looked into her blue eyes, such a pure color. "Look, Lind, I'm not stupid. If you want sex, you have to open your legs. You don't want sex."

I got out the bed, trying to get a grip on my frustration and grabbed my boxers up off the floor, sliding them back on, before sitting on the edge of the bed. My elbows on my knees, I rubbed my hair with both my hands. Feeling her shifting in the bed, I turned to see her slipping back into her bottoms.

"I let you do it before," she said.

"Let…" That was the key word here. "Lind, 'let' is very different to 'want'. I don't want you to let me do anything. I'd rather not do it."

I stood up. "I'm going back to my room. I'm gonna go down to the gym for a bit. What do you want to do today?"

She looked like I'd punched her in the gut. Pale, afraid, and doubtful too.

I carried on. "You said you prefer the pool. Let's hang out by the pool today, then."

She nodded.

"Shall I knock for you in a couple of hours?"

"Yeah." She breathed, like she was gonna say more.

I didn't wait to hear it. I didn't want to hear anymore. I grabbed my clothes and walked out into the hall, semi-naked.

There was a couple out there with a kid. They stared at me, no doubt judging this as a walk of shame. It was, but not for the reason they were thinking.

Ignoring them, I headed straight in to my room.

In there, I dropped my clothes onto the bed, and hit the side of my fist against the wall.

When was I gonna learn?

Lindy

When Billy knocked for me, he'd obviously just got out the shower, his wet hair was waxed up, he'd shaven, and he smelled nice. He had a white tee on with the shorts he'd worn yesterday, and a towel hung over his shoulder. He looked strong and domineering, and… like Billy—except his blue eyes flashed and his jaw was taut. I didn't know if I preferred him in a white t-shirt or a dark one. I'd thought dark, but the white against his sun-tanned skin looked good, and it seemed to define his muscular build more. I wanted to touch.

Wanted. See it was more than let. But that was my brain talking. My body had a mind of its own.

"I'll just get my towel." I couldn't keep looking at him. I felt too awkward. This was a mess and I'd made it. Everything I touched turned to a pile of crap.

He leaned a massive shoulder against the door, holding it open as I grabbed my towel. I didn't take my backpack, so we could go in the water easily.

"You okay?" he said as I walked past him out into the hall.

"Yeah." He seemed deflated not really angry. Just frustrated. "You?"

"Oh, okay. I might need to sort myself out later, after our little game this morning, but hey, that's not going to be anything new…"

What was he on about? I didn't ask him; this was a minefield I was tip-toeing through. If I asked, the whole thing would explode in my face again. I wanted the Billy of yesterday back. "Cheer me up."

He glanced at me.

"I know I'm an idiot, I'm sorry, forget it, and just cheer me up."

"How do you want cheering up?" His shoulder's relaxed a little, and a smile twisted the edge of his lips, accepting that I'd chosen to walk away from the minefield.

"Tell me jokes." He'd always been good at remembering and telling jokes, and when we'd shared a place at college I always used to say that to him when I was feeling down. Hours of my time had been spent sitting on the sofa with my legs tucked up under me, with him leaning on the back of it, throwing joke after joke at me.

He threw me a sharp smile, accepting the olive branch I'd tossed at him. "Okay…"

When we got down to the pool, I was laughing and breathless, and he was laughing at me, not his jokes.

"I can't believe you really find that shit funny."

"I like your shit. You should've gone into stand-up, you have the timing."

"And the stupidity."

I brushed my fingers along his cheek as I dropped my towel on a lounger, "and the courage…"

He made a scoffing sound. "The courage to make a fool of myself. That would be about right."

"You're no fool, Billy."

"Yeah, well…" His words ran dry as he threw his towel down and looked away from me, then stripped off his tee.

A hot tingle gripped tight in my belly at the sight of his chest. The tingle slid down between my legs.

It was want. I longed to reach out and touch him.

He looked at me as he slid his shorts off, leaving only his swim trunks on. "You stripping, or you gonna swim fully clothed?"

I'd put the dress I'd worn last night on over my bikini, and now I held my breath as I stripped it off. I knew I had to. If I was gonna get more confident in bed, I had to get more confident about my body.

I'd talked to my counselor over the cell while he'd been in the gym. I'd told her everything Billy had said. I couldn't talk to Mom about anything, so it was good to have a new person who was there to listen, and I'd got on well with her from the first moment I'd met her. She'd been really understanding. Not judging, or commenting, just listening.

After I'd finished, she'd asked what I thought about it. I'd told her he was right. She told me I had to deal with my issues, but she'd said it was probably just because of everything that had been going on, and not to worry about it. To just relax and do what felt right.

The conversation had made me feel a lot better, and now I was just trying to relax and not pressure myself into going too fast. She'd said I had to take things a step at a time. Look at my own body more and learn to like myself… Then the rest would follow.

But stripping off was hard.

Billy watched me, or rather my body. His gaze lifted when I threw my dress on the lounger. "Do you want to lie down or get straight in the pool."

"Can we get in the pool?" I hated being on show and there were a lot of people lying around the pool. I just wanted to be in the water and out of sight. My head was having a hard time dealing with the exposure. I felt like a beacon crying "ugly" with flashing lights, even though no one around us looked at me.

I turned quickly and walked to the pool, to sit on the edge and slip in. But Billy grabbed me and swung me up into his massive arms.

"Billy!" he was gonna throw me in the water. "My makeup!" I squealed at him.

"That's boring, Lind." He dropped my legs back to the ground. "Why even wear makeup down to a pool?"

With that he turned away and dived into the deep end, slipping beneath the water like an arrow, all smooth, elongated muscle and sinew. He was big, but his muscle was loose. His shoulders mostly looked relaxed and not stiff at all.

I sat down on the edge as he reappeared on the far side, then used a fast crawl stroke, his face slipping in and out of the water. Some women around the pool watched him. He had a good body, the definition in his abs and pecs was gorgeous. Their observation didn't annoy me. I was proud to be here with him. I'd watch him if I was a stranger.

I lowered myself in carefully, and with my head up so my face didn't get wet, I swam breaststroke toward where he was swimming into the shallow end. Trying to keep my hair out of the water as best I could, though I could feel the end of my damp ponytail trailing on my shoulders.

There was a bar serving drinks in the water on the far side of the pool and a couple of people sat on stools in the water, leaning on it, talking to the bartender.

There was a kids' pool the other side of the complex, with slides and stuff. it meant there were no kids around here to splash me.

Billy got to the end of the pool and stood up in the shallows, facing me with his elbows on the side, looking casual and handsome, smiling at me as his leopard tattoo shifted like it really clawed his chest.

That leopard looked angry. It bothered me. There was something weird about it. It looked cool and colorful. It was a work of art... But it screamed anger and I knew how that felt.

Beyond Billy's shoulder, a girl on a lounger watched him.

"Hey tortoise," he said as I swam up.

"Hey." I put my feet down on the bottom and my fingers slipped to pull the hem of my bikini bottoms more snugly over my ass. It had slipped up while I was swimming.

"There's a girl behind you thinking you look mighty fine."

He laughed. "Well, nice to know that someone thinks it, Lind." The implication was I didn't.

I leaned back into the water and then started swimming backwards doing an invented stroke, still trying to keep my head up. "I think so too."

He came after me, catching hold of my ankle as it lifted, and pulled me back, but then he let go and started swimming on his belly next to me, doing the breaststroke. I turned and swam next to him.

"Well I think you look pretty good in that bikini. I like stars. I might be making some wishes."

My bikini was dark blue with little stars all over the material, and there wasn't much of it. It tied either side of my hips. But I'd liked the little halter-neck top. It had a gold star between my breasts. I'd bought it to wear under clothes, though. I felt self-conscious now.

We didn't talk as we finished the length and then swam back, both of us using breaststroke. Words span around in my head. I wanted to pick the right ones.

He stopped, standing up in the pool and leaning against the side again. I caught the same girl watching him.

"Come here." He reached out and gripped my arm, pulling me closer, and then his arm stayed around me and I put mine up around his neck, holding his gaze and letting him capture all of my attention.

"Sorry about earlier." His fingers lifted a lock of my hair that had come loose from my ponytail and tucked it behind my ear. "But you do understand."

"Yeah." I swallowed back my fear. Just relax and get the words out. "But my head does want you, Billy, it isn't just *let*. My body just doesn't know how…"

He sighed, his gaze getting more intense. "What about Jason?"

"What about Jason?" I didn't understand.

"Your body doesn't know how… What about Jason?" His hand slipped to the small of my back, like he thought I was going to move away and tried to stop me.

"You heard what Rachel said. I told you—"

"I mean did you want? Or did you let?"

God, the honest truth. I whispered it, "Let."

His eyebrows went up. "Lindy, for years…"

"I told you, my body doesn't know how."

His hands came up and gripped my head and then he spun me against the side, kissing me, his tongue pressing into my mouth. When he broke the kiss, he said over my lips. "I can teach your body how. That's no hard deal."

He kissed me again, his hands slipping under the water and gripping my hips, his thumbs pressing down on my pelvic bones. I'd hated Jason touching my hips, it had just reminded me how uncomfortable I felt about my size, but Billy's touch was different, it said… I like.

The next thing I knew his pelvis was pressing against mine and it wasn't just his fingers saying "I like"; a hard erection pressed against my belly, and his hands slid around to slip into the back of my bikini bottoms and gripped my buttocks.

When he broke the kiss he didn't let go and he didn't move away.

My fingers swept his wet hair off his brow.

"So then, I guess I am up for seeing where this goes." He looked down at me with bright eyes. "If you are, and the offer's still open."

I took a breath, feeling like the ground shifted underneath the pool. "The offer's still open and I'm up for seeing where this goes too."

My arms were up on his shoulders as he lowered his head and kissed me again, and this time his tongue kept teasing mine.

Gently knocking against it, until I realized he was trying to get me to move my tongue in the same way he was. I tried. But then he broke the kiss and lifted his head. "Kissing is like a game of tag. By the way, you're it."

Shit. He kissed me with an open mouth, but didn't use his tongue. It was a challenge. I felt hot and stupid as I slipped my tongue past his lips. I had never done that with Jason. Stupid. But—I had always let—never done.

Billy's tongue stroked over mine, receptive and encouraging. I tried to relax and think about what would feel good. After a minute he pulled back, breaking the kiss again, and pressed his forehead against mine. "Overthinking babe. Just do what feels right?"

"Okay." I tipped my chin up and pressed my lips to his, then ran my tongue over his lower lip, 'cause Jason had always used to do that to me, and I wanted to know what it felt like to do it. Then I pressed my mouth hard against his, feeling bold and determined, and fought against my head trying not to overthink but just do.

His palm settled at the back of my head and his mouth and his tongue answered me, pressing just as hard back, as his pelvis pushed against me. A warm, sharp delicious pain pierced my belly, thrusting down between my legs.

A game of tag. I'd tagged him and he'd taken over. I let him lead for a while, but then fought for command of the kiss. My palms pressed against his cheekbones as my fingers clung in his hair.

I was breathless when we stopped kissing and I'd lost any awareness of all the people around the pool.

"Do you want a drink?" he asked.

"Yeah."

"Better wait until my erection goes down, though, hey?"

I laughed. Shit. I felt like I had never kissed anyone before. But then the only other person I'd kissed was Jason. How did we get things so wrong? He was fine with Rachel.

I sighed at myself. Angry with myself. With my lack of confidence and fear. It had held me back. I wasn't going to let it anymore, I was going to face my demons and beat them down. I had to just deal with everything, whatever, I couldn't keep running from things…

And if I could find a sanctuary in Billy… then cool… I did want it. Desperately.

Lindy

We'd spent all day around the pool, messing around in the water, and when we'd had a drink at the bar Billy had told me to open my legs as I sat on the stool in the water, and then he'd stood between my thighs.

His hands had been touching me all day, resting on my thighs as we'd been drinking at the pool bar or at my waist when we'd just been standing in the pool. When we lay on the loungers in the sun, he'd pulled his up next to mine and rested his hand on my lower back, until I'd said move it so I didn't get a tan mark. Then instead he'd rested his hand by my side, and his little finger had kept nudging the first curve of my breast.

He was so different to Jason.

Jason had never touched me like that.

But then if Jason had continually touched me in a way that constantly implied he was thinking about sex, I'd have told him to leave me alone.

I'd pushed him away.

This time I was trying not to. But then I didn't want to tell Billy to leave me alone. His touch was different—reverent. Like he loved touching me. It made my nerves tingle with expectation, and I'd got damp, like I'd got damp touching myself, and hot. I felt really hot, even though the day was not that hot. It was an internal heat, flaring and simmering under my skin. Like he'd switched something on.

The last time we got in the pool, when the area had started to empty and only a few people were left around, he became more daring. When I sat on the stool at the bar in the water, his palm slid up my thigh and his thumb brushed over my bikini bottoms, rubbing just for an instant, then his hand slid away.

He did it a dozen times, running his hand up my leg as we talked, then brushing over the part of me that was already sensitized and throbbing for him to do more, then he slid his hand back down my leg.

I tried to remember to breathe and talk at the same time, acting like there was nothing going on, because there was another couple sitting two seats away from us.

Then he pulled me off the stool into the water, nearly getting my hair wet and splashing my eyes, and tugged me out into the deeper water, to kiss me. There his hand slid up over my ribs and his thumb snuck beneath my top, reaching right up to stroke over my painfully hardened nipple a couple of times.

People might have seen, but he hid his action with his body.

When he broke the kiss, his hand slipped away, pulling my top back down to make sure I was covered, then he leaned to my ear. "Your room or mine?"

"Mine," I answered, panic swamping me.

This was new to me—this feeling. I didn't just want him; I was desperate for him. If I didn't have him, I didn't know what I'd do; how I would fix the intense buzzing and burning throbbing in my blood.

He'd spent a whole day on foreplay. That is what he'd been up to in the pool, sensitizing me. Making me want it. He'd said he knew how and he did.

Now I had to face up to this decision, though.

When we approached my room, despite my longing, fear tangled in my belly, like a ball of rubber bands, as more and more were wrapped around it.

We hadn't put our clothes back on. Billy had all our clothes draped over his shoulder and a towel about his waist. I had my towel wrapped around me and tucked in over my breasts.

One of his hands gripped mine firmly, his fingers threaded

through mine. I'd swear he knew I'd had an impulse to run and he urged me not to.

Terror, desperation and desire whizzed around in me like fireworks on July 4th.

I wanted him to keep me focused.

I didn't want to run.

I wanted to do this—to feel what it was like to enjoy having sex.

"Where's your room key?"

"In the pocket of my dress."

He let go of my hand. I wished he hadn't. My cowardice became ten times worse.

He slipped the clothes off his shoulder, hunted it out and handed it to me.

I slotted it in the door. The latch clicked. My belly plummeted to the soles of my feet.

I shut my eyes as I went in, praying for courage as my hands shook. My belly was Jell-O—the hunger and desire I'd burned with outside the door, smothered.

He threw all our stuff on my bed as the door shut.

I didn't know if I could do this.

"Shall we shower?"

He didn't know I was in full-on panic. I was too messed up, I couldn't answer.

He took my silence as acceptance, gripped my hand, pulled me into the bathroom and into the shower, tugging off his towel. Then the fingers of his free hand pulled off the towel covering me and he tossed it on the tiles outside the shower.

There was room for two. "My makeup," I said, as he turned it on.

The water poured down on us.

"Please tell me you don't wear makeup in the shower." His pitch was low and strong, no-nonsense. You-are-just-going-to-do-it-as-I-say. "You must wash it off sometime."

His hands gripped my hips, over my pelvic bones and pressed me back against the tiles. His big body unnerved me. He was broader and stronger than Jason.

But in a way it was like a dare…

I wanted to be different, and if I could be different with Billy, I could be different with anyone. I wanted to feel what all that strength could do.

We'd done it before and I'd liked the feel of his muscle moving between my thighs. That's what I'd imagined the other day, but I knew he'd been holding back.

I wanted to know what he'd held back, what doing it with Billy, properly, would be like. It was going to be nothing like doing it with Jason.

He kissed my jaw and by my ear, beside my eyes. Nudging little kisses. They sent tremors through my nerves. Fear and desire went to war with swords inside me.

"I don't like people seeing me without makeup." My head tipped back against the tiles as his kisses travelled to my jaw again and on to my neck,

"Why?" The word vibrated on my neck, as his hand clasped my breast over my bikini top, then his lips and teeth nipped at the sensitive skin on my neck.

I was hot between my legs; I'd never had that sensation with Jason.

The water poured on to my face, and his head, and his back, running down.

His other hand slipped inside the back of my bottoms and gripped my ass.

"Because, I don't like it. I feel naked without makeup." I said the words to the steam filling the air above us. It was hard to breathe. An iron bar of panic wrapped around me.

With Jason I'd never thought about sex, my mind had wandered around, drifting from one thought to another, never really absorbed in what he was doing… But he'd never done anything with the insistence and force that oozed from Billy.

His head lifted.

I met his dark-blue gaze.

It reached right into me, as his hand slid down beneath my breast, pressing over my ribs. He knew my brain had put on the brakes.

"So this is back to a lack of confidence. You told me yesterday you don't like your body and now you're saying you don't like your face. I don't get you, Lind, you're the most assertive person I know. You've bossed Jason around for years. Remember I lived with you. Where does all this insecurity come from?"

"I don't know. That is why I have a counselor, to help me unpick it."

His lips tilted in an odd smile. It questioned and showed his doubt.

A memory of my first visit to her struck like a lightning bolt. My gaze dropped to his shoulder. As my hands gripped his waist, clasping muscle. "I'm like my Mom… That's all I've worked out so far. I get it from her, a need to be perfect. To never fail. To never look weak, or ugly, or…" I took a breath as I thought of the truth—of how much pain that meant.

How was a person ever perfect in an imperfect world?

My makeup hid my imperfections; I couldn't take it off.

In my second session, I'd learned that was what I was best at—hiding anything and everything that made me imperfect.

I was good at covering up what was really going on.

I had learned that from Mom too.

That was why the counselor said I'd slipped up and got so depressed. She'd said I should stop hiding and try to let things out. Talk to people…

I couldn't do that.

But I had to deal with the stuff going on in my head and not hide it.

Oh shit, understanding rose like the sun. Makeup was a part of that. A way for me to wear a disguise and hide behind it emotionally, not just physically. I *was* like Mom…

Billy pressed his mouth over mine.

He'd known my thoughts had gone to places beyond him. That was how it had been with Jason. I'd never really been with him when we'd done it—*it had been let.*

For a minute I'd forgotten Billy was even here.

I shut my eyes. Gripping the muscle at his waist more firmly.

He was here.

And I was here.

His tongue slipped into my mouth.

Instinct pulled at me. *Play tag.* Like we'd been doing all day.

He broke the kiss. "You have no idea how beautiful you are. You don't need makeup, Lind."

Shit, the timbre of his words tingled through my nerves, racing through my body.

Jason had told me I was pretty. Frequently. I'd never really believed him.

But the way Billy said it…

I lifted onto my toes and pressed my lips against his. One of his big hands came up and embraced the back of my head, his long fingers separating as his whole body pressed me back against the tiles, his erection straining to get out of his swim shorts. I fought to keep up with his game of tag.

I could not forget he was there now if I tried.

His body called to mine. What he did wasn't only in my head, but in my blood and my nervous system. I shook, but it was not from fear anymore. Anticipation tumbled around us.

Both his hands slipped into the back of my bikini bottoms. They curled and massaged my buttocks. He did it to arouse us both, pulling me against him and then letting me fall back against the tiles.

He was desperate.

I'd never felt that in Jason.

Jason had always been gentle and tolerant, slow, and deliberate—always making sure I was okay when he progressed. But

I'd told him no a lot. He'd never pushed, or urged, or encouraged.

Billy was doing all those things, his whole body was insistence, but not in a way that made me think he wouldn't stop. If I said stop. I knew he'd stop.

But he didn't make me want to say stop.

I wanted him to continue.

One hand ran up my back. The bow behind my neck was tugged and undone. Then the bow in the middle of my back. My bikini top fell loose.

I'd always done it with Jason in the dark, under the covers. I'd never liked him looking at my body. This was a hundred times different. It was daylight; it poured in through a skylight. Nothing was hidden.

Vulnerability cried out in my head again but Billy didn't give me time to let fear take hold. My top was pulled away and his mouth left mine, then a second later it closed over my breast, as his hand held it. His other hand was still on my ass, gripping and massaging. It slid further down, his fingertips tantalizingly straining to reach my sensitized swollen flesh.

Lord.

Shit.

I had never felt like this. My head fell back against the tiles, my fingers curling and gripping in his wet hair as the water kept on drenching our sexual game.

Jason had sucked my breasts. A ton of times. But now the sensation pulled inside me, not just an external feeling, an internal pull, as if a cord stretched from my nipple to that part of me the video on the internet had told me to touch.

I wanted Billy to touch me there.

Ah… Jason had always been gentle.

Billy was not gentle. His suck was hard and insistent. There was no way my brain was wandering away from this.

"Oh." Had that sound come from my mouth?

This was so different.

His fingers let go of my ass and slipped out of my bikini bottoms. I didn't want him to let go.

The bow at the side came loose.

I shut my eyes as he gripped my ass again, and his other hand let go of my breast, then freed the other side of my bottoms.

My poor brain grasped at every sensation, hidden in the darkness behind my eyelids.

My heart thundered out a racing base beat.

His mouth pulled at my breast and his hand came back up to knead it with a firm grip as my bottoms fell onto the shower floor. I was naked in the daylight.

I shut my eyes tighter and bit my lip, pushing aside the fear that hovered over my head. This was vulnerability beyond anything I'd know before.

But fear had just become another dimension adding to the intoxicating things he did.

I thought his hands would get more intimate, but they didn't. The suction on my breast pulled free, my nipple sliding off his tongue. Play tag. I wondered if in the future my breast could play tag with his tongue too.

His mouth pressed over mine; a hard, firm kiss as his fingers gripped my ass again and pulled me tight against him, only this time my skin was brushing against the cotton of his swim shorts and the pressure of his erection rested against my belly.

It was erotic—tantalizing—as his tongue played in my mouth.

Billy.

My hands slid down his back to his butt and gripped the firm, round, muscle through his swim shorts.

His hand moved to take them off.

He'd thought I'd asked for that. I hadn't, but I guess if this was going further that had to be done, and I wanted it to go further.

This was so beyond normal for me. Jason had never done anything like this, never been urgent.

Billy pushed down his shorts, they slipped to his feet, then he kicked them away, still kissing me.

His flesh pressed against mine.

This is going too fast!

Billy's fingers curled around my buttocks, reaching beneath. I thought he was going to lift me. If he had I'd have said no, as panic flared like a forest fire.

But he didn't.

He dropped to his knees. I gasped.

I felt sick.

My fingers gripping either side of his head, I tried to pull him up. "Billy! No!" I didn't want this. I wasn't ready. "No! Please! I can't!" My voice pleaded pathetically for him to stop when I couldn't pull him up.

Billy

Lindy's body had gone rigid the minute I'd dropped to my knees, and her grip bracing my head was like a vice trying to pull me up. She sounded panicked.

I looked up, my fingers still gripping her ass as the water rained down on me.

Her fingers clawed on my neck, pulling.

"Relax, Lind."

She shook her head, all her muscles still tight with anxiety. "I don't do this. I don't like it." Her dyed lashes held droplets of water as her blue eyes reflected her urgency—terrified.

She was weird. My brow squished, my lips twisting—probably telling her I'd thought that. "Well, I do, Lind. So are you gonna let me?"

Shit, why had I used the word let? Want… She didn't want. And I didn't want her to let.

Her head shook, her teeth cutting so hard into her lip it turned white on the edges.

I stood. This wasn't going any further.

As I moved, my erection brushed her leg and hip. It had not

acknowledged her denial.

My hands still holding her bottom, I rested my forehead against hers, sighing out the desire, raging to do what I'd planned.

We'd been playing all day. My body was like one of those sprung toys, all coiled-up and ready to jump, with a sexual energy that wanted to explode. I breathed out, "Why?"

"'Cause it's strange."

"Why strange?"

She fell back against the tiles, slipping out of my hands.

"It's too intimate."

"Intimate in what way?"

"Billy, stop tying my words in knots!"

"How else am I gonna understand…" Exasperation touched my pitch.

The stupid girl started crying.

Way to kill a moment. That put the fires of desire right out. There was nothing even smoldering. My cock got the text. *It is not happening.*

I wrapped my arms around her and pulled her against me. Her head fell against my shoulder, her face pressing into my neck.

"I take it you and Jason never did that."

She shook her head.

What the fuck had they done? Just the missionary position and nothing else?

The water poured down on us.

"Sometimes you have to face your fear."

She pulled away. "I'm not afraid. It's just… Letting someone that close—"

"Is too intimate…" I finished for her.

Her body shivered.

Frigid, Rachel had said.

Rachel could only have got that definition from Jason.

Lindy had hated sex. Just done it—in the missionary position.

Frick.

She'd trapped herself in with this discomfort. No wonder they'd ended.

"I suppose this is down to your stupid obsession with how you look. Cause you think I'm gonna see something you don't want me to… That I won't like… Lind, you should let the guy be the judge of what he likes. Believe me, everything down there is only going to turn me on. I'm a guy, you're a girl, and I'm not gay, so I'm pretty sure it's all gonna be okay."

My pinky finger was on her neck, her pulse raced like mad beneath it.

She was truly terrified, like she had a phobia.

I kissed her. Kissing had seemed to work pretty well in the pool for helping her forget she was only wearing a bikini.

I moved one hand, slipping my thumb across her belly to brush the skin above the place she was terrified I'd see and hate.

I ran it lower.

She was Hollywood.

Why go frickin' Hollywood when you had no intention of letting anyone down there?

Weird girl.

Her muscles slackened a little as she started playing tag with my tongue and her arms came up around my neck, but her movements were hesitant. She didn't trust me anymore.

If we were starting up again and going further, I just had to do it, and let her deal with it—or stop me again. One or the other.

My thumb ran down and touched her. Her whole body jolted. But it was kind of sexy to have that much influence over her.

I broke the kiss. "You okay?" I said against her cheek, as I brushed her again, and moved to kiss her neck.

She swallowed. Hesitating. "Yeah."

"Tell me at any time you're not."

"Okay."

"But I'm going to do what I want, Lind, because you're beautiful and you need to know it, and you need to get over this stupid thing, and not care what anyone else thinks."

The heat of her breath brushed my shoulder as water poured onto my back, but she didn't say no. She was going to try to brave this out.

I didn't want her to be brave. I wanted her to want me to do it.

I rubbed her a few times more, until she stopped jolting and her arms settled more heavily on my shoulders as she relaxed, her tongue dancing around mine, fighting to keep up. Her thoughts were on our game of tag. I slid my fingers between her legs and two into her.

She gasped. Her arms tightening back up, clinging rather than embracing.

I broke the kiss. "Still okay?" I brushed my lips over hers before she could answer—gently, teasing her senses.

She pulled back, her gaze meeting mine, as she nodded. "I'm okay."

I guess they had done this.

"Think about how things feel—nothing else. Focus on sensations."

She shut her eyes nodding again, and leaning her head back onto the tiles. It looked like sacrifice. *But my head does want you, Billy, it isn't just let. My body just doesn't know how...*

Well I was gonna teach her body how, and her head would have to catch up.

She had said she wanted.

I kissed and bit her neck, my fingers drawing in and out.

She'd been turned off, but she was moist, and her internal skin soft like satin. My painful erection pushed at her hip and my thumb brushed her too, to hold her mind on me.

She started relaxing, her weight resting against the tiles.

I longed for her to move—to rock against my hand. But this was only acceptance, not participation. Let... She stood still, just limper than before.

But she'd said she wanted.

I brushed kisses across her cheek, then whispered in her ear. "If kissing is tag, then sex is a competition, honey. You're meant to fight for it."

"Fight for what?" Her eyes flew open. She had been thinking of me and what I was doing, the assurance shone a bright sparkle in her eyes.

"For your end. Race me to it, or tease me and hold it back. Rock your hips against my hand."

"I can't, that's—"

"You can do anything you want."

"And if I don't want."

"Trust me, you'll want. You wanted to get better at this. If you want to get better, then you're going to have to be brave."

"Okay."

"Rock your hips." My last words came out sharp, but she needed someone to push her through her barrier of fear.

Her hips moved and brushed my erection as she rocked them forward into my hand. I groaned. I couldn't help it. Her head turned, her gaze catching mine like she thought I'd forced out the sound.

"You are beautiful, Lindy. You really need to know it."

I dropped to my knees. It was probably too soon, but I just couldn't hold back. The girl was Hollywood, brushing into my hand, and it called to my tongue.

I kissed her belly. Her muscle stiffened, but she kept moving. I kissed her hip bone, then swept the tip of my tongue from there to her belly button. Then from there I started kissing a pathway down as my fingers and my thumb worked.

Lindy

I wanted to cry, and scream… and melt. The water running over my body sucked me into a pool of sensation—pleasure—terror.

My fingers gripped hard in his hair and his tongue touched me.

I'd never understood why people wanted to be this intimate.

But I knew Jason was with Rachel.

He'd always wanted to do it with me and I'd never let him. It was just too weird, too personal. Too close to imperfection and people seeing the truth about me.

"Ahhh." Billy didn't seem to care.

His tongue played. I kept moving my hips. Following the rhythm he set with his fingers. Each time I rocked forward his tongue waited for me. Teasing the sensitive spot his thumb brushed when I pulled back.

My fingers clasped tighter in his hair as the terror ran away like the water dripping off us. He was right. I wanted this.

His fingers increased their pace. In. Out.

I leaned all my weight against the wall, my thighs quaking with a desire to give way—to fall and let him do whatever he wanted.

He wasn't going to stop. I didn't want him to. The only thing to do was do as he'd said—race.

When I was younger I'd had a competitive streak as strong as him and Jason.

Don't think. I shut my eyes tighter. All I could see was black. Race!

My fingers pulled his head and his tongue back to me when he took it away as I rocked back. I didn't go so far back either, teasing him, using the sensitive tip he was after as bait for him to chase.

Sensations wrapped around me, tying me up in a charm, like he'd been doing all day in the pool.

Involuntarily my fingers released his hair, then gripped it again as I rocked forward, using his pattern of invasion as a guide.

"I like it." I whispered into the steamy air. My eyes still shut so I could hide from the girl who'd said that.

His tongue wasn't there when I rocked forward. "Thank fuck for that..." A deep rumbling laugh stirred up a new sensation... "Lind."

I opened my eyes, looked down and met his dark-blue gaze. The onyx circles at the heart of his eyes were really wide.

"Race me..." The words rolled over gravel in his throat. It was a challenge.

He was on.

I pushed against his fingers as they invaded, and held his mouth to me, learning every trigger for the sensations roaring up inside me, and moving my body to intensify every little thing.

It had not felt like this when I'd lain on the bed alone.

People said eating chocolate was as good as an orgasm. Oh Lord, no. Chocolate did not feel as good as this.

But then an odd new feeling peaked and swelled—"You're gonna make me pee."

He glanced up laughing. "You won't pee. And even if you did I wouldn't care. Just relax." His thumb released its pressure as he looked back down, at me, watching his thumb brush over me, admiring what he saw with an awe that was crazy.

Then without looking up he leaned forward and his lips settled over the sensitive place his thumb had brushed and he sucked.

Shit. My fingers gripped in a spasm of desperation in his hair, as sensation roared through me—he'd said I'd want him to do it.

I wanted.

Was that my breath releasing in pants into the steamy air in the shower.

Yes.

Billy. Oh, Billy.

This was so crazy. Heat burned under my skin, a need to race…

He sucked harder and his fingers pushed right up into me, with a hard thrust…

I shut my eyes, falling back against the tiles as it came in on me—the wave of sensation I'd discovered yesterday morning— rolling over the top of me, but now it swilled through my body like a tsunami, rushing into every limb and every nerve.

"Lind." My name was agonized hot breath as he pulled my hips further forward, and then his tongue invaded me.

I was Jell-O. My thighs shook, my fingers clinging in his hair.

This was why Jason had left me. This is what he'd discovered with Rachel.

No wonder. *No wonder…*

Jason had never touched me with any determination, ever. Why? Why had he not been able to give me this?

Pounding out a hard rhythm of need, my heart pumped heated blood around my body, as my soul fell into this new intoxicating world.

Liquid gold scorched through my veins.

It was no longer a choice to press back against Billy. I had to. My body cried out to. My fingers clasping clumps of his wet hair as the shower poured out more water on to us.

His tongue pushed into me, as his fingers gripped my buttocks, pulling them apart, and teasing me with the closeness of his fingertips. Nothing I'd ever seen Billy do had been half measures… He was a full-on guy…. Even in this…

Oh heavens. That sensation was coming again.

My body jolted and I slid a little down the tiles on the wall. My legs had no feeling. The wave of sensation ripped through me, swilling around my body, then sucked back, like the wave had done on the beach, and he took full advantage, his tongue moving deep within me… I could be in no doubt he liked this…

Billy stood. The grip of his fingers, now holding me up as his tongue pressed into my mouth.

He tasted weird. Of me.

I kissed him back with a new desperation to our game of tag, but then he gripped my hand, lifted it and put it against his erection.

I couldn't.

"Billy I—"

"It's okay I don't want you to do the same. Just help me jerk myself off, you're surely not mean enough to leave me hanging…"

My fingers beneath his, he wrapped them about the hard column of flesh.

I looked into his eyes, not down… He didn't look away, like he understood I needed him to look at me.

He moved his hand, running mine up. I was scared again. *Relax.* I heard the word in his voice.

Fight it! I didn't want to be afraid anymore. I wanted to be happy.

I stopped letting him control my grip and held him harder.

He groaned.

I pressed my tongue into his mouth, taking over the game of tag. He sighed a breath into mine. When I lifted my weight off the tiles, my breasts brushed against his chest. His body shook, then his hand suddenly moved mine faster—up and down—in swift, firm strokes.

He broke the kiss. His breathing heavy and his eyes dark.

My other hand gripped at the first curve of his buttock, as my gaze clung to his.

His strokes got faster, moving my hand, and a dimple cut into his cheek as the muscle in his jaw bunched. He was clenching his teeth.

I had never watched Jason orgasm.

Billy's gaze clouded, like he couldn't focus on me anymore, and he cried out. His hips grinding into our joined hands, as his flesh pulsed, pumping out a sticky fluid on my belly.

He leaned forward, his cheek pressing against my wet hair as his free arm came around me.

He was riding the wave.

Now I knew what Jason had felt when we'd done it. Why he'd liked it, and why he'd wanted to do it more. Because it felt good.

I hadn't thought about being naked, or what I looked like, or about Mom for at least half an hour. But those feelings crashed back in on me now as he pulled away.

He looked down, letting my hand go. The back of his fingers ran over my belly, as his other hand moved me beneath the water to wash it clean.

"You okay?" he said, looking back up.

I nodded. Then I admitted, "Apart from feeling a crazy load of awkward right now."

"You don't need to feel awkward." His pitch dropped. "That was awesome." He looked away, reaching out to the dispenser to squirt some of the free shower gel on his palm. "I'll wash you. Then you can wash me."

He even washed my hair, massaging shampoo and then conditioner into it, combing his fingers through it and making me hold my head under the shower. Next he put soap on a washcloth and carefully washed my makeup off. No one had seen me without makeup since I'd been fourteen… not even Mom and Dad. But then I had never seen Mom without makeup ever.

I shut my eyes, nausea tumbling in my belly. I was completely naked—standing before Billy. He was the only person who'd seen me like this.

The cloth ran over my body, exploring every curve. I didn't open my eyes, just tried to breathe and not think, and not panic.

With all that strength, he was really gentle.

When he finished, the water still cascading, he pressed a brief kiss on my lips. "You can stop hiding and open your eyes now."

A jolt flipped something in my belly, sending up butterflies.

He gave me the cloth. "Wash my back." he turned.

He was making me do all this stuff with an insistent determination, daring me not to pull back, to take his challenges, but he was also doing it wisely, making this a little easier for me.

I ran the soapy cloth over the broad expanse of his back, following the contours of the muscle down to his hips. I understood a little why he wanted to touch me. He had a hot body. I mean everything was right proportion, right place… built like art…

He'd touched *me* like he'd thought I was hot…

I ran the cloth over his buttock, and then slid it to the other side.

He held still. Letting me do whatever without comment.

He was daring me…

"Turn around."

He did.

I hadn't looked down before. I looked at the nest of dark hair and his penis hanging limp.

This still scared the hell out of me. It was way too personal. I looked up and caught him watching me. He smiled.

I smiled, though it was timid.

He gripped my hand and pressed it and the washcloth on his belly. "Don't lose your nerve now…"

I held his gaze and smiled, determined. My hand moved up first, to his chest. Then I looked down again and watched, following the cut of his pecks, tracing the lines of his leopard tattoo over mounds of hard muscle. His muscle jolted beneath the cloth as it passed over his nipple. He had a sprinkle of dark-brown hairs that trailed downwards, narrowing toward his groin.

There was nothing that put me off.

I didn't want to stop touching him, and even when I got down to his junk I carried on, getting as intimate with him as he had with me. He laughed.

A little weight lifted from my shoulders as I laughed too, my gaze flicking up and catching on his for an instant. I had never laughed over anything sexual. Sex had been sufferance and torture for me, and I'd tried to be right and had been so horribly wrong.

Tears blurred Billy's face.

He gripped my hand. "Do my hair for me. Then we're done." His pitch was deep and gravelly.

Were we going to get into bed and do it properly? Excitement warred with panic.

When I spoke to my counselor next time, I was going to talk about this. I had something wrong with me. I knew it now. Why did I get so afraid of being intimate and exposed?

Rachel had called me frigid; Billy said weird.

Why was I different?

I didn't want to be different.

I shut my eyes as I reached over to the dispenser beyond him. Fighting to ignore the screams in my head reminding me he was looking at my face when I didn't have makeup on. He could see me. The me I hid—the me who always seemed to fail. The me who hurt so bad. The me who felt too guilty to fight that pain. I had no escape, only the chance of somewhere to hide.

I opened my eyes and he smiled at me as my hands lifted to rub the shampoo into his hair. I desperately wanted to tell him to turn around again. But I didn't, I held out, knowing he looked at my face the whole time.

When I was done, he stepped under the water, not waiting to be told, and his hands lifted to rinse the shampoo out himself. I guess he knew I'd reached the margins of my limit.

He turned the water off, then grabbed a big towel from the rack beside the shower and tossed it at me. "See you in the room, I need a pee."

Nervous and shaking, I wrapped the towel around me. It brought a sense of security as I walked back into the bedroom.

It was the same room I'd walked into an hour ago and yet it felt different.

Everything was different.

A part of me just wanted Billy to go, so I could lie down and try to put everything that had happened into a place in my head.

I hadn't understood myself; I was beginning to. I needed time to think, and I needed help from my counselor.

But I'd taken a step forward today. I could never go back.

"Do you want to go out and get something to eat?" Billy's towel hung from his hips, tucked in below his belly button. Even his belly button was beautiful.

Did he know I'd freaked a bit?

"Yeah, I could do with a walk. I don't think I am gonna be great company, though. My head is spinning with stuff, Billy."

If I walked outside, would I discover an apocalypse had hit the world?

Maybe the streets were full of zombies.

Or maybe it was just me...

"I'll go back to my room and change."

I nodded, not sure what to say.

Chapter Seven

Billy

When I knocked for Lindy, she had on another flimsy little cotton dress. It flowed to mid-thigh.

I guess the one thing she didn't mind about her body was her legs.

But her makeup was back on. The layer of foundation presenting flawlessness and hiding if she blushed. Her painted cupid's-bow lips smiled at me. The fake color not much different from the skin beneath.

Tonight's eye shadow of choice… a pale brown-and-gold blend.

At least it looked natural. She did look beautiful, but I had a feeling her makeup hid something.

She'd looked better without it to me. She had nothing to hide.

"Ready?"

"Yeah."

A different purse hung from her shoulder, a little tan one, but again it had a long strap and it dangled to hang just below her ass, drawing my eye to the suggestion of the curve of it through the flowing cloth of her dress.

Her jacket hung in her other hand.

"Here…" I held out a hand to take it. Then I held it up so she could slip her arms into it. She was gonna get cold in that little dress.

I didn't really want to go out to eat. I was hungry for food. But I was hungrier for her.

I'd have just taken her to bed for three hours had this been my choice and maybe ordered something in. But Lindy was a whole barrel full of hang-ups, and taking things too far too quick was probably a bad idea. So I was taking her out and giving her time to adjust to the idea that she'd let me do a really intimate thing.

It had scared her to death, but she'd enjoyed it, the sweet intensity of her orgasm had been the defining answer to that.

She made me laugh.

She was such an anomaly.

I wanted to call Jason. My thumb had actually hovered over his name in my contacts. But I hadn't called. What the fuck had my best friend been doing leaving her with all this garbage in her head? Okay, I knew Jason was not the pushy type. If she'd said no, he'd have just taken no full stop and not touched a discussion about why. But he could have convinced her there was nothing wrong with her body…

Didn't they call it body dysmorphic disorder, when someone was obsessed by imagined flaws in their figure or face?

We'd been told all about that stuff when I'd been working toward my degree. We'd been warned that some people didn't need to exercise, they needed psychological help.

That was Lindy.

At least she was getting it now.

I gripped her fingers and slotted mine in between hers, squeezing tight. "You didn't need to put your makeup back on. You're really pretty without it."

She stopped walking, her hand tugging mine. I stopped too, turning to look at her.

Her forehead had crinkled and her narrow plucked and tinted dark eyebrows lifted high. "Why do you have to be so challenging?"

I yanked her into an embrace, pulling her into me and wrapping my other arm around her, because *I love you.* I had a great big pool of feeling inside me that had been there for so long with no outlet, and now…

Now she was in my arms and she'd let me do stuff Jason had never done. I laughed a little, to disguise the feelings going on inside me. But it came out weird. "You ought to know me by now, I'm always challenging." I let her go. "Why do you think I went into being a personal trainer?"

She started walking again and I turned walking next to her, gripping her hand. "Because you like exercise and you want to do it all day."

I laughed. "Because I get a kick out of challenging people, making them do more than they think they can. It's rewarding. It gives me a buzz."

When we got to the stairs, I let her hand go, and instead my hand ran along the rail. She held back, so I walked on ahead, talking. "Your boyfriend may have been calling the shots as captain of the football team, but I was always the motivator. Coach would even let me do the talks in the huddle 'cause I got them moving. In fact, when I pack up playing, I'm gonna coach kids."

"You still play football?" She sounded surprised; I thought she knew all this.

"Yeah, for fun sometimes, you should come down and watch. Meet the guys. Some of them you'll remember from school."

When I glanced back she was busy thinking about something. "What?"

"Nothing. You're just surprising me."

The sun hit me when I stepped outside. It was warm when you were out of the shadows and the wind. I turned, waiting for her to catch up the couple of paces she was behind me, then I wrapped my arm about her shoulders. "Do you want pizza?"

"Yeah, okay."

We shared a couple. She ate more than she had done the other nights. She surprised me when she picked a fifth slice. I looked at her. "So what is it exactly you don't like about your figure, Lind?"

She put the pizza she'd been about to bite back down on her plate and her face screwed up at me. Maybe I'd picked the wrong moment to ask...

"Why?"

"Just because..."

"Just because..." She mimicked before picking the slice back up and taking a bite. But once she'd swallowed it, she said, "I don't like my hips, or my ass, or my thighs... or my belly. Happy?"

A lopsided smile pulled at my lips—her moody pitch made me want to laugh. "Well, I don't see anything wrong with any of those things. They all looked pretty awesome to me."

"Billy—"

"Billy, nothing. Listen to me." I leaned forward, looking at her. I wanted her to get this. "There is NOTHING wrong with you. You're perfect, in fact every woman in this place would probably give a couple of thousand dollars for surgery to look as good as you— "

"You're wrong." She shook her head. "You're just being sweet, and it's kind of you, but I know, Billy. I'm not blind..." she took a breath, "...and if there is nothing wrong with me, why would Jason go off with Rachel?"

I was going to answer, but she didn't let me.

"And don't you dare lie to me and say she isn't prettier than me. She's skinnier and better looking."

"Lind, she—"

"Don't lie, Billy, tell me honestly, do you think she's hot?"

That hit me back, because being honest, you'd have to be completely blind not to think Rachel was hot to some degree.

"There! See! I'm gonna pay the check." I hadn't even finished, and besides she'd paid last night.

I caught a hold of her wrist and pulled her back when she moved to stand up. "No. I'm paying, and I'm not finished eating, and we're not finished talking." Perhaps my voice came out too harsh, but the girl's self-destruct button was annoying me now.

When she sat, I swilled down my mouthful of pizza with beer and wiped my mouth on my hand, eyeing her critically. She was going to listen to me… "Lindy. Hands up, I admit Rachel is hot. But so are you. You saw it at school. You were the high school queen, and you gloated. So what's changed?"

"I grew up." She stuck her tongue out at me.

"And got even more beautiful. What is wrong with you? You're messed up, Lind."

Her lips pressed together and then frickin' quivered, and moisture glittered in her eyes… "I know I'm messed up. That's why we're here, remember…"

I reached out and gripped her hand, my thumb rubbing over her palm as my fingers hung on, while she tried to pull away. Maybe I'd taken this too far. "Look if you really hate yourself that much, you can just exercise you know, do yoga or something. But if you are asking for my opinion, there's nothing wrong with you. You look amazing."

I opened my hand, letting hers go. She pulled it away, looking down.

She didn't believe me.

Time to put up the white flag. "Do you want to go down and walk on the beach?"

"Yeah."

"Come on then." We left the rest of the pizza uneaten, and I headed over to pay, pulling out my wallet as she walked out the door.

When I met her outside, she had her arms wrapped around her middle. A flash memory of Lindy, head cheerleader, laughing and smiling at some joke, spun into my head. She'd been flirting like crazy with Jason, trying to get his attention; it was before they'd started going out. That girl was very different to this one. What the fuck had happened? Jason? I wanted to call him… He might be my friend, but he deserved kicking for leaving her in this much of a mess. Had he never told her she looked good. He'd definitely let her get away with hiding herself. What was wrong with him?

I wrapped my arm about her shoulders and turned her to the beach. "Okay, then, tell me why the desperate need for me not to see you without makeup? Is that all part of your warped opinion of yourself?"

"Are you on a warpath or something?" Annoyance rung in her pitch, but she didn't pull away from me, instead she tucked in against me as we walked, though she still clutched her arms about herself.

"Just tell me."

She looked ahead. "My eyebrows and eyelashes are too pale—"

"You're blonde." She didn't continue after I'd interrupted.

"Sorry, don't stop, keep talking." The girl was tiny, tucked under my arm, I really didn't get how she could think herself too big.

Her cheek brushed against my chest. "My face isn't symmetrical."

So. No one's was. I bit my tongue.

"I hate my nose and my eyes aren't level, and—"

Okay enough. "And who gives a shit? All those things together make what looks like a perfect face to me. You seriously have that body dysmorphic thing. You don't see yourself how everyone else does." There were other people on the beach, and as her head lifted from my chest I pointed to a woman a few yards away from us. "Are you bigger or smaller?"

Her head spun to look at me as her arms fell. "Bigger." She sounded shocked that I'd ask the question.

"Smaller," I answered, "by a mile. Her..." I pointed at another woman.

"Bigger!"

"Smaller. Much. What about her?"

"Bigger..." She sounded irritated with me now.

Stopping her, I gripped her chin and made her look into my eyes, in the last light of dusk. "Wrong again, smaller. Are you more beautiful than that woman?"

"No—"

"Yes, Lindy. What's in your head, is wrong. And without makeup, by the way, you're fricking awesome." I pressed a sharp, hard kiss on her lips before letting her go, and then turned to begin walking again. "Talk to your counselor about it. You need to get your thoughts rewired."

"You're a bully," she said as she walked beside me, a foot away.

"And you're a drama queen."

She huffed at me.

"Look Lindy, you are gonna have to get used to the fact that I am here to do what's best for you, and that includes stopping you from beating yourself up over a pile of garbage that you've invented in your head."

Her arms came up and clutched her sides again. She didn't answer, just carried on walking.

I'd helped a ton of people in my job, but I didn't know what I could do for her. She was defeatist. She had no desire to change, and unless people wanted to change, they weren't going to.

But I wasn't defeatist. I'd waited years to be with her like we were now, like we had been this afternoon.

I looked up from the beach to the walkway along the street. The tattoo place I'd had my leopard done at was up there. All those emotions roared and clawed. I had a chance.

I looked ahead at Lindy, defeated, deflated, and tiny compared to me. I'd help her get sorted, somehow.

Over the top of the noise of waves rolling in, I heard music. It came from further along the beach. Some guys and girls sat around a fire near our apartments. A couple of them played guitars while the others sang along.

I shouted to Lindy. "You'll be okay!" She stopped and turned around, waiting on me to catch up. When I did, I said. "But seriously speak to your counselor, because you have it wrong."

I wasn't qualified to fix her head; it was too messed up, and it wasn't really my role. I was here to be her friend… and… and who knew what else would come…?

"Come here." I lifted my arm.

She looked at me, then came back to me. This time she wrapped her arm about my waist, as my arm fell across her shoulders. Pain gripped tight and hard in my chest. I still couldn't believe she was here with me, like this. Was this afternoon a dream?

We walked the rest of the way up the beach in silence, listening to the music.

"Shall we sit down and listen to them play?" she asked.

"If you want."

It wasn't a song I knew. It sounded like something the guys had written themselves, kind of a ballad. The group around them rocked in time, sang, and laughed, having a good time.

About ten yards away from them, Lind stopped, looking up at me. "Let's sit here."

I nodded.

She shivered as she sat and tucked her dress beneath her.

"You cold?" It had got really cold now it was dark.

She smiled up at me. "A little."

I stripped off my sweat top. "Here."

I got a big smile for my chivalry. "Thanks." She slipped it on over her jacket. It swamped her. I was probably triple the size of her. She really was tiny.

I dropped down onto the sand next to her and sat with my knees bent up, like she did, letting the sound of the waves and the dudes playing guitars wash over me as I knocked the sand off my hands.

"You'll be cold now…" Her head tipped onto my shoulder, her hair brushing over the skin of my bare arm, as the breeze raced up the beach blowing it back off her face.

"I'll survive."

The guys playing their songs, changed tune and upped their tempo. I wrapped my arm about Lindy and tapped out the beat on her shoulder as we listened.

The guys were really going for it, heads rocking, feet tapping, as a load of girls in their group got up and started dancing on the sand.

Lind watched them. "I can't remember being like that. Was I ever like that?" She hadn't taken her eyes off them.

My fingers gripped her shoulder for an instant before subconsciously going back to tapping the rhythm. "When we were at school, yeah. Don't you remember that party at Josiah's? When you girls all got up and did that stupid dance you'd made up to a song."

Her head lifted and she glanced at me. "God, I'd forgotten that. That was our last summer wasn't it, just before prom. Everyone jumped in the pool too."

"Yes, we did."

She laughed. "I pushed Jason in."

"I remember and he pulled you in when you lifted a hand to help him out, and you went crazy 'cause he got your hair wet…" I stopped…. "Did you have an issue with your appearance even then?" I remember her always being perfectly made-up for as far back as I had memories of her.

She looked back at the guys playing guitar. "Yeah."

Shit.

One of the guys playing looked up and caught us watching through the legs of the dancing girls.

His gaze caught on Lindy and stayed there for a couple of minutes before he looked away.

"Did Jason know?"

Lindy looked back at me. "I guess. He knew I didn't like him touching me in certain ways, and that I never liked him seeing me undressed or without makeup."

"The guy's an ass. I'm gonna tell him when I see him, he should have told you you are fine."

She moved away from me and got up. "He did. All the time. He just wasn't a bully like you…"

It wasn't said with anger or bitterness, or even as a joke, it was just a statement.

She brushed the sand off the back of her dress.

"Shall we go back up?"

"If you want."

The music had got louder and wilder. I saw the guy look at her again. Then the other guitarist looked up too and followed the gaze of the guy looking at Lindy. They were both blonde-haired, and they had a really similar appearance. I guessed they must be related.

I caught hold of Lindy's hand. "I'm not bullying you, I'm helping you…"

We started walking up the beach toward the steps leading to the apartments.

I still wanted to smash Jason's head against a wall right now. What the frick had he been thinking, leaving her obsessed by a false perception this long?

When we got up to the landing leading to our rooms, my heart beat faster. I knew what I wanted to happen tonight. But I didn't know if Lindy was on the same page still, or if she'd changed her mind…

When we reached her room she stopped, stepping away from me. I met her gaze. "Will you sleep in my room again tonight?"

I sighed. That wasn't quite the invite I wanted tonight. I'd hoped to be pulled in with a sentiment that said, I want sex. But it was a start. "If you want?"

"I want."

"I'll go wash up in my room."

"Okay."

It had got really awkward now.

As she went into her room, I turned to mine and slotted the plastic card in to free the lock.

I went into the bathroom and used the toilet, cleaned my teeth, then stared at my image in the mirror, my fingers gripping the sink.

I'd been into Lindy for years and now I had a chance with her I'd discovered the girl I'd been into wasn't who I thought…

Did it make a difference?

No.

I pushed off the sink and straightened up.

Whatever… I was here to help her.

I ran my fingers through my hair and ruffled it up, happy with how I looked. Then I blew out the air in my lungs. Why did I feel nervous?

Chapter Eight

Lindy

I still had Billy's sweat top on. Its warmth and the smell of his aftershave surrounded me. I'd lived with him for three years, I was used to his scent. It was reassuring.

I pulled it off over my head, stripped off the jacket I had on underneath, then took off my dress and got a t-shirt to sleep in.

What Billy didn't know was I didn't even like looking at myself naked.

Once I'd covered myself, I unhooked my bra and slid the straps off my arms, then pulled my bra out and dropped it on the pile of clothes on my bed.

I moved the whole pile to a chair and went into the bathroom. I was brushing my teeth when Billy knocked.

My belly did a spin. What was going to happen tonight? I didn't think it would be nothing.

Feelings and images from this afternoon coiled up inside me and twisted in my head. I was trying to make sense of everything. I bit my lip as I stared at myself in the mirror. Billy knocked again. My lipgloss had worn off; my lips looked pale and thin.

A third, impatient knock hit the door.

Turning away from my reflection I went to let him in.

He'd changed clothes. He had on shorts made out of sweat-pants material and a black loose sleeveless tee.

As he walked in he took out his wallet and keys then he dropped them on the chest by the bed.

My heart pulsed out a base rhythm in my ears as he gripped the hem of his top. He pulled it up over his head.

My gaze soaked up his abs. He couldn't see me looking, his eyes were hidden in the cloth.

I'd rubbed a washcloth over his abs—I wanted to touch… My palms literally itched, the coil in my belly unwinding in a way that made a sweet ache tingle downwards.

"You gonna take your makeup off?"

Damn he'd caught me looking. I glanced up. Was he pushing again? I didn't want to. I wanted everything to feel easy and normal.

"Take it off," he urged, before I even answered. He must have seen the answer in my expression.

The pupils in his eyes had dilated in the low light thrown by the only lamp switched on; it was next to the bed. It made his eyes look bigger and darker. But his gaze was still warm. Long, dark eyelashes fell and lifted, then his eyebrows rose.

They framed his eyes in a way that increased the aura of his intensity and strength.

If you didn't know him, you'd probably be scared of him, but he'd never scared me. He had always been big, likable, Billy—who could make me laugh, argue and shout at times—but always feel better.

"Go on then…"

I wish he'd stop pushing me…

I turned and went into the bathroom. My skin needed cleansing, whether I put my makeup back on or not, and in there I could get my heart rate and my panic back under control.

What I didn't expect, though, was for him to follow. As I stopped in front of the mirror, I caught his movement behind me, and then in the reflection I saw him lean a shoulder up against the door jamb.

I looked at him through the mirror. That stupid angry leopard scratched at the skin across his chest. "Do you have to watch?"

"Yeah. If you are gonna get comfortable with people looking at you."

I looked away, picking up my cleanser and the cotton-wool wads. "Have you watched other girls take their makeup off?"

"No, Lind. It's not what generally gives me a kick."

He'd never brought any girls back to the apartment when we were at college. I knew he'd had relationships, though, but they'd never been serious. He'd never brought a girlfriend over to Jason and I and introduced her; but I'd heard people say things, like "Billy spent the night with…"

I'd heard a girl was angry because she'd never heard from him after something had happened and about four times in the three years we'd shared a place, girls had come up to me with comments and messages they'd wanted me to pass on to Billy.

I'd never passed them on. I'd figured if Billy had wanted anything to do with them they would have gone straight to him.

I looked at him in the mirror as I wiped the cotton wool over my skin, stripping off the foundation. "You're freaking me out, you know that?"

"I'm just watching." His massive arms folded over his chest, covering the leopard's head, but I could still see its claws stretched out. That stupid worn-out leather bracelet dangled from his wrist too.

"Well, I wish you wouldn't."

"It's good for you. Think of it like medicine."

"Oh right." My pitch had soured. Inside I panicked. Why couldn't he see I was scared? I turned around, my hand dropping. "Please…"

"I saw you this afternoon without makeup. So this is nothing new—face the fear."

My belly lurched. This time it had nothing to do with the quality of his body. My hand shook as I turned back to the mirror and began again.

He wasn't going to give in. So I had to.

My heart rate pounded as I dropped the foundation-stained cotton wool and prepared another, then began again. It took me a couple of minutes to get all my foundation off, especially with my hand shaking.

I looked at my eyes and my lips in the mirror. Which first? My gaze caught on his.

His lips twitched up at one side, suggesting a smile, though he didn't let it form. "Just do it… I think your beautiful… remember that?"

He's seen you before.

I shut my eyes and began wiping off my eye shadow. Right now I hated Billy Worrall.

It hadn't felt so bad this afternoon when the water had been running over us. I hadn't felt quite so naked and vulnerable…

I didn't just feel sick, it was like I was gonna be sick. "Billy…" It was a plea for him to turn away as I opened my eyes.

"Go on…" Heat burned from the dark blue, urging, encouraging, reassuring—but saying he was not gonna let me get out of this.

My hand shook when I reached for another wad of cotton wool. "Why are you making me do this?"

"I'm not making you. I've asked you. And you want to be free of the trap you've made for yourself otherwise you'd have just said an outright no and told me to get the fuck out…"

True.

I stared at myself, not him, as I ran the cotton wool over my lips and wiped off the last of the lipgloss, leaving them pale. My mouth looked so thin, and my eyes bland…

But my insecurity had lost me Jason.

The earthquake inside me stole the ground from beneath my feet. I didn't like who I saw in the mirror. The girl who had no life or color. She was ugly.

I gripped the sink; I would be sick or faint…

Billy moved, his arms unravelling. He stood behind me. My gaze was pulled to his in the mirror. His fingers gripped my chin, holding it steady.

"This face is beautiful. Do you hear it? I mean really beautiful. More beautiful than when you cover it with paint…"

He turned my head and moved around me, and before I said anything, or had chance to think anything, his lips pressed down on mine.

My arms came up to his shoulders. *Kissing is like a game of tag.* His tongue brushed into my mouth and stroked mine, then withdrew. *You're it.*

I shut my eyes and joined the game, forgetting what I looked like as my tongue went into chase, reaching into his mouth to catch the tip of his.

His hands slipped to my buttocks and the small of my back as the edge of the sink pressed into my hip from the force of his response.

Kissing Billy was so different to kissing Jason.

He broke it, and the power in his big arms lifted me up through his grip on my ass.

My arms held harder around his neck. "Billy!"

His deep chuckle was a tremor through my chest as he carried me out of the bathroom.

"I haven't finished!"

"You've finished…"

My legs wrapped around his thighs as he reached the bed and started leaning me backwards, his knee dipping the mattress. "Billy…"

Fear pulled my lungs tight, making it hard to breathe. This was happening too fast again. Everything with Billy was full on and fast.

He let me go, once he'd laid me on the bed, with a quick, sharp kiss on my temple.

As he straightened, I sat up, my legs curling to cross in front of me, my hands settling in my lap.

He toed off his sneakers. "You're not lying down?"

I didn't answer; I didn't know what to answer. My head was too busy shouting that my face was naked…

He stood there, his eyes challenging. "Are you letting? Or do you want to? Or do you just want to spoon?"

Cut straight to the point—that was Billy.

With Jason, I'd spent half my life trying to guess what he thought, because he wasn't good at speaking his mind; he'd been too nice. He avoided confrontation. He'd walk out or give in rather than argue with me.

"I don't know…" I took a breath. "But I was enjoying kissing you…"

"Okay, so there's a challenge. Do you want me to persuade you to want?" His lips parted in a big grin. "I can do that, if that's what you're after."

I shrugged, a chill lifting goosebumps on my skin; my belly filling up with a thousand butterflies.

"Okay, I'm getting into the bed. Dressed or naked?"

"Naked." I swallowed, I'd seen him naked, it would just make things easier if we did do it, it would save me debating over whether or not I helped him out of his shorts… and that would be terrifying.

You're no better than Jason. You're a coward, Lindy Martin!

Billy hooked his thumbs into his loose shorts, then bent.

I turned away, onto all-fours, and crawled across the bed to the far side, to pull back the covers.

When I slid under them, I looked up. Billy got in the other side, all hard-honed, sinew and muscular flesh, the cut of his muscles moving beneath his skin.

He looked at me, "Considering you want sex you're all wrapped up… I don't know how you think I'm gonna get at you…"

I let my death-grip on the comforter loosen, he tugged it down, just a little, a grin parting his lips, and made a girlish scream.

"Ahh. He saw me!"

Laughter bubbled out from my throat. He was crazy. But that's what he'd wanted me to do—laugh.

Heat burning under my skin, as the laughter died, I rolled to my side, one hand tucking beneath my head on the pillow as I faced him. He leaned on one elbow looking at me, the comforter over his hip.

I loved his eyes; blue and big, outlined by those amazing lashes. Jason had nice eyes too, but they were brown. Billy's blue eyes were striking.

I turned leaning back to switch the lamp off.

"Uh, Uh. Keep it on. You need to conquer your fears, and I need to see if you're letting or wanting." He stared at me for a minute. "That is, if we do it at all. You can say stop anytime you decide."

I nodded as awkwardness rattled through me.

His hand touched my hip, over the tee I had on. "So we're starting with kissing and seeing where it goes..."

I nodded again, biting my lip.

"But If you want me to kiss you, Lind, you're gonna have to come a bit closer."

He wanted me to be the one who moved because he wanted to be sure I wasn't just letting. I got what he was doing—pushing me again—making me make the choices.

I shuffled over, my hand lifting to the back of his head, and my fingers sliding into his short hair. "I'm not letting you, I like kissing you. I liked it this afternoon—"

"Liked..." He laughed. "That's called faint praise, honey. I am gonna have to do better this time. Like really isn't a compliment."

"This afternoon was good, it's just, I'm... It feels weird."

"Good is as bad as liked, but I know what you mean, you feel nervous still. So kiss me and stop feeling nervous."

One of his arms slid beneath my shoulders and his other hand, that had been on my hip, slipped to grip my buttock as he leaned in to kiss me.

When his tongue pressed into my mouth, his hand moved to my thigh and pulled it up onto his hip.

There was no escaping Billy. He wasn't going to wait for me to get over my awkwardness, it might well happen never; he was going to make me want him…

My belly flipped with that odd delicious ache I'd discovered today.

He had an erection already, and he rubbed it against my belly as his hand moved to my buttock. His tongue withdrew, then slipped back into my mouth, simulating sex.

The guy was making me wet. I was going to let him do it.

But there was that word. Let. I didn't want it to be let, either. I wanted to want him to do it to me.

If kiss is tag, then sex is a competition. You're meant to fight for it. Fight for your end. Race me toward it, or trick me, tease me and hold it back.

I wished Jason had been a bit tougher and told me I was doing it all wrong, then maybe he wouldn't have left me.

Billy broke the kiss and his fingers slipped to grip my t-shirt. "Shall we get rid of this thing?" He tugged it a little, not upwards, just outwards, shaking it.

He'd seen me naked once already, but it didn't make the idea of taking my t-shirt off any easier.

"You know you can trust me. I'm not gonna screech 'freak' when I see you…" He joked.

"It's not funny…"

In bed there was no difference in our height. I looked straight into his blue eyes. The teasing light died and instead concern glowed there. "I'm not making fun of you. I'm trying to make you feel easier, that's all."

"I know."

"Well are we gonna take it off then?"

I took a breath, trying to work up courage, and push down the terror tearing through me. "If you want…"

"But do you want?"

I huffed out the breath… "Yeah." I did, but I wished he wouldn't keep pushing me to make the choices. It stepped me up the rungs of an anxiety ladder heading toward panic.

"Well then…" He sat up a bit, leaning over me and flicking back the covers so he could get a hold of my t-shirt, and he started lifting it. But I hadn't realized he'd meant to take the covers off too, and my heart went nuts. I gripped his hands.

"Relax, I swear I won't do anything you don't want."

Shit. I shut my eyes, nodding and letting his hands go. Nausea rolling in my belly, I arched my back as he pulled it over my breasts, then I leaned forward, lifting my arms, so he could slip it off.

"Open your eyes, Lind, you look like this is torture. You're kind of ruining the moment…" My eyes flew open and I swallowed against the dryness in my throat. His dark-blue gaze caught on mine. "Remember you can say stop anytime you want. So there's no need to panic…"

I nodded, but my hands shook as they rested against his sides, ready to continue.

"You know you're gonna have to take your panties off too if you want this to go any further. I'm leaving that to you so I know that's what you want."

Awesome. I slipped my hands under the covers and slid them off, lifting my hips then my legs, doing it all out of sight, before letting my panties drop onto the floor next to the bed—vulnerability thrusting a knife into my chest.

He didn't look me in the eyes now. I think he knew. But as he threw my top on the floor too, his gaze dropped to my breasts. "You like your breasts, right?"

I laughed. What a silly question. "Yeah."

"Good. So do I." His head dropped and his hand lifted, and then he gripped my breast and flicked the peak of my nipple with his tongue before circling it in a slow, gentle caress.

How did that do stuff in my belly?

Then finally he sucked, and as he sucked the connecting sensation in my belly pulled tight. How could he do that? It hadn't felt like this with Jason—ever.

He lifted his head, "Are you still thinking about what I'm doing, or are you thinking of something else?"

I couldn't answer. He wouldn't want to know I'd thought of Jason, images of him when we'd been together had filled my head.

Billy's blue eyes stared at me. "Just keep your mind on me and what I'm doing... If you want to get the best out of this..."

I had a feeling he knew my mind had slipped back to Jason, or maybe he thought it was fear. I hoped he thought it was fear.

"Lind?"

My mind had wandered again.

"I want this." I answered, breathlessly. I did. I needed to get Jason out of my head, and I needed to—

"Well then," his head bent, and the rest of his words came as warm breath sweeping over my breast, "compete. There's no fight in you; you're just lying here. Do something, Lind. If you don't wanna touch me, touch yourself."

"Myself?"

"Like you did the other morning..." He looked up, flashing a challenge in his eyes.

"How's that competing?"

"Believe me, that will make me wanna come." His gaze was dark and intense.

I shut my eyes as his lips brushed a kiss on my breast, then he tracked a path of kisses to the other side.

Biting my lip I slid my hand beneath the comforter.

Was I actually gonna do this?

He sucked my left breast.

I bit my lip harder and closed my eyes tighter. If I didn't open them I could pretend I was alone.

My fingers found my sensitive spot and rubbed.

"Rock your hips," he whispered over my breast. My whole body jolted. He wasn't even gonna let me pretend I was alone.

"What are you trying to do to me?" I said into the air, my eyes still shut as a tremor ran over my skin while his fingers played with one breast and his lips taunted the other.

"Make you enjoy this so much you are never gonna care what your body looks like again… or use the words liked or good."

There was a promise…

I touched myself more determinedly as he sucked me harder, this was a competition that didn't seem to be involving him. But right now I didn't care. I was thinking about what he did, and what it would be like to have him moving between my legs, giving me sensations that could make me forget everything.

A flush burned under my skin.

His fingers slipped down across my belly as he nipped at my breast with his teeth.

Frick. His flat tongue pressed and rubbed, easing the pain he'd just caused.

His fingers brushed my inner thigh.

My free hand clasped a fistful of his hair and my other hand stilled.

"Don't stop, honey." The warm air of his words teased my damp nipple.

I kept my eyes shut and carried on, gripping his hair and rubbing myself, and when his fingers slid into me I pressed my head back into the pillow with a soul deep sigh. His touch was gentle and tender.

No nothing Jason had ever done had felt like this. He'd always been gentle, but not with the knowledge Billy had. Billy was gentle but he knew where to touch.

I bit my lip again, my hips tilting up of their own accord.

"Yeah…" He breathed over my breast as his fingers got more active, and I moved my hips to the pattern as they slipped in and out.

Just keep your mind on me and what I'm doing.

I wanted to. I did.

Billy.

My fingers clasped even tighter in his hair, probably hurting him, as my body got lost in the avenues of feeling. Billy tied my belly up in knots.

The soles of my feet pressed into the sheet as his fingers reached deeper. My hips moved more strongly. *Competition. A race.* I was racing him with my fingers too, working just as hard as he was inside me.

Something wrapped around me stealing the air. Shallow sighs left my lungs. I burned.

This was ten times what I'd felt when I'd done this alone.

Oh.

Ah.

Exclamations came constantly in my head but I didn't have the confidence to let them out of my mouth, they left my throat as sighs as I hid in the darkness behind my eyelids, letting him touch me…

Let?

Nothing about this was letting.

I drank in what he did.

What are you trying to do to me? Make you enjoy this so much you are never gonna care what your body looks like again. Rock your hips.

Hidden behind my eyelids, I could be that person. My hips lifted against his invasion, over and over as he played with me, and I played with myself.

Then…

Oh then… The end stole up on me. It raced in—hitting me like a sneaker wave.

Oh my God. Oh… My… God… It crashed into me. This feeling… This thing… It ripped into my body, sparking in my nerves and racing through my blood, to my fingertips.

I gripped his hair so tight I'd pull it out.

He'd lifted his head and his fingers had stilled in me as my toes gripped the sheet. I didn't know what had happened in the last few seconds. I'd left even time behind.

I breathed hard as I came back to earth and opened my eyes, forcing my fingers to open and let go of his hair as my hips dropped back on the mattress.

He smiled, his fingers sliding out of me. Then he brought them up to his mouth and sucked them.

A tremor tingled in my belly as those fingers left his mouth and brushed across my lips.

I bit his index finger.

He laughed.

"How was it?"

"Good. I want you, Billy." My blood hummed the words to a tune written by nature not me.

"Well that's convenient, 'cause I want the hell out of you…" He was already moving but turning away…

My heart kicked. What was he doing?—Reaching for his wallet, getting a condom.

The little silver packet slipped into his fingers. He ripped it open.

I rolled onto my back and bit my lip as he put it on.

I didn't want to watch. This delay let the heat drip out of my blood and cold fear creep in.

Then he turned back and moved over me.

The comforter slipped down further so it lay over his hips and left everything above bare. He could see everything.

But then so could I.

"Ready?" His voice came out deep and heavy, loaded with emotion, like this meant a lot to him, as his weight pressed on his hands, dipping the bed either side of my shoulders.

His hips hovered over my parted thighs.

My heart pounded out a manic beat. The sheer size of his body gave me a sense of dark and dangerous, but when I met his blue gaze, I saw gentleness—Billy. Kind-hearted, lovable, Billy. My friend.

"Yeah."

"Don't shut your eyes," he ordered, as he angled things. I lifted my hips without even thinking, because I wanted him there.

He didn't ease into me like he'd done the time we'd done it in the SUV—and like Jason had every single time we'd done it—Billy shoved into me, a sudden hard invasion. It filled me up.

"Oh." The exclamation escaped my lips. He had so much force in his muscular thighs and they pushed mine wider, and all the air out of my lungs.

"Keep your eyes open," he ordered again, when I would have shut them. Then he was pulling out. My super-sensitized internal flesh grabbed at the sensation as a beautiful pain pulled at my consciousness. I'd swelled down there, as I had in the shower, blood throbbed sensation between my legs.

"Oh." The sound slipped out as he pressed back in.

He smiled.

I gripped his muscle-packed shoulders.

He could cast spells. He'd been into Harry Potter when we were kids. I remembered that. "Wizard," I breathed as his hips kept moving.

He did odd things, angling his hips, and pulsing on the edge, and... and... "Billy!" My fingernails cut into his shoulders as another sneaker wave hit out of nowhere, smashing into me.

Then he moved faster, smiling, pushing in and pulling out, over and over, the muscles in his thighs working hard.

Our gazes clashed. "You're not fighting me, Lind. Fight for me..."

I bit my lip and shut my eyes—

"Keep your eyes open."

Oh Lord. My eyelids snapped up and I pushed my hips against him hard. I tried to catch his rhythm. If kissing was tag, this wasn't like a race, it was a dance... a blissful dance.

My body had woken up. Been switched on. Turned on... No wonder people said that.

Hot. Sweating. My mouth dry… My blood hummed… "I'm gonna come again." This time I felt it approach, it simmered, rippling through my body, threatening to pull me back out to sea.

"I'm gonna come too…" Emotion burned in his eyes.

He looked down, watching our bodies join.

I stopped moving. "Frick, don't stop, Lind. Don't stop…"

I started again, shutting my eyes, because he wasn't watching me, and let sensations skim through my nerves and take hold.

The fact that he watched made my skin burn hotter.

Sound left my mouth every time he pressed in and I pushed up.

He increased the pace. I followed his lead.

A race. A dance. Move and counter move.

He penetrated harder, hitting me roughly…

The wave hit. It swilled into me, like it smashed into a narrow rock pool on the shore.

The earth rocked around us; he didn't stop, but took over. The winner of the race, pounding into me, hitting my body with a force that kept my temperature up and the sensations spinning inside me.

Fighting. Racing. Pushing toward his end.

My fingers clung in his hair, holding on. All I could do was hold still against this onslaught and let him do as he wished. There was no more dancing and I couldn't race against this, I'd never win. He wasn't allowing me back to earth until he'd got to his end.

My head pressed into the pillow and my toes curled gripping the sheet. Let… But it wasn't that sort of let. This was nothing like anything that had happened before.

I came again, the feeling even more intense. How could it happen again, when I was still high on the last one?

"Ahhh." Billy shouted, announcing his end, a low animalistic roar of sound, as he pushed in deep and hard. He pulsed inside me, holding still, his body rigid.

I opened my eyes. He looked at me, but his gaze had clouded. He shut his eyes and a low growl left his throat as he withdrew then rolled off me. Then he laughed. "Shit." His hand came up and gripped his hair.

His body glistened with sweat in the light from the bedside lamp, making the ridges and hollows across his chest and abdomen more beautiful. The comforter rested over his groin, revealing that little cut of muscle at his hips.

He'd only just finished and I wanted to do it again.

His leg bent up beneath the comforter. "That was something…"

I guess he wasn't disappointed. He breathed hard, his fingers still in his hair. Then he sat up, his eyes opening. "I better go get rid of the condom."

When he disappeared into the bathroom, I pulled the comforter up. My arms held it over me. I'd been disloyal to Jason. I'd cheated. He'd dumped me months back and had a completely new life—a wife and kid. But my heart still belonged to him. I'd broken that— and discovering I could enjoy sex with Billy, Jason's best friend, made everything all mixed up and wrong.

Tears tingled a path down my cheeks. I wiped them away as I heard Billy pee.

I felt awkward. I was back in the room, naked beneath the comforter, lonely and scared.

He came back in naked, beautiful, big and confident.

My heartbeat pulsed out appreciation. The ache between my legs reminding me there was no doubt my body liked his.

I swallowed against the dryness in my throat. "Can you get me some water?"

"Yeah, course." He turned to get a bottle, then threw it on the comforter in front of me.

I sat up, holding the comforter over my breasts, opened the bottle and sipped from it as he got back in bed.

I put the bottle down on the chest beside the bed. When I turned back, he lifted his arm. "Come here."

I did but I cried again, my arms reaching about his midriff and then clinging as he held me against his chest. I got his velvety skin wet.

His fingers brushed through my hair. "What are you crying for?"

"Because it was good."

"And that's made you cry…?"

"Yeah, it doesn't feel right. I don't know. I shouldn't be here. It's like it's a dream and I'll wake up soon," *with Jason*.

His fingers stroked through my hair. "It's okay. It feels like a dream to me too. Switch out the light and we'll go to sleep. Maybe it'll feel more real in the morning."

I rolled away and flicked the switch, then lay on my side, facing away from him and curled up. I didn't know what had hit me or what was wrong with me. I had too much going on in my life. I'd escaped it for an hour of bliss but that made the burden of reality even heavier…

This wasn't a dream. Jason wasn't ever coming back.

But it wasn't the thought of Jason making me cry anymore. It was Mom. How could I have forgotten about Mom?

Billy moved behind me and curled around me, spooning; his breath caressing my shoulder.

Chapter Nine

Billy

I'd been watching Lindy for ages, my head balanced on my palm, as I lay on my side next to her.

For a girl who hated sex she'd been hot last night. It hadn't ever been that good with anyone else. But maybe that's 'cause it was her. *It's like it's a dream.* I got that emotion.

Lindy and me.

The girl I'd wanted for as far back as I could remember…

I wanted to touch her face. But I didn't want to wake her.

I was the first person who'd seen her like this. Without makeup. Truly naked.

Lust twisted in my belly, tangling up with the love playing guitars in my heart.

How could she not see how beautiful she was? She looked pretty frickin' awesome to me. The naked tone of her lips was a very light pink. Her black-tinted eyelashes flickered. My gaze lifted to the thin lines of her plucked eyebrows; she'd tinted them too. But her cheekbones were strong and natural and her nose had that cute little upward tilt. My fingers itched to play with the waves in her blonde hair as it spread over the pillow. I'd stroke a finger along her nose too, touching because I could, sweep a finger along her jaw and down the column of her neck. Her skin had tanned since we'd got here so it didn't look so pale.

The girl was beautiful.

Her eyes opened.

"Hey." I said, my voice deep.

"Hey."

My fingers brushed her hair off her forehead, then ran the path I'd imagined… before coming back up her neck to touch her pale lips. They parted.

I wanted to have sex with her again, but I wouldn't. I figured she'd want me to leave her alone to get used the idea. Frick she'd cried. What had that been about? I'd chickened out of forcing a real answer from her. I had a feeling the truth would hurt. A huge, heavy stone, a lump of scared weighted down my belly, afraid the real answer was—*I was thinking of Jason*. That's why I'd wanted her eyes open, so she saw me. But she'd shut them at the end and then she'd cried.

"How are you?" The husk of emotion echoed in my voice as her bright-blue eyes looked questions. I avoided the ones I wouldn't want to know.

"Okay. Did you sleep okay?"

"Uh huh." I played with her hair, threading it through my fingers.

Her hand lifted and rubbed over my hair, then down my cheek. "You're all prickly, you need a shave."

I laughed. "Yeah."

"What do you want to do today?"

Stay in bed with you and have sex with you over and over again… But seeing as that wasn't an option. "The surf is meant to be up today, do you mind if we go down on the beach and I take my board?"

She smiled. "If you want. I still can't believe I didn't know you could surf…"

"Yeah, well the summer I learned, you and Jason had buried yourselves in a love-nest. You had no interest in what I was doing…"

She frowned.

Dumb error! Why had I mentioned his name?

"We did not, we—"

"You did." I turned and got up, seeing as I'd invited Jason into the bed with us, I was getting out. "You wouldn't let him do anything without you. He'd have dropped me, like you dropped all your friends, if I hadn't gone to the same college as you guys." I talked with my back to her, picked up my shorts and top and pulled them on.

"Are you angry with me about that? That sounded angry…"

And she sounded confused. I wasn't surprised I didn't really know where it came from.

Old pain and jealousy.

I rubbed the leopard on my chest. I'd spent that first summer here fighting myself, mastering the waves and mastering my head. Trying to convince myself Jason and Lindy were together and that was it. I'd had to stop jealousy eating me up—he was my best friend. I hadn't succeeded and I had come here every summer since, doing the same thing. But then when I had gone home last year, I'd discovered that Jason had gone to New York…

I turned back.

She leaned up on her elbows, the comforter barely covering her breasts.

She was beautiful—I'd had sex with her.

Air pulled into my lungs. I breathed it out. "I'm not angry. I was just a bit messed-up myself that summer. The waves got me through it."

"How come I didn't know?"

"Because you never asked, and like I said, you and Jason were holed-up. I'm gonna go back to my room, shower and shave, turn up there in an hour and I'll get you breakfast."

She smiled, a look in her eyes that said "please like me". It wasn't a smile I was used to from Lindy. Had I always overlooked her lack of confidence or had she hidden it? "I'll see you in an hour." A "please like me" pitch caught in her voice too.

I smiled back, walked over and pressed a quick kiss on her lips. She didn't have to work me. I loved her. I'd never succeeded in getting her out of my head. The leopard on my chest had been the outside view of the inner pain that clawed at me whenever I was with her. "See you in an hour."

Lindy

As soon as the door shut, I got up, went into the bathroom and looked in the mirror. My naked face hit me. I hated it. I turned away and sat on the toilet to pee, gripping my head.

What happened last night was me. I hadn't dreamed it. My nerves hummed with the sensations he'd taught my body and my thighs ached.

I showered, running a soapy cloth over my skin, while images of his hands attacked my brain.

Then I retreated into the person I knew, hiding behind makeup. But in the mirror I could still see that new person. I was different. I'd experienced things I hadn't known existed.

I picked a cherry-pink bikini to wear, then pulled on my denim shorts and a pale-blue sleeveless tee. I covered it with a purple sweat top. I slipped my feet into my sandals, grabbed my backpack, took a deep breath, and then set off to knock on his door.

He was shirtless with wet, ruffled hair. The leopard cut its claws into his shoulder. He turned away. The cargo shorts he had on, hung low on his hips, flashing those taught lines of muscle that came up across his pelvic bone, and when he turned the top curve of his butt.

"Take a seat," he said, with an easy smile, pointing at the sofa bed, that was folded back into a sofa. His holdall was open on the floor, with his clothes piled messily in it.

I sat down and looked up at him. His room smelled of melted butter and frying tomatoes.

He grabbed a jug of whisked eggs. The muscle in his abdomen clenching and shifting as he tipped the eggs into the pan with the tomatoes.

"When did you get food to cook with?"

"When we got here. I'm a big boy, I get hungry." He threw me a grin over his shoulder, patting his flat belly with one hand as the other stirred the eggs.

My wits scrambled like the eggs.

I leaned back and lifted my feet up on the sofa. "How many girls have you been with? I don't remember you properly going out with anyone at college..."

He glanced over his shoulder, his eyes wide. "Why? It doesn't matter."

"Nope it doesn't, but I just want to know. You know about me..." I left Jason's name unsaid.

Billy sighed, his shoulders lifting and falling as he stirred the eggs. "I have no idea. Quite a few. I haven't counted them. I'm a guy..."

I didn't say anything; it didn't really matter. "But you never brought anyone back to the apartment."

"Because it would have felt wrong with you..." He stopped, taking a breath as he shifted the eggs off the heat. Then he looked at me. "With you and Jason in the apartment. So I always kept it out of the apartment. But you two didn't go to parties. I did."

That was true. "So you had hook-ups..."

"I hooked up with girls, who wanted to hook up with me. There was nothing in it and no one was let down or disappointed; they knew what we were doing." He had his back to me again, dishing up.

Disappointment curdled in my belly. I didn't even know why. "Was that what last night was then? A hook-up?"

He turned with my plate of eggs and tomatoes. His blue eyes intense and penetrating. "Last night was last night. It was just about you and me and no one else, and we'll see where it goes, shall we?"

"Yeah." My brain was too troubled to think beyond twenty-four hours anyway. He sat down and we ate, without speaking.

When he'd finished he got up and put his plate in the sink. "I'll take you down to the beach and get you settled then get my board and wetsuit out of the SUV."

"Okay. I'll wash this stuff up while you get a top and some shoes on."

He laughed but turned away as I went to the sink.

I'd spent three years living with Billy and Jason, I'd cleaned up after him before. But now everything was different. There was no Jason, and me and Billy had had sex last night. Good sex!

My heart pounded guilt into my blood.

Billy hunted through his stuff, then went in the bathroom.

I shoved the guilt away, kicking it in the ass. I deserved to live. Mom would not be upset… and Jason wouldn't give a shit.

The scent of Billy's aftershave came into the room before he did. "You ready?" He leaned over my shoulder and took the cloth I was wiping the drainer down with.

My belly wobbled like Jell-O and the floor tipped sideways.

He caught my arm. "You okay?"

Had I started falling?

"Yeah," I pulled myself together, straightened up and stepped away.

"Put your stuff in my safe, then if you want to come in the water with me, you won't have to worry."

"I'm not going in the water."

He gave me a half-smile. "Whatever, come on."

He grabbed the rug that we'd used the other day from the floor near his holdall and tossed it over his shoulder as we left the room, his hand hovering near my back. Then as we walked down to the beach, his fingers settled at my waist.

It felt comforting, but odd.

When he lifted the blanket to throw it on the sand, I stopped him. "No, I'll wrap it around me, I want to be able to watch you surf."

"Okay." He flashed me a smile. Both of us were tiptoeing around awkward today. "But I can get one of the other blankets from the SUV. I'll put this down and get you a non-sandy one to put around you.

Once he laid it out, I sat down on it, my knees bent up and my arms wrapped around them as he ran off back up the beach.

The breeze blowing up from the ocean made me shiver and whipped up the sand, tossing it around like a shifting magic carpet flying low over the beach.

I liked Billy, and what we'd done, but my heart still ached for Jason… and my body was full of pain for Mom.

I watched the waves crash up onto the sand.

Waves had kept crashing over my life for years, and like the sand I'd got pulled, thrown and blown around on the tide and breeze. I had no control over anything. This was not where I wanted to be. Things would never be how I wanted them to be… I couldn't control fate… I couldn't stop what was happening. I was gonna lose Mom, like I'd lost Jason…

A girl's squeal disturbed my distracted thoughts. The people who'd been around the campfire last night had a game of frisbee going on a few yards away, and a girl had dived and missed a catch. The rest of them laughed, but one of the guitar-players walked over to help her up.

He glanced my way and caught me looking. I looked at the waves.

Billy was gone ages, letting my mind play around, overthinking everything.

If Jason had been more honest with me about how bad our sex was, and helped me understand that, like Billy had done… What would have happened then? Would he not have gone to New York and met Rachel? Or maybe gone but not been drawn to her?

I sighed, moisture clouding my gaze and pain punching at my belly.

Billy's feet kicked the dry sand up beside me. I looked across as he set his board down, then tossed the extra blanket at me.

"You okay?" He'd seen the moisture in my eyes.

I took a breath and shoved my sadness away. "Yeah."

He stripped off his sweat top and tee.

Every time he stripped it flipped something in my belly.

His nipples stood out from discs of darker brown. Jason's skin had been pinker than Billy's.

I shut my eyes. I really should stop comparing them.

When I opened my eyes Billy stood in his swim shorts, the muscle in his thighs and arms moving as he pulled his wetsuit over his feet. Once it was on both legs up to his knees, he rocked his hips as he pulled it up over his massive thighs. The thing clung on every curve.

He grinned at me when it hung from his waist. I think he liked me watching.

He slid his arms into it. It wasn't easy or seductive, but the action had his abs and pecs shifting, and I watched that wondering how someone could make their body look so good. But then he did spend hours and hours working out. It was his job…

When his arms were in, his hand lifted and combed his hair back, then ruffled it.

A low note of laughter caught in the back of my throat. He didn't have any product in it today, so it didn't stand up straight anyway, but that was why he'd instinctively ruffled it. It was cute the way he did that.

His gaze came back to mine, a look of uncertainty in it. It was the first time I'd seen Billy look uncertain. Had he heard the noise of laughter escape my throat? "Sorry, it was just the way you rubbed your hair, you do it all the time. Only this time, there's nothing in it to spike it."

He gave me a twisted smile that was not sure if I was teasing in a cruel way.

I took a breath. "I prefer it not spiked."

"Do you now? What, like I prefer you without makeup…?"

He'd caught me. My lips parted in a smile. "I guess so."

He pulled the zipper of his wetsuit up, stopping my eyesight gorging on his ripped abs. "Difference is though, Lind. I'm not shit-scared by what you think about me leaving the stuff out of my hair."

True.

"Are you gonna come down to the ocean and watch?"

"I can see you from here."

"I know but walk down there with me. I feel guilty leaving you alone here. I'll put my stuff on the blanket to stop it blowing away."

I'd had years of Jason leaving me behind when he went running, and we'd argued about that, lots. Or rather I'd argued and he'd just gone off for a run. Billy knew.

"Okay." I got up. Between me and Jason, before we split, things had been well-worn and predictable—comfortable. Things with Billy were odd and unknown—so strange.

Stop comparing!

We were avoiding facing things today, because I guess neither of us really knew what difference last night had made.

It had just been sex.

But sex had changed everything...

Billy walked beside me carrying his board under one arm, his other hanging limp. Then about halfway down, he reached over and caught hold of my hand, and his fingers threaded in between mine. "You seem sad."

Tears burned in my eyes. I am sad. I have so much to be sad about... If you knew... But I can't tell you...

I swallowed them back. That was how things had been between Jason and me. Me sad and unable to speak and him not understanding or talking. He'd just turned away to avoid the conflict— and gone out for a run—while inside I'd screamed—you go, you escape me. You have your fun and forget I'm here!

I looked over at Billy's blue eyes. My belly fluttered like I had a bird in it, not butterflies. "Not really, just thoughtful. But, hey, no more than normal lately. I'm not gonna suddenly feel better because we had good sex."

His lips twisted. "I know, Lind, but for the record… it wasn't just good sex, it was awesome sex."

At the ocean, he let my hand go, but then his hand gripped the back of my head and he pressed a kiss on my lips.

When he pulled away his fingers lingered in my hair. "See you in a while."

"Okay."

He turned and ran into the shallows, a slow jog. For a muscular guy, he could move easily.

When he got into waist-height he threw the board down and pushed it out a little bit further.

I watched him go deeper and turn his head sideways to avoid the breakers crashing into his face, gripping the board as it tipped up, then went over the wave. On the other side of it, he pulled his body up onto the board. I only caught glimpses of him as he lay on it and paddled out deeper still.

The next time I saw him, he came back in on the surf, riding the brow of a wave, still lying on the board, but while I watched the white spume race about him, he gripped the board and pushed himself up to stand on it, then steered it with his feet.

It looked effortless. He balanced easily, his arms hanging loose, just the power in his thighs and calves cutting a path for the board through the racing water.

I was in awe of him. The shape of his body. The cut of his hips into his waist. His broad shoulders. His simplicity. His calm nature. The way he supported me. His passion.

He really was something out of the ordinary, and nothing like Jason. My stupid heart still didn't seem to know Jason had left me, though.

Stop comparing!

Billy rode the surf into the shore until he was only a few yards away from me. I watched until he jumped off and dropped into the water, lifting a hand to me.

I lifted my hand. Smiling.

He turned to push the board back out.

I turned away, then walked back up the beach. My arms folded over my chest, pulling the blanket tighter around my shoulders. It was really cold today; the wind was strong. I glanced around the beach. Dozens of people had come down to fly kites. They bobbed and danced on the air, catching and taming the ocean breeze.

My gaze fell as I reached the warmer, dry sand, watching my toes sink into it until I got to the blanket.

When I sat down, I bent my knees up, watching the ocean. I couldn't see Billy.

I should have brought my cell down, then I could have played games while he surfed. I didn't want to be alone.

The misery I'd left at home crept in. I'd been pushing it away, slowly escaping, the last couple of days but I could never escape it, I shouldn't even be trying… Guilt—I hate you. Pain—I hate you. Fear—I hate you. *FATE—I FUCKING HATE YOU!*

This is where loneliness left me… with time to think. I didn't want to think.

"Hey! Watch out!" Something light hit my shoulder and bounced off.

A frisbee.

"Sorry!"

I picked up the frisbee and looked up. It was one of the guys who'd played guitar last night. "Yours?" I held it up.

"Yeah, throw it over."

He stood about a dozen feet back from the blanket. The only way I'd have any chance of throwing it near him was to stand up. I stood. The blanket falling off my shoulders. I spun the frisbee at him, trying to cut it through the harsh breeze racing up the beach. It went wide.

"Whoa." He reached over, laughing and diving for it. He caught it before he, and it, hit the sand. His blue eyes bright with laughter.

"Quite a challenge, do you wanna play?"

It would be better than sitting alone thinking. "Okay."

He got up, brushed the sand off, then threw the frisbee to someone else before walking my way, holding out a hand.

""What's your name? Mine's Nial." His grip was tight and warm.

"Lindy." The wind blew my hair around, all over my face. When he let go of my hand I tucked my wayward hair behind my ears.

He pointed over to the other guy who'd been playing guitar last night. "That's my brother, Sawyer, and…" He went on to name the eight or so people who played the game, another five or six of them sat on rugs near where they'd had a fire last night. The frisbee game went on around us.

"You listened to us last night, right?"

"Yeah." I didn't see any reason to lie.

"Well if you liked what you heard, we're playing at Jackson's Bar tonight, why don't you come?"

I looked for Billy in the ocean.

"You could bring your…" Nial hesitated asking a question.

What was Billy to me? "Friend," I picked the only answer I knew to be true.

The frisbee flew past, about a foot away from Nial's head, as if someone reminded him he was supposed to be in the game.

He looked over his shoulder at his brother, his lips quirking to the side, then he looked back at me. "Come on, let's play." His fingers gripped my arm and pulled me into the game. His fingers were long and narrow. He had Jason's build, a little shorter than Billy and thinner, but still muscular, just in a more athletic way.

A lot of teasing went on in the game, people pretending to throw one way then throwing the other, deliberately making it go high or wide to get the catcher out. For the first half hour none of the others threw it to me. Nial always did and he never made the throws hard. But then gradually I got absorbed into the game and I had to keep my eyes open as everyone started throwing to me, and not easy catches.

A couple of the girls tossed questions too.

"Where are you from?"

"A small town not far from Portland."

"Are you on vacation?"

"Yeah."

I hadn't socialized for months, and even when I had, for the last year it had only been with Jason's family. This felt good. Something buzzed inside me.

Sawyer threw the frisbee at me, from way across the ring and it went wide. I lunged for it and fell, catching it an inch off the sand.

"Cool move." Nial came to help me up, gripping my forearm as I still held the frisbee off the ground.

I laughed, struggling to my feet.

"Lindy! Lindy!"

I looked down the beach to see Billy walking up with his surfboard under his arm.

His wet hair was stuck to his forehead. It made him look different—aggressive. "Lindy!"

"Looks like your *friend* wants you…"

"His name's Billy. Maybe we'll see you tonight. Thanks for asking me to join in. It was fun." I lifted my hand a little, then turned and ran down the beach to meet Billy.

"Hey." My voice came out breathless as I reached him, but a smile pulled my lips apart. "Did you have fun?" I walked beside him, matching his pace. Water dripped off his hair and his wetsuit, and he smelled of salt.

His brow furrowed and his eyes narrowed. "Yeah, 'til I saw you with them. What were you doing with them?"

"Playing frisbee."

"Obviously. I mean why?" We'd reached the blanket. He put his board down on the sand and began unzipping his wetsuit.

"Because they asked."

"Who asked?" His wetsuit was now gapping open all the way to his groin, revealing the cut of his abs, that had strange sensations twisting around in my belly, stirring up a potion of memories.

His hand lifted and swept back his wet hair.

"Nial. One of the guys who played guitar last night. His brother, the other guitarist, is called Sawyer." I didn't list the other names, I'd forgotten half of them anyway. "He was being nice because he saw me on my own. They're playing in a bar here tonight, so we could go along and listen if you want."

He huffed out a breath but didn't answer as he started peeling off his wetsuit. There was no denying he had a good body. I glanced over at Nial and saw him make a throw, his lean arm stretched out. That was the body shape I was used to.

Once Billy had stripped his wetsuit off he pulled his shorts back on over his swim trunks, then looked at me. "Aren't you gonna lay down."

"It's too cold to catch any sun today."

"Then I'll go fetch the tent poles and blankets. Sit down."

I did. He pulled his t-shirt and sweat top on, then his fingers combed through his hair and ruffled it. It brought a smile to my lips, especially as my gaze went to that stupid leather bracelet. I was gonna cut that off for him.

He looked at me, not going, but instead dropping down to kneel beside me on the blanket. "I know you still don't think you're attractive, but that guy does—"

"Nial?" I picked up the spare blanket and wrapped it around my shoulders again.

"Yeah, he was staring at you last night when they played, I saw him. I know you didn't."

I didn't know what to say. "He threw the frisbee and it hit my shoulder."

"It was a move, Lind. He thinks you're hot."

I looked at the game of frisbee, that had carried on.

"Have you got the hots for him?" Billy's pitch got lower. I met his dark-blue gaze. It asked more questions than that one, burning with accusation and disappointment.

Was he angry? I didn't know if I fancied Nial, but I knew I was not ready to commit to anything… not with Billy or anyone… I couldn't get caught up in anything right now… I… Then what had last night been? Foolish probably. Not thought-out. But I didn't regret it. "I don't know, but if I did, Billy, it hardly matters. You know I'm not ready to get into anything heavy, I'm too messed-up right now…"

The emotion in his gaze punctured and he looked down as he got up again. "I'll go get the stuff for our den."

What had he thought last night was? He hadn't ever had a serious relationship, so he can't have thought it anything special. But I wasn't asking him. I didn't want to get into difficult conversations. He'd said in the beginning we'd just see where things went. That was all I wanted, easy, unpainful, uncomplicated, escape. That was what he'd given me.

Chapter Ten

Billy

I hadn't said much to Lindy on the beach, or as we'd walked back up to the apartments at around five. I hadn't gone back into the surf either. To be truthful, I was pissed with her. After what we'd done the night before I didn't like the thought of her anywhere near another guy.

But that was being a jerk, jealous and selfish, and those were the feelings I'd tried to conquer in the summers I'd spent here. They could eat my innards out if I let them—I was done with them. She had to do what she wanted.

Though every time I thought of that guy, it still made my skin crawl like I had bugs all over me, and my teeth clench.

I had to stop myself from growling at her when we discussed where to go eat. She held out for the bar—to watch Nial and his brother Sawyer play.

Bullshit.

I'd only just got her, after years of watching her, and now she liked someone else. What was wrong with her? What was wrong with me?

In the end we agreed a compromise. We went to a diner and then went on over to Jackson's Bar.

When I ordered our drinks a swell of emotion frothed around

me like I was riding the crest of a wave. I wanted to do harm to someone tonight. I was riled up and ready to fight—for her. Ten hours before I'd thought I knew where I stood; I'd stepped through the gates of heaven. Now I was back on the stairway down to hell, where I'd been wallowing for years.

"Hey, guys." Nial's cheery welcome had all the muscles in my back stiffening and the hair rising on the back of my neck.

Fuck.

I turned.

"Do you want a drink?" He looked at Lindy.

"I've already ordered."

He looked at me and held out a hand. "Hey, Billy. Nice to meet ya all, I'm Nial." The guy was playing with me.

I wanted to punch him right in the face, and then maybe in the gut too, but that was not an option. Instead I gripped his hand really hard and felt the bones in his fingers crunch, warning him to back off. "Likewise."

He knew he was stepping on my territory, I could see it. But he looked like the sort of guy who didn't give a shit, and the complete opposite of me.

He had blonde curly, unruly hair a couple of inches long, light-blue eyes, and he was shorter and thinner than me—different coloring, but more like Jason.

I let his hand go. It dropped to his side as he shook it out like I'd hurt him.

I was glad.

He looked at Lindy, a half-smile playing on his lips that said I hadn't put him off. "You gonna come and sit with us?"

"Okay," she answered without even looking at me for agreement.

Awesome.

The barman slid our drinks across. "There you go."

I turned around and was gonna get my wallet out, but Lindy laid her hand over mine. "It's my turn."

Great, now Nial had more ammunition. He knew she wasn't

letting me look out for her. It opened a door for him. He'd think she didn't care about me…

But then maybe she didn't. How the hell did I know? All we'd done was have awesome sex. The sarcastic, bitter pitch in my head made me angrier still. But we hadn't discussed commitment, and maybe, 'cause she didn't know anything about sex, she hadn't known how awesome it was.

Shit.

I clenched my teeth as I picked up the bottle of beer, then let Nial lead us over to the people Lindy had been playing with today. Lindy walked ahead of me, talking to him, and when we got over there, there was a chorus of greetings and lots of people smiling at her.

She smiled back, full-on mouth-open, with happy sparkling eyes, and a this-is-amazing face.

Well now I felt like shit, 'cause if this made her happy, when she'd been feeling so down she'd tried to end it all, I really should get over myself and be happy for her.

Everyone talked over one another, making space for us to sit in the ring of three tables they'd clustered together. Lindy talked back, animated and excited. I hadn't seen her do that for years, not since we'd been at high school.

When she'd chased after Jason at high school, she'd laid in wait for us around corners and come out with the biggest smile, saying, "Hey!" like she was surprised to bump into us and hadn't been there waiting.

She used to catch up to us on our way home, with a pile of books in her hands, struggling like they were too heavy so Jason would offer to take them. If I had, the answer was, "But Jason goes my way, so he can do it."

"Billy…" Her palm settled on my thigh, tiny in comparison.

She'd said something. I hadn't heard. At least she wanted me in the conversation. She hadn't forgotten me.

I stumbled through some interaction, my gut twisting as her

hand stayed on my thigh. I wanted it to be the two of us back at the apartment, exploring bodies and getting to know each other better. I was terrified it wasn't the same for her.

She was everything to me; I'd been nothing to her. What if we had awesome sex and then I was relegated back to nothing?

Nerves prickled up my spine.

"We've got to go play." Nial and then Sawyer stood up.

I watched them set up and tune their guitars as Lindy carried on talking with the others, mostly the girls. It had been years since she'd had girlfriends. I really should notch my attitude down a level or two.

Lindy laughed at something one of the girls said, a proper laugh. You'd think she didn't have a care in the world. She wasn't thinking about the way she looked now, or about Jason. I wished I'd been the one to make her laugh that easily.

When the guys started playing, the bar went silent. They were good. I'd give them that. They could make music, and their group of friends who clearly knew all their songs began joining in with the lyrics as Lindy watched, bright-eyed with happiness. She was enjoying this. I shouldn't be angry with her.

My fingers beat out the rhythm on my thigh, nervously, the thigh that still had Lindy's hand on it.

That hand grounded me and occasionally it moved, brushing up and down a little as she talked, or gripping a little when she laughed.

The guys took a break after they'd played four songs. Nial jumped down off the dais and came straight over to us. "Do you all want another drink, we're getting some beers in."

The guy came over from the bar with a whole tray of open bottles, and people started grabbing them. "Thanks," Lindy answered. She'd drunk soda so far.

I looked at her. "Your meds…"

"It's just one." Her pitch said, *get lost, Billy,* and the look she threw over her shoulder was just like the ones my little sister Eva threw when she thought I was being annoying.

Great, now I'd fallen into the fun-spoiler bracket.

She'd got happier. I was pissed off.

Nial took the vacant seat the other side of her. The girl had gone to the restroom. He started talking, leaning forward to just speak to Lindy. I couldn't hear because of the noise in the busy bar and then Lindy's hand lifted off my thigh and she turned to face him.

Bullshit.

Fighting an urge to grab Nial by the throat and shove him up against a wall, I put my beer down, stood up and headed for the restroom myself, curling my hands into fists and then forcing them open again.

I looked myself in the eye in the mirror as I washed my hands after. "What the fuck are you doing? Get a grip, Billy. Let the girl enjoy herself, there's no harm in it."

That was what my brain thought—but my body and my instinct screamed to tell the guy to get the fuck away from her and just drag her out of here.

When I went back in the bar the guys were playing another song and Lindy was up in front of the stage dancing with their friends.

Nial's gaze followed Lindy's movement. He hadn't seen me come back in.

I watched her too, as I walked across the room. Lindy wasn't used to dancing like they were. For years we'd line-danced; it was the thing back home. Jason's mom had got her into it, and Jason had never been any good at it. It had been my one in with her for the last few years. She'd always chosen to dance with me over Jason. When I got close, she spotted me. She hadn't seen Nial watching her.

"Billy! Come and dance." She held her hand out, the other one still gripping her bottle of beer, that was already half-empty.

Awesome, this night was gonna end on the bathroom floor.

"Come on," she urged, her hand reaching further out to me as she smiled wide.

There was no point in not. I wasn't gonna be the killjoy.

Leaving my beer where it stood on the table, knowing it was likely I'd have to pick her up later and be the sober one, I went to her. Her arms settled up on my shoulders, one of her hands still holding her beer bottle. It bumped against my back as she moved.

She was so much shorter than me, with just her flats on she only came up to my chest.

My hands gently gripped her waist as she rocked and bounced to the rhythm of the music.

"You okay?" I bent to her ear to ask.

"Yeah, fine."

"Good." The smell of beer mixed up with the mint gum she'd been chewing earlier and her perfume. My nose brushed her brow. She looked up and met my gaze, hers cloudy from the beer.

I kissed her, forgetting Nial and everyone else in the bar, and her fingers ran into my hair as she played chase with my tongue.

She hadn't forgotten me.

The song changed, and I came up breathless, as she did. We stared into each other's eyes then as we kept moving. She was not thinking about anyone but me. I knew it. A light switched on in my heart, and something gripped it sharp and tight, just like she'd had a hold of it for the last several years.

I was pathetic for a big guy, really…

Lindy

"Am I sleeping in your room?" The question was uncertain as Billy's eyes shone dark grey and black in the electric light of the hall.

"If you want?"

His big hand cupped my cheek. "No, Lind, if you want?"

Yes, I wanted. Just the thought of him coming into my room stirred up memories and a deep, sweet, pain, gripped low in my belly. "I want…" *You.* The last word wouldn't come out. It still felt disloyal to Jason to want someone else—his best friend.

When my card key slid out of the door Billy's mouth came down on mine and his fingers pushed the door open, drawing me in.

Last night we'd prepared for bed. Tonight was different. Tonight it was like he'd been hungry and wanting me for hours. I'd never felt any hunger in Jason. But then he'd probably held it back because if he'd been like this, he'd have scared me.

It scared me with Billy, but in a way that made my heart race, like going on a rollercoaster. I wanted to be scared. I didn't want him to stop.

He pulled the sweater I had on over my head, then gripped my dress. But before he could take it off I yanked his shirt, pulling it more out than up. I wasn't used to Billy's way of doing things, but I didn't want to be vulnerable—the only one naked.

He got the hint and with a twisted smile, and heat burning in his eyes, he undid a couple of buttons, then pulled it up and off, the muscle in his chest and arms moving.

For the first time I let my urge to touch run. My fingertips brushed his skin, following the lines of muscle. He had an awesome body. I preferred it to Jason's. Was it wrong to say that?

Billy was a granite force of strength, and I needed that to stand on; the foundations of my life were so frickin' rocky.

I flicked his belt from the buckle. He chuckled, a deep, heavy sound and then his fingers settled back on my dress and fisted.

I looked up and met his gaze a moment before he lifted it. Humor or rather pleasure—happiness—sparkled in his eyes. Soul-deep happiness.

I couldn't even remember what that felt like. But I could remember the pleasure he'd taught me last night… I wanted it. Desperately.

I let him take my dress off over my head. No. I wanted him to. *Fight.*

I got his button, freeing his pants.

He unhooked my bra, leaning around me.

My hands slipped into the back of his pants, cupping his butt, forcing the zipper down. His fingers slid into my hair and we kissed. I got lost in it, my tongue chasing his. My hands gripping at the muscle of his ass.

He broke the kiss. "Lay down, Lind."

The pace of my heartbeat ratcheted up a dozen notches and tingles did a line-dance through my nerves as I stepped back, slipping off my sandals and sitting on the bed.

He pushed down his pants, and boxers, taking everything off and straightened up naked.

I scrabbled backwards across the mattress, lying down before him, sacrificing everything for the moments of freedom I knew were coming as he bent to get a condom out of his wallet. I didn't care that I only had on my panties, I didn't care about anything except what was coming next. A beautiful freedom.

The thin leather bracelet he wore stood out on his thick wrist as he slid a condom on, making this tough guy look subtly vulnerable, dispelling the threat of the leopard climbing his chest.

When his knee came down on the bed, dipping the mattress, he didn't come to me, instead his hands gripped my panties and slid them off. I shivered as he did it. Reality, awareness and fear kicking in. But then his hands caught hold of my thighs and pulled my legs open.

I cried out, half-moan, half-shock. A rush of something, something addictive and terrible all at the same time, tore through me. But before I could react, his mouth was on me, down there. I was a little drunk. My brain didn't have chance to catch up with the idea of it, but oh! It didn't matter. I didn't care. My fingers gripped in his wax-spiked hair, fisting and pulling at it as his tongue played games.

Race him!

The tips of his big fingers pressed into my thighs as I pushed up against his mouth, following the movement of his tongue. I thought of the things I'd thought of when I'd touched myself. Only this was beyond anything I could imagine.

Oh shit. Billy.

Next time I did it to myself I was gonna think of this.

A battle. A race.

I pressed up against his mouth over and over, searching out the movements that delivered the best shocks of pleasure, sparking small explosions under my skin.

It was no hardship to focus on what he did… What he did was crazy, his tongue licking, pressing in and then his lips closing around me, and—sucking…

"Ahhh…" The sound slipped from my lips.

His teeth caught my sensitive spot with a little tug.

I laughed, my fingers clasping even tighter in his hair.

Why didn't I feel self-conscious with him anymore? Because he showed no sign I had to be self-conscious.

Had I always sensed I might lose Jason? That he'd never really loved me. Was that why things had never been right?

But then Billy didn't love me. This was just sex. Maybe that was it, maybe he gave me permission to just have sex and enjoy it, and not worry about what I was, or wasn't, or what life would become.

His lips settled over the sore spot he'd bitten and sucked with a stupid gentleness as his fingers slipped inside me. I came undone, breaking in half. Splintering. Shattering. Swamped. My breath only shallow, short panting…

"Billy." His name slipped from my lips as he came up over me, his thick thighs between my legs, and then he pumped into me with a pace and skill that had my nails cutting into his back.

I raced—fought to make him lose control and come too. To make him want the hell out of me, like I wanted the hell out of him.

I was so drunk on sex. I didn't care about anything but this.

Breathy noises filled the room. Sweat leaked over my skin and glimmered on his and the air held a musky scent. Sex. My thighs wrapped about his waist. I curled the soles of my feet on the back of his buttocks as he worked harder, growling at me as I pushed up against him.

This was sex. What Jason and I had done had been nothing. I

could understand why he'd gone now. Of course he would have been tempted away by this. I got it.

Billy plummeted into an orgasm with a hard thrust. I fell right along with him—free-falling through space as the weight of his hips pressed me deeper into the mattress.

I escaped to heaven. Maybe in a few months I could escape here and meet Mom again, as she used to be...

I wished I had discovered this long ago. Maybe then I wouldn't be in so much pain.

I could get addicted to sex.

As he went off to the bathroom to get rid of the condom, I slid under the comforter, too exhausted to even bother with finding my clothes, or going to check my makeup.

I few moments later the lights went out, and Billy came under the covers next to me and pulled me against him with a hand splayed over my belly.

We fell asleep spooning.

Lindy

My cell buzzed. It was in my purse on the floor, near the door.

The bedroom looked like a warzone, with our clothes everywhere.

I chucked the covers back and got up to get it.

Billy didn't wake.

Mom. My heart pounded at the sight of her image smiling at me on the screen. My hand shook. I really shouldn't drink with my meds, my belly was a queasy hole today.

The things Billy and I had done played through my head. I hadn't cared. I still didn't. I'd escaped.

"Hey. Mom?"

"Sweetheart—"

"Is everything okay?"

I carried the cell into the bathroom, shut and locked the door, pressing the thing up tight to my ear.

"Yes, there's nothing to worry over, darling. I called to check you are okay, that's all. Are you?"

With my back against the door, I slid down onto the cold floor tiles. "Yeah, Mom. Better than I've been in a while. I needed this vacation. Billy was right. It's good for me."

"And you two are getting along?"

"Yeah…" A huge question hung inside me and it sounded in my voice. What was happening? What was Billy? What were we? We weren't just friends anymore. But what then? I wasn't ready for anything complex, and painful… I hurt enough.

"You're sure?"

"Billy has been really good to me."

"You remember your counselor is calling today?"

"I know."

"Good, honey. Well I want you to know I'm okay, and you keep enjoying yourself. You deserve to be happy."

But how can I be?

The hole inside me filled up with love—for her. "I love you."

"I love you too, honey. We'll see you next week."

"Okay."

"Goodbye." She blew a kiss down the cell.

"Bye." Pain cut into my heart as the call went dead. I swiped the tears off my cheek.

Shit my makeup.

When I stood up, my reflection in the mirror showed mascara and eyeliner smeared around my eyes and my foundation looked like a mask. Then I looked at my body.

I reached for my robe hanging on the back of the door and slipped it on, I didn't want to look at myself. I picked up the cleanser to wipe my makeup off.

In half an hour I'd showered, reapplied makeup and the girl in the mirror looked more like the person I knew.

When I went back into the bedroom, Billy was still asleep, lying on his side, his long, thick black lashes resting on his cheeks, the leopard rising and falling on his pecs as he breathed.

I sat on the end of the bed, with my knees tucked up and clasped in my hands.

His arm rested on top of the comforter.

The stupid leather bracelet wrapped around his wrist beckoned me to look out the scissors from my makeup purse and cut the thing off. It held too many memories of a time my life had been unrestrained… Everything had been sparkly, glittery, fun and expectation then. I got up and went into the bathroom to get them.

I'd wanted to give the bracelet to Jason, but Jason hadn't wanted it, Billy had stretched out his arm. "Tie it on me. I like it." I'd done it and smiled smugly at Jason to make him jealous.

He hadn't been jealous. He was always too laid back to bother about mistrust, or anger… I wished he'd argued with me when we'd been together if he didn't like the stuff I'd said, or done. Maybe then we'd have fallen apart earlier and I'd have understood that we weren't right.

But Billy… I searched through my makeup purse. What were we? He suited me in bed. He liked me like that and just looking at him made my belly shiver. I found the scissors and headed back.

But there was a confusing swamp of feelings in me, too many to unpick.

Was I using him, like I'd done with that bracelet?

He made me feel better. But beyond that? Where was this going? Why? What were we doing? Was I making another stupid error? Being selfish just because he was willing to give? What if I repeated history, and blindly took, only to wind up getting hurt?

I couldn't answer any of those questions.

"Hey."

His eyes opened just as I reached to cut the bracelet off.

A smile came from deep inside me. I loved his dark-blue eyes. Something warm and heavy twisted in my belly. "Hey."

"What are you doing?"

"Cutting off this stupid bracelet I gave you years ago."

"No." He moved his arm away and he looked angry. "I like It."

"Why? It was a childish thing."

"Lind, I've had it years; it's a part of me. I don't want to take it off. It's part of who I am."

I didn't know what to say as I sat on the bed holding the scissors.

He took them off me and put them on the chest of drawers beside the bed.

"How long have you been awake?" He lay back down, his hand settling behind his head.

"A little while."

"Long enough to pretty yourself up and hide behind your makeup, hey?"

Was that said out of annoyance? Shit, why did I have no clue how to even be me anymore? I didn't know whether to challenge him or not. I was confused, worn-out by surviving.

He leaned up on to his elbows and the comforter slithered further down his chest. "I oughta go down to the gym this morning…"

"That's okay, my counselor is calling me at ten."

"Then we'll make a date for breakfast after, okay?" He hesitated like he didn't know what was going on between us either.

I'd spent years stepping around the shattered glass of my life. "Yeah." I breathed.

"Unless you wanna get back into bed, to give me a workout…" His smile turned crooked and wicked.

I shook my head, panic suddenly rearing, I was too confused right now. "Nah, go down to the gym. I'm not in the mood."

His eyes turned mat, then a look of concern passed across his face. "You, okay?" He sat up and reached for my hand, the comforter slipping all the way down to his belly.

The guy was a whole pile of caring. Really I should have always been into Billy not Jason. But Jason had been the guy everyone hungered for. Billy had just been the friend of the best-looking guy. I'd overlooked him.

I couldn't overlook him now. "I'm okay."

He squeezed my fingers then let go of my hand. Perhaps he'd guessed I needed time to get everything in order in my head. Or maybe this was weird for him too.

"I'll get up then and get out your way."

I nodded.

He slid out the bed, naked and started gathering up his clothes, to get dressed.

I stood up and went to watch the ocean from the window. The waves were huge today, crashing up onto the beach.

My cell chimed the notes to say I'd got a text. Billy picked it up and threw it onto the side of the bed near me.

I picked it up and smiled.

"Who is it?"

I looked up. "Nial."

"You swapped numbers with him?" His eyebrows had lifted and his pitch was tainted with annoyance.

"He's inviting us over to his folks' place, they're having a pool party out there today."

"Great." Billy turned away, grabbing his shirt up from the floor. "Us, or *you*?" He looked back at me, then pulled it over his head.

"He said, '*we're having a pool party round my folks, do you want to come.*' He knows I'm with you…"

"Maybe, and maybe not."

"Billy—"

"Never mind, I'm being a douche. Tell him we'll go. Get his zip code and I'll drive out. Then if I hate his company I can leave."

Billy's pitch had a hard edge I wasn't used to. "Are you jealous?"

One eyebrow lifted this time. "Should I be?"

"No." But shit, it felt good to know he got jealous. I liked his anger. Emotion said he felt something more than nothing. Maybe I mattered to him more than I had ever mattered to Jason…

"Then just make sure he knows that, Lind." His eyes threw the same message at me. Then he turned and walked out, leaving an aura of possessiveness behind. I loved it.

Chapter Eleven

Billy

"This is it! Right here!" Lindy shouted as we saw a set of huge black cast-iron gates. I made the turn and pressed the buzzer on the intercom.

"Hi."

"Hey, it's Billy and Lindy."

"Awesome. Come on in."

A moment later the gates opened.

His folks place was a fucking ranch. Horses ran around in a field on the right-hand side of the track I drove up and I passed stables before reaching the house. The house was huge.

Great, this was a ploy to win her with rich-kid status. I couldn't compete.

He came out as I pulled up in front of the house. There were half a dozen cars parked out there.

I killed the engine. Lindy jumped out as I opened my door.

"Hey, Lindy!" Nial waved at her.

I gritted my teeth and got out, slamming the door behind me. He glanced at me with a twisted smile. "Billy." The guy knew I didn't want to be here. Hell, he didn't want me here. But I was here.

Lindy started telling him we were late because we'd got a little lost. I walked up behind her and slotted my arm about her waist.

Her muscle jolted, like she didn't like me claiming her, but she didn't push me away.

"Come on in…" Nial encouraged. "We're out back, by the pool."

Lindy pulled away from me, following him and talking as I trailed behind like an idiot.

As soon as we got round there Nial stripped off his tee, flashing his skinny abs at her. "Are you coming in?"

He didn't wait on her answer. He turned and dived into the water.

I looked at her. "What do you want to do, are we going in the pool?"

A hesitant smile curled her lips—temptation and terror at war.

She'd said over breakfast she'd told her counselor about being too hung-up on her looks. Apparently the woman had gone on about it being something Lindy could work on… I supposed most of the time she talked about her split with Jason, and she couldn't fix that…

"Yeah," she said in a low, breathy voice. "Let's get in the pool."

"With no t-shirt on?" I winked at her.

She flashed me a smile. "With no t-shirt on."

I didn't know where the sex we'd been having was leading us, but we were closer, we weren't just friends anymore.

Everyone else was in the pool, so we'd have looked dumb if we'd hung around the edge anyway.

I stripped off my t-shirt and saw a couple of the girls look. Lindy smiled at me as she slid her shorts down first, taking her sandals off too. I unbuttoned my jeans and spotted Nial watching Lindy as she stripped off her tee.

"Hey, Lindy. Get me a beer, and help yourselves!" Nial shouted from the pool.

I figured it was to keep her out of the pool so he could watch her longer. "I'll get them, Lind. Do you want something?"

"Just a cola."

Instead of diving in, she went over to the steps and climbed down. No doubt to protect her makeup. Nial wasn't the only one checking her out, though, as she did—I was too—and I had a feeling a couple of the other guys also watched her.

She had a good body, no matter what her stupid head thought.

When she was in the water I turned, got myself and Nial bottles of beer and snapped the caps off. Then did the same with a bottle of cola. I carried them over to the pool and leaned over to hand Nial his. When he swam to the edge, he smiled at me. We both knew the game he played, pitching for my girl. But really nothing said she was my girl.

I made him tug the beer out of my hand. Just to taunt the guy. He smiled at that too, then turned and swam over to where Lindy was, surrounded by the girls.

She had a full-on smile and talked in the way she'd used to at school.

Nial might piss me off, but being involved with this group was good for Lindy.

I put my beer down on the edge of the pool. Straightened up, then lifted my arms and dived in. The water absorbed me and I opened my eyes, watching everyone's legs. I spotted Lindy's bikini. Today's was bright yellow. Her hands were under the water and her fingers slipped along the line of the seams on her ass, pulling it down a little as it'd ridden up.

When I came up out of the water, her taste was in my mouth, even though it couldn't be. She'd got lost in sex last night, forgetting about her body, her makeup and even Jason. She'd only cared what I did.

But even though Jason hadn't been in her brain, I wasn't sure about her heart. I had a feeling he'd still been in bed with us.

I took a deep breath and shook the water out of my hair.

Lindy looked over and smiled at me as I smoothed my hair back. Some of the other girls said, "Hi."

"Hey. I'm just gonna get my beer."

I swam back to the side.

Lindy laughed at something. Her laughter made sharing her worth it.

I picked up my beer and swam one-armed, to the shallow water, where I could stand up.

"Hey." A girl's hand touched my shoulder. As I turned her fingertips slid down over my leopard. "I like your ink. It's cool."

"Thanks." I took a sip of my beer, as the water in the pool lapped at my pecs, sensitizing my nipples.

She moved to the edge of the pool and rested her arms along the rim, letting her feet float, trying to look casual and sexy, by my guess. "What's with you and Lindy?"

That was the question I'd been debating. I shrugged.

"She said you aren't dating."

No? Then we were just having sex. That kicked. I sipped my beer.

"If nothing's really on between you two…" She glanced at me with a smile, saying I'm interested.

I shook my head. "Thanks, but no thanks."

"Let's play volley ball, we've got enough for two teams!" One of the other girls shouted across the pool.

"Where did you guys all meet?" I asked the girl next to me.

"We all live around here."

I sipped my beer. Sawyer and Nial started picking people for teams.

"Have you known Nial and Sawyer long then?"

"A couple of years. They moved out here three years ago."

And now you let them play pack leaders…? They all did everything Nial and Sawyer said. It was like being back at school. Jason and Lindy had been the Nial-and-Sawyer type… They'd had an aura that pulled people their way… Look how that ended… I looked at Lind and sipped my beer again.

She stood talking to Nial as the water swayed around her shoulders, getting the tip of her ponytail wet.

I'd lay good odds that Nial had picked her first.

"You're on my team, Billy!" Sawyer yelled over.

That figured…

"What about you and Lindy?"

My eyebrows lifted. What about me and Lindy?

"Where did you meet?"

"At school and we shared an apartment at college. We've known each other years."

"But you kissed last night, and neither of you say you're dating…" Her lips quirked with sarcasm.

I took the hit, lifting my beer bottle in salute. "She was with my best friend at college, I shared their place."

"Awkward…" She laughed and then swam off to join the group of people around Nial. I downed the last of my beer and then swam over to Sawyer's half of the pool. Of course we had the deep end, to make it harder.

Lindy

"That's it. You guys win!"

Nial gripped my arm when Sawyer called defeat. "Hey, Lindy, come help pick what pizzas to order." We'd thrashed Sawyer's team. But they'd had the deep end of the pool.

I waved at Billy, then turned and walked through the water. It lapped at my breasts.

I'd spent the whole afternoon laughing. Billy and I had been on opposite teams, and every time the ball had come near him, he'd hit it in my direction, like we were having a one-on-one game. He'd kept smiling at me every time I looked his way, and he'd grinned each time he'd knocked the ball at me.

We hadn't been able to talk, there were too many people and too much water between us, but I still felt like we'd spent the day together, because of all the non-verbal communication we'd had going on. I couldn't remember having non-verbal conversation with Jason—actually that was a lie, I could—when I'd glared at him for doing something dumb or annoying.

He'd accused me of forcing him into stuff when we'd split. I guess his non-verbal communication had been just going along with me, when really he'd been pissed off and hated me.

Nial pressed his palms down on the edge of the pool and hauled his body out of the water. It streamed across his skin. He really did look a lot like Jason—bodily—not his coloring. He was blonde and blue-eyed; Jason had brown hair and brown eyes.

I gripped the rail by the steps and climbed them carefully, looking down to double-check my bikini still covered everything it should. I hated my belly. It wobbled a little while I moved. I glanced at Billy, his eyes were not watching my belly; his gaze absorbed my ass.

I pulled my bikini bottoms out of my butt cheeks and heard him laugh.

I swear Jason had never once, in all the years we'd been together, ogled me like that… But at Christmas I'd seen him watching Rachel like that.

"Come on, Lindy…" Nial rubbed his body down with a towel.

"Here." He threw me a towel.

I wrapped it around me and tucked it in over my breasts, hiding myself beneath it.

"What's your favorite?" He looked at me over his shoulder as he turned toward the house.

I smiled, following him. "Something spicy."

"What about Billy?"

I laughed. "He's a meat feast guy."

The marble tiles in his parents' house were cold under my bare feet.

"I'll get the list and we can work out how many pizzas to order and what." Nial walked a bit ahead of me, along a wide hall that had various doors leading off into sitting rooms, a dining room, den and a study. Every room had exquisite decoration. His parents must be really rich.

When we got to a massive kitchen with a wide central island. He pulled open one of the cedar-wood drawers and dropped a take-away pizza menu onto the black granite top. He slid it over my way, leaning across a peninsular of units that jutted out in front of a long table and chairs.

Mom would love this kitchen…

I looked at the menu, ignoring the open wound weeping inside me.

I hurt so much, and a day messing around in a pool with a pile of new friends wasn't going to take the hurt away. This was a vacation, the little escape I'd needed to regroup. It wouldn't fix anything permanently. Nothing was permanent. I'd learned that in the last few years.

"How many do you reckon for all of us?" Nial pushed.

I looked up and found him staring at me.

Jason's eyes had been a warm, deep-brown; Billy's dark intense steel; Nial's were endless soft blue sky. Out of the three of them, I preferred Billy's dark stormy steel eyes.

I looked at the menu, shoving the memory of Jason aside. Pain lanced through my heart. He'd never loved me, though he'd said "I love you" all the time. He'd thought he'd been in love… and then he'd met Rachel, and learned that his heart really didn't give a shit about me… Billy had more interest in me after just having sex than Jason ever had.

"What do you think?" Nial came around beside me and his fingers touched my arm. "Lindy." His hand lifted to my chin, bracing it and then he leaned in…

Shit.

My hands pressed against his naked pecs, his cold nipples under my palms.

A shiver of wrong ran through me.

The things-don't-feel-right sensation I'd felt with Jason whenever we'd had sex. Maybe because he hadn't really wanted me.

With Jason my body had screamed, no!

With Nial…

"I don't want you to do that."

"No?" Nial's blue eyes glittered with confidence.

Confidence exploded in me too. The sort I'd had at high school. I believed in myself. Jason may never have been into me, but Billy and Nial were, so there couldn't be anything massively wrong with me. Could there?

"No, Nial, I'm sorry, I'm not in a good place right now, and things are kind of up in the air with me and Billy… I'm not interested in you like that. Sorry. But I'd still like to be your friend. We've had fun hanging out here."

He shrugged and laughed at the same time. "Oh, well it was worth a try. Billy is a lucky bastard…"

My ego glowed in a way it hadn't for years. "Thanks."

"But no thanks…" he finished, laughing before looking down at the pizza menu. "Alright, then, help me pick. How many?"

Chapter Twelve

Lindy

Billy's arm lay over my shoulders as we walked back along the corridor toward our rooms. I was tired; I think he was too. We'd been playing around in the pool all day. After we'd eaten, the guys had put a loud-speaker system on and played music into the pool area, and things had gone a little mad.

Nial hadn't been any different after my rejection. That had felt good. He'd still flirted and laughed, dancing with me. Lightness swelled inside me tonight. I hadn't had a drink, but I still felt drunk.

"Are we sharing again?" Billy said in a low, deep pitch as we reached the door of my apartment and stopped.

I smiled at him. "I want to…"

His blue-grey eyes glowed. "Awesome." The word was heat across my lips as his head came down. Longing burned through me when his lips pressed against mine, scorching me on a backdraft of memories from the last couple of days; eagerness catching in my belly.

He took the card key from my hand, slotted it in the door and when the lock clicked loose and a green light flashed he pulled it out and pushed the door open. "Go on." His hand set a gentle pressure at my waist, encouraging me to go first. Something flipped in my belly—anticipation.

When the door shut, he said, "Lind, do me a favor tonight, go take your makeup off before we get into bed? I like you with no makeup. Don't get me wrong. I like you with it… But it's just, I'm the only one who's seen you with no makeup. I like that. I want to go to bed with that you."

The tight grip lifted from my belly to my chest.

I stepped forward and touched his cheek, then lifted to my toes and kissed his lips, briefly. "Thank you, Billy. For being so sweet."

His lips broke apart in a wide smile and his hands braced my head, then his lips crushed mine, just for an instant. "Go take off your makeup."

Billy was in bed when I came back. He'd left a single lamp on next to him. I ran to get in. I was naked. I had never got into bed naked. Shame, exposure crashed through me as I moved, but I ignored my fears. Billy liked what I looked like; he wanted me naked. He threw back the covers and I dived in.

I laughed as he threw them back over, covering me up.

He understood how big a deal this was. Thrills beyond my physical desire for his body skimmed through my nerves as I snuggled up against him and he turned to face me.

His palm rested on my hip, then slid up to cup my breast as he kissed me.

I played that now-familiar game of chase with his tongue, as his long fingers massaged my breast and his thumb kept brushing over my nipple. My hands were in his hair.

He broke the kiss. "I want you to touch me, Lind."

My eyes got wide. He always had to push at a boundary. But his boundary-pushing worked. I slid my hand down and touched the rigid column of flesh that pointed up at me. It jolted as my fingers touched his tip.

He laughed into my mouth as my fingers pulled away. "You aren't hurting me. I'm just sensitive there, that's all. Touch away."

I smiled as his lips came down on mine again; my heart and soul floating in zero gravity.

Billy was easy to open up and be sexual with.

I touched him, stroking a fingertip along the taut velvet skin of his erection, while his hand massaged my breast and his tongue pressed into my mouth. Then I gripped him, taking him in my fist as he'd taught me in the shower the other day, and ran my hand down, then up.

His sigh of hot breath filled my mouth, and his hand slid down between my legs, then a long finger slipped inside me.

Sensations swirling around I didn't know what to concentrate on, touching him, fighting for who would reach the end, or the delicious stroke of his finger.

I shut my eyes, capturing different moments from each. I ached for him. Pain weaved through my middle. The texture of the solid mass in my hand, the pressure of his tongue sweeping over mine all played games with my senses…

He leaned more over me, forcing me to roll to my back as his caress got more determined, wanting to win the game. I ended up just gripping his cock and giving in, as he sent me over the edge of a tidal wave. I wanted him in me. Desperately.

I gripped his hips and pulled.

He laughed instead, rolling onto his back and pulling me with him. "Come here…"

"What?"

"Get a condom and go on top."

"What?"

He pulled my upper arm, his grip urging me to move. "Get a condom, put it on me, and straddle me."

His massive strength struck at another boundary. The boundary was gonna shatter, I didn't even argue. I just wanted him in me.

His wallet rested on the side by the lamp he'd left on. My hand shook as I reached for it, and pulled a condom out. I couldn't open it, my hands shook too much. He took it off me, opened it, then held it out to me.

It was a dare. A test. To see if I'd do it. I did, my hands still shaking as I rolled it down the length of him. I didn't think about the intimacy or the oddness, I thought about how good it was gonna feel.

I sat astride his thighs.

"Up," he ordered, tapping my thigh. The black circles at the heart of his eyes swelled wide.

I kneeled up, and then his hands gripped behind my knees, urging me forward.

One hand left me, grabbed his cock and angled it upward. "Now come down…" his deep throaty voice cut the air.

He knew I hadn't done this before. I looked down at the trail of dark curly brown hair leading to his groin, as the familiar pressure of his penetration absorbed my thoughts.

"Oh." The sound came out of my mouth as he filled me up.

He gripped my hips.

I met his gaze, his dark eyes shone in the light of the lamp. "Ride me. Rock. Lift and drop. Do whatever feels good to you."

Yeah, *he knew.*

I'd become entirely vulnerable. This way he could look at my face and my body the whole time. His gaze skimmed down across me to prove it, but the appreciation and desire burning in his eyes and flickering in a muscle in his cheek dismissed my terror. Whatever I thought of myself, there was no doubt Billy liked what he saw.

Of course this way, I got to look at all of him too. My gaze and fingers fell on his middle, skimming over his abs. The smooth ridges and hollows. I cupped his pecs.

I'd touched Nial's chest earlier; it hadn't been the same. I was turned on by touching Billy. My fingers opened and my palms pressed down as I lifted up.

His leopard clawed beneath my right hand, capturing my gaze and his fingertips pressed into my thighs as I dropped and lifted again.

"Rock forward as you go up, Lind, catch my tip with the

movement as you come down…"

Who had he learned this stuff with?

"Ooo." I didn't care. I shut my eyes and did it again. "Ahhh." Another sound of pleasure and discovery leaked out of my mouth.

The back of his fingers ran over my breast, then touched my chin.

I opened my eyes and I met his dark gaze.

"Have you ever ridden a horse?"

"A long time ago."

"But you learned how to rock your hips to command it to walk without words."

"Yeah."

"Go on then."

"What?"

"Ride me like that for a little while, then go back to what you were doing."

His husky words touched me like his fingers. "Shit." He shut his eyes as I moved. "That is it, Lind. Shit."

I kept moving, grinding against him as it kicked sparks up through my body from the sensitive spot I'd learned this week was the heart of happiness during sex.

"Oh Billy." I got damp, swelled and burned.

His fingers massaged my thighs, gripping and releasing with my movement, his hips working against my rhythm in a slow race.

Fight. Tease.

I went back to doing what I'd done before, lifting up, sliding to the very tip of his length, then flicking my hips back. He hissed out a breath, then bit his tongue.

I slid back down and rocked forward, for my own pleasure, catching the bud on his pubic bone and hair.

"Lind. You're good at this."

I felt good at it. Scratch that, I just felt good.

"Fuck." His fingers dug really hard into my thighs.

"Shit."

"Oh my God."

"I am not going to last much longer if you keep doing that, Lindy."

His fingers clawed on my thighs, like he hung from a cliff edge.

I lifted one more time, just to push him to the limit, then went back to rocking on him, and arousing myself. I was so hot, sweat crept over my skin.

His breath became shallow, and his eyes looked like glass.

He made me feel… sexy…

"Lind." Awe carried my name into the air on his breath.

I looked at his chest, my fingers splayed over the leopard, and went back to lifting up. His hips pressed up as I came down.

I met his gaze—it overflowed with adoration. What the hell did he see?

"That's it," he hissed.

"Yeah." His voice caressed me with approval.

"Shit, Lindy…"

Pleasure played across his face and burned in his eyes. His breaker was rising. Mine rose to.

A sweet ache swelled in my belly, growing in intensity, getting ready to break into a wave of foamy white water frothing through my nerves and my fingertips gripped his chest. "Oh." I shut my eyes when it hit me in a flood, swirling through my blood. I couldn't hold myself up. I fell, gripping the sheet either side of him.

Billy braced his arms around my shoulders and thrust up into me, over and over, not letting the flood slip away. His thrusts striking me with the pressure of a fist, all his powerful muscle focused on invading me until he'd come too, with a loud growl of emotion, pain and pleasure breaking his voice.

When I came back to reality, exhaustion claimed me as one of his hands braced my head against his shoulder while the other gripped my buttock.

He combed his fingers through my hair, then kissed my forehead. I didn't move. I was happy where I was, using his body as a mattress. He was solid and dependable. His fingers kept combing through my hair.

I'd found heaven. Nothing else mattered but him.

But ultimately reality had to return. Nothing in life was dependable. Everything had a conclusion. I couldn't control anything.

I rolled off him on to my back, and watched as he got up and went to the bathroom to get rid of the condom.

Sadness settled in my soul again. There was no escape…

"You okay?" he asked as he slipped back beneath the comforter.

"Yeah." I smiled half-heartedly. No. Nothing in my life was okay. *Liar, this was okay…*

"Come here." He lifted an arm. I could have turned and spooned like we normally did, but I wanted to be held and comforted. I turned to face him and he smiled, rolling onto his back as I pillowed my head on his leopard.

His fingers played with my hair as I fell asleep, his leather bracelet catching my ear.

Chapter Thirteen

Billy

I picked up Lindy's case and slid it into the back of the SUV as she watched, her arms crossed over her body, her hands gripping either elbow.

She'd been quiet since yesterday. She obviously wasn't looking forward to going home. Since we'd met Nial and Sawyer and their crew, we'd spent every day with them, doing something. Last night we'd sat down on the beach, round a campfire, listening to them sing, in just the same way we'd first seen them.

Their presence had pissed me off a lot, but it had been making Lindy smile a lot, so I'd kept my mouth shut. I had her alone at night, when we went to bed.

I'd miss that.

We still hadn't talked about what the sex was about. I had no idea if it was gonna continue in some way, or if, when we got home, that was it… Did she consider me her boyfriend… or was I just an on-the-rebound guy?

Shit, that would stink; if she'd just used me to get over Jason and when we got back home we were done. That would be a major-league kick in the balls.

The leopard clawed my chest as I loaded up the last of our stuff. That had been a promise to myself, not to get trapped by jealousy. I was gonna keep that promise now. I wasn't gonna be the guy left hurting like hell anymore.

I slammed the back door shut, then turned to Lind. Her gaze lifted, she'd been looking at the asphalt.

"You ready?"

"As I'll ever be."

I smiled reassuringly. She didn't echo it. Just turned to get in. I moved ahead of her and got the door. She didn't look my way as she slid into the seat.

I went round to the driver's side, pulling the keys out of my pocket.

Home.

This was gonna be shit.

She didn't talk while I drove. She seemed no happier than she'd done on the drive out.

When I pulled up in front of her parents' house, I was in the dumps too. I didn't want to let her go.

Her cell buzzed and as she looked at whatever text had come in she smiled for the first time today. Admittedly not jubilantly, but it was a smile.

"What?"

She looked at me. "Nial said he's got a gig sorted in Portland in two weeks. He's inviting us to go meet up with them there. Shall we go?"

Shit! All my self-preservation and promises slipped through my fingers like dry sand running away. "What the fuck for?"

Her eyes widened at my bark.

"The guy's been sniffing around you for a week. Why are you encouraging him?"

"Billy—"

I hit the wheel with the heel of my palm, frustration rearing its head and my internal leopard roaring. I glared at her. "Billy nothing! You've been flirting with him and sleeping with me for a week, Lind. You need to make up your mind what you want. Who you want!" *I am not playing fucking second place to another guy in your life! I did that for too long with Jason!* Fortunately I was still controlled enough not to let the last bit spill out of my mouth, but I shoved an accusing finger in her direction.

"Billy—"

She looked confused and horrified. I didn't care. I'd had enough of her playing games with me. "Lindy! You've been fucking me! Why the hell have anything to do with him?"

Her brow creased above her nose, her narrow eyebrows pulling down. But instead of answering or shouting back, she shook her head, her eyes glittering with tears. Then she turned and opened the door.

"Lindy!"

She slipped out of my reach and out of the SUV before I could grab her arm and stop her.

Shit.

I released my seatbelt as she ran up the path to her house. I opened my door. "Lindy!"

She disappeared into the house.

"Fuck!"

I was a douchebag at times. I'd spent two weeks making her feel better and then brought her home and shouted at her. "You are an A-hole, Billy Worrall." I slipped out of the SUV to get her stuff.

Her dad came out.

Great. Now I was gonna get it. Mr. Martin was known to hold grudges.

"Lindy asked me to come fetch her stuff." He didn't look or sound angry. I opened the back of the SUV.

"Yeah." That was all I could think to say.

"How is she? Is she feeling any better?"

She had been. Guilt threw a fist at me. Not only for the argument but because I'd been having sex with his daughter for over a week with no clear intention.

That was a lie, I had intent, I just hadn't checked out what hers was—apart from wanting to come. She'd achieved that numerous times. Go Billy! The end.

I handed him Lindy's case. "She seems better. We hung out with a group there, and she enjoyed that."

"Good." He smiled at me. "Thank you for taking her away, Billy. I think she needed a vacation. I appreciate you helping her." He picked up Lindy's backpack and slung it over his shoulder.

Guilt threw another punch at me. "Yeah."

"Well then, Billy. I'm sure we'll see more of you. You've been a good friend to Lindy." Mr. Martin turned his back on me and carried Lindy's stuff up to the house.

I looked at the windows. Nothing moved behind the netting. I wondered if her mom was in there counseling her on avoiding me… Maybe… But who knew as no one had seen her mom for months.

But I sensed Lindy watching—probably cursing me…

"You idiot." I slammed the rear door shut and headed for the driver's side, angry with myself.

Fuck it.

Lindy

"Sweetheart, you look better."

Billy drove off and I turned away from the window as Mom came into the room. "You look pale."

"I'm fine. Don't worry about me, Lindy love. I'm worried over you."

I went to her. "You don't need to. I promised I won't do it again…" I'd stopped the tears from falling when Billy had shouted at me, but now they came.

I'd wanted to hit him. It was bad enough coming home… Why had he turned on me? Usually I'd have shouted back, telling him what I thought. But today I was too fragile. "Mom." I breathed in her perfume as her arms came around me and mine wrapped around her. She'd gotten so thin.

"Honey." Her fingers ran over my hair.

I could feel her ribs as I held her.

"Don't cry, sweetie."

I pulled away, wiping my eyes. The pain I'd been suffering for years cut into my chest. I wished it would just go away, but it would only go away if Mom got better or… I couldn't think of "or". I didn't want to lose her—but she wouldn't get better. "I'm sorry. Billy and I argued."

Dad came in as Mom gripped my hand and he glanced at me. I didn't want him to know I'd argued with Billy. He wouldn't understand. I smiled at him, biting my lip.

He nodded. "I'll put your things in your room?"

"Thanks, Dad."

"It's good to have you home."

I should have said, it was good to be home, but the words stuck in my throat.

Mom brushed my hair off my cheek. "Come and sit down with me and share. We'll put it all to rights…"

Tears blurred my vision as I curled up against her, my arms slipping about her waist as hers rested across my shoulders. "Now tell me everything…"

I wished I could tell her *everything*—and everything would be right.

My cell vibrated in the back pocket of my pants. It would be Billy. I didn't look at it.

"We…" I told Mom about Nial and Sawyer and their friends, and Billy being a jealous jerk—it wasn't so charming when it made him shout. But I missed out the bit that we'd had sex numerous times. I just told her we'd been kissing.

Billy

'Hey, come on, Lind, answer me. I said sorry.' I tapped the send icon and watched the little bar slide across.

My cell made a zippy sound, announcing the text had gone.

No reply came back.

She'd ignored my calls, messages and texts yesterday as well as today.

I threw my cell onto the passenger seat. Frustration boiled so bad inside me, I could smash the stupid thing.

I got out to go meet another client, shoving Lindy out of my mind.

If she could do it to me, I had to learn to do the same.

I'd forgotten how many reps two of my clients had done. And all the guys accused me of working them too aggressively.

At lunch I decided enough was enough when she still didn't pick up my call but pushed it to answerphone.

I wasn't like her…

I drove to her house.

As I walked up to the door, my hand tapped out a nervous drumbeat on my thigh.

After I'd dropped the knocker three times, I stood back, my hand running through my hair. Then I messed my hair up again to spike it, rather than leave it flattened.

Shit. My heart thumped like crazy. It felt like I breathed exhaust fumes the air was so scarce.

Someone walked along the hall toward the door, a figure moving beyond the net that covered the door. I rubbed my sweaty palms on my sweat shirt. I had humble pie to eat.

I'd glared at my stupid dumb leopard last night, reminding myself the plan was not to let envy keep clawing at me. But my head just couldn't help it.

"Mrs. Martin." Her mother opened the door. OMG. She had changed.

"Billy?"

She looked really thin. "You okay?" Maybe it was rude to ask, but last time I'd seen her she'd been about 20Ib heavier. But that had been a long time ago. Anyway, if she'd lost weight deliberately, she'd lost too much. It made her look drawn underneath her makeup.

"I'm fine, thank you, Billy. I guess you're here to call on Lindy but I'm afraid she's not here. She's at the Macinlay store if you want to see her. I know she'd hate to have missed you."

I wasn't sure she'd care that she'd missed me, and I certainly wasn't going down to Jason's store to have it out with her. "Thanks Mrs. Martin, I've got to get back to work, but would you tell her I came round."

"Yes, dear."

I turned away, angry again, my internal leopard scoring my skin.

I climbed back in the SUV.

My clients this afternoon were gonna get a hell of a workout. What the fuck had she gone down to Jason's store for?

I smashed my palm on the wheel and gritted my teeth.

Why couldn't the girl get it? He didn't want her anymore.

I grabbed my cell, slid up my contacts and called her number. It rang four times, then went onto answer.

"Please leave a message after the tone."

"Lindy! If you are down at the store, thinking you have a chance with Jason now; you need to get your head screwed on straight. Because there's a reason you two were shit in bed! He never loved you, and you never loved him! Just admit it to yourself!"

I ended the call, growling at my reflection in the rearview mirror, and tossed the cell aside before slipping the gearshift into auto and slamming my foot down on the gas.

Fuck it! Fuck her! I'd had enough.

Chapter Fourteen

Lindy

Nervous sensations did a line-dance over my skin. This was a crazy thing to do. But Billy had been pushing me to break boundaries and I was never gonna move on unless I smashed this one to pieces.

My hand shook as I pushed the door open. The bell above it rang to tell people working in the store I'd come in.

Shit, this place—the smell of wood polish on the floor, the sound of the bell, stirred deep in my soul. Tears clouded my vision. This store had been a massive part of my life for years. It had been my second home. My sanctuary… Until Jason had left me, and then—how the hell could I have stayed?

I'd lost everything all at one go.

Jason and I had planned to run his dad's store together. No, that was a lie. He hadn't wanted it at all. That had been my plan.

He'd gone to New York, left me to it, and then come back less than a year later with someone else—to do what I had planned for the two of us —and he'd rejected. No. He had not rejected it, he'd rejected me, even then.

My chin tilted as I forced myself to walk on, controlling my breathing so I didn't sound panicked. I panicked internally. I wanted to run right back out.

"Lindy?" Surprise raced through Jason's wife's pitch—but not horror or anger.

She stood behind the counter, wearing a carrier that had the baby snuggled up against her breasts.

Jealousy plunged a sharp dagger into my right breast.

"Can I help you?" She started to walk out from behind the counter.

I lifted my hand, to stop her. "It's okay. I haven't come to cause trouble. I just… May I speak to Jason if he's here?"

Her expression said, why, but she didn't say the word. "Hang on, I'll text and ask him to come out here."

Her cell was on the counter by the cash register, she picked it up and typed quickly.

I bit my lip as I waited. I bet Jason wouldn't want to talk to me, but I knew he would talk to me. He may have let me down badly, but he was a nice guy. He hadn't wanted to hurt me. He had, though.

Rachel's gaze lifted from the screen of her cell to me. "He said, he'll be right out."

I took a deep breath, praying for courage. "How's the baby?"

She smiled, a really wide smile. "Saint is perfect. We love him like crazy."

We…

Her and Jason.

The word made me itch. Jason and I had been we! But that was old and gone, and I had to smash that boundary and think of myself as me.

"Lindy! Hey!" My heart did a weird flip when I heard his voice. I turned and looked at him. Rachel's presence was a massive ball of tension behind me.

He went over to her first, reached out, gripped the back of her neck, and pulled her forward as he leaned over the counter, then he kissed her.

It was a brief kiss. When he broke it he ran a hand over the baby's head

"You'll wake him." Rachel said quietly.

Jason chuckled, "He's fine." Jason looked happy about the baby, really calm, laid back, and glowing. Nice.

He smiled at her, his lips parting as he slipped one hand into the back of his pants. I knew the gesture.

When he turned to me, his other hand lifted and combed through his hair. They were both gestures that said he felt awkward.

I'd got very used to those silent expressions of his reluctance to fight, mostly in the last year of our relationship.

His other hand fell and also slipped into his back pocket.

"Jason."

"Lindy."

"Can I talk to you privately?" There was no way I had the courage to speak in front of Rachel—*the girl he'd left me for*.

He glanced at Rachel, his handsome face apologizing to her. Jason was devastatingly beautiful. Billy did not compare to him in that.

"Sure," he said, facing me again and then lifting his hand. "Come out back."

"Is your dad not there?"

"Nope, he's out with suppliers. Come on." He waited for me to walk ahead, his hand still out. I did, self-consciousness slashing a blade through my thoughts about the width of my thighs.

Rachel had had a baby a couple of weeks ago and was like a pole.

Stupid. I'd stopped caring with Billy, because he hadn't cared. But Jason had spoken without words, by finding someone prettier and thinner than me.

I pushed open the door of the office. Familiarity hit me. I'd spent so many hours in here, talking with his dad or him, sorting files, ordering stock.

I missed the store as much as I'd missed Jason. But the emptiness that had been inside me for months wasn't there. I didn't miss him anymore. But I still missed the store.

"Do you want to sit down?" His hand indicated the chair his

dad used and I noticed the open web page on the computer Jason must be using. It was the online gaming magazine he'd developed. I'd heard about it and looked at it.

I looked back at him. "No, I won't take long."

One hand ran through his hair and then both slipped into his back pockets again.

Great, he was defensive.

I took a breath, for courage, then let the words I'd practiced come out. "I came to say sorry. I didn't pick here to take the overdose to hurt you…" *I just consider this place home…* "And I didn't mean for you to find me."

His familiar brown gaze absorbed every word, then his hands slipped out of his back pockets. "Billy already told me. You don't have to— "

"But I needed to tell you myself, and I want… I want to say I forgive you…" His expression twisted, like he was gonna dispute that, but I carried on. "I know we had to split. You couldn't have stayed with me, you didn't love me, and I get that you fell for Rachel."

There, I'd drawn a line on the past. I could move forward now.

"Lindy." His eyes softened to pools of caring. It was the way he'd looked at me before he'd gone to New York and his arms opened.

I was crying before I knew it, crumbling into him. His arms came around me. Mine slipped about his waist.

This had always been right between Jason and me. He'd felt safe, like the store—home. They'd been the places I'd gone to feel better.

"Lind." His hand stroked over my hair, as my cheek pressed against the muscle of his chest.

But I missed Billy's bigger solid bear hug of reassurance.

"I'm sorry too." Jason's voice rumbled low in his chest. "I know I hurt you. I just want you to be happy as well. And Rach wants the same…"

Her name reminded me that I didn't have any right to draw comfort from him now. I pulled away, wiping my eyes. "Sorry."

"Lind, you don't need to be sorry for being upset. You have a right to be upset, and I'm sorry it's my fault. But I can't change how I feel, and now, if either Rach or I can do anything to help you, we will."

He smiled, and I tried to smile back but my lips quivered as tears clouded my gaze.

"Come on, come and talk to Rach." He gripped my hand and started pulling me out of the office. A part of me wanted to plant my feet and not budge. But Rachel wasn't gonna go away, she worked in the store, she lived in the town, I was gonna keep seeing her everywhere. It was half the reason I'd spent the last six months hiding away. If I was gonna draw a line on the past and move on, I guess I had to get used to the idea of seeing Rachel around too.

Swallowing back my discomfort I let him tug me down the aisle leading to the counter. Rachel stood there. She smiled, but her eyes held a questioning look.

She wasn't bothered that Jason held my hand, though. She was one hundred percent confident in what they had together… I saw her gaze change, passing to him and smiling just for him.

Happiness.

I wish I could be happy. I wish everything in my life was certain and secure.

"Rach…" Jason squeezed my hand then let go. It was a reminder of how things used to be when his security belonged to me. "Lindy came to make peace with us. I told her we'll do whatever we can to help her be happy."

I hadn't really come to make peace with them. I'd come to find peace myself. But—

"That's awesome, Lindy—" Rachel smiled one of her hands patting under the baby's bottom on the carrier.

I swallowed, plucking up courage. This had not been what I'd planned; it took everything one step further beyond comfort, but that would be one step further to putting the past behind me and finding a way to live… "I'm sorry I was mean to you when you first came here."

"You had a right to be mean. I know that. I'm sorry I was mean back."

"That's okay—" It really wasn't, but I was letting it go now. Letting everything that had happened just become history so I could live today.

"I know you'd find it hard right now. But if you could stand it, Lindy, I'd like to be your friend. Maybe in the future... I don't have any friends here..."

Tears made her hazy. I needed to go. Being friends—that was a step too far. But I didn't want to just walk out. "Can I see the baby?" I'd been terrified of seeing her with the baby. It seemed like she had everything I'd dreamed of with Jason, the store, a family, happiness... It was one last fear to kick in the face and then I'd go.

"Sure." She turned sideways. The kid was in a huddle. All I could see was his face and his dark hair. He had a pouty mouth, a squished little nose, and his eyes were shut tight. He was only four weeks old. I hadn't expected her to be in the store.

"He's cute."

"I know, isn't he...? He's adorable..." Rachel said.

Jason laughed. "Until he cries or shits. Although the face he makes when he shits is pretty cute."

Rachel laughed.

They were solid. He was with someone he loved now. He hadn't loved me. The words echoed like a chant. "I better go." I looked at Jason then at Rachel, and nodded my goodbye. I had no place here. It was her place.

The door shut on my past with a bang.

"I'll walk you to your car," Jason offered.

"You don't have to—"

"I want to."

I walked ahead. He followed me out into the parking lot. "Thanks for coming in to talk..."

I shrugged. "It's time I moved on. I just need to focus on me and getting things together."

His hand flicked my hair back off my shoulder, a gesture he'd done a thousand times when we'd been together. Then it fell on my shoulder. My heart remembered his touch. It was excruciating. I had no right to it. I didn't want it.

"You'll be okay, you'll meet someone else."

I shook my head and shrugged. I wasn't looking for that. I had too much going on… "I just need to get my life straight."

His hand fell away. "Yeah well if Rach or I can do anything to help, get in touch."

I nodded. But I wouldn't ever ask him for help.

"Let me get your door." Jason may have kicked my heart out of the state at Christmas, but he hadn't done it because he was mean. He was full-on nice. He just hadn't loved me.

I got in, remembering how I used to slide the window down and he'd lean in and kiss me. But the memory was like a dream, and shadowed by images of the good sex I'd had with Billy.

"For the record… it wasn't just good sex, it was awesome sex…"

I wound the window down to deny the emotions and fear rubbing up against each other and starting off a tornado in my head.

He smiled and tapped the roof of Mom's car. "I'll see you around, Lind. But make a deal with me whenever we see each other let's say, hi."

I nodded. "Okay. See you around."

Trying not to let him see how much my hands shook, or let the tears come until I was out of sight I slipped the gear shift into first and pressed down on the gas.

My heart screamed—get away from him. Tears slipped onto my cheeks as I drove off.

Billy

"You're early, Billy."

I threw Eva a bitter smile and chucked the SUV keys and my

cell down on the kitchen counter. "I'm not in the right mood to go to the gym." She was standing beside the fridge pouring herself a glass of juice.

"Ah, my poor big brother's still in a bad mood?"

"Don't." I warned her.

"Did Lindy upset you?"

I lifted a hand to clip her, but she dodged it, laughing.

"It's not funny, Eva."

"Billy has heartache…"

"One day, when you're older you're gonna fall for some guy and know how it feels to love someone who doesn't love you back."

She poked her tongue out at me.

She'd known about my infatuation with Lindy for ages. Thankfully she'd never told anyone. But as soon as Lindy and Jason had split she'd been on at me to push for more than friendship… She didn't get how complex things were.

"Why did you go away with her, then?"

"Because she needed a friend."

"Doesn't she know by now you want to be more than her friend?"

She knew. But it didn't seem to make any difference. I still didn't have a fucking clue where I stood with her. Gripping the countertop I leaned forward, anger and envy scorching through my veins.

How to make Lindy love me? Why had she gone to see Jason? Why did she keep letting Nial chase her?

"Sorry." Eva's hand settled on my shoulder.

I looked up. "You don't need to say sorry. It's hardly your fault. Just whatever you do, don't say a word to Lindy."

"Haven't you told her how you feel?"

"No." I wasn't gonna thrust my neck in a noose.

"Tell her." Eva pressed, her blue eyes bright and vehement.

I lifted my eyebrows. "No way. She'd laugh at me."

"You think she'd be that mean. I don't. I know Lindy's had a hard time lately but she's always been a friend to you."

"Let me underline that, A FRIEND."

Her hand patted my shoulder. "If she doesn't fall for you Billy, she's blind."

I gave her a hug, my baby sister, who wasn't such a baby anymore. "Well, then, she's been blind for a lot of years..."

"But she was with Jason. Now she's free..." Her warm breath heated my shoulder, then she slipped free of my grip. "...and you're a catch, Billy."

"So says my little sister." I chucked her under the chin. "I think you're biased."

She gave me a big smile. "Of course I am. All my friends are in love with you."

"Nice to know I can impress some girls then."

"You impress lots of girls, and you know it."

But not the one I want.

My cell vibrated, rattling on the counter.

Lindy's name flashed up as a message showed.

I picked the cell up. 'I hate you! Why do you have to be such a douchebag now?'

What? That was vicious.

'Hey.'

'Don't say hey, like you did nothing."

'Why?'

'It makes it even worse you don't know... I hate you, Billy!"

I held the cell up and showed Eva. "I don't think Lindy agrees..."

Eva's eyebrows lifted as she picked up her juice. "What did you do?"

"I don't know."

"You'd better call her and find out, then." With one last smile thrown in my direction she left me in the kitchen and headed for the den.

Awesome.

I looked at my cell. At least Lindy was speaking to me now.

Sliding the screen over, I went into contacts and picked up her name, then pressed the call icon. "Hey, Lindy."

I leaned back against the counter.

"I don't know how you dare call me!"

"Why?"

"Your stupid message. If you are down at the store, thinking you have a chance with Jason now; you need to get your head screwed on straight. You're a douche, Billy!"

She ended the call.

Shit. I'd left that message in anger hours ago. I'd forgotten about it. I called again.

"Lin—"

"Go away! I don't want to talk to you!"

She cut the call.

Fuck. Gritting my teeth I called again. "Hear me out!"

"Why should I?"

"Just—"

"You had a go about Nial yesterday so I texted him and told him it was best we didn't keep in touch, and now this thing with Jason. What is wrong with you? And Mom said you came around here. You had no right to come here without asking. She doesn't want people calling here! I don't want to talk to you! Go away!"

The call went dead.

I tossed the cell on the counter, giving up.

Whatever. Let her be in a mood. I wasn't the one messing around. She'd had sex with me… She couldn't do that and then keep chasing other guys.

But she'd told Nial to get lost!

Victory cheered inside me as I blew out a long breath and I hit the side of my closed fist on the counter. Dammit, it was not a win.

I went to get some juice from the fridge and drank it from the carton, staring at my cell, not sure how I'd managed to make a mess of things within hours of getting home.

The leather bracelet Lindy had made years ago slid up my wrist.

My cell rang, playing out *Clarity by Foxes*.

It was Jason.

"Hey. When are you gonna return my calls and come out for a drink again?"

I smiled. "Hey. Tonight if you like. I could do with someone to talk to."

"Cool. Rach can drive, then we can both drink."

"No, I'll drive. If I drink too much, I'm only gonna be cursing."

"Why?"

"Never mind. I'll tell you later."

"What time's good for you?"

"Half seven…"

"Done. That gives me a chance to help Rach get Saint to sleep."

"He sleeps?" I laughed.

"Yeah. Pretty good. We normally get a couple of hours' peace before he's hungry again." There was that proud daddy pitch.

"Family life's got you all roped in."

"I know. I love it. I'll see you later." The guy was smiling; I could hear it down the cell.

Whatever Lindy had gone in to say to him today, it hadn't annoyed him. But then he'd been so frickin' happy lately maybe even if she'd ranted at him, it wouldn't dent his mood.

"Okay." I ended the call. I'd go down the gym for an hour after all. Pumping weights and working out would help me fight my frustration.

I wanted what Jason had with Rachel between me and Lindy. Well, minus the kid. But the relationship, yeah.

Chapter Fifteen

Billy

"Billy! Hey! You okay?" Jason had waited outside the bar. We gave each other a masculine hug. I had my friend back.

I shrugged. "Let's get a drink."

His hand rested on my shoulder as we walked into the bar, then slid off.

"How's Saint? How's Rachel?"

"Saint's fine." He grinned, but then his smile fell a little. "But Rach's moods swing from one extreme to the other lately, and sometimes so fucking fast it's crazy. She's a like riding a rollercoaster. I hang on as she races up and down. It's 'cause she's given up her meds to breastfeed. So one minute she is laughing like crazy over nothing and so excited she can't sleep. One night I found her making Saint a blue birthday cake he's too young to eat. Then the next hour, she's quiet and tired and all she wants to do is hug Saint. But she's determined to keep feeding him. She won't give in. And if that's what she wants, I'll keep hanging on. She's had a shit life so far, she deserves to do what she wants." He smiled again. "I'll get the beers; you get us a seat."

I headed for the farthest, quietest, corner of the bar and sat at a table. Jason came over with two bottles and sat facing me. He slid one of the bottles across the table to me.

"So what's made you down then? Where'd you go away to anyway?"

Ignoring the second question I answered the first. "Lindy and I have fallen out again."

His eyebrows lifted. "She came down to the store today—"

"I know. That's partly why. 'Cause I told her to stop chasing after you—"

"She wasn't chasing after me. She came into the store to draw a line on the past."

"To what?"

He'd taken a drink from his beer. He wiped his mouth. "To make friends and put it all behind us. She apologized. I apologized. She forgave me, and then she talked to Rachel too."

"Lindy?"

A tilted smile tugged his lips. "Yeah, Lindy."

"I didn't expect that."

"Neither did I. I thought she was gonna shout at me when she asked to speak to me alone."

"And what did she say?"

"That she accepted I'd moved on, and she wanted to move on too. We agreed to say hi when we see each other… I mean we were together for years, it feels really weird when she crosses the street to avoid me."

Thanks for the punch in the gut—*we were together for years.*

I knew that. My hand ran through my hair, Lindy's words washed over me. I shut my eyes and messed up my hair again so it spiked.

I was a douche.

"You okay?"

I looked at Jason. "Yeah." I finished my beer. "I'll get us another."

"I thought you were driving?"

"I have a lot of muscle for the alcohol to disappear in, one more won't do me any harm."

He lifted his bottle in a gesture of thanks.

When I got to the bar, I slipped my cell out of my back pocket. "Two more bottles." I ordered them, then opened the texts and found Lindy's name.

'Hey, I owe you an apology. I'm sorry. I just talked to Jason, and he told me what you said at the store. I am a douchebag. Sorry.'

As the guy put the bottles down on the counter, my cell vibrated.

I glanced down as I reached for my wallet. 'Yeah you are! And what about the Nial accusation?'

Smiling, I took the hit in the gut, put my cell down and paid. When he turned to the cash register, I replied, 'Hey.' I was still pissed off about Nial.

'What about Nial?!'

'Sorry.' I had no choice but to clear the air.

'Accepted.'

'Thank you.'

'You ARE a douchebag, though!'

'I know.' I looked up to see the guy hovering with my change. Dropping him a dollar tip, I picked up the bottles and headed back to Jason.

A smile touched my lips.

How did she do this to me? Make my heart leap around at her will.

I pushed Jason's bottle across the table as I sat, then leaned forward and asked a question I couldn't resist. "When you were with Lindy, was she hung up on what she looked like?"

His eyebrows lifted. "Why?"

"Just tell me, was she? I mean I've noticed lately how she's always made-up and I've never seen her in a bikini. She's always kept t-shirts on when we've gone swimming." That was a lie, I had now. But… I hadn't before we'd gone away.

Jason frowned, asking why I was asking again, without saying the word.

I held my silence, pushing him to speak.

"I guess."

"You guess. You must have known."

He looked awkward. "Okay then, I'd say yes. She never liked… Well. Whatever. I don't think she'd want me talking to you about that."

No she definitely wouldn't.

I sat back. "Did you never try to do anything to help her get over it?"

His brow furrowed. "How?"

"Tell her there was nothing wrong with her, for a start." My voice came out more aggressive than I'd intended.

"Seriously, are we talking about Lindy? The girl who doesn't listen to anyone…"

"Yeah. But you could have been more forceful, you could have made her get it."

"Made her?" He shrugged. "I could never make Lindy do anything. Good luck if you plan to."

My free hand ran through my hair. Shit. I'd flattened it again. I roughed it up, then let my hand drop and met his gaze. "She needs someone to help her. You didn't. You fucked her up." It seemed that now that my leopard had laid off Lindy it was clawing at Jason.

His brow screwed up. "Fucked her up?"

One hand clutched my beer, my other slapped down on the table. "Why the hell did you keep her hanging all those years; you can't have loved her?"

He shook his head. "Where is this coming from?"

"From the fact the girl is a mess and you're to blame. It's obvious you care way more for Rachel… So why the hell did you stay with Lind all those years, just screwing the girl up?"

"I do care more for Rach, but how the fuck could I know the difference before? When Rachel hit me like a tornado, it was only then I found out what I felt for Lindy was just a breeze, like she was a sister. And everything about Lindy and me was about her. You know that. She chased me to get with her. I couldn't have done anything different. She wouldn't have let me!"

I leaned back. "You were too weak. You should've just stood up to her."

"And I guess you've got yourself down for that." His eyebrows lifted.

"Well, someone's got to help her."

A smile pulled his lips sideways. "I do remember you slept with her when she and I were still together, you know."

"So. We had that conversation."

The smile split his face, then he laughed. "Do you like her?"

"Of course I like her. I lived with you two for three years…" I shrugged and took a swig from my beer bottle.

His eyes narrowed and he leaned forward. "Okay, then, I mean do you more than just like her?"

Shit, my gaze turned to a group of guys behind him. I swallowed, then focused back on Jason. It made no difference to him now. "Probably. Possibly. I don't know." *I did know*.

His head tipped back as he laughed, then his hand came up and smacked my shoulder. "Well if you like her. Tell her."

I lifted an eyebrow at him. Lindy was not ready for a declaration. But surely she knew I *liked* her. "And if when I tell her she runs for the hills?"

"Ha. Ha. She may."

I made a face at him as my free hand began tapping a rhythm on the table.

Jason leaned forward. "Seriously, if you and Lindy get together, I'll be glad for you."

I gave him a sneer in answer. "Why? 'Cause then you can forget you're guilty of messing her up?"

"That," he smiled and nodded, then said in a deeper voice, "and, I want Lindy to be happy, so if you like her then I am all for it. You have my approval."

I grimaced. "I don't frickin' need or want your approval, and neither does she. If we get together it will be nothing to do with you."

He leaned back laughing and smiled wide again. "You're caught. You really like her."

I've been caught for years. I didn't admit that to him. My cell started ringing, the beat of *Clarity by Foxes* filling the air.

I pulled it out my pocket. Lindy.

"Hey." I didn't look at Jason. I looked beyond him as I answered. I didn't want him to guess it was her.

"Hey, is that all. You said you were sorry, and then nothing. Do you want to come over and pick me up?"

"I... I..." Shit. I stood up nodding at Jason, and began walking out of the bar.

"Where are you? It sounds noisy."

"Hang on a minute."

The cold night air hit me as I went outside. It was dark. "I'm at a bar with Jason, I've come outside so I can talk."

"You're with Jason?"

"Yeah, we came out for a drink."

"Oh." She sounded like all the air got knocked out of her.

"Why did you call?"

"To ask if you wanted to come over and pick me up, so we could go somewhere."

"Where?"

"Well just for a drive or something, but if you're already out—"

"Jason will want to get back early anyway. He won't want to stay out when Rach is at home with the baby. I'll come and pick you up after we're done."

"Okay. Text me when you leave the bar then, and I'll wait outside."

"Okay. See you in a while."

She hung up. With no goodbye, no I missed you. Nothing. What was up with her? She was so hard to judge.

Slipping my cell back in my pocket, I headed in.

Jason leaned back in his seat staring at the bottle he held in his hand.

"You alright?" I prodded.

He looked up and smiled. "Yeah. Just getting my head round you and Lindy being an item."

"We're not an item, and, fuck, do not say that to her, she'll run a mile. We're just friends." *Friends who fuck.*

Jason's eyebrows lifted. "That was her calling, wasn't it?"

"Yeah." I may as well admit it, I'm sure my expression had given it away anyway.

"What did she say?"

None of your business. "She wanted to see me, that's all."

"That's a good sign, though, isn't it?"

"Jason. She's hung up on you. She still thinks of me as a friend."

"She said today she wants to move on."

"But saying it and doing it are two different things."

"You were the one who just had a go at me for not standing up to her. Stand up to her and tell her you want to be more than friends."

Friends who fuck. "I don't want to scare her off."

He made a face. "Okay, so now you know working out Lindy is tough. I never succeeded, so good luck."

I changed the subject then, I wasn't comfortable talking about her with him. It felt too like I was going behind her back.

When we finished our third drink—a cola, 'cause I was driving and Jason was a lightweight when it came to beer—we agreed to call it a night.

"I'll call Rach to come pick me up."

"No, I'll drive you home."

"But you have Lindy to go and see."

"It won't take long."

Grinning at me he got up. "Come on, I'd hate to be the thing that holds you two apart any longer."

Now there was a statement.

I didn't text her; I called her. "Hey, I've just dropped Jason off at his place, I'm coming over now."

"I'll come outside and meet you."

"See you soon."

"Yeah."

"Bye."

"Bye."

All very *friendly*.

I slotted the gearshift into auto and put my foot on the gas, but I couldn't rush; it was a built- up area. My belly did jack-jumps and my hands were fucking shaking when I saw her as I turned into her road. She stood under a streetlamp a little up the road from her house, her arms clutched across her middle and her eyes looking out for my SUV. She had on a short skirt and a loose sweat top. Her bare legs looked pale in the electric light.

When I pulled up opposite her, she ran across the road, yanked open the passenger door, and got in. I smiled at her. She wasn't smiling; she looked as haunted as she'd looked before we'd gone away.

"You okay?"

After she pulled the seatbelt on, her hands slipped under her thighs as she looked at me. "Yeah."

"Where'd you wanna go?"

"Out to the lake." She bit her lip.

"Okay." I gunned the engine and headed off. She never said a word as we drove out there. But it was only a few miles out of town.

The track was dark and rugged, the SUV bounced through the potholes. I pulled up behind the trees in the parking area, to make sure if anyone else came out here we'd be less likely to be seen. It was private property, but we all used the place for a little privacy now and then. Putting the SUV in park, I switched off the engine.

Lindy started moving immediately, having unclicked her belt she climbed across the middle. I pulled the lever to slide my seat back as she straddled my hips.

"I want to do it." Her cold hands pressed against my cheeks and then her mouth came down on mine, and as I opened my lips to participate, her tongue pressed in.

This was no game of chase. This was her dominating me.

I gripped her head with both hands and pushed her back. "Lindy."

"What?"

"Don't you wanna talk?"

Her lips twisted with a bitter smile. "Not really."

"What about going to see Jason and Rachel today."

"What about it?"

"Don't you want to talk about it?"

"No." Her hands fell to my buckle and started unthreading my belt.

I gripped her hands as she leaned back to look at what she was doing, using the lines of moonlight stretching through the trees and reaching into the SUV. "Lind, slow down."

She looked up, her eyes all dark in the shadows. "Why?"

"Because you're going too fast. Give me a chance to catch up."

"Oh." She looked down.

I wasn't even aroused.

Her gaze met mine. "Sorry." But then her hand slipped free of mine and she started rubbing me through my pants.

Shit. What was the point of arguing? I gripped the back of her neck and pulled her mouth back to mine, but this time I led the kiss, as she made me hard. Not that it was difficult when she was sitting astride me in a short loose skirt.

Her tongue wove about mine, with determination. She wanted to get herself off and fast.

I wasn't gonna stop her when two weeks ago she'd hated—and been terrified of—sex. Maybe this was a breakthrough.

With my fingers buried in her hair I pressed my tongue into her mouth.

She slipped my button free then undid the zip of my pants. Her cold hand grasped me and began moving up and down.

I kept kissing her.

After only moments, she moved awkwardly in the space between my seat and the wheel to get her panties off. "Have you got a condom," she breathed over my lips as she straddled me again.

"My wallet's in my back pocket."

The muscle in my abdomen contracted hard as I lifted to let her get at it, and within moments she had me sheathed and rose up, ready to—

Shit.

Press down.

Her mouth pulled away and she looked down as I gritted my teeth, battling the immediate desire to release into her warmth.

Shit.

It felt good to be in her again.

She moved fast, and hard, leaving me nothing to do. I couldn't move and keep up with her in the seat of the SUV. She was definitely working to get herself off.

My fingers gripping in her hair, to try and calm her down a little, I shifted my hips forward so I was better positioned to press back. Then it was a full-on fight for who broke first.

I think it only lasted fifteen minutes; it certainly wasn't long, but my end was mind-blowing.

"Ahhh." My cry filled the small space around us as I came riding the back of her orgasm. Her internal muscles had clasped around me, pulling and throbbing with fluid warmth.

We'd steamed the windows up. If anyone else had pulled into the parking lot, I wouldn't have even known.

I pulled her lips back to mine and kissed her. Then let her go.

Instantly she pulled off me and climbed back over to the passenger seat, picking up her panties. "I've got a tissue if you want it?"

She drew it out of the pocket of the loose sweat shirt she had on and held it out.

"Thanks." I started sorting myself out, as she slipped her panties back on.

When I did my buckle back up, she looked over. "You'd better take me back."

"Now?"

"Yeah, I told Mom I wouldn't be long, Dad is on a shift."

Great. I knew her dad was in the habit of driving out here at night to check there were no trespassers. If he'd found us his gun would've been pointed at my head.

"Okay. When am I gonna see you again? Do you want to do something tomorrow night?"

She glanced at me. "You can pick me up again if you like, but I don't want to go anywhere, and I can't stay out long anyway."

I put the SUV into reverse and looked behind me to back out. "What time then?"

"Nine?"

"If that's when you want."

"Yeah."

We drove home in virtual silence. I tried asking her a couple of things, but got one-syllable answers, so I gave up. When we got to her parents' she'd have just leapt out the SUV, but I stopped her, reaching over and catching hold of her wrist. "Lind? Don't I get a proper goodnight?"

She turned back around, smiling hesitantly and leaned over to kiss my cheek. "Night, I'll see you tomorrow." Then she turned back and slid off the seat, jumping out the open door.

Weird woman. How the hell was I supposed to know how to handle her?

Chapter Sixteen

Lindy

I shut the door quietly, as I heard Billy's SUV turn the corner at the end of the street.

"Lindy!" Mom's call reached along the hall from her bedroom.

"Mom! Is everything okay?!" I'd hoped I wouldn't wake her.

"Yes, sweetheart! Are you okay? Where did you go?"

I headed to her room. I'd left her in bed. "Mom?" She lay beneath the comforter. She looked really tired and worn out. Pale.

Her hand lifted.

The ache in my chest ate at me as I held out my hand too and walked over. When I reached the bed I gripped her hand, slipped my sandals off and sat on the covers next to her.

Would she be horrified and disgusted if she knew what Billy and I had just done? "I'm sorry I woke you."

"You didn't sweetie, I was awake anyway. I'm not sleeping well lately."

No wonder she looked exhausted, my fingers tightened about hers, holding on…

"I went out to see Billy"

"Have you two patched things up?"

"Yes, I guess so, kind of…"

"Kind of…"

I loved her gentle smile, the one that encouraged me to open up. We were close, probably because I was an only child. I'd been spoilt. She and Dad had never had any reason not to spoil me with love and stuff. There was only me.

What was I going to do? How was I going to cope?

Her fingers squeezed mine a little more firmly, though not hard. But then they let go.

"Mom?"

"I'm fine, sweetie. Tell me what happened."

"We made out." The heat of a blush crept up my skin, but hopefully my makeup hid it… I swallowed.

Her eyebrows lifted. "You and Billy?"

"Yeah."

"Are you dating?" Her blue eyes asked the same question.

"I am not really ready to—"

"But you like him. I mean, like that, you are not just letting him fill Jason's place? It is not just because you're lonely, sweetheart?"

I heard the tiredness in her voice. It was hard for her to speak.

"No… I… I don't really know what it is, but he makes me feel better, and he takes my mind off… Off everything else…"

She smiled weakly and her hand lifted again. I held it for a moment.

"I could read to you if you like, and you could just shut your eyes, Mom. It may help you sleep."

Her eyes had already drifted closed. She opened them again, looking at me. "That would be wonderful, darling. I'd like that. Read me something light and romantic. I don't want anything heavy."

"I'll go pick something."

Letting go of her hand I stood up.

Chapter Seventeen

Billy

Fuck, I was confused. I didn't know where I stood with Lindy.

For two weeks I'd picked her up and driven her out to the lake, to do it, then driven her back. Not every night, but most nights. And nothing else. No dates. No dinners. No telephone calls… The girl was insane. Her and Jason had hung out constantly; they'd been attached at the hip. They'd done everything together. Me? I was only good for sex…

My hand ran into my hair and clasped it as I watched the guy I was working with doing the one hundred sit-ups I was counting off. Sixty-seven, sixty-eight, sixty-nine…

I didn't know how to change things. What to say to her?

I was scared if I challenged her, the whole thing would turn to dust. I loved her. I'd loved her for years.

Then it had been my secret painful obsession. Now it was addiction.

Every day I got my shot, a fix of Lindy. Agitation rumbled around in my gut constantly when I wasn't with her. I felt sick with need—and fear—'cause I just didn't believe she was gonna stay with me. All she seemed to be doing was using me…

Was she?

Would she?

"Fuck. That must be one hundred, Billy!" The guy stopped, his face twisting in an expression of agony.

Probably. I'd lost count.

My hand fell then lifted again to rub my hair and mess it up, so it wasn't left flat. "One hundred. Now we'll go for a run." At least then I didn't have to frickin' concentrate.

When I got home later I saw Eva's backpack in the hall. Mom and Dad weren't home, though. I was glad, 'cause my whole family had started noticing my constant bad mood, and Mom had been getting negative about Lindy. She would interfere if she got too wound up, and I didn't want that.

I threw my keys on the counter and headed to the fridge for cold milk.

Every muscle in my body was locked up with aggression and annoyance that had no vent. I'd go to the gym for a while and pump some weights, then pound a punching bag. That would give me an out for a while.

"That's disgusting, I hate how you drink it from the carton."

I lowered the milk carton and wiped my lips as I turned to face her. "Eva."

"What's up?"

"Nothing."

"You look like you're ready to kill today. Your forehead's all scrunched-up and angry."

I really needed to go punch the bag. Sighing, I tried to get my muscles to knock off and relax. Lindy and I were having a night off the sex thing. I was going out with Jason.

"Is it Lindy again?"

I grunted acknowledgement.

She walked over to get some stuff from the fridge. "I'm making a sandwich, do you want one too?"

"Yeah." Maybe it would stop my belly doing fucking jack jumps.

I took another swig of the milk.

"Don't you dare put that back in the fridge!" She glared at me.

I was just about to.

Laughing, I set it on the counter instead, as she set down all the stuff to make a snack.

I leaned my elbows on the counter and dropped my head, as my fingers combed into my hair. The questions that had been firing at me all day started off again. Was Lindy using me? What the fuck was I to her?

"It is Lindy, isn't it?"

My head lifted.

Eva idolized me; that was something to hold on to. "It's Lindy, but don't meddle, and make sure Mom doesn't either. It's for me and Lind to work out, no one else."

"No one knows you're seeing her, so how the hell could anyone else meddle."

"Leave it, Eva."

"I don't get why you two just don't tell people."

"Because she doesn't want anyone to know right now."

"Why?"

I shrugged. Who knew?

"Billy…" She lifted her hands and would have hugged me, but I held up a hand to tell her no.

She went back to sorting out the food.

"She's still getting over Jason. It's gonna take time. I'm okay with being patient."

"Her and Jason split up months ago. He's married with a kid; she needs to get over it and move on."

A bitter sound left my throat. "It isn't that easy for her, and like I said, I've been patient long enough. I can wait a little longer for her to make up her mind."

"She's seeing you; surely she should have already done that…"

I shrugged. You'd think so. "Can we change the subject…?"

Billy

Jason stood outside the bar, on the driver's side of his dad's truck, leaning through the window and talking to Rachel, who'd obviously driven him down here.

I was gonna drive him home. If I got drunk I reckoned I'd be pathetic and blubbing like a baby in my beer. I wasn't getting drunk.

"Hey!" I shouted.

He turned smiling. "Hey."

Mr. Family-man.

Jason's whole body said how happy he was.

Walking up to the truck I saw Saint strapped in his carrier seat, fast asleep, on the passenger side next to Rachel. "Cute."

"'Til he screams," Rachel answered.

I smiled. "Hi, Rach. How's the new mom?"

"The new mom is exhausted. That is why I don't mind Jason coming out for a drink with you again. Saint kept us awake last night. I'm going home and going to bed."

Jason grinned at her. "And sleep, honey, you've spent too many nights awake when you're on a high. I'll see you later."

"I'm down now. I'm exhausted. You know I'll sleep. I love you."

"Well, if you start feeling too down, call me. I love you." He leaned into the truck and kissed her before stepping back to let her reverse out.

Envy hit me hard in the chest, winding me, as Rachel drove off. Jason lifted a hand. So did she, before pulling out of the parking lot. They were so together. People spoke about soul mates—they were soul mates. You could see it.

I wanted that.

Him and Lindy, they'd spent all their time together until he'd gone to New York, but it was obvious how wrong that had been—it had never been like Jason and Rachel.

I wanted the same thing with Lindy.

I was her soul mate.

It had all just got a bit muddled when we were young. She'd made an error and fallen for Jason's pretty face. I wanted her to fall for me now, and fall hard.

"Shall we get a drink?" Jason's arm came about my shoulders as we turned. "Hey. Cheer up..."

"What?" My face must have slipped into my now-habitual look of Lindy-based frustration.

"What's up? You looked pissed."

"Sorry I'll get in a better mood." We walked over to the bar as Jason's arm fell.

Shit. I shouldn't talk to him about it, but he was my best friend and he knew Lindy better than anyone—and I just needed to vent.

"Two beers," I said to the guy behind the bar, holding up two fingers. My other hand pulled out my wallet. The guy popped the caps off the bottles, then slid them over the bar.

"Have you seen how Rach can knock a beer cap off on a counter? She learned it from one of her mom's guys. I tell you, that girl was dragged up not brought up. She makes me laugh half the time, the stuff she comes out with. She loves having Mom and Dad as her Mom and Dad, she's started calling them Granny and Gramps since Saint was born."

I laughed; his complete domestication was funny. A year ago he'd been the one determined that his life would be better than small-town Oregon.

"What?"

"You. You're sure different with her."

He picked up his beer. "Shall we stay at the bar?" He glanced at two vacant stools at the end.

"Yeah." I picked up my beer and followed him down there. We both propped an elbow on the bar once we'd sat. Whenever we'd hung out in bars until now, Lindy had always been there, leaning on his shoulder or gripping his arm.

I missed her. Watching her face as Jason talked. Being able to make a laugh rip from her throat and catch the flashes of her smile.

That sound had been rare in the last couple of years.

A frown crunched my brow as I lifted my beer and took a drink.

"Go on, then... What is it? What's getting you down?" Jason

pushed, having taken a swig from his beer.

"One word—Lindy."

"Ah."

I shouldn't talk, but… "She and I have been hooking up."

His eyebrows shot up. "Hooking up? You are not talking about my Lindy, then."

"Yes. Only she isn't yours anymore and if you say that you're gonna make me hit you, and she's not the girl you knew anyway…"

"Wow." His eyes got wide and his hands reared, palm out. "No war from me…" His hands fell on his thighs and he leaned in. "But when you say hooking up—"

"I mean hooking up." I sighed. "When I went out of town I took her away with me. We messed around at first, but then it became… more—"

"That is not like, Lindy." He leaned back, shaking his head. "But why are you annoyed about it?"

"I want more." A smug sensation rattled through my body and probably slipped into my voice. "She likes it with me. In fact she can't get enough of it. I keep getting booty calls from her."

"Lindy!" His eyebrows lifted, but then he laughed.

"It's not funny. She's fucking me around and I don't know what she's thinking, or what the fuck to say to her."

He bit his lip to stop his laughter, but I could see it in his eyes.

"You know her better than anyone. Tell me what to do!"

He smiled before taking another shot of beer. Then looked me in the eyes. "Stand up to her. Like you said, I never did, that's where I went wrong. Tell her you want more or it's nothing."

But I didn't want it to be nothing.

"Billy." His beer bottle clunked down on the counter. "Don't put up with her shit like I did. If she's still into me, it's only in her head, it isn't in her heart—she never enjoyed sex with me." A single eyebrow lifted, punctuating that.

"But that was because she's obsessed with what she looks like. She worried too much about getting naked…" Shit. I was saying too much.

Too late. His expression said he'd got the message. "She's over that, she gets naked with you…"

I held his gaze. "Yeah."

"Well that is something, 'cause I don't remember ever seeing her naked."

I shouldn't be having this conversation, I was betraying her, but if I didn't, how was I gonna sort it out? "I taught her to like it but it's back-fired…" Shit, if I was telling him stuff, I might as well tell him it all. "I liked her the whole time you two were together—"

"The whole time?"

"Yeah." I looked at my beer bottle. "I wanted to be with her before you two started dating."

"Are you kidding me?" His fist hit my arm, but it wasn't a punch, just a knock.

I looked up, heat burning in my skin. Fortunately the color I'd captured on the coast probably hid my awkwardness. "No."

His eyes flashed confusion, then his gaze turned to his beer. "Shit."

"Sorry."

He swigged some of his beer, then looked at me again and shrugged. "It doesn't matter, her and me are over. But did you hook up with her when I went to New York deliberately?"

"No, it just happened… I told you that. She got upset. I comforted her. But I'd wanted her for so long, I messed up and kissed her, and she kissed me back 'cause she was thinking of you… and then, well… I took it too far. She never wanted it that night."

"But she does now…"

"Yeah…"

My cell vibrated in my pocket.

Lindy. Had she'd frickin' heard me. 'I know you're out with Jason, and I know we agreed we wouldn't meet up. But I really want to see you. Would you come and pick me up after.'

"Shit."

"What?"

"Lindy." I handed Jason my cell. There was that eyebrow lift again as he read it, then he looked at me.

"A booty call?"

"A booty call."

"That girl has changed."

I smiled. "Well I like that she's changed. I just don't know where the fuck I am with her. She never talks about going out someplace, or even says we're dating… I don't think I'm any more than a friend to her still."

"So how are you going to reply?"

"I'm gonna go see her."

Jason laughed. "Have you had a massive thing for her for years, then?"

I held his gaze. This was honesty in its rawest form. "Yeah."

"Shit. I won't lie, that makes me feel weird. We shared a fucking apartment with you…"

"I know. Tell me about it."

"Do you like torture or something?"

"I must do. 'Cause she's got me all tied up."

He laughed and drank from his beer, then lowered it to the counter. "So what do you want from me?"

"A plan?"

"Like I said, just have it out with her. If I had done that, I'm sure we'd have discovered long before we did that we weren't right for each other. Maybe you and her are right. Maybe she just needs to get it. You know what Lindy is like, full of opinions. She has her way of doing stuff, and everyone else just has to come into line. Call her on it." He laughed then, before grinning at me. "Tell her she can't have any until she makes up her mind. That's what a chick would do. Hell that's what she used to do to me."

Shit, he made me laugh, and I should not be laughing at that. Oh, my God.

Putting the brakes on would be weird, though. But I had a gut feeling he was right—and things couldn't keep on as they were.

I needed closure one way or another.

I needed to get on with my life, with or without her. I couldn't keep living with pause pressed.

I looked at my cell and texted back. 'Okay. I'll call when I drop Jason off.'

':D'

Cool. This was gonna be one hell of a night. My heartbeat rocketed up to the manic pace of a base beat. It pounded through my blood.

Billy

As Jason walked up the driveway to his parents' house, I called Lindy. "Hi."

"Hey, Billy." Her voice was bright.

"I'm just leaving Jason's." In contrast, my tone came out flat; the muscles in my back knotting. I didn't like the person Lindy made me—the anxious fool. I'd made her happier, but the problem was, for us to work, I needed to be happy too.

"I'll see you soon. I'll come outside."

"Okay." I cut the call.

My head held images of Jason and Rachel, and the easy way he'd leaned in through the truck window earlier. Stuff was relaxed between them. He'd never been like that with Lindy, he'd been too busy pleasing her.

Somehow I'd ended up dragged on to the same path. How had that happened?

Shit. Jason was right. I had to face up to her.

When I pulled into her street she stood on the sidewalk, in the place she always waited, her arms crossed over her chest, like she was cold. But the night wasn't that cold.

When I drew to a halt she pulled the door open and climbed in, smiling. "Hey." Her expression was warm.

"Hey. The lake?"

She pulled the belt over and popped it into the slot, looking at me with a wide smile. "Yeah."

I pressed down on the gas and pulled away, my heart still playing that base rhythm.

"I know we said we wouldn't meet up, but I was itching to see you." Her hand reached over and gripped my thigh, squeezing it a little.

She didn't see anything wrong in this. She didn't think it was weird…

I kept my focus on the road, illuminated by the beam of the headlights.

"Are you okay?" Her voice expressed concern when I didn't do anything to respond, and her hand slid off my thigh.

I glanced across and threw her a slight smile. "Yeah." *No.*

"What did you and Jason talk about?"

You. "Just stuff…"

"Anything interesting?"

"It depends what you call interesting. He told me his cousin Richard is getting into lots of trouble. The crowd he hangs 'round with are bad news apparently, the Doyles."

"I heard that. Is Jason trying to talk sense into him?"

"Yeah, but he hasn't got time to pull his cousin out of that bullshit, he's got Saint and Rachel to focus on."

"Yeah." The answer was quiet.

Because she was jealous? Because she still thought she loved him? Why?

The conversation died until I pulled into the parking spot we'd used every night since we'd started coming here.

She unclicked her belt. "Let's get in the back."

Awesome! No time for conversation again.

There was something wrong with my head, there must be, 'cause I was a guy, this should be my fucking idea of heaven—a pure sex relationship.

But I loved her.

I'd loved her for years.

This was not what I wanted.

When her fingers gripped the door catch she must have sensed something in my mood 'cause she stopped and glanced back. "You, okay? What's wrong?"

"Nothing." I may as well do it with her one more time, it may be the last time, and I was gonna make a memory I could hang on to for the rest of my days. "Come on."

I released my seatbelt and slid out when she did.

We got in opposite sides of the back of the SUV, like the last few times I'd seen her.

It had got sordid for me, like she was a hooker. Not that I had ever picked up a hooker.

"Take your jacket off," she said, already stripping off her sweater. She had on a short, fluid cotton skirt and a camisole-type top.

Lust caught hard in my belly and gripped at my balls, tingling to the tip of my cock. I wanted to be in her no matter that this was sordid. Maybe secretly I was the dominatrix type... Letting her be the boss of me. But then that wasn't what turned me on, just her body turned me on.

I took my jacket off, as ordered, and tossed it over onto the front passenger seat. Then her fingers began unbuttoning my shirt.

From a girl who couldn't stand to be touched and had to shut her eyes and bite her lip to endure sex, she had gone from one extreme to the other... Her fingertips ran over the skin of my torso, brushing across the contours of my abs and pecs as I watched in the moonlight shining through the back window.

She lay on her back, moving her legs either side of me as I kneeled.

"Come on." Her fingers pulled my belt from the buckle, then her cold hands were unbuttoning my jeans.

"Can't we take it a bit slower tonight?" I just wanted her to value this, but I was rock-hard for her and she knew it as her hand slid inside my boxers.

Shit.

Ahh. Shit.

She'd learned how to touch me just right, and she didn't hold back.

"I have to get back to the house," she whispered up at me, as she touched.

It was always the same excuse. I have to get back home. Why? For fuck sake. What did it matter if she was home in one hour or two?

Her hand let go of me, and she pressed her heels into the leather seat covers either side of me, lifting her hips to slip off her panties. Then she turned and shifted, sliding them down her legs and off, as I rested back on my haunches watching, my jeans hanging open and my dick bouncing out the top of my pushed-down boxers, fully aroused and aimed at her. Right now that was where my brain was—in her panties, or rather not, her panties weren't a barrier anymore.

Shit. Her fist gripped and worked me again. She pulled me along like I was on a leash.

How had she undermined me so easily?

Jason had felt snowploughed—she was doing the same to me, just in a different way.

But right now—shit—my blood hummed with need and I didn't give a fuck. Her cotton skirt had slid up her thighs, revealing everything. My temperature shot up ten degrees as her hand left me and she touched herself when I went down on all-fours over her.

I played right along with her hand, touching her, and then sliding two fingers into her damp heat.

A whisper of a sigh left her mouth and she shut her eyes, ending her own little game as I took over, but then she pushed her hips up against my fingers.

She was fighting to get to orgasm already, letting her mind search every sensation. I watched her expression, looking for signs that meant I'd done something right. I wanted everything to be right for her—so she would stay with me—*love me.*

One hand on the leather seat holding my weight off of her, the other touching her, I nipped and sucked at her neck. Her body arched. She'd put her hands behind her back to undo her bra.

A shiver of lust ran up my dick, as she lifted her top and her bra so I could kiss and suck her breast, and then she undulated against my hand as I sucked hard on her pointed nipple.

The girl was gonna have me coming any moment… any moment… Shit, *she* broke, all over my hand, throbbing about my fingers, sticky and hot.

I slid my fingers out of her and lifted them to my mouth to suck her flavor off them, ready to power into her.

Her fingers pressed on my chest. "Condom!"

"Shit."

She didn't wait for me to get it, but pulled my wallet from my back pocket and helped herself.

She had it out and on me in moments.

My brain was a fuzzy babble of want as I pressed into her warmth and her inner muscles welcomed and gripped at me.

I was frickin' insane for her. I was lost. She had me in chains.

Both my hands pressed down on the leather seat, as hers ran under my open shirt, over my back and buttocks. I looked down, watching myself entering her, working her slowly, enjoying every sensual second as she pushed up against me.

She wanted me to go faster. I wasn't going faster. I wanted to hang on as long as I could. It could be our last time…

Fuck. She was good now. The Lindy of a few weeks back was long gone. She was rocking up against me and shifting her pelvis so the different angles added to my pleasure.

I gritted my teeth, trying hard not to come, thinking of anything but what she was doing… refusing to be hurried.

This was a true battle.

I bit my lip to cover a growl, when she caught the tip of my dick with a crafty movement.

"Come on, go faster." Her hot urging hovered in the humid

air around us as a desperate plea. It was said because she really needed it, not 'cause she just wanted it.

I gave in, pumping hard and fast, striking at her most sensitive spot with each thrust, her legs opened wider, and her toes slipped into the back of my jeans, over the top of my thighs.

She came in seconds, her legs limp and her fingernails scoring my back. I carried on, determined not to let this end yet. I worked brutally for minutes and minutes more, making her come over and over again, until with a whimper of pure bliss her fingertips slid down and gripped at my buttocks as she came one more time. That had me. I went over the edge with her. Falling like a stone into a deep ravine and tumbling hard. I shut my eyes. Shit. Shit. That was probably the best orgasm I'd ever had. It blasted through me like a jet engine and left me empty.

My heart slowed to a calmer rhythm and breath returned to my lungs. I opened my eyes to find hers focused on me.

Her fingers combed through my hair. Her eyes said she had a deeper feeling for me than friendship. But, how did I know?

I sighed as I withdrew from her.

"Here." She gave me a tissue she'd brought from home, to put the condom in, like she did every night.

The bitter sordid feeling twisted a knife into my gut.

When I moved back to put my clothes straight, she slid her panties on, then did her bra up and straightened her top.

I knelt on the seat, my arm along the back. I had to face her off and get the air clear. I needed to push this to get it right.

"Lind…" She sat with one knee bent up on the seat so she could face me, and the other leg on the floor of the SUV, her hand curled in her lap.

I willed her to say what I wanted her to say, but I could see she just wanted to go home.

"Yeah."

I held her gaze. "What are we doing? Are we dating or what? Are you my girl or what?"

Her forehead squished up in a frown.

What the frick was so confusing?

"Billy—"

I heard the denial—rejection—in her pitch. My hand fell off the back of the seat.

If anyone ended this, I was. I was gonna be in control. I wasn't gonna let her push and pull me around, and I couldn't stand to hear her say, *nothing.* "It doesn't matter, whatever it is, it's over."

"What?" Her eyebrows shot up. The word stung with accusation and anger.

My hand lifted and flung my irritation at her. "I don't want this—"

"What do you mean?" She moved toward me.

I leaned back. "I mean, I don't want to be your sex toy—a sex-only thing. I can get that anywhere. That isn't what I'm after with you. I won't drive you out here again. That's it, we're done, okay?" Why did I say okay? I didn't care if she was okay with it. I wasn't.

"Billy…" Her fingers gripped my shirt, like she had something to say, like she was gonna fight for me, but if she'd intended to, the fight died on her lips, cause she let me go and turned away instead. "Will you take me home?"

"Sure." Course I'd take her home. I wasn't gonna leave her out here…

She unlatched the door and slipped out. She was in the passenger seat by the time I climbed back in to the driver's seat.

She stared ahead as I reversed out.

She didn't say anything and I didn't know what to say, so I said nothing either.

This had turned into a pile of shit. But I knew where I stood now. Nowhere.

I had to get over her, get her out of my soul. There was nothing there on her side, beyond lust. And lust was not enough for me.

As soon as I stopped outside her house, her belt was undone, and she leapt out the SUV.

The door slammed without a goodbye or anything.

My teeth clenching on my anger and hurt, I hit the wheel with the palm of my hand. "Fuck it." I'd blown it. But then in reality there had been nothing to blow.

My obsession with Lindy had to be over.

Gripping the wheel hard, I gunned the engine and pulled off, leaving the pain I'd endured for years behind. I'd lived with it long enough.

Lindy

"Lindy? Lindy, honey?" Mum shouted as I ran into the house and straight past where she lay on the couch. "Lindy!"

I couldn't speak to her, not now, I just needed a minute to pull the shattered pieces of me together, but when I got into my room, that wasn't what I did. I slammed the door shut, fell against it, gripping my head in my hands and cried as heartbreak poured out of my soul and I slid to the floor.

Why had I thought a guy would want me? Nobody wanted me! I wasn't meant to be happy! I was meant to be miserable! I sobbed noisily into my hands, glad no one was here to see.

I hated Billy and I hated Jason. I hated fate and God and life...

If I didn't know it would hurt Mom and Dad too much, I'd just get rid of myself... But I knew how selfish that had been now, and I couldn't consider it again.

I stood up, angry with them both: Billy and Jason. Oh... and with myself. My mascara-smeared face glared back at me from the mirror on the chest of drawers bedside my bed. I threw it at the wall. It crashed against it and smashed.

"Lindy! Lindy!" Dad's voice rumbled along the hall outside my room. "Lindy! Are you okay? What is it? What happened?" He tried the door, but I'd flicked the catch when I'd slammed it shut.

The handle rattled. "Lindy, open this!"

Just go away.

"Lindy!"

He wouldn't go. I knew he wouldn't. Not after I'd taken an overdose. He was probably picturing all sorts of hideous stuff right now. I took a breath as tears streamed down my cheeks.

"Lindy?" His voice was quieter. Perhaps he'd heard me crying.

"I'm coming. Just give me a minute." I went into my bathroom and ran the water, grabbing my washcloth.

"Lindy?"

"I'm wiping my face! I'll be there in a moment!"

I dipped the washcloth in the water, staring at myself in the mirror. I'd have seven more years of bad luck now, after breaking the other mirror.

Tears welled in my throat. What did it matter, my life couldn't get any worse, and who the hell cared what I looked like? Why was I so bothered about looking good when no one cared?

I threw the washcloth in the water and left it there, going to open my door. Dad stood outside, his hands on his hips and concern in his eyes. I loved Dad. But he didn't know how to connect with me, what to say…. It wasn't his fault. Nothing was his fault, and he was going through this too.

Seeking comfort, I did something I never normally did. I stepped out of my room and slipped my arms about his middle. His arms came around me and I started crying again, sobbing into his cotton shirt. Then I realized that his body was shaking too. He was crying too. I didn't look up, just held him even tighter as his damp cheek rested against my hair and we cried together.

"Dwayne! Lindy?"

Dad pulled away instantly, wiping the tears off his cheeks.

I wiped mine away too.

He smiled at me. "I know it's hard, Lindy love. It's hard for me too. But we will get through this. We'll be okay. Now come in and sit with your mother for a little while so you can put her mind at rest?"

I nodded, my gaze clouding. I wiped the tears away, and took a breath to stem the urge to sob. I didn't know how anything would be okay anymore. The last few weeks, when I'd had Billy to go to, to escape into, things had got bearable. But now…

Chapter Eighteen

Billy

"When are you gonna start smiling again?" Eva slid a plate of pancakes across the counter to me. I sat on a stool on the opposite side, not smiling. I felt like shit.

"Have you heard from Lindy lately?"

I met Eva's far-too-perceptive gaze. "Not since her text. that said, you're a jerk. I hate you."

It had come just after midnight on the last night I'd dropped her back at hers.

"She's the jerk. I can't believe she doesn't see what you feel for her. I—"

My teeth gritted, neither did I. "Stop it, Eva, I don't want to talk about it."

"But—"

"Have you and Lindy parted ways entirely then?" Mom walked into the room, interrupting Eva before she could launch into her favorite everything-that-is-wrong-with-Lindy-Martin speech, I'd heard it a lot in the last few days. Eva no longer thought Lindy was nice. Sleeping with, and then ignoring, her brother equaled "not nice" in Eva's eyes. To me, it just equaled pain.

"Yes, Mom." I think so. I hadn't told my family yet but I'd been looking at places to live in Portland. I figured this time I was better off making a clean break and getting away from here. I needed to put Lindy behind me. While I was still here, knowing she was only up the road, she was constantly in my head, messing me up.

"Well, honey, you know we are all here for you if you want to talk." Mom's hand slid onto my shoulder, gripped, then fell away.

"I know."

Dad had spoken to me the night before. My family were close, but it meant they all knew way too much of my business. At least they didn't broadcast it, though.

I started eating the pancakes.

"I'm sorry it didn't work out, sweetheart," Mom added.

So was I.

"I'll tell her what a bitch she is, if you like?" Eva grinned at me with an evil eye, ready for a fight on my behalf.

I swallowed my mouthful of pancakes. "Just leave it, Eva, she didn't do anything wrong—she just doesn't like me like I like her. It's not a crime and it's not her fault." *It's just, sad,* and like being kicked in the balls and punched in the gut.

"Like I said, she's the jerk." She tossed me a smile then headed off to finish getting ready for school and go catch the bus.

"Are you sure you're okay. Can I do anything?"

"No, Mom, just give me some space to be down. I'll get over it and then I'll be fine."

She gave me a concerned smile, worry hovering in her eyes, then nodded and turned away. My cell rang out *Clarity by Foxes* and vibrated on the counter beside me.

I had to change that ringtone.

I glanced down. Jason. We'd been talking a lot since Lindy and I had split. It was like old times, we were close and reliant on each other. The only difference was there was no Lindy standing between us.

Maybe some good was gonna come out of all this.

"Hi."

"Hey, do you feel like a drink?"

"If you want."

"Don't sound so keen."

"Sorry, yeah, okay, whatever. I probably need to."

"Rachel wants to come out with us, is that okay? I think it would be good for her. She's in one of her crazy happy moods." He laughed. "So watch out, because she's going to be burning energy talking…"

"If you want, if she wants…"

"Again, not so keen."

I laughed. "Whatever." I should really get to know her more, if Jason and I were gonna be close again. It would be a novelty to be close with him and not jealous. The image of the leopard marking my chest presented itself, a reminder to move on. "Okay, that would be cool. I'd like to get to know her better."

"You're not gonna secretly start liking her, though? She's a little addictive when she's up, it's catching."

I laughed. "No, you're in the clear, I'm done with that."

"Rachel will drive. She can't drink anyway 'cause she's breast-feeding. We'll pick you up at eight, after Saint's settled. Mom is gonna look out for him."

"The family life…"

He laughed.

"Sure. See you then."

"See you later. Have a good day."

"And you." He hung up. I put my cell down, to eat my now-cold pancakes.

"Who was that?" Eva asked.

I glanced over to see her head stuck around the door. "Jason. He asked me to go for a drink again…"

"It's good you two are spending more time together."

"Thanks. What are you now, grown from my little sister into my mother?"

She smiled as she came over, and then she messed up my hair, 'cause she knew I hated that. "Nope, just the little pain in the ass, who's gonna hang around her big brother for the rest of her life. I love you, Billy. Lindy is blind and stupid"

"Thanks. But you won't be around for the rest of your life. You'll find a guy and then you won't be interested in me."

"I wish." She smiled before walking off to go get her school stuff.

"Do you want me to run you to school, Eva?" Mom offered.

"No I want to catch the bus. There's a boy I like on there. Maybe he'll be the one to convince me my big brother isn't the best guy in the world… I'm working on him." She looked from Mom to me, throwing me a sparkling impish smile.

I laughed. She disappeared.

Shit, I had been chasing Lindy since the days we used to all pile onto the school bus. It hit home how sad my obsession with her was.

I needed to man up and move on.

Billy

Watching Jason with Rachel was interesting. He was so relaxed it made me realize how tense he'd always been around Lindy. He'd held himself in with Lindy, careful of everything he'd said and done, not with Rachel. They laughed a lot and talked constantly and he was right, she was in a crazy, bubbly mood—smiling constantly, teasing him and laughing loudly. Making him laugh too.

Whenever he told me something, she'd finish the story.

They were a pair. Completely in tune and together.

The times I'd gone out with him and Lindy, we'd had quiet conversations, this was raucous.

Rachel told me about when she and Jason had gone out for their first night together, and Jason had had a major hangover. He didn't seem to care that she teased him, and his eyes glowed in the low light of the bar as he looked back at her laughing too. "So does it matter I'm not used to getting as drunk as you?"

She laughed, "No, in fact I think it's cute."

He finished his beer as I ordered another. I think he was on his fourth, I was on about my… tenth maybe? Busy drowning my sorrows quietly—I couldn't get loud sad drunk with Rachel here and in her super-bright mood—so I was aiming for oblivion instead.

I liked them together. I liked her. She was good for him.

I wished Lindy could see it and get that, maybe then she'd move on too.

At ten-thirty I started to think about heading home. My cell went off, vibrating in my pocket—*Clarity by Foxes.*

Shit I had to change that.

I took it out.

Lindy.

Fuck

We hadn't spoken for three weeks.

Standing up I turned away as I answered, "Lindy," catching Jason's gaze and lifting my eyebrows as he stopped talking.

Lindy

"Lindy." When Billy spoke I took a breath, longing for the right words, but he didn't wait for them. "I told you, I'm not gonna be your sex toy anymore and I'm not giving in."

The tears already rolling down my cheeks grew stronger as I tried to catch my breath but couldn't. A sob came out, on a sound of desperation.

"There's no need to cry." The sound of people talking and music made him hard to hear. "Just… don't call me, okay…" The words slurred a little, like he'd had a drink.

But I had no one else to call! "Billy!" His name came out on another sob. "My mom is dying, she's in the hospital. Will you come? Please! I need someone here!"

"What?" His pitch changed from irritated and defensive to concern. The Billy who had taken me on vacation to help me escape.

"She has cancer! She's dying!"

"No, Lind. What? What did you say?"

"Mom has cancer! She's in the hospital! She's dying, Billy! I don't want to be here alone! Will you come?"

A sharp intake of air echoed from my cell. "I'll come. Oh shit I can't drive, I've been drinking."

It got quieter, like he'd been in a bar and gone outside. My tears fell in rivers. I couldn't breathe; every breath became a sob.

"Don't worry. I'll get there. Where are you, Portland?"

"Yeah, in the Providence." I'd known this moment was gonna come, I'd known for so long—but knowing and living with it…

"I'm sorry, Lindy. I'll get there." The slur had gone, and determination burned in his pitch.

The cell went dead, my hand dropped and I slid down the wall. I ended up on the cold, tiled floor, and leaned my forehead on my knees.

The pain I'd lived with for four years bombarded me like a stinging sandstorm, stealing my vision, my senses, and leaving me lost.

Billy

I had a feeling I'd paled as I walked back in the bar. My hand gripped in my hair.

Had Mrs. Martin just discovered she was sick? But that didn't sound right, not to be rushed in with cancer when it was just diagnosed.

I was sure I looked confused when I got back to the table and grabbed my jacket off the seat.

"Don't tell me you're going to go see Lindy?"

I didn't have chance to reply. Rachel stood up. "I'll take you. Jason and I can get home to Saint, then."

I took a breath, shaking my head. "I'm not going to hers. It was Lindy, but she's at the Providence hospital in Portland—"

Jason stood. "She hasn't—"

My hand came up. "It's not Lindy, it's her mom. Mrs. Martin

has cancer. Lindy said she's dying. Lind is really cut up. I said I'd go there."

"I'll drive you." Rachel was already moving, the keys in her hand.

"Fuck, that's crazy." Jason followed. "We'll get you there."

"What about Saint?"

Rachel glanced back at me as we walked out. "He'll be fine with Granny. I'm worried about Lindy. That's terrible."

"Yeah…" What the frick… I needed to get there and talk to her. Find out what was going on.

As Rachel drove I sat in the back seat of Jason's dad's truck watching the darkness, not seeing a thing. This was mad.

"Surely Miriam must have known…" Jason said, his head turning against the rest, speaking over his shoulder.

"Who knows." We were all in shock.

"But it's cancer, that doesn't just spring up on you."

I kept thinking about Lindy being so down and upset after the overdose. What if… Shit.

My fingers ran through my hair, then I messed it up to spike it again, before my hand fell on my thigh and started tapping out a beat.

Frick.

Rachel dropped me at the front door of the hospital. "Thanks, bye, I'll—"

"We're not going, we'll come in."

My eyebrows lifted.

"Billy, she's not my girlfriend anymore, but I was with her for ages, I still care about her." He glanced at Rachel. "Rach gets that."

She nodded. "Yeah, I wanna know she's okay too."

But she wasn't okay, and I didn't think she'd want them here. "Just stay in the front waiting area then 'til I find out if she's alright about you being here."

"Okay, Rach will go park up, then we'll meet you in there."

"Just sit and wait, I'm gonna go find her first. She may not want you around."

"Okay." His voice was tight and uncertain. He didn't want to be shut out. But surely he had to get that he had no right to be here now.

"This is about Lindy, no one else, Jason."

"I know."

I shut the truck door. My jaw locked and my hands clenched as I walked into the hospital and up to the reception. "What ward is Mrs. Martin in, Miriam Martin? I'm a friend of the family. My..." I still didn't know what the frick Lindy was to me. "My girlfriend is there, it's her mom..."

"Are they expecting you?"

"Yeah."

"I'll call up and check. What's your name?"

"Billy Worrall."

The woman looked away from me as she picked up her phone. "Hey. I have Billy Worrall in reception, he says he's connected to Miriam Martin through her daughter. Can you check if that's true before I send him up?"

She glanced at me, smiling a little, as I leaned on the counter watching her. My breath probably stunk of beer. A couple of minutes of silence passed, then she said, "Okay, thanks."

She looked up at me as she put the phone down. "You can go on up to the ward."

"Where is it?"

"On the first floor, turn right once you get out of the lift and it's the first door."

"Okay."

I wiped my sweaty hands on my jeans. I'd been mean to Lindy; *I don't want to be your sex toy.* What the fuck had been going on in reality?

When the lift doors opened on the first floor she was there, and she didn't wait for me to step out but rushed in lifting to her toes, her arms wrapping about my neck.

I held her too, and shit, there was that thing inside me, that addiction, that clawed and roared at the feel of her. I held her tighter. The familiar smell of her perfume capturing me and saying home. "Lindy." My fingers stroked through her hair as the lift doors started shutting.

"Shit." I let her go and pressed the hold button. She moved away from me, her arms crossing over her and gripping either side of her ribs. "Come on," I gripped her upper arm and led her out. She'd been crying, a lot, her eyes were red-veined and puffy and full of shimmering saline.

A tear escaped.

In the hall outside the lift I wrapped my arms around her. Her forehead pressed against my shoulder as she cried.

For a minute I said nothing, my hands just stroking through her hair and rubbing her back.

When she pulled away, wiping the tears off her cheeks with the back of her hand, I said, "Is your dad here?"

"He's in with Mom, I had to get out, I can't stop crying and it's not fair on her."

My fingers gripped her upper arms. They were bare, she just had a t-shirt on. "Did you know?"

She nodded, tears flooding her eyes.

"How long for?"

"Years…" The answer came on a sob, and then her arms were about my middle and she clung to me.

I gave her a minute, my heart pounding.

Years?

"Do you want to go somewhere to talk, get a coffee or something?"

She shook her head against my chest.

"What do you need me to do, Lind?"

"Just hold me."

I did for a minute, but then the hall we stood in rocked. "I'm sorry, I need to sit down. I was out with Jason. I've had too much to drink."

She pulled back and looked at me. Then she nodded. I couldn't tell what she thought.

She turned to lead me along the corridor to a door she pushed open. "This is the day room, we can use it."

There were a load of chairs in it, a TV on the wall and a table in the corner with a stack of magazines and secondhand books.

She crossed the room, pulling me after her, and sat down on a chair in the corner. I sat in the one at right-angles to it, leaning forward and resting my forearms on my thighs. My head spun.

She slipped off her chair and instead sat on the floor with her back against it.

"Isn't the floor cold?"

She shook her head, as her arms crossed, like she was hugging herself.

"How long have you known, exactly?"

She glanced up at me. "Nearly four years. She had breast cancer. When she got diagnosed it had already spread; it was in her lungs, and lymph glands and her spine. She could have had chemo and a ton of invasive operations, but they said it wouldn't mean she was okay, it would just give her more time. She didn't want to spend her last years sick or Dad to see her with her hair falling out."

Was she kidding me? *Or Dad to see her with her hair falling out.* Surely having more time mattered more than that...

I shook my head at her when it clicked. Lindy had inherited her I-need-to-look-perfect gene from her mom. But why not tell anyone? "Why didn't you say something to me, I mean if not before, why not tell me when we were away?"

"Mom doesn't want people pitying her. She wanted us to deal with it as a family."

"While you suffered and fell apart...?" Shit, so many things started clicking into place. "Is that why you took the overdose, not because of Jason?"

Her blue eyes looked up at me, searching my expression for judgment. "Partly, but not because of that particularly... It's just...

This is hard… I don't want to live without her and I didn't have Jason to turn to anymore. I got messed up… I know it was wrong now, but at the time, I couldn't think straight."

More tears rolled down her cheeks.

I rested a hand on her shoulder, feeling like the douche she'd called me a few weeks ago. I'd cursed her in my head for not getting over Jason. It wasn't Jason she hadn't got over.

Her temple fell against my knee as she clutched her legs against her chest. "I don't want to let her go, but there's no choice."

My fingers brushed over her soft hair, releasing the scent of her shampoo. Lindy grounded me. She made me feel real and alive. And her… What was I to her? "I'm sorry."

Her head tipped back and her eyes met mine. "Me too. Sorry you felt like I was using you, I guess I was. It's just, it felt good to get out of the house, escape… and sex with you… made me forget everything for a little while."

I brushed back the strands of her hair that had got stuck on the tear tracks. I probably shouldn't say what I was about to say, but I was drunk, and I had to get it out… "What am I to you, Lindy? I mean do you like me, think I'm hot… What? 'Cause I have no idea."

She didn't answer.

Fuck it, I was just gonna throw all my cards on the table and leave her to show her hand too. "Lindy, I love you. That's why I'm asking. I've loved you for years. I wanted you before you were even seeing Jason. But you always looked at him not me." I took a breath. "Now I know you see me, but what do you see?"

Her forehead crunched up. "Since—"

"Since before Jason."

She looked even more confused. "But we shared an apartment with you at college…"

"I know. Believe me. I spent those years in agony." My smile twisted, maybe turning bitter.

"But you… We all got on…"

"I only went to the same fricking college as you to stay near you. See how bad I have it for you now?"

She shook her head, her gaze clouding. It didn't look like she appreciated my confession. Fresh tears dripped from her tinted eyelashes, dropping onto her bent knees.

"Come here." I pulled her up off the floor, onto my lap and she turned sideways, her arms sliding about my neck as I rubbed her back. "Sorry, I didn't pick the best moment to tell you, did I?"

She sobbed against my neck, her tears soaking into the collar of my shirt.

"Mom is dying, Billy."

Yeah, wrong moment. My confession got swept away as she sobbed as hard as she'd done when I first came up here. I held her. That was what she'd asked me to do. Just that.

It was about ten minutes before she pulled away, sitting up and wiping the tears from her cheeks; her eyes redder and puffier. She sniffed. "Sorry."

"You're entitled to have a good cry."

"I ought to go in and talk to Mom and Dad for a moment, then, when I come out, we can go down to the café and get a coffee. You probably need one if you're drunk."

My lips twisted in a lopsided smile and I caught her chin in my fingers. "I didn't say what I said 'cause I've been drinking, it's the truth."

Her eyes stared back at me. "I believe you. I just… I need time to get my head around it, and you need to sober up."

I nodded. Was I slurring my words? I didn't think so. But I bet I did have beer breath. "Okay." My heart clenched with a bitter pain. She didn't feel anything for me. I was an idiot.

She got up. I caught her hand. "Hey, I forgot, Jason and Rachel are downstairs, they drove me in."

"Why?"

"'Cause I've been drinking…"

"No, I mean why are they downstairs? Are you going to go

again?"

I stood up too and gripped her head in my hands, tilting her face up to look at me. "No, Lindy. I'm gonna be here for as long as you need me now."

"Then why did they stay?"

"Because Jason was worried about you, and Rachel. They both want to support you too. I warned them you might not want them here, but Jason insisted on hanging around. He said he still cares about you and Rachel agreed."

Her gaze shuttered, turning inward. She was thinking, remembering stuff about Jason, probably.

There was that knife cut of jealousy inside me.

"Hey." My fingers brushed her hair back from her cheek. "If you don't want them here, I can tell them to go…"

Her gaze came back to me, new tears sparkling in her eyes. "No, it's okay. Why don't you go down while I go see Mom, and then I'll come down and find you?"

"If you're okay with that?"

"Yeah." She nodded. "I'll see you down there."

She turned away, her hair slipping out of my fingers. My hand lifted to my hair as she walked out, combing through it, then I roughed it up.

A part of me left with her. I wasn't a whole person without her. I'd been crazy the last few days to think I could forget her. I couldn't forget her.

My hands slid into my pockets as I left, heading for the elevator.

Jason stood up as soon as I got down to the main reception. "How is she, have you seen her?"

"Yeah. She's a mess, as expected. But she said she doesn't mind you being here. She's gonna come down in a while, then we can go get a coffee."

"And Miriam, how's Miriam?"

"Dying. She has breast cancer. Or rather it started off as that but now she has it loads of places. It was diagnosed four years ago, but it had already spread beyond any cure. She didn't want anyone to know… She has weeks or days left, that's all…"

"Shit…" Jason hissed.

"Oh my God." Rachel stood up.

"Why the fuck didn't Lindy say something…?" Jason's hand gripped behind his neck.

"Because Miriam didn't want her to. Because Miriam was the one who passed the I-must-be-perfect gene on to Lindy. Because Miriam didn't like the thought of being pitied, or watched…"

"Lindy changed the summer break before we went to college, completely. She turned moody and angry. She was always opinionated and bossy, but that summer…" His hand fell to his side. Rachel gripped it.

I could see the guilt hitting him. He had a ton more to bear than I did. They'd been together and he hadn't known…

"Crap." The swear came out on his breath.

"Hey, Lindy!" Rachel called across the room. I turned to Lindy as Rachel added, "I'm really sorry to hear about your mom." Rachel's voice was still bright and bubbly, like it had been at the bar and it echoed about the reception area.

"Me too," Jason added, "tell Miriam I'm thinking of her. I called Mom. She'll pray for her."

Tears shone in Lindy's eyes. I moved to meet her as she walked the last few steps and slung my arm around her shoulders. She leaned against me, in a way that seemed instinctive.

The scars jealousy had cut in me healed a little. Her arm settled about my waist in return, and her other hand rested on my abs. The heat of her breath seeped through my shirt for a moment, as she hugged me before pulling a little away, but her arm stayed around me, and mine stayed around her.

Jason looked at my hand on her shoulder. It was weird having Lindy up close to me with him here. I caught his gaze and he smiled. But it was an awkward smile.

A tremor of insecurity spun through my belly.

This may be odd but he had to deal with it—and so did I.

"I want a coffee," Lindy said, "shall we go to the café?" She did her best to act normal, but I could hear her discomfort in her voice.

Jason and Rachel turned and walked on ahead. My hand slipped from Lindy's shoulder and gripped her upper arm instead, holding her back. "Are you sure you're okay with this?"

Her head turned and her gaze caught mine… "I feel as if I'm dreaming. I'll wake up, and this will never have happened."

"I wish that for you too, Lind." But I couldn't fix it, and I wouldn't want time to go back four years anyway. If it did she'd still be with Jason…

Her arms slipped about my middle, and we held each other again for a moment. I hurt for her—for what was happening with her mom—but it felt good to hold her.

"You smell of beer," she said, as she let me go. "We'd better go get you a coffee so you can sober up."

I laughed.

She gripped my hand and led the way.

Rachel and Jason were ordering theirs when we got down there. I gripped Lindy's hand more firmly, looking at the guy who was serving. "Two coffees. One large and black. Do you want something to eat, Lind?"

"No, I couldn't, I'm not hungry. My belly is a mess."

"What about a cookie, you don't want to get ill. You need to feel well enough to support your mom."

Tears glittered in her eyes. "Okay."

Jason picked up their tray as ours was being loaded. "Where do you wanna sit?" He looked at Lindy.

"By the windows, if that's okay. This place feels like it's closing in on me."

My fingers lifted and brushed through her hair as Jason walked away. "I'm sorry."

"For what?"

"For all of this…"

"It's not your fault, Billy."

"I know, but you deserve to be happy…"

More tears glittered. I needed to drink my coffee so I stopped ramming my foot in my mouth.

She wiped at the corners of her eyes and took a deep breath as I picked up the tray, steeling herself to face Jason and Rachel, I guessed.

"We really don't have to go talk with them if you don't want."

"No, what happened is hardly important anymore, is it?"

Those words swept over me and seeped into my blood. She didn't care about Jason anymore. Was that what she'd said?

She walked ahead over to where Jason sat beside Rachel.

You drunken jackass, Billy. What she meant was—since her mom is dying what did her ex matter?

She slid into the seat nearest the window. I set the tray down and sat next to her, then handed her the coffee and her cookie.

Awkwardness hung in the air as Lindy faced Rachel.

"I really am sorry about your mom." Rachel sought to express concern but her words still poured out full of vibrant sound, tripping over each other. "If I'd known—"

"What?" Lindy interrupted, "You two would not have got together? That would be dumb, because it's obvious you and Jason were made to be together." She looked at Jason, "And he and I never were…"

I slipped my hand beneath the table and lay it on her thigh. Immediately her hand slid underneath and laid on mine, her fingers settling between mine.

Pain caught hard in my chest.

"I know," Rachel answered, smiling, with a little infectious sort of laugh. "But what I was gonna say, was, I would have been kinder to you. Definitely."

"But that would have just been pity, and I wasn't being kind to you—"

"That was a little justified…"Jason whispered. "You must have felt like fate was beating you up. No wonder you didn't want me to go to New York. You should've just said, Lind…"

"Mom didn't want people to know…"

"But…" He stopped talking, glanced at Rachel and smiled, then finished looking back at Lindy. "We were engaged. I was supposed to be a part of your family."

Jason gripped Rachel's hand while it rested on the table.

"But then you two wouldn't have met," Lindy looked from Jason to Rachel and smiled. Rachel grinned.

Lindy looked at Jason again. "And if you'd stayed here with me, you'd have ended up hating me. You didn't love me. It was always gonna end badly, wasn't it? You were right."

I didn't know if it was really what she thought, or if she'd just resigned herself to it now—like she'd said, it really didn't matter anymore.

My fingers squeezed her thigh gently; she squeezed my fingers in return.

Shit, it was wrong to feel good that she'd come out and admitted she was with me while her mom was dying. I was too drunk; I sipped my coffee.

Jason asked how her dad was.

The conversation after that was clumsy and full of pauses, as all of us avoided any more difficult subjects, but it wasn't unbearable, and Lindy held up. As soon as she'd finished her coffee, though, she looked at me. "I need to go back up. I want to go see Mom."

"We ought to get back to Saint, Jason. He'll be missing us and I need to feed him." Rachel said.

He glanced at her. "Yeah." Then he looked at me. "Do you want a ride back?"

I looked at Lindy. "Do you want me to stay and hang out here with you?"

Tears filled her eyes and she nodded.

"It's okay. I'll stay."

"I need the restroom before we go," Rachel said, standing up as Jason started moving out the way.

"Me too," I rose as Lindy's hand lifted off mine.

"I'll wait here," she said.

I looked back at her. "Okay."

Then I realized she'd be left here alone with Jason. She didn't seem bothered, though.

Lindy

When Billy walked away with Rachel, Jason slid into the seat opposite me and gripped my hand. "I'm sorry, Lindy, I really am." His face blurred as tears filled my eyes. His fingers wiped one off my cheek. "I wasn't all that good to you, was I? Not really."

It was weird to have him touch me again when I needed comfort. But… It didn't feel right anymore. Sniffing, I wiped my own tears away. "No, you had it right. I chased after you and pressured you to want me; you never really did."

"That sounded all hard and cold, Lind. But I don't think that's what you feel inside. You and Billy, is it going somewhere?"

"I don't know… I can't think about the future…"

"From what he's said to me, he sounds right for you—"

"What did he say?"

His smile twisted and he blushed a bit. "It doesn't matter, it just sounds like you and him get along way better than you and I ever did."

I didn't disagree, it was true. I looked down at his hand holding mine. It didn't even feel reassuring anymore. It didn't feel anything but odd—and wrong... "I guess, we could go wait for them over there, rather than make them come back here." The awkwardness of him touching me, and being so close, was too much.

"Yeah." Letting go of my hand, he slid out of the seat. I did too. But when I stood up, he captured me in a hug. He'd been my comfort for years. He was so much leaner than Billy, and a little shorter, my head rested against his shoulder, not the solid mass of Billy's chest, and my arms fit further around him. But it was wrong now. He didn't feel strong enough to protect me.

Billy was right for me…

I let Jason go and stepped away, letting go of him mentally, not just physically.

He was my past. What I'd thought we'd had, hadn't even been true… And I didn't care anymore.

"Ready?" Billy's voice caught at my heart and stirred it. I looked past Jason to see Billy walking over. I left Jason behind.

"Hey." I hugged Billy and his big arms came around me.

This was where I belonged now, with this solid, secure guy—who'd just said he'd loved me for years…

Chapter Nineteen

Lindy

Mom breathed slowly with her eyes shut. Dad sat by her bed, his arms crossed over his chest and his head bowed forward, asleep.

I sat in the chair on the other side of the bed.

Mom still clutched the button that would release the morphine from a drip into her arm. She opened her eyes. She hadn't been asleep.

"How are you?" I whispered.

She gave me a wobbly smile. "Surviving, honey."

I leaned forward and covered her hand. "I wish I could do something… Anything to make it better…"

"I know, and so do I… But we can't."

Tears clouded my gaze. That was why I hadn't stayed in here, because I kept crying, and crying was no good to her.

"I'm sorry. You're growing up, Lindy, and I won't get to see you married or my grandkids… Not physically at least." She shut her eyes on a sigh, that sounded heavy with exhaustion. "But I will come back as an angel and watch over you. I'll see them." It was the promise she'd made to me from the day this had begun.

I squeezed her hand. She pressed the button so the drip released the pain meds. That was why she had finally decided to come in here—she'd been in unbearable pain and finding it hard to breathe.

She'd been crying for hours.

She didn't open her eyes again. I leaned forward, resting my forehead against the hand I held. It lifted from beneath mine, and I moved, then I rested my head on the blanket and she stroked my hair. I wanted to keep my mom. I didn't want to lose her.

"Thank you for being my mom. I've been lucky to have you. You've done so much for me." My voice got muffled by the blanket.

When I was a kid we'd gone cycling and swimming, and spent days and days together. She wasn't just my mom; she was my friend.

Her fingers combed through my hair. "You know we could cry over all the years we don't have, or we can smile and be glad for all the years we have had, and all the things we've done."

Pain swelled in my heart and new tears tumbled on to my cheeks. I sat up, wiping them away. She'd opened her eyes.

"I am glad, Mom. I'll remember everything and tell my kids everything so they know you... But... I still don't want to let you go..."

Tears shimmered in her eyes too. "I know, sweetheart, but it is nearly time now. I am in too much pain. When I go I'll be glad God's been good enough to take me, and then on the other side I can watch over you without pain."

Tears rolled down my cheeks. I was being selfish. It was time for her to be free of illness... "I'm sorry, I can't stop crying."

"Dad said Billy came up to the hospital with Jason and Rachel?"

"Yeah."

"And?"

"I asked Billy to come..." I took a breath. "He was out drinking with Jason; he couldn't drive. Rachel brought him up here and they hung around. I had coffee with them but they've gone now..."

"And Billy?"

"He's still here."

She gave me a weak smile. "Do you think he's the one who'll hang around forever?" Her body jolted when she finished speaking and her breath caught and hitched with a spasm of pain. I ignored it, she hated fussing and fussing wouldn't change anything.

That was one of the reasons she hadn't wanted to tell people—she didn't want to be fussed over.

I didn't know how to answer.

"Do you like him a lot or a little?"

I smiled. "A lot… In some ways more than Jason…"

"And—"

"He said he loves me, Mom. He said he loved me all the time I was with Jason."

She let go of the button for the morphine and her hand settled over mine as it lay on the blanket, patting me. Her smile twisted, then tears glittered in her eyes. "Well, the good Lord is a mystery to me, but that is one answered prayer. I wanted to know you had someone to turn to and you'll have Billy."

I cried noisily, sniffing and sobbing.

"Climb up and lay next me. Let me hold you." She patted the bed.

I did, trying not to hurt her, but I had learned a long time ago how to be careful when I held her, and it was wonderful to have her arm about my shoulders and her fingers stroking through my hair as I fell asleep. I didn't know how many more times I would feel those things.

Billy

The sound of the door creaking woke me. I was bleary-eyed and anxious when I saw Lindy walk in to the day room. My head thumped as I sat up. Shit. I wish I hadn't had so many beers.

I stood up, my hung-over brain rolling around in my skull.

Her eyes were still red and puffy from crying.

I glanced up at the clock. It was 2a.m. My hand lifted and ran through my hair as she came toward me.

"Hey. You okay?" Of course she wasn't.

Her eyes filled with tears. I opened my arms. "Come here…"

She did, holding me tight. I'd seen Jason hug her earlier. It had punched me in the chest. I'd endure watching the two of them long enough in my life, but then I told myself there was nothing between them anymore.

Her cheek pressed against my chest, her damp tears soaking into my shirt as she held on to me. My heart took comfort in it.

Shit, I was being a selfish bastard tonight.

My fingers combed through her tangled hair.

She pulled away a little. "Sorry, I fell asleep."

"So did I."

"Mom was holding me…"

I didn't know what to say to that.

"She told us to go home… Dad's getting the car. I said we'd meet him out front."

"Okay." I swallowed. There was no moisture in my throat.

"Will you stay at mine?"

"Will your dad be okay with that?"

She nodded. "I told him. He's fine."

"Okay."

"You want to? You don't mind?" Her eyes were deep pools of doubt.

My hand cupped her cheek. "Lind, of course I don't mind… I'm here for you…"

She nodded as a tear tumbled over. I wiped it away with my thumb.

"Do I smell bad? I bet I smell like a brewery?"

She laughed, though it sounded a little choked. "You smell just fine, and you feel even better. Come on."

She gripped my hand and pulled me after her.

"Is your dad really alright about me staying over?"

She looked back and smiled. "Billy, he may be a cop, but he is human. Jason used to stay over lots."

That wasn't what I really wanted to hear…

When we got outside the cold night air hit my hangover. I shivered as her dad pulled up. I got the door of the front seat for Lindy. She slid into the car smiling at me. Then I got in the back.

"Mr. Martin." The back seat was way too small for me.

He looked over his shoulder and acknowledged me. "Billy."

This was weird. I rubbed my hair, then realized I had flattened it earlier and spiked it again. I didn't know what to say to him. So I didn't say anything. *Sorry to hear about your wife,* sounded dumb. I sat back and looked out the window.

As they talked about Lindy's mom, I tried not to listen. I didn't want to intrude.

When we got to their house, I got out as soon as her dad parked up and got Lindy's door for her. I still felt awkward, but I wasn't running.

Shit only about six hours ago, I'd been sitting in a bar moaning about her to Jason and Rachel. I felt like a bastard right now.

"You, okay?" I whispered, gripping her arm as her dad walked ahead to open the door.

"Yeah, do you want a coffee or something before we go to bed?"

Damn something hard and elemental bit into my gut. I was gonna share a bed with her in her parents' house. "No."

She looked up and gave me a slight smile. "Nor me. I'm tired."

I let go of her arm and put mine up on her shoulders as we got to the front door. Her dad had left it open and gone in.

She stopped and turned, looking up at me. "I like it when you hold me. Jason held me earlier—"

"I know."

She gripped my hands… her gaze holding mine. "It felt wrong… It feels right when you hold me."

I smiled at her, pulling my hands free and wrapping her in my arms. "And believe me, it feels just as right for me to hold you…"

She sobbed against my chest, so I kept holding her. But then she pulled away. "Come on, let's go to bed."

She went in first.

I followed her, trailing behind. I'd been in her parents' house a ton of times. But this was different.

She headed to her bedroom at the end of the hall. I knew where it was. I had never been in it.

As she flicked on the light I saw she had it painted in a pale blue and childish fluffy clouds covered the blue ceiling. Her curtains were a girly clutter of bright, different-colored small flowers, and the room was neat and perfectly tidy. Completely Lindy.

"I'm gonna go clean my teeth and get ready for bed."

I nodded, as I heard a door bang along the hall. Surely this must be weird for her dad.

I sat down on her bed as she disappeared, rubbing my hand over my face. I didn't start getting undressed.

A few hours ago I'd been in the bar thinking her and me were history, and now, now I was in her bedroom with her dad's approval while her mom lay dying in a hospital back in Portland...

She came back in.

I straightened up and looked at her.

"Do you want the bathroom?"

I nodded and got up, reminding myself we'd shared a room for two weeks at the coast.

In the bathroom, I looked at myself in the mirror. I looked like shit. I used the toilet, washed my hands and my face, and cleaned my teeth with some toothpaste on my finger. Then I went back into the bedroom. She was wearing cotton pajamas. She slid into the bed.

"You okay?" she asked.

"Yeah." I didn't look at her as I stripped my shirt off. I looked around for where to put it.

"Put your clothes on the chair."

Her clothes were piled there.

I toed my shoes off, unbuttoned my fly and stripped off my jeans. I left my boxers on.

"Can you turn the main light out?"

"Okay."

As I switched if off, she switched on a lamp by the bed.

We'd done this when we were away... but... it felt real tonight...

Like she was my girl. I'd never had a proper girlfriend… ever… Because forever I'd just wanted her.

I slid into bed next to her…

"Turn the light out."

She did.

"Let me hold you."

She slid across the bed and came into my arms, and everything that had felt wrong for weeks became right as her head settled on my chest.

Her cold hand touched the skin over my ribs.

Instinctively my fingers brushed through her hair. "I wish you'd said something, Lind."

"I couldn't. Mom didn't want us to."

I sighed and squeezed her against me. "Well, just know now you can talk to me. I'm here for you…" I hesitated. "I love you…" It felt so good to say those words aloud to her and not keep them strangled inside me.

She took a breath; it drew across my skin. "Thank you…"

My fingers stroked through her hair. "It's okay, I don't expect you to say it back. But I just want you to know…"

She nodded. Then her tears wet my skin. I held her harder until sleep claimed me.

Lindy

Dad knocked on the door. "Do you kids want coffee?"

My eyes blinking, I sat up then looked down at Billy. "Do you?" He looked really tired when his eyes opened.

"What?"

"Do you want coffee?"

His expression crunched in confusion, but he said, "Yeah."

"Yes please, Dad!"

I heard him walk away. Immediately I slipped out of bed. Leaving Billy there. "I'll be back." I hurried out into the hall to find Dad.

He was in the kitchen. "Have you heard from Mom?"

He turned and smiled at me. "She's fine. She had a peaceful night. We can't ask for any more than that."

I leaned on the counter as he filled the kettle. "When will you go to the hospital?"

"In a couple of hours. She wants to be moved to the hospice today, though, Lindy, love, and then we are going to have to work out a routine. She won't come home again now and you have to keep living. She knows that. She doesn't expect you there every hour of every day."

Tears clouded my vision.

"Come here."

I went to him and let him hold me, and held him. "We are going to get through this together, sweetheart."

I nodded.

"And we'll be okay and your Mom is going to be okay too… We just have to learn to let her go, and make the passing as easy as we can for her…" More tears came. I knew all of this, in my head. But my heart…

"Mr. Martin. Lindy." I turned to Billy. He'd put his shirt and jeans on, but his feet were bare and his hair messed up, and stubble shaded his jaw.

I smiled at him. He looked hung over. "You didn't have to get up."

"I didn't like to just lie in bed." He looked at Dad. "Can I do anything?"

"You can look after my daughter." Dad smiled, then turned to the kettle as it whistled to say it was boiling.

Billy looked at me, his hands slipping into his front pockets as he shrugged.

"You've been doing a pretty good job so far, Billy, just keep going." Dad didn't look back, but lifted the kettle to fill the coffee pot.

Billy smiled at me.

"You have." I walked over to give him a hug but a cell rang

playing out *Clarity by Foxes*. It wasn't mine or Dad's.

"Shit." Billy turned and headed off toward the sound, that probably came from my room.

I looked at Dad. "I want to ask him to stay here…"

"That's okay, darling. I'd rather you aren't here alone when I have to work."

I hugged him again while the coffee brewed. Then I turned and filled mugs for Billy and I.

When I took them in the bedroom, Billy was sitting on the bed talking on his cell.

He looked up and smiled a little at me. "She's okay."

I smiled too, putting his coffee down on the side next to him. "I'm round hers."

"Yeah." He looked at me again. "Jason's mom says if you need anything, just ask… Did you want her to cook you some dinners or something… and would your mom want her to visit?"

I shrugged. I didn't know if Mom would, and I couldn't think about anything else.

Billy looked away. "She, or I, will let you know."

"I know." He looked up at me again. "He says he's thinking of you… and Rachel is too."

"Tell them thanks."

"Did you hear that… she said thank you."

"Alright, we'll let you know."

"Bye." He touched the screen ending the call as he looked at me. "It's weird talking to Jason when I'm sitting on your bed."

I smiled. "It shouldn't be, him and me were over ages ago…"

His gaze caught on mine asking. *And you and me?*

I turned and sat down next to him. He leaned forward, rubbing his hands over his face and hair, like he was trying to wake himself up. My fingers settled on his back. I loved the way his back narrowed from his broad shoulders, angling into his hips. My fingertips skimmed over his shirt. "I don't know about us, Billy. I can't really think about the future right now. But I know I want you with me, and not just to have someone here. But because I want *you* here."

He straightened up. "What are you doing today?"

"I don't know; I'll probably go with Dad to visit Mom. They're gonna move her into the hospice today. But Dad is discouraging me from spending too much time with her. Billy… I'd really like it if you'd stay here for a few days?"

"Sure, I don't mind. But I have some clients today. Will you be okay if I go to work?"

The guy just oozed concern. "I'll be fine."

"What if I go home after work, pick up some clothes and stuff, then call you when I'm ready?"

I nodded. "Okay."

His fingers cupped my chin. "Sure."

I nodded again. "Sure. Mom is going to be in the hospice weeks. I can't stop living."

He let me go. "Well then," He looked down and pulled his shirt up to his nose. "I stink. I'm gonna go home and shower, and I'll see you later, not drunk, and not hungover."

I smiled at him, leaning back on the bed as he bent to pull his shoes on. "How will you get home?"

"I'll walk. It'll clear my head."

"Call me when you get home."

His lips twitched into a lopsided smile, that twinkled in his eyes too. "Okay."

When he had his shoes on he leaned forward and as his palm braced the back of my neck that stupid leather bracelet brushed my skin. He pressed a kiss on my lips. Then he said over them, his gaze looking right into mine, "I love you." The words skimmed a shiver down my spine. I really believed them. It had never felt like that when Jason had said them to me.

As he turned away, I stood up. "You know you've always worn that bracelet—"

"Yes, Lind. It is because you made it and I know you made it for Jason, but you gave it to me and it's all I've ever had to hold on to…"

I didn't know what to say. "I'll walk you to the door."

Dad was still in the kitchen. Billy lifted his hand to him. "Bye Mr. Martin, see you later."

"Goodbye, Billy."

Outside on the porch I hugged Billy, my breasts loose underneath my pajama top. It felt as intimate as being naked. It was because he'd said he loved me.

He smiled at me and his fingers brushed beneath my chin, before he turned and walked away.

There was a warm, squeezing sensation in my belly, that I didn't remember ever getting when Jason went away. When Jason had gone to New York I'd missed him worse than bad, and when we'd been at college I'd wanted him near. But it wasn't the same.

I gripped the wooden pillar of the porch, watching Billy walk up the street, his hand lifted and combed back his hair, and when it lowered, it hesitated then lifted again and ruffled it to spike it.

I'd watched him do the same thing so many times. The gesture touched a soft spot in me. I smiled to myself, but then he looked back and he grinned when he saw me watching, lifting a hand. He turned to walk backward a few paces too and pressed a kiss on his fingertips and then blew it to me, before lifting both hands and making a heart shape.

I blew him a kiss back, then he turned away, and with a tight ache in my chest I turned to go inside.

Jason was absolutely right. We had been wrong together. I had said it yesterday, but had still not wholly believed it. I believed it now. Nothing Jason had done had ever been so sweet as the way Billy adored me.

Billy did love me…

Wow! A big smile pulled my lips wide when I went in to Dad.

Billy

Dad opened the door. "Where the hell have you been?"

"Hey, Dad." I gave him a stupid grin. I should feel shit over what was going on for Lindy, but I couldn't help the fizz of happiness. I'd said I loved her and it had made her smile and her eyes glow; she hadn't run for the hills.

"You could have called your mother at least. She's been frantic thinking you're lying dead on the side of a road… She's been awake half the night"

I was too wiped-out to get into an argument. I walked past him into the living room. I'd been through an emotional washing machine and then tumble-dried.

"I was with Lindy."

"Lindy?" Mom appeared.

"Yeah, Lindy. I have to get to work. Can I get into the kitchen and make a coffee?"

"I'll make your coffee. You sit down and tell me why you are spending more time with that girl…"

I laughed at the condemnation in her voice as she turned to get my coffee.

She looked over her shoulder. "It's not funny."

"We're together…"

She stopped dead and turned back. "No."

"I spent the night at her's. Her mom is sick. Mrs. Martin has cancer. She's dying. Lindy called me up when I was out with Jason and Rachel and asked me to go into the hospital and sit with her."

"So she's using you again…" I looked over as Eva walked in; she had her pjs on.

"She's not." I looked back at Mom. "Will you put the coffee on? I need to go shower; I have to work today."

I looked back at Eva as I headed across the living room. "Apparently her mom has been sick for years. That's why she's been so weird…"

"Years? Miriam?" Dad challenged as I passed Eva.

"Yes, Dad. She didn't want anyone to know. She's embarrassed about it. You know what Lindy's mom is like…" The same as Lindy—too worried about what others think.

"But that's foolish…" Mom answered. "I haven't seen her for a while but I thought she was just hiding away because of Lindy going off the rails. I thought she was embarrassed by her daughter—"

"Nope, Lindy didn't even fall to pieces over Jason, she fell to pieces 'cause her mom was diagnosed terminally sick four years ago." I looked at Eva. "So, even if she is using me, I don't give a shit anymore, because I make her feel better and I told her I love her and you should have seen the look in her eyes…"

"What look?"

"Like she thought it was awesome…" I grinned. "Mom, I'm gonna go shower. Will you make the coffee…?"

She nodded. Dad caught my gaze and nodded too.

I'd been cross-examined and the jury was gonna discuss. I doubted the verdict would be good. None of them believed Lindy was for real…

I did.

For the first time ever.

The grin was still on my face as I stepped into the shower.

Chapter Twenty

Billy

When I got in the SUV and picked up my cell, my hand shook a little. Partly 'cause I'd drunk too much last night and partly 'cause even though I'd been upbeat earlier, now it was time to find out if Lindy wanted to see me, doubt kicked.

I was gonna text, but that was cowardly. I found her number and called.

It rang a few times as I tapped my fingers in a rhythm on the wheel. Then it went into answer. "This is Lindy, I'm busy. Leave a message and I'll call back."

"Hey, it's Billy, I've done working. Call me if you want me to come to the hospital, or anywhere else."

The words echoed in my head as I ended the call, *or anywhere else.* That sounded pathetic. Please need me, Lind. Please love me back.

I threw my cell on the passenger seat, turned the key, revved the SUV and glanced in the side mirror before I pulled out.

My cell rang "Shit."

There was a car behind me; I couldn't pull straight in. I flicked my indicator and drove another couple of hundred yards then pulled back in and parked. My cell had stopped ringing.

It was Lindy.

I called her back. "Lind?"

"Billy." Her voice came out breathless like she was glad it was me. My heart did a stupid back flip. "You're done working? How did it go?"

"Great, apart from fighting a pounding headache. Are you at the hospital? Did you want me to come there?"

"No, Mom's moved to the hospice, but yeah I'd like you to come here." I could hear her smiling. Was that stupid?

"How's your Mom?"

"A little better now she's settled in here and on the pain-meds she needed. We had a long talk today. She's sleeping now."

"Do you want to go home, then?"

"No, I'm gonna stay until four, but she said she doesn't mind you coming in the room, if you want to…"

Did I want to? For Lindy, I guess I did. "Okay. I'll get out of my gym gear, then come."

"Thanks, Billy." Her words sounded like they came from her heart.

"You're welcome, Lind. I'll be as quick as I can."

"I'll meet you in reception. Text me when you leave home."

"Okay."

"Bye."

"See you soon."

"Okay."

I chucked the cell back on the passenger seat, looked in the mirror, then pulled out.

We'd moved on—she was my girlfriend, and yet I still wasn't sure where we stood.

No one was at home when I got there. I showered and threw some clothes into a backpack to head out.

When I went back into the living room, Eva and Mom were in there. "I'm gonna pick Lindy up from the hospice, where her mom is, and then I'm gonna stay at hers for a few days."

Eva stood up, all bristling little sister. "Billy—"

"Don't you want me to be happy?"

"That is what I want, but she makes you unhappy."

Mom stood too. "I feel sorry for the Martins, but that does not mean I wish you hurt."

I dropped my backpack on the floor, looking at them both. "Okay, it's nice you care, but... Let me deal with it!" I glared at Eva, then Mom. "I'm going all in, and giving this the best chance it has."

Eva's eyes narrowed. The irritated look of a teenage girl.

Mom touched my arm, like she was about to try and talk sense into me. "Billy—"

"No. You know how much I want this. Just give me space and time to see if I can make it work."

Doubt and worry surged through her gaze, while Eva's eyes burned pure anger. Neither of them had any faith.

I had faith.

I looked at Mom. "Stay out of it." My pitch held force.

Her hands lifted, palm out. "Okay. But you know what I think. I've warned you."

"And you know what I think too," Eva threw her cent in.

"Eva, you've never had a boyfriend. You can't give me relationship advice."

"I have a boyfriend. The boy on the bus asked me out!" Her voice lifted to a squeaky squeal.

I shook my head and grinned at her. "You have a day-old relationship and now you think you know it all. That does not make you the perfect mentor." But I didn't like the thought of Eva dating any more than she'd choose Lindy for me. "Come here." I lifted my arm. She came over and hugged me. I hugged her too. "Being with Lindy is good for me. Whatever happens, I know I'll have given it a shot. And you... well, you look out for yourself and make sure this boy adores you like you deserve."

She laughed, slapping a palm against my abs to push me off.

I looked at Mom. "Trust me? And be nice to Lindy." I turned

my gaze on Eva, saying the same thing.

"Of course, I will be nice." Mom answered. "Miriam is sick. But I just want you to be happy."

"I will be."

Mom came over for a hug. I set her away quickly. "I need to go, I'll see you later." I picked up my backpack.

"Would you tell Miriam we'll pray for her…"

"I think it's too late for prayers, Mom."

"It's never too late."

I smiled.

"Give my good wishes to Lindy too," Eva said.

I lifted an eyebrow at her. "Yeah?"

"Yeah, her Mom's sick, even if she is a bitch to you."

I smiled at them, then turned away. They had to get behind me on this.

In the SUV, my backpack on the back seat, I texted Lind. 'Just leaving. Text me the zip code.'

'Cool. Here it is. :D I'll see you soon'

'See you soon.' My thumb itched to type "I love you", but I figured it was best not to overdo the use of those words when she didn't feel the same.

Billy

When I walked toward the reception, Lindy came out of the doors and as soon as she reached me she lifted to her toes and wrapped her arms about my neck.

She smelt good and she felt good. But I'd seen her hugging Jason like this too many times—it was too weird.

I had to make it different.

I squeezed her tight and picked her up. Her arms grasped me tighter as her face pressed into my neck.

"I love you, Lind." The words couldn't stay in me anymore.

When I put her down, she smiled.

Her hands gripped my head, then she lifted to her toes again and kissed me. Just a quick press on my lips.

My heart did that flip thing again.

She gripped my hand and turned, pulling me toward the hospital. "I'll take you up to see Mom. She's actually looking forward to a new face."

Mrs. Martin didn't look as bad as I expected, propped up on pillows, she had her makeup on. She smiled. But she looked tired, too thin, and she had a drip going into her arm.

"My Mom said to say she wishes you well… and you, Lind." I looked over at her. She was busy painting her mom's nails, she smiled at me. "Eva said it too."

"That's sweet of her." She had no idea of the animosity my family felt toward her.

"Yes, that's very kind," Mrs. Martin added.

Lindy looked at her. "Why don't you let people visit you, Mom, now you aren't in so much pain, it might be easier—?"

"I think that may be nice."

Lindy smiled, warming to this theme. "What if Billy's and Jason's moms organized a rota so people came for half an hour each day, then you would have some different conversation, but if you get tired you wouldn't have to keep up appearances for long."

Lindy looked at me. "Your Mom would do that, right?"

I nodded. "Yeah."

She looked back at her mom. "That's the way to go, Mom."

Mrs. Martin smiled a little – it was tight. It was the first time I'd got a hint of how much pain and discomfort she must be in. "That would be a pleasant relief," she said looking at me before sighing out a careful, shallow breath. She was tired now. She wanted me to go, I could tell.

"I'll talk to her."

Lindy blew on her Mom's freshly painted nails, then laid her mom's hand on the covers. "We'll go and let you rest before your dinner gets here, so you'll be able to eat." She'd noticed her mom was getting tired too. "Dad is coming again this evening. I'll come back tomorrow."

Her Mom's eyes shut, but a smile played at the edges of her lips. She whispered. "Please tell him if I'm asleep, to come sit next to me and hold my hand. I'll know he's there."

"Of course." Lindy smiled. "I'll refill your water before we go in case you want a drink."

She picked up the jug and disappeared, leaving me alone with Mrs. Martin. I stood up, to follow Lindy, but I'd been sitting on the other side of the bed to Lindy and before I could move Mrs. Martin caught hold of my hand. "Billy…" It had hurt her to say my name and reach for me.

I looked down and met her gaze, sympathy cutting into my soul. "Yes, Mrs. Martin."

"Do call me Miriam, Mrs. Martin sounds so formal and cold." She tried for a smile, but it didn't really work, it was too twisted by pain. "I want you to know Lindy's been going through a hard time—"

"I know Mrs… Miriam. But—"

"You think a lot of her, I can see that. I don't expect you to take responsibility for her, but just be gentle with her… look out for her for me, when I'm gone, and give her time. She was heart-broken when Jason went to New York, and when I go…." A tear rolled down her cheek.

Gripping her hand in both of mine, I sat back down. "I'll make sure she's okay…" But I didn't think it was just Jason Lindy had been heartbroken over… "Don't worry about Lindy. Even if she doesn't want me around I'm gonna be around for her."

The door to the room opened. I let Miriam's hand go and straightened up. Lindy caught my movement as she came in with the full water jug, and her eyebrows lifted, as if to say—*what?* I just smiled.

Lindy
When we got back to mine, as I got out of the SUV, Billy grabbed

his backpack from the backseat.

Something flipped in my belly when I saw him walk around the SUV with his backpack over his shoulder—in a good way. We had roots threading out into the ground.

New memories to replace those of Jason.

I walked ahead of him. When we got into the hall, I said, "Why don't you dump your stuff in my room."

He smiled at me. "Okay. Who's cooking dinner?"

"Me. You're the guest."

"Guest? Is that what I am?" His eyebrows lifted.

I smiled at him. "And my boyfriend! You are that most now."

"Good. I just wanted to check nothing's changed since yesterday."

He dropped his backpack and grinned at me.

"Nothing's changed, Billy." I put my arms up around his neck as I said it, and his head lowered, then we kissed.

It felt like I hadn't kissed him for weeks, I'd been so used to Jason's kisses that those came to mind more than Billy's version. It was nothing like Jason's—full-on. Because he really loved me? Maybe that had always been the difference. Jason had held back on me because he never had.

We kissed for ages, with a mutual need to keep cherishing each other. I could sense how much he felt for me—it had been there back at the beach too and my body had known it.

He broke the kiss, and rested his forehead against mine. "Do you wanna eat now? It must be exhausting trying to keep upbeat around your mom?"

I pressed one last kiss on his lips, than turned away, slipping from his hold. "It is. What do you want?"

"What do you wanna cook?"

"Pasta is the easiest thing. I can whizz up a tomato sauce."

"Pasta with tomato sauce it is then…"

He followed me into the Kitchen, leaving his backpack on the floor and leaned on the counter, talking to me while I got every-thing out and started cooking. He was so easy to have around. I mean Jason had been nice and I'd always thought of him as my friend too… But Billy made me laugh twice, and his smile glowed in his eyes when I looked at him. He was glad to be with me.

We sat at the table to eat, still talking.

I'd sat with him and eaten dinner a ton of times in the past. We'd lived in the same apartment after all, but again, it was different, because now I knew behind that easy swagger, the quick smiles and jokes that were said with a sparkle in his eyes, was love.

We carried our empty bowls to the kitchen. "Dad is gonna be out for hours. Did you want to go to bed?"

"Now there's a blunt offer."

I left my bowl in the sink and turned. "How would you have had me offer?" I wanted to be worth all that love.

He leaned around me to put his bowl in the sink too, his free hand touching my waist, then straightened up, looking me in the eyes. "Well, you could have just come up and kissed me…"

He kissed me.

My belly and my knees wobbled like Jell-O.

When he broke the kiss, his lips moved to my ear to whisper in a deep pitch. "Will you come to bed with me?" He took a breath, then said in a lighter tone. "That is how you do it."

I laughed, my arms slipping around his neck as I lifted to my toes, then I whispered in his ear. "Yes."

It didn't matter that Mom was sick, excitement and expectation still roared through my senses. This was escape, but not only that—there was a whole ball of emotion being blown around on a hurricane in my chest.

He lifted me off my feet and threw me over one massive shoulder. "Ahhh, Billy! This is not romantic."

"You won't be thinking about romantic in a moment."

I smacked his ass, then squeezed one perfect pert butt cheek, laughing as he walked along the hall to my room. "You're nuts."

"Nuts in love…" he said, tumbling me down on the bed. I bounced on the mattress as he straightened to strip off his tee.

"I love your chest."

"I love you!"

I laughed as he leaned down.

"Come on, let's get these off." His fingers undid the button on my jeans. I lifted up, letting him strip them and my panties off, smiling at him.

"Take your top off," he said, his fingers unbuttoning his jeans, while he toed off his sneakers.

I stripped off my top, then undid my bra as he peeled everything off below the waist in one move. "Sexy." I breathed.

My bra came off, as one of his knees hit the bed. "Nope, you are the sexy one, get over here."

I tumbled back on to the bed, laughing as he pulled my knee to drag me down. But how could I laugh when Mom was so ill? Guilt slashed its knife at my face.

"Lind?" He saw the change, leaning over me and stroking my hair away from my face. "Okay?"

"Yeah, it's just… Mom… I feel like I shouldn't be happy, but… you make me feel happy."

"She wants you to feel happy, at least some of the time, you know she does. There is nothing wrong with you being able to keep living and enjoying life. That's what your Mom wants. She told me. When you went out the room, she said, you'll get down, but she asked me to help you get over it—"

"I'll never get over it…"

"Okay, that was the wrong words. I mean you'll learn to live with it, and she urged me to help you work out the path to that point."

My fingers stroked through his hair. "Will you?"

"Of course I will, my heart's stuck by you all these years, Lind. Do you really think it's gonna desert you now?"

"No…" I believed him.

"Do you still want to have sex or are you not in the mood now?"

"I'm still in the mood." I pulled his mouth down to mine.

It wasn't just sex, though, he was making love to me—cherishing and worshipping me, his gentle fingertips skimming over my skin as he kissed me, making me forget everything but him.

"Billy…" My hand gripped the back of his head suddenly, when his fingers slid into me.

We didn't kiss as his fingers worked, but our gazes held and my fingernails dug into his scalp.

I shut my eyes and my whole body arched when the orgasm ripped through me in a flood tide. Then it was him in me. Working hard, making me think of nothing but him again. His body, his size, his masculinity, his gentleness—his love.

My fingers pressed into the flesh of his buttocks as he worked quickly, fighting to make me come again. I was insane for him when we did this.

"Ahh!" I tumbled over once more and my flesh just became his as he manipulated and maneuvered me into positions to intensify the pleasure.

When he finally came, it was about an hour later and I was boneless and exhausted, my face smashed into the covers, where I had fallen at one point, being on all-fours. I rolled onto my side on the bed, laughing. He wrapped an arm around me and pulled me against his chest. I fell into a chasm of sleep. I hadn't slept for days.

Lindy

Music woke me. *Clarity by Foxes*.

Billy's cell.

I rolled over and sat up, the comforter slipping to my waist. Billy moved too, his hand searching for his cell on my chest of drawers. It wasn't there.

He got up and reached for his jeans. His cell was in the pocket.

His palm rubbed his face as he straightened up and answered it. "Yeah."

I looked at the clock. Eleven.

"What?"

"Okay."

"Who is it?" I asked. He turned and looked at me.

"It's Jason. Rachel's missing."

His hand lifted to stop me saying more. "Hang on a minute. What, Jason?"

"Where do you think she's gone?"

"Sure, course I will."

"I'm at Lindy's."

"Yeah."

"Okay."

"I'll call you when I'm in the SUV."

Billy dropped the cell on the bed, then immediately started to put his jeans on.

"What is it?"

"Rach had a bad day. She left the house about two hours ago. He doesn't know where she's gone. He wants help looking for her."

Billy picked up his tee.

"I'll come too." I slipped out of bed as I said it.

"Are you sure? You don't have to."

"She came to the hospital yesterday to support me… I want to."

"Okay, hurry then. Jason sounded desperate. He's worried."

"Why?"

"Saint's been crying all day and Rach is off her meds because she's been breastfeeding. He thinks she's hit a massive low. He's worried she'll do something bad…"

Shit.

I dressed really quick, but Billy was ready before me and hovering at my bedroom door with his keys in his hand. "Come on," he said, as I zipped up my sweater.

I smiled at him, then hurried ahead of him. "So where do we look?"

"I don't know, everywhere. I told him I'd call when I was driving."

"Give me your cell, then."

As we walked out to the SUV, I looked up Jason in Billy's contacts and called him just as I got into the passenger seat. Billy gunned the engine.

"Jason."

"Lindy?" His voice rang with doubt and fear, and he was breathless like he'd been running.

"I'm with Billy, we're in the SUV, are you in your truck?"

"It's parked at the store. I've been looking everywhere around Main Street. I just don't think she's here." I imagined his hand gripping in his hair as he stopped and looked around.

"Where else do you think she might have gone?"

"I don't fucking know. I can't think, Lind."

"Take a breath," Billy was already driving toward town. "Where do you two go? Where does she take Saint? Where would she feel safer and secure—happy?" Those were the things that had pulled me to the store the night they'd found me.

He let out a sigh, then took a deep breath. "The park maybe! We run there and she takes Saint there loads. She loves the park."

"Which one?"

"Both."

"We're near Lower Park, we'll go there. You look in Upper Park."

"Okay." The cell went dead.

I looked at Billy. "He's panicking."

Billy glanced at me. "I know. It must be bad."

Neither of us said anything as he drove.

When we got there he pulled into the parking lot and as soon as the engine died I leaped out, leaving Billy to lock up.

"Where do we look?" I shouted.

"I don't know, call Jason again." I turned to see Billy glance at the cell still in my hand. I called Jason as we started walking, hurrying into the park.

"Hi." I think he thought it was gonna be Billy this time.

"We're here. Where should we start looking?"

"Along the river. In the playground." His breathless voice

brimmed with anxiety. He was running as he spoke. "I can't see her here! Rachel! Rach!"

"Billy, you run along the river path, you're faster than me. I'll head to the playground. Jason, do you want to stay on the cell?"

"Yeah."

His fast breathing sent a rhythm through the cell as he ran.

I started running too, as Billy was absorbed by the dark heading for the river path. I wasn't fast. The boys were the sporty ones. I'd enjoyed being a cheerleader but that was more about agility than speed. Energy flowed into my muscles—adrenaline, fear. I wouldn't want anything to happen to Rachel.

Six months ago I'd hated her so much I could have scratched her eyes out, but the emotion in my chest now was compassion and concern. I liked her. Oh my God. Had I just said that? But it was true. When I'd spoken to her at the store and in the hospital, she'd been nice.

I like her.

"Rachel!" I shouted out her name. But there was no answer.

"Is she there!" Jason's breathless voice roared down the cell.

"No, sorry, I was trying to see if she'd call back."

"Rachel!" I heard him shout at the other end of the cell. But I took it there was no answer as a few minutes later he shouted again. "Rachel!"

So did I. "Rachel!"

The night was really dark, but there were lamps dotted about, illuminating the park for people who wanted to be out here in the evening.

"Rachel!" I heard Billy shout from the river path, much further into the park than me. What if she was in the water? It might be too late.

"Rachel!" I called again.

"Rach!" Jason's voice echoed from the cell.

I didn't understand. She'd been fine yesterday, smiling and talking excitedly. I knew what it was like to want to duck out of life and just get away… But Rachel had Saint and Jason, and she seemed like she had the perfect life… Why would she come down here?

I ran on, with Jason's breaths a rhythm seeping through the cell into my ear.

"Have you seen her?" The passion and intensity I heard in Billy's voice for me rang in Jason's for Rachel. But it didn't hurt me to hear it anymore. He loved her, and I didn't even care.

"No, but I'm not at the play park yet."

I carried on running, starting to get tired and out of breath, but then I came around the corner and the shrubs surrounding the path opened up. "I think I see her!"

"What?" Jason's desperate breathless response came through the cell.

"There's someone sitting on a swing. She has long hair, and she's tall and thin like Rachel."

"I'm coming." The call went dead as I ran on toward the figure.

It was just a silhouette cast by the lamp shining down on the play park. Whoever it was sat with their head down, leaning against a chain, gently moving the swing a little with their feet.

"Rachel!" I called as I got closer. The figure had blonde hair, like hers.

She looked up and even though I was yards away, I saw a vacant glint in her eyes. "Rachel." I said more gently as I stopped running and got closer. She didn't get up. She didn't do anything other than look at me.

"Billy!" I yelled into the darkness facing the river. I couldn't hear him anymore, he was too far away. "Billy!" I yelled again. "I found her!"

I didn't wait for an answer, but moved closer, my hand out. I felt like I was approaching an animal that might run or bite. I didn't know how she'd react. "Rachel, Jason called us. He's worried. Are you okay?"

She didn't say anything. Just looked at me blankly.

Looking down at Billy's cell, I called Jason again and lifted it to my ear. She still hadn't acknowledged that she knew who I was, or that I was even there. "Yeah." His voice echoed like he had the cell on speaker in the truck.

"She's here. She's just sitting. She's not talking."

"Call 911, I'll be there soon." I ended the call, to let him concentrate on driving.

"Rachel, are you okay? Can I do anything?"

She shook her head, then whispered, "I'm sorry."

I squatted down as I typed 911 into the cell. "You have nothing to be sorry for."

"I do. I'm not a Mom." I could hear the echo of the black hole she was in—isolated and tragic. I had been there only a little while ago.

But yesterday she'd been fine… Happy…

The call rang. "Hello, emergency…"

I stood up again and turned my back on Rachel. This was so strange. Me, helping Rachel… "I'm with someone, she has bipolar. She doesn't seem with it… she's not been taking medication."

Billy appeared, running out of the shadows, over the grass. He leaped over the low metal fence surrounding the play park like it was a hurdle.

I carried on talking to the woman on 911, giving her the address and more details about Rachel, and then listening as she tried to keep me calm.

Billy squatted down and spoke to Rachel, breathing hard and rubbing her shoulder.

Jason arrived a few minutes later sprinting along the path from the parking lot at full throttle. He was super-fast when he ran. He probably could have run professionally but he'd never taken it that far.

I breathed out… maybe because I had held him back… I'd always complained about him spending time running… I had been a bit of a bitch to him at times, I suppose.

Jason wiped tears off his face as Billy moved out the way.

Jason knelt in front of Rachel, gripping both her hands. "Rach…" There was so much pain in his voice. "You scared the fuck out of me. We had a deal, that you'd call when you get down, remember? You didn't call me."

She didn't say anything, just looked at him.

"Mom's with Saint, he's gone to sleep. He was just gripey. Dad's gone to get some powdered milk for when he wakes. Everything will be okay, but Saint is missing his mommy…"

"I can't do it…" Rachel whispered.

"You can," Jason answered with absolute confidence. He had total faith in her, even though right now the way she looked, she was right…

"You're going to be fine. The hospital will get you back on your meds. Everything will settle down, and I'll go to New York and sort that asshole out. Okay? So you have nothing to worry about, except just keeping well."

Tears tracked down Rachel's cheeks as we heard the siren of an ambulance. "I don't want to go to the hospital," she whispered.

"I know," Jason answered, "but it's the safest place for you until you get straight. I'll come with you, and I'll spend as much time there as I can, and Mom will bring Saint in, and everything is going to be okay, Rach."

She bent forward, her forehead resting on Jason's hair. I could see how much she loved him, craved him. It was in every movement of her body, no matter that she was trapped in utter despair.

Jason moved, his arms going around her as he stood, picking her up, cradling her as her arms wrapped about him, clinging hard. "It's going to be okay. I promise. I promise, honey."

Something grabbed hard at my heart as I watched him carry her toward the park entrance and heard the ambulance getting closer.

I followed as Billy walked next to me.

I didn't know what to think as odd sensations twisted around in me. But none of them were jealousy.

Compassion. Pity. Respect. Regret. Sorrow… Hope… Craving…

He really did love her, and she loved him. What was between them was nothing like anything I'd known.

The compassion and pity was for her. Respect—for him. Regret, sorrow, hope and craving… those feelings all span from selfish need. I hadn't had that with him. I wanted it. The battle in my chest between all those feelings made it difficult to breathe.

The medics took Rachel from Jason's arms when we reached the parking lot, and then immediately they gave her an injection.

Billy caught a hold of me and hugged me hard as Jason hovered near Rachel.

I hugged Billy back. All the stuff in my chest calmed and eased, and settled down.

I pulled free, turning. "Jason." He looked at me. "I'll come down and work in the store on Monday. You are gonna want to be with Rachel. I'll work every day for as long as you need me."

He smiled, giving me a tender look. It was the way he'd looked at me when we'd been together, with kindness, and appreciation— never the heart-wrenching, overwhelming love he looked at Rachel with. "Thanks, Lind, that would be awesome. You don't have to, though. I'll understand if you don't want to—"

"I want to help you." I did. I was over him. I was over being jealous. I didn't want him, I wanted Billy now anyway.

I looked at Billy. His eyes shone with that special look of deep affection. I leaned against his chest, against the leopard that roared and clawed beneath his clothes. His arm came around me, sheltering me.

"I'll come in for eight-thirty so you or Darren can tell me anything that's changed."

Jason's smile twisted, in an expression that said, thank you, but he looked tired and worn down.

I didn't understand. "How come Rachel is so upset? She was really happy yesterday… and then today…"

His hand lifted and his fingers ran through his hair. "It's

chemistry, Lind. That's bipolar. There's a lot of stuff going on for us, and Saint has kept her up all night… But even if there was nothing going on, she could just go down, or shoot up for no reason when she's off her meds… She wanted to breastfeed… I guess now she has to give that idea up…"

Leaving Billy's comfort I stepped forward, reaching out to touch Jason's arm. "You're good for her. You two are right together."

His smile split, but at the same time moisture glistened in his eyes. "I love her, no matter what."

"I know." My hand fell.

"Mr. Macinlay, we're ready to go!" One of the medics called from inside the ambulance, as another headed to the driver's door.

Jason glanced at them, lifting a hand, then suddenly looked back at Billy. "Shit, the truck, would you take the keys 'round to Dad. He can come get it in the morning."

"Yeah." Billy held a hand out to catch them. Jason threw them over.

"See you later," Jason said before turning away.

"When she's more with it, tell Rachel I'll be thinking of her!"

He looked back at me and smiled again. "You can come visit if you want, she'd love that. It'll make her feel better. She has never stopped feeling guilty."

I smiled in return, without answering.

He turned away and climbed into the ambulance.

Did I forgive her?

I guess I did.

Jason had never been right for me.

I looked at Billy as the ambulance doors shut.

I had a chance to discover real love now… I never would have done if Rachel hadn't come into Jason's life.

I forgave her—and him.

Billy wrapped his arms around me as the ambulance pulled out and I leaned against him.

He brushed my hair back behind my ear, "Shall we go 'round

to his parents now?”

“I guess so, we can tell them what’s happened then too.”

Chapter Twenty-one

Lindy

So many surreal things had been happening in my life lately, stepping over the threshold of Jason's parents' house was another. It was a long time since I'd been here, and I had been a different person then.

The last time I'd come here had been for their Christmas party. Jason and I had already split and he'd been here with Rachel. His parents hadn't liked her and she and I had had a battle of words.

She'd won.

Like she'd won Jason. I'd hated her then, and for months after…

Now? I think I did like her.

Billy gripped my hand harder when Ester, Jason's mom, invited us into the living room and offered us some coffee. Darren sat in his usual chair. He smiled at me. I'd worked in the store with him since I'd turned sixteen. He'd been a dad to me too.

"Lindy, love." He stood up.

"Darren." I let go of Billy's hand to hug Jason's dad.

"The circumstances are horrible, I know, but it is good to see you again. I felt like I lost a daughter." He let me go as tears fought to be freed, but they didn't run over.

Maybe I had exiled myself in the last few months rather than been pushed out. No one had ever asked me to leave the store. I

294

could have still gone in to see Darren, if nothing else.

"Jason sent us 'round to give you the keys for the truck." Billy held them out. Darren took them.

"He's gone in the ambulance to the hospital with Rachel," I explained.

"How is she?" Ester asked.

"Not good, I guess. Shall I help you with the coffee?"

She nodded and like old times, I followed her into the kitchen to talk. "Rachel seemed really down, and yesterday she was really up."

"Saint was crying," Ester said. "I have been telling Rachel all day, it is just how babies are, but the poor girl takes everything so personally when she hits a low, and then of course there is this thing with the father. He refuses to do a DNA test, and they need to prove he is the father before they can get him to sign any papers to allow Jason to adopt Saint."

I hadn't known any of that. I knew he wasn't Jason's. I just hadn't known it was complicated, or that Jason was trying to adopt Saint. But I should have known he'd do something like that, that was Jason all over. He was the saint-like one. Maybe that was why Rachel had picked the name.

An odd part of me was proud of Jason.

Ester turned with a mug in each hand. "And how are you, dear? We haven't spoken to you for so long, and it is such dreadful news about Miriam. If we can do anything..."

I took the mugs from her, leaving her to bring the others as *déjà vu* tumbled through my head. I'd done this numerous times when Jason and I were together.

When I walked into the living room, though, it was Billy sitting on their couch. His big, muscular body making his presence known. I didn't miss Jason, or the life I'd had with him anymore. I was happier and better with Billy.

When I sat down, I told Darren I'd work in the store again for as long as he needed me. He seemed pleased. Then Billy and Ester started planning the rota Mrs. Worrall and Ester would create, so

Mom could have a visitor every afternoon.

This was all weird. Mom and I had been completely isolated and we needn't have been.

A whimpering sound disturbed the conversation. I saw a row of red lights on a monitor on the side play up and down in time with the sound. The pitch got sharper and and the lights swung right to the end of the line when a full-on wail rang out. It was a call. *Someone come get me!*

"Saint. He's due a feed," Ester clarified.

I smiled as she got up.

"It will be the first time he's been fed from a bottle, so let's see how we get on..."

It would be a big deal for Saint not to have his mom feed him.

A couple of moments later Ester walked back into the room carrying the sweetest baby. He had dark hair, but it was just a cloud of fine, wispy strands like a halo around his head. His little cheeks burned red and warm as his sleepy eyes blinked at me.

He had a stripey baby-grow on and his chubby long legs dangled. He'd be tall, but then Rachel was tall.

"Do you want to hold him while I go warm his bottle?" Ester said to me. My gaze lifted from Saint to his grandma. Odd sensations twisted and tied a knot in my belly.

Want. Longing. But not jealousy.

"Yeah." I lifted my hands and she came over and gave him to me. He weighed more than I expected.

I balanced him on my lap, my arm cradling him as Ester disappeared. He looked at me—the stranger—and grasped my hair. He was so cute.

Billy's palm settled on my back and rubbed it.

I'd told him after I'd taken the overdose that I'd done it because I couldn't stand seeing Jason with this kid. Billy probably thought this was hard for me. It wasn't. Not at all. Not now. Nothing that had happened in my life was the fault of this tiny little human being.

I gripped his hand, getting him to free my hair and his fingers closed around my thumb instead. I looked at Billy "He's sweet."

When I'd been with Jason all I'd wanted was the two of us to settle down with a house and kids—I'd been desperately seeking "normal". With Mom sick and me messed-up, I'd thought being a mom and wife would put everything right. It wouldn't have.

I still craved those things, eventually, just not yet.

There would be a right time for me and a right person—I hoped the right person was Billy. I felt like it would be Billy.

Ester came back into the room, carrying the bottle.

"You can try feeding him if you want, Lindy."

I wanted. I lifted my hand to take the bottle.

"Try leaning him back and then put the teat to his lips, and let's hope he doesn't think about the different feel when he starts sucking and gets the warm milk."

I did. He fidgeted a lot, whining and pushing the teat out of his mouth, but I cooed and persisted as Billy watched and rubbed my shoulder.

Saint twisted toward me. It was like he was looking for a breast. I changed the angle of the bottle and ran it over his lips again, so milk leaked a little. Finally he opened his mouth, latched onto the teat and sucked, his little hand resting on my sweater over my breast.

It was awesome.

His eyes shut, and his tiny eyelashes rested on his cheeks.

Ester started singing a nursery rhyme and Darren whispered. "Rachel always sings to him when she's feeding, it'll make him a little more settled. I'm sure he knows you're not his mom, but if we can keep things as normal as we can for him we will."

Rachel had said she couldn't do this, but it sounded to me like she was a pretty good mom, really.

When he'd drunk half the bottle, Ester told me to sit him up, and then she took him from me so she could wind him, walking around with him pressed to her shoulder as she rubbed his back.

She gave him the rest of the milk.

"Rachel must be missing him." I couldn't imagine what it would be like to be separated from him if he was my son. My heart would ache so bad…

I thought of Mom, of how much it must be hurting her to leave Dad and me… But she was resigned to it, I knew that, because she was in too much pain now, she was ready to go. Dad was right. I really needed to help her go and feel comfortable and content to leave me. In the weeks she had left, I needed to find the person I was going to be when she had gone, and show her I would be okay. That was the best thing I could do for her.

Ester stood, with Saint held to her shoulder as she rubbed his back again. "We'll make sure he goes in to see Rachel tomorrow. Hopefully she won't be in there too long."

I nodded.

"Jason said I should go visit her."

"Oh, she would like that. She has kept beating herself up over hurting you."

I nodded. The world seemed such a different place today. For years I'd been trapped by what was happening to Mom. Now I could see everyone had something going on in their lives. "Has Rachel made friends here?"

"Not really, the bipolar makes it difficult. She has us but—"

"Well, I'll try and help her—"

"You have enough going on with your mom—"

"I know, but I could do with rebuilding friendships too, I've been hiding away because of Mom."

"Well, we shall do what we can to help you and Miriam, Lindy. If you need anything you must call and I can make extra dinner for you to take home to feed you and Dwayne."

"Thank you, I know Dad will appreciate it, and if I'm working at the store, I'll want to spend my evenings at the hospital."

"You can have some time out every afternoon too, Lindy, I can cope for a couple of hours on my own," Darren added.

Déjà vu… How many times had I sat here listening to Jason's parents offering to support me?

When Ester went to put Saint down to sleep, Billy and I left. We didn't speak until we were back in the SUV. Then he said, "You okay?"

I looked at him. "I think so. I think I am better than I have been in a long time. I don't feel jealous of Rachel. I am happy for her and Jason. Does that sound stupid when Rachel has just been admitted to the hospital?"

He smiled, his hand reaching over to grip my knee. "No. It's good."

"It's thanks to you."

"No, it's just you learning to deal with it all."

"Because you've helped me."

"You'd have probably got there in the end anyway." His hand came up and stroked through my hair before he turned away and started the engine.

I floated home like I was living in a dream, and I slept really well.

Chapter Twenty-two

Billy

When I woke, I had Lindy's head pillowed on my chest. Her hair spread out tickling my skin as she breathed.

I lay still listening to her breathing, absorbing the weight of her small hand on my belly and her leg over my thigh, thinking about last night.

Shit her mom in the hospice, Rachel in the hospital… What was wrong with the stars?

Then I thought of Lindy holding Saint. She'd looked so natural feeding him. It had pulled a cord, excruciatingly tight, around my heart. I wanted kids with her one day—and a house, with a yard for our kids to play in.

But only when she loved me as much as I loved her.

I'd seen her look at me last night; when Jason had come to fetch Rachel. I'd watched her, watching them, and then she'd looked at me.

She'd looked at me in a different way, as I treaded on nails and eggshells, trying not to break anything, but let this be what it should be, and hoping the music that I heard playing between us would start playing in her head too.

She knew what I felt about her. I was just gonna keep saying it, and showing it, and hope the spell of it wrapped around her and made her feel the same.

I shut my eyes and a deep breath sucked into my lungs. The movement made her stir and start to wake.

Images of Mom's and Eva's angry, disbelieving faces hovered behind my closed eyelids. I needed to get them on my side. On mine and Lindy's side. I'd have to take her 'round there today.

She sat up a little, blinking sleep from her eyes. My fingers stroked through her hair.

"You okay?"

"Yeah." She turned away to get up, though. "I'm gonna go call the hospice and check Mom had a good night, then I'll call Jason and find out how Rachel is."

"Okay, but let's visit your mom later and I'd say it's best we don't crowd Rachel for a couple of days. Why don't I call my mom and ask if we can go 'round for lunch. Then we can tell her about this rota thing…" *and make them fricking like you again.*

She smiled and nodded. "Okay."

After she stood, she slipped on her dressing gown, then left the room.

She had no idea my family hated her now and I wasn't gonna tell her. She didn't need to know.

When we walked in to my house, Mom, Dad and Eva stood in a row, like the bloody defense on a football pitch, about to charge.

My hand rested on Lindy's shoulder, making it clear I was gonna protect her. I stared at them, saying without words—*don't cause any trouble, be nice.*

Lindy's arm surrounded my waist in return and she leaned into me.

Eva's gaze dropped, looking at Lindy's fingers as they pulled at my waist.

I hoped Eva saw things were different.

"Lindy." Mom said stiffly, turning away. "Do you want to come help me dish up."

Shit, if she was gonna interrogate Lindy I'd strangle her.

"Billy," Dad said, "Let's lay the table." Frick this was an ambush, they'd planned to split us up for some reason. Eva smiled at me, confirming it, then disappeared into the kitchen, following Mom and Lindy.

"If Mom says anything mean to her…" I ground out as Dad turned and gave me the tablecloth.

"She won't, she's just—"

"Testing her. I know. It's bullshit, Dad." I flicked the cloth out over the table then grabbed the cutlery from his hand, trying to get this done as quickly as possible so I could get into the kitchen to help her.

Lindy

"It's nice to see you, Lindy."

Some sort of undercurrent flowed into the room, right along with the Mrs. Worrall's words. I glanced at Eva. There was something in her eyes as she smiled.

Neither of them sounded like they were really happy I was here.

"Thank you, Mrs. Worrall."

"How is Miriam?"

"Not well, but coping better now she's in the hospice."

"Here, would you tip the salad into this dish and toss it in the dressing while I get the plates out? Eva, can you put the lasagna on the table?"

An empty bowl and a large packet of salad leaves stood on the side. I pulled the packet open as Eva took the lasagna away.

"So Billy said you two are dating now…" Why did that sound like annoyance?

My forehead scrunched, at the cold and clinical pitch in her voice and I glanced at her, but she wasn't looking at me. "Yeah."

"And how long have you liked him for…?"

She was asking something else, not that, but she still didn't look at me. I picked up the bottle of dressing and drizzled it over the lettuce. Eva came back in.

I swallowed, trying to work out the answer to whatever Mrs. Worrall was not asking… "I'm sure you heard we got closer before Christmas." There were enough rumors. Heat brewed under my skin. "And Billy took me away a couple of months back. We have kind of been on and off since then, because of Mom being ill. But now we're properly on. You don't mind him staying over mine do you?"

I looked at Mrs. Worrall and saw Eva standing behind her glaring at me.

Didn't she like me?

Mrs. Worrall faced me, a look of speculation and deep intensity in her eyes. Like she was trying to look inside me to see an answer to the question she hadn't asked. She judged me badly.

Oh my God. They didn't want him at my place, or me here. They didn't like me. They didn't want him dating me.

Billy came in and my heart leaped, flying out to grip a hold of him. Not literally, just metaphorically. Really Billy came to me, our gazes locking, and mine probably telling him how relieved and pleased I was he'd come in here.

His arm wrapped around my shoulders.

He knew.

He knew they didn't like me.

"Mom," he said in a deep pitch. It warned her to leave me alone.

What had I done to them to make them hate me?

Billy's fingers squeezed me against him, like he knew I'd panicked. I turned to him, my arms wrapping about his waist and clinging as he talked over my head. "Have you heard about Rachel?"

"Yes, she's in a hospital isn't she?" Eva said.

"Yeah, she disappeared last night, Lindy and I found her down at the swings in the lower park. She's been off her meds because she was feeding Saint and her bipolar has reared up. We saw Mr. and Mrs. Macinlay last night and told them what had happened."

"Oh," his mom said.

"Lindy and I are gonna go visit Rachel, tomorrow probably, after work, if Jason says she's up to it. Lindy is going to go back to working in the store as well, until Rachel is better at least."

"Oh." The second, oh, of acknowledgement was different. Some thought had leaked into her pitch.

"Yeah," Billy said in an odd tone, like it was meant to mean something.

Gaining courage and telling myself to stop being so stupid, I let him go and straightened up. "We talked to Ester last night about sorting out a visiting rota for Mom. Mom didn't want visitors at home, she's been too ill and too worried about what people think. She's lost touch with everyone. But I've persuaded her to let people visit. She needs more company than Dad and I. We'll bore her stupid if it's us all the time, especially as the doctors think it will be weeks before…" I couldn't say the word, die… "So it would be good if her old friends spend some time talking to her. She gets tired, so people would only need to pop in for half an hour. Ester has agreed and maybe you could help her set it up, if that would be okay?"

Sympathy touched Mrs. Worrall's gaze now. Pity. Mom would hate it if she just turned up out of pity. "Of course, Lindy. I'll call Ester in the morning and we'll sort something out, and maybe we can both go up and visit Miriam tomorrow while you're working."

"Thank you," I nodded, and looked at Eva, who was still staring at me.

Did they not like Mom either? I wanted to ask… But how did you ask a question like that.

The conversation was stilted and awkward at times over dinner. But every time I felt uncertain, Billy caught a hold of my hand and squeezed it, and I glanced up at him and smiled a thank you. It didn't really matter what his family thought. It only mattered what he thought.

Every time I looked at him a warm, mushy feeling tumbled around in my belly.

It *really* didn't matter what *anyone* else thought about us being together. I was glad we were together.

Chapter Twenty-three

Lindy

Life was so strange. How could it settle into a pattern and feel normal when Mom was dying? But it did. It had.

Working back in the store gave me a new focus for my thoughts. I knew Mom was ill, but the hospice was safe, and she had friends again, who helped her. Every lunchtime I went there and did her hair, her makeup and her nails before she had a visitor so she felt good before they came in.

Billy and I visited early in the evening together and when Dad got there we left him and Mom alone. I know Dad mostly just sat and held her hand because by then she was really tired.

I had friends too, and my best girlfriend—Rachel. That is how bizarre my life had become. But she's the only person who seems to understand how hard it is watching Mom die.

Rachel hadn't seen her mom since she'd been really young. She'd run away from home. Her mom had bipolar too, but had never taken any medication. Rachel understood what it was like losing her mother, just in a different way.

Our friendship had started when Rachel had come out of the hospital. She'd been really doped-up, and not very talkative when Billy and I had visited her on the hospital ward, but after she'd got home they'd gradually balanced her meds, and we'd started having heart-to-hearts—about Jason and Billy—about love—about life.

We'd spent hours talking at Jason's parents. I'd just gone round to keep her company, but talking to her had started getting addictive because she'd had such a colorful life. I would have a heart made out of iron if I hadn't been moved by some of the stuff she'd said.

Two months on from that, she came down to the store regularly, with Saint. Just to talk and help out, and at lunch we often headed over to the diner to eat and talk. I'd introduced her to some of my old friends from school too. Friends I hadn't seen for years who I had reconnected with.

I was starting to get my life on track.

And I had Billy.

He stayed at mine a lot, but not every night. When I went out with friends, he stayed away.

I missed him, though, when he didn't sleep over, and I missed him when he didn't come out with me, but I knew I couldn't become reliant on him like I had on Jason. I had to make myself happy first. That was one of the things that talking to Rachel had taught me and my counselor agreed and encouraged.

Rachel loved Jason, but it was Rachel who'd turned her life around after she'd met him.

"Hey, Lind." Jason, walked into the store from the back office, carrying his laptop. Rachel stood on the customer side of the counter. She turned around.

"Jason."

"Honey." He put the laptop down on the counter. He often sat out here working now, even when Rachel wasn't around.

Saint was tucked up in the carrier, in front of Rachel. Jason rubbed his head then pressed a kiss on it. Saint made a croaky little sound as Jason straightened and kissed Rachel, his fingers cradling the back of her head.

I smiled. I liked watching them together. They were good together. It didn't make me jealous; Billy and I were good together too.

My cell rang.

It was probably him.

I picked it up. It wasn't Billy's image, though. It was Dad's.

"Hey…"

"Lindy…" I knew from his pitch. "The hospice called. I'm on my way there. Can you get someone to give you a lift?"

Tears flooded my eyes and spilled over. I wiped them away. "Is she unconscious—"

"Not yet…"

Mom had been getting worse, but… "How long?"

"They said her heartbeat is really weak. It could be hours, Lindy, love."

I cried, sniffing back tears and trying to breathe. "I'll get there." I couldn't say anymore.

The call ended. Dad probably wasn't able to speak either.

Tears running in rivers down my cheeks, I turned to find Jason behind the counter. "Lindy?"

"She's dying. I need to get to the hospice."

"I'll drive you."

"No, I'll call Billy. His last client was in town, he'll be near here."

My thumb had already found his number. I touched call. It rang three times as I held the cell to my ear, my hand shaking.

"Lindy, I'm—"

"Billy…" I sobbed. "It's Mom, I need to get to the hospice…"

"Where are you? At the store still?"

"Yeah."

"Okay, I'm coming… I'm sorry, I'm gonna have to call this session short, you'll have to do a cool-down on your own, my girlfriend's mom is really sick…" He ended the call.

I turned to grab my purse.

"I'll get your coat." Jason's voice was heavy with concern.

Rachel touched my arm and gave me an understanding look.

I couldn't stop shaking. All the years I had known this was

coming—the last few weeks… Nothing had prepared me for the pain in my chest… Nausea twisted in my belly.

Jason brought my coat out and held it up for me to put on.

Tears flowed onto my cheeks, as pain stole the air from lungs, and fear made me tremble.

A customer walked in. "I'll handle it," Rachel said quietly, as Jason gripped my arm.

"I'll come outside and wait with you," he said.

He kept a hold of my arm as we walked. Then outside, before the steps, he hugged me.

I didn't want him to hug me. I wanted Billy's broad chest, big arms, and the heartfelt emotion he showed for me. "Honestly, I'll drive you up—"

I pulled away, feeling stung. I didn't want him to. I wanted to be with Billy. "No, I'll wait for Billy." My voice was sharp. The old me I guess. The short-tempered bitch, but that was just because I was so worried over Mom, and panicking.

I needed Billy.

Jason rubbed my arm. I sensed he wanted to say, *it'll be okay*, but it wasn't gonna be okay. The end was here. I was losing her.

We stood there for about five minutes, waiting until Billy's SUV pulled up. He'd sped here, and he leaped out the driver's seat as I hurried down the steps, Jason followed.

Billy pulled the passenger door open. He had his work gear on: shorts and a tee. I threw myself into his arms, he was already moving to hug me and he gripped me hard and tight. It felt so good to have him here. He smelt of fresh sweat from working with clients, but I didn't care. Even the familiarity of that wrapped around me.

I love you. The words slipped through my head. It was the first time I'd thought them—but I'd felt them before.

I didn't say them to him, it wasn't the right time.

"Come on, let's get you there." He turned away, holding the door as I climbed in and looked at Jason. "Thanks."

Jason's lips closed and an understanding expression passed across his face as I shut the door.

There was nothing to say...

Chapter Twenty-four

Billy

The coffin gradually disappeared out of sight, then the men let the tapes they'd lowered it with drop. Lindy stepped forward and threw a white rose down on to the coffin. When she stepped back her hand searched for mine. I gripped it hard, making sure she knew I was around for her.

Her dad bent and picked up a handful of soil and threw that down. It made a sprinkling sound and then he threw a red rose, and that made no sound at all.

Something hard gripped my heart and my vision distorted with tears.

I hadn't been in the room when Mrs. Martin died. Lindy thought she wouldn't have wanted me in there. Lindy had said goodbye with her dad.

We'd got up there in time for Lindy to speak to her mom and say a last "I love you", and her mom had gripped her hand and then slipped into unconsciousness. She'd been unconscious for five hours before she'd passed. I'd waited in the dayroom, promising Lindy I wasn't going anywhere as she'd just sat and held her mom's hand.

Lindy had talked me through it all afterwards, several times. I was encouraging her to keep talking. I thought that was the most important thing—that she felt as though her mom lived; because she did live, in Lindy's heart and in her memories, and she needed to keep those memories alive.

Tears tracked down my cheeks and Lindy sobbed. I think everyone here was crying. If they weren't they had hearts of stone.

Others came forward to throw soil down on to the coffin and say their goodbye, including Jason and his parents, although Rachel stayed back.

Lindy stood in silence, watching. I knew her thoughts were not silent. I bet she cried out a thousand words in her head.

I couldn't even imagine being in her position and yet she seemed to be coping. I mean they'd had long enough warning...

The first thing Lindy had said to me when she came out of her Mom's room, after she'd passed was... "At least she won't be in pain anymore... It was time..."

But it must hurt to lose the mom she'd been so close to and they had been really close.

I was not just crying for poor Miriam and the years cancer had stolen from her life. I cried for Lindy too, and the years she would have to live without her mom.

Lindy

"Lindy, dear, how are you? Go and find Billy and take a break, you must be exhausted." Billy's mom rubbed my arm, leaning past me to put another plate of sandwiches down. The church had been packed full of people and now Billy's house was full of people and everyone wanted to talk to me and offer condolences.

Billy's mom had kindly offered her house up, so she could host and take the pressure off Dad and me, but I still felt like I should host.

The whole thing was emotionally exhausting.

I'd lost Billy an hour ago, and lost the drink he'd given me an hour ago.

"Where is he?"

"Outback, in the yard with Jason and his cousins."

Billy's mom, Susan, had taken me under her wing in the last few weeks. Billy had let on a few weeks back that his family had all known for ages how much he'd thought of me, and that now we'd got together they were all waiting for me to rip his heart out. So I'd gone out of my way to make sure they knew how much I thought of him. Though he still didn't know it yet… I loved him.

"Go on, dear. You escape and go out there for a little while."

"Okay." It took me a while to get out though as so many people stopped me to say "How sorry I am", and "If you need anything." The town had turned its back on me last Christmas when it had found out I'd slept with Billy before Jason and I had split. Now they couldn't do enough for me. I didn't really care about their shallow sentiments.

Billy spotted me as soon as I got out the door. He had a bottle of beer in his hand. He put it down and lifted his arm. Jason, Rachel and Jason's cousins all stood around, in black dresses and suits. Rachel had on a black dress too. She was so skinny you'd never know she'd had a kid.

I slotted under Billy's arm as I reached them, and it came down over my shoulders.

I love you. Those words had echoed in my head a ton of times since the day Mom had died, but I still hadn't said them aloud, it didn't seem right to say them now. He'd think it was just because of everything that had been going on and how good he'd been to me. I wanted him to know when I said them that it was just about him.

"You, okay?" he said in a low pitch as the others kept talking.

"Yeah. Just taking a breather."

"If you need me to do anything, or stay hanging around with you, just ask…"

"You're okay, you're doing good…" I knew he'd do anything for me, absolutely anything…

He kissed my temple, and I hugged his middle, as Jason said

something to him.

Then Jason's cousin Richard chimed in a defensive pitch. "I don't know why you all have it in for Ryan..."

"He keeps getting you in trouble." Jason's voice rang with the depth and command he'd never used when talking to me—until the end. "You should drop him."

"I'm not dropping him. He looks out for me, and I look out for him. That's the way it works with the Doyles"

"In a jail cell..." Billy scoffed. "Why the hell are you hanging with the Doyles? The whole family is trouble."

"They look out for each other."

"Exactly!" Jason said more aggressively than I had ever heard him. "They look out for themselves!"

"They don't give a fuck about you..." Billy added.

"That's not true." Richard threw back before taking a drink from his beer, while his eyes looked from one person in the little group surrounding him to another.

They'd got Richard pinned, then. Everyone had been talking about his friendship with Ryan Doyle for ages. I hadn't paid any attention to it. I had too much of my own stuff going on, but apparently in the last year, from what I'd heard, Richard had changed completely and got into loads of trouble because of the Doyles.

Jason caught hold of Richard's arm and turned him away from everyone else, I could hear him speaking in a hard, whispered tone, obviously giving his cousin an earful, although I couldn't hear the words. I'd never known Jason be like that. I guess his family were really pissed off with Richard over it.

Billy ran a hand over my hair. I looked up.

"Do you want me to sleep over tonight, or would you rather be alone with your dad?"

Billy's dark-blue eyes shone with understanding—and love. "I think he needs me tonight. We agreed we'd sit up and watch some old home movies, and drink, and say our personal farewell to her like that."

"She's not gone, Lind. If she's still in your head and your heart, she's still alive… Just without pain."

He said the sweetest things. I smiled. I hadn't smiled all day. "I know." She was with me. She'd said she'd watch over me as an angel, and I felt her. I had done since about six hours after she'd died. It was truly like her spirit hovered in the air I breathed—watching, caring—loving—and smiling at Billy's tenderness.

His head bent and he kissed my lips. It was just a little press of his lips against mine, but it said so much more. *I love you,* the words were in my head again as I held his gaze.

"I love you, Lind." My smile lifted but I still didn't say the words back. He must know I felt them anyway. I was sure my eyes said it.

Chapter Twenty-five

Lindy

"Billy,"

"Lindy? What's wrong?" He'd heard the tears in my voice, just from his name spoken on the cell.

"It's Dad. Will you come over and pick me up? Can I stay at your parents' tonight?"

"Sure. I've just finished, I'm packing up, can I shower at yours—?"

"No, Dad and I have fallen out. I don't want to hang around. Pick me up and shower at yours. If that's okay?"

"It's okay, I'll be there in half an hour. I'll be as quick as I can."

"See you soon."

"I love you, Lind."

He ended the call. My hand holding my cell dropped as Dad knocked on my bedroom door.

"There is no need to make such a fuss, Lindy. It's just dinner."

"At our house!" I didn't get up. I didn't want him in my room. He came in anyway, opening the door, stepping inside and then leaning against the wall, the door handle still in his hand.

"At my house."

"At Mom's house! I don't want her sitting at the table—and if you let her stay!" Tears streamed down my cheeks as anger tied knots in my belly.

"Lindy, be sensible. Life has to continue—"

"In a year, or two years, not now. Not so soon. Mom only died four months ago!"

"And she was sick for years. I want my life back. I am entitled to move on, Lindy. You have Billy."

"It's not the same. She was not my wife! Didn't you love her?"

"Of course I loved her. But she was sick for a long time and I have grieved for a long time… It's time for me to build a life again—"

"I HATE YOU!" I threw the words at him, standing up. I had to get out. Get away from him. I couldn't believe he could be so disloyal. That he could forget her so easily.

"I'm going out," I said, grabbing my coat and pushing past him. He caught hold of my arm, but I pulled it free.

"Lindy—"

I covered my ears walking past him. "I don't want to hear what you have to say. Billy is coming to get me. I won't be home tonight…" I glanced back. "So you can do whatever you want with this woman! But don't expect me to ever like her!"

I ran along the hall and out the door, letting it slam shut behind me—away from him, away from the house and away from the memories I couldn't face.

How could he?

How could he!

Mom!

I ran down the steps and out into the street. I thought Billy would come from the left, so I headed that way, running, but after a few yards I slowed to a walk, sobbing as tears streamed down my cheeks.

"Mom, I'm sorry. He isn't the dad I thought I knew." I said the words out loud, to her, to the sky, looking up.

"I thought he loved you." But how could he have loved her and forget her so quickly? I didn't get it.

She was still with me. She had a physical presence in me and around me. How could he just move on?

I stopped walking, squatting down and covering my face, and then kneeling on the sidewalk. I hurt so much inside. I hurt for her. For the life she was going to miss. Over Dad's betrayal. Tears trickled in paths down my cheeks, as my hands dropped.

He hadn't just betrayed her, he was betraying me too!

Billy's SUV pulled up next to me. I cried even harder. "Lindy!" He'd jumped out and stood next to me. "Lindy, what are you doing out here? What's wrong?" He came down on one knee.

I turned and held him. I couldn't stop crying.

"Come on, let's get you over to mine."

He picked me up. I clung to his neck and pressed my head into his shoulder. He had that sweaty end-of-a-work-day smell––I loved it.

"Let's get you strapped in and get you somewhere where you feel safe." His voice came out calm and strong as he pulled the door open, holding me so easily.

I missed him holding me as he left me on the seat and pulled the strap across, like I was a kid being buckled up.

I gripped his hand as he clicked the belt home, smiling, my tears finally drying up.

Billy just knew what I needed.

He smiled too, then shut the door and walked around to the other side of the SUV.

When he got in the driver's seat, he turned the engine on, then glanced at me. "What upset you?"

I started talking as he looked in the mirror and then pulled out. "You know Dad joined that dating website a month ago? Well, he told me today he has met some woman on it. He's seen her twice and he's asked her around to dinner. Tonight. To meet me!"

He looked over at me. "Shit!"

"I know, right. It isn't weird of me to be angry is it? Please tell me!"

He glanced at me, his expression stiff. "It isn't…"

"I can't believe he did it, and he thinks there's nothing wrong with it!" I carried on rambling, crying and complaining as he drove, and Billy was pure Billy, listening and letting me rant.

When we got to his parents', he pulled onto the drive and parked. I wiped the tears off my cheeks with my sleeve.

When he killed the engine, he didn't move to get out, but turned to me. "Are you okay, are you ready to go in?"

"I love you." The words burst out of my throat.

Freeing my belt, I leaned forward to hug him. "Oh Billy, I really do. I have for ages, but there has never seemed a right time to say it, and I give up, because there will never be a right time."

His fingers ran over my hair. "You don't have to say it, sweetheart."

I sat back. "But I want to, because I do. I LOVE YOU."

He laughed. "Have you been drinking?"

"No!"

"Do you want to tell me about your dad?"

"I've been telling you about Dad. He's a traitor!"

"That's a harsh word, darling…"

"Maybe, but he was supposed to love her. To love us!"

"He does love you." Billy's arm came around me and pulled me against him, as his other hand stroked through my hair.

"How can he?" I answered against Billy's collarbone, the scent seeping from his work gear invading my senses.

"Because he is a man, Lind. You have me, and he needs someone to turn to for comfort."

I sobbed against his sweaty tee.

"Just think about it. It isn't wrong that you're angry. Of course you are gonna be hurt and find it hard. You loved her in a different way to him. But she was his other half, and he's been hurting for a long time. He's looking for a way to ease his pain, and for him, that's through another woman, that's all, Lind."

I'd just been breathing as I listened to the rumble of words in his chest.

I sat up. "I hate you when you talk so fucking logically."

He laughed. "You just said you loved me…"

"I do… but not when you agree it's okay for Dad to move on and forget all about Mom after four months…"

"I'm not saying I agree. I wouldn't be moving on if it was you. Shit, Lindy, I hung around waiting on you to notice me for years. That isn't like me. But your dad is your dad, and I can understand why he might turn to someone. He hasn't forgotten your Mom. He's just learning how to live with the memories of her—that's why he's looking for another woman."

"Well, I don't care. I hate him looking for another woman. I don't want to be around any other woman. I don't want to be introduced to them. I don't even want to know or think about them."

"Then I've got an idea…"

"What?"

He twisted in his seat, his leg hooking up over the gear shift and he gripped my hand. "One day, Lindy, I'm gonna get down on one knee and look up into your eyes and ask you to marry me, and when I say it, I'm gonna make it a magical moment you are not gonna forget. You'll treasure it—we'll treasure it—for the rest of our lives, and we'll tell our kids all about it. But that day, and that moment, isn't now. I know you're not ready. But until it's the right time, and the right day, and you've healed properly from everything you've been through, then why don't we just get a place together…?"

He took a breath.

"We spend so much time sleeping over each other's, I've been feeling like I want somewhere that's just our place for weeks, but when your mom was sick, it wasn't the time, and then I thought you'd want to stay with your dad and not leave him alone… But now… If it would be easier… Why don't we just get somewhere together in Portland, rent a place, no commitments—just see how it goes…?"

I gripped his hand. "When you ask me to marry you, Billy, I am gonna say yes. I will be so happy. But you are such a good guy, because you're right, it's too soon. I couldn't be happy if we got married now. But when it's the right time, I am gonna walk up the aisle with a beaming smile." My gaze caught and held his. "But for now, yes, I do want to get a place together, that is just what I need. Thank you. I would love to live with you and build a home together, a place for us."

He smiled at me, his fingers wrapping around mine, and he opened his mouth. I knew what he was gonna say. "I love you," I said it first. "I really do. More than I ever loved Jason. It's like you are in my blood, flowing around in my veins, and you make my bones ache when I'm around you and when I am not around you I have a hole in my belly that wants to be with you. I love being with you. I just love everything about you…" Another tear rolled down my cheek as I smiled. His free hand came up and wiped it away. It was a happy tear now, though.

"I love you too."

"I know." I laughed.

"Come on, let's go tell my family the news. But we'll tell them after I shower. I stink. And then I'm gonna take you out to some swanky restaurant in Portland and we'll celebrate. okay?" His hand rubbed over my hair, messing it up.

"Yeah."

"Oh God, Billy." I sat back. "I don't just love you, I need you, though. You know that, right?"

"Yeah, because I need you too, Lind. I always have. Come on, let me go shower and then we can break the news to Mom and Dad, and Eva."

When we walked in, I could tell they'd seen us sitting outside in the SUV talking; his Mom and Eva had questions in their eyes.

Eva was still a little wary and suspicious of my motives, but Susan had been nothing but sweet to me and considerate, trying to be like a mom to me, and replace my own. No one ever would, but I really appreciated her being kind when I knew she was upset I had been breaking Billy's heart for years.

She'd learn I wasn't gonna do that ever again...

"I'm just gonna go shower, Mom," Billy said.

"Do you want dinner?" Susan answered, her gaze slipping to his work clothes and then looking at me, obviously wondering why I was here so early.

"No, I'm taking Lindy out to dinner."

"Okay." She smiled at me as Billy pulled on my hand to lead me on.

"Are you gonna wait in my room?"

I smiled at him. "If you want." I knew what that question really was. When I get out the shower do you want to have sex? Longing, want—and need—twisted up in my belly. I nodded, following him, pulled along by his hand gripping mine.

Billy

The water ran over my head in rivers—*because I do love you. I LOVE YOU...*

I LOVE YOU.

Shit.

Lindy had really said that.

A huge great, fat smile parted my lips.

I laughed out loud.

She'd said it. I'd sensed it, but who knew with Lindy...?

She'd said it!

Wow.

The words had exploded in my chest, like a firework shooting off.

After all this time... After years... The girl I loved—loved me!

As my hands rubbed the shampoo into my hair, the leather bracelet slid around on my wrist. The bracelet she'd given me when she was fifteen that I'd never taken off. Faith paid off. I'd always known what she knew now. That we needed each other...

We were soul mates.

I tipped my head back, washing out the shampoo and letting the water run over my body as I smiled again, rubbing the shower gel over the leopard on my chest. The damn thing felt more like a pussy cat now; it didn't scratch me at all.

Awesome!

I laughed again as I washed off the last of the soap. Then turned the shower off, grabbed a towel and wrapped it around my waist.

No one was in the hall when I walked through, and when I opened my bedroom door I found Lindy undressed and in bed.

Smiling, I slid the bolt on my bedroom door to lock it.

Now was the time to get our own place…

She flicked the covers back, giving me a get-in-here smile. I let my towel slip to the floor and dived on the bed.

She laughed as her hand came up and gripped my wet hair, just behind my ear. "I want to make love to the man I love."

"You'd better go on top then, if you're taking control." I rolled to my back and she came over me, straddling my hips. I gripped her thighs. I was already erect just at the thought of this, and she didn't wait, she slid down onto me, already wet.

My fingers clasped as she moved, rocking forward and up. I bit my lip as lust thrust a dagger deep and hard into my groin.

Her little breasts swayed and her hair slipped from her shoulder to her back as she smiled down at me, so obviously happy when less than an hour ago I'd found her crying in the street.

She loved me. I'd given her happiness.

I was gonna give it to her forever. My grip on her thighs firmed and I took over, I just wanted to send the girl into oblivion, and she was so light it was easy to hold her up as I pushed my hips up and shoved into her, over and over, in a hard pace that had her in spasms and dripping all around me in moments.

Her body tipped forward, her fingers clawing into my shoulders as she hung on and I assaulted.

It didn't feel different. She'd loved me for ages. I'd known it—but now she'd said it.

I claimed her body even more aggressively, and she panted and sighed, making little squeals of pleasure. Fortunately my bedroom was right at the end of the hall…

She broke again, on a sharp cry, and I followed her there, shutting my eyes and soaring high with her.

Shit.

"That was beautiful." Her fingers combed through my wet hair.

I opened my eyes, looking into the blue of hers and smiled. Then I slapped her ass. "Come on, get dressed! Then let's go tell my parents the news."

She grinned at me, pressed a kiss on my lips, then climbed off me and got up. As I toweled my hair dry, she snuck over to the bathroom with her clothes, to have a quick wash.

Then, when we were both dressed we headed off to face the inquisition. Lindy had a tell-tale just-done-it glow, though, that I bet Mom would spot. But so what? I'd taken her mind off her dad.

Mom was dishing up their dinner when we got down there, and she and Eva were in the kitchen.

I looked at Dad, "Would you come into the kitchen a minute?"

His eyebrows lifted, but he rose and followed us in there.

"Mom," I had Lindy's hand gripped tight in mine. Mom carried on dishing-up as Eva stared at me, then looked down at mine and Lindy's joined hands. I glanced back at Dad. "Lindy and I have decided to rent our own place; somewhere in Portland. We'll start looking tonight."

Mom dropped the pan and spoon she'd been holding on the counter. She didn't look at me, though, she looked at Lindy. "And that's really what you want. You're sure about this?"

Lindy nodded. "Yes, absolutely, we both agree it's the right time. It's too early for longer-term commitments yet. Billy has been really sweet. He's giving me time to get used to Mom being gone, but we both want to be together, and… why wait?" She took a breath. "When we love each other." She gave Mom a little smile and shrugged.

Mom seemed to look hard at her, like she was judging if it was the truth or not, but then she came forward to hug Lindy, hard, like she was really thankful. Lindy let go of my hand and hugged her back.

I looked at Dad. He just nodded his approval, then said, "I'm happy for you, son. That's fine by us." He lifted a hand. I shook it. It was like graduating again. He slapped my shoulder before turning to go back into the living room.

Eva flew at me. "I'm so happy for you," she whispered in my ear with her arms wrapped around my neck. I lifted her off her feet. Pretty much like that kid she'd been dating at school had done in the last few months. The girl had been walking around on air.

"Thanks." I whispered back. Then I set her down and let her go, smiling, as she turned to Lindy and hugged her too.

"You better look after my big brother..."

"Oh I will," Lindy answered, looking up at me. "He is gonna get back all the love he gives... and I owe him years of it. I'm in some deep debt."

When Eva let her go, I hugged my girl. Lifting her off her feet too, and kissing her near her ear, then whispering. "I'll never be able to love you any more than I do and I do not regret a single day. Now I am gonna just make sure that you know every moment how precious you are to me, and how much I need you."

She laughed, a delicious soft sound. "Same..."

Author's Word

What happened when Jason went back to New York is at the end of Just You, the story of Jason's work friend Justin, who he knew when he met Rachel. Jason's and Rachel's story will also continue in the next book in the Starting Out Series, and you'll hear more about Lindy and Billy too.

So where did my inspiration come from for I Need You? Well, I was never like Lindy at school. I hung around with the popular people and I had a friend like Lindy, the prettiest in the school year. In comparison, I was always insecure, self-conscious, awkward and hard on myself. I never had lots of boyfriends at school; I did not come into my own until my late twenties, when I finally believed in and liked myself.

But I discovered when I met the people I thought were perfect after school that they too had suffered numerous insecurities. Most of us have something that pulls us down and holds us back.

In my head I am still very much a new adult, but I have the advantage now of having faced and survived many hardships and those have made me a stronger person who has learned self-belief. If I can help others reach that point at an earlier stage through my books that is what I would like to do.

Like Lindy, push your boundaries, face up to your insecurities, blow them out of the water, and you can be whoever you want to be and achieve whatever you want to achieve. Self-belief is always the first step.

For more information about my New Adult romances find me on facebook https://www.facebook.com/JaneLark.NABooks and follow me on Twitter@JaneLnabooks.

Bonus Material

Rachel and Jason's story started in *I Found You* and is available to buy now. Read on for an exclusive sneak peek at chapter one below!

I Found You

Chapter One

The beat of the music pounded through my earphones, drowning out the loud rattle of the subway trains. I was in the zone. My heart was racing, my feet striking the pavement with the rhythm of the bassline as I ran.

The monotony of city life swamped me in the day, but running brought me back from it at night.

God, I missed home, and fuck it was cold.

Too cold to snow. I heard the words Dad always repeated. I'd always thought it a myth. Was it ever too cold to snow? I didn't know, but people had been saying it all day.

The pavement was dry, not icy. Dry with cold. There was no moisture in the air, only the cloud of my breath, as my lungs filled and then exhaled with the pace of my strides.

Maybe it was true. God, there were so many myths in the world. Like, New York City was the place to be. It still felt like new shoes to me, like it just didn't fit.

The asphalt felt firm beneath my sneakers.

I looked forward, trying to increase my pace and energy, burning away the doubts and disappointments I'd felt since I came to the city.

At the end of the bridge there was a figure, caught in the middle of a beam of orange lamplight, like some illuminated angel. I generally only saw other guys jogging on the bridge path. It was rare to see anyone else.

It was Thanksgiving in little over a week and Christmas in a few weeks. Lindy was pissed I wasn't going back home, but she'd made up her mind to come to me for Christmas.

Was that good or bad?

The figure was facing the Brooklyn Bridge, probably looking at the reflection of the lights glinting and shifting on the dark water. It was mesmerizing when you focused on it.

The Manhattan Bridge was never busy, probably because of the noise of the trains. The environment didn't inspire pleasure, so it wasn't a place for tourists. But it was a good path for running: long and straight, and normally empty.

I ran harder, my eyes focusing on the figure.

The person hadn't moved. They held their hands up, gripping the metal grill above them.

The pose seemed odd. A little desperate. It wasn't casual.

My imagination shifted, no longer picturing angels but a horror movie. The way the lamplight shone down on the figure was like they were in the sights of a hovering helicopter, or a beam from a UFO.

I thought of Christmas again, and ached for home. But I wasn't going home. I had to conquer New York.

The light shining down on the stranger suddenly took the form of a Godly benediction once more. The person's arms shifted, stretching out, similar to a crucifixion pose, hands wide and high as they looked upward.

I was getting nearer.

My fingers were numb with the cold, even inside my gloves, and my ears burned as the frost nipped beneath my hood. Running should've kept me warm, but it was twenty-one degrees Fahrenheit, way below freezing point.

Fuck, now I could see the person ahead was standing in a t-shirt. Their outstretched arms were bare.

"Hey!" My heart rate thundered as I ran on, wondering what sort of sketchy city-nutter I was running toward. What were they doing wearing a tee in this weather? It didn't look like a homeless dude, but…

My breaths grew more uneven.

The guy ahead hadn't heard me.

I pulled my earphones out. "Hey!"

Still no recognition. It was like they were in some sort of trance.

My feet pounded on the concrete.

It wasn't a guy, it was a girl. I'd seen the long hair way back, but hadn't been sure. Plenty of guys had long hair. But now, I could see.

I knocked my hood back. I didn't want to scare her. "Hey!"

Nothing. Not a single sign of recognition and I was only yards away. She was wearing skinny jeans and sneakers with her tee.

Her hands moved, catching hold of the wire like she was going to climb it, then her foot lifted, seeking a grip on the railing.

Her arms bracing her weight; her other foot lifted. What the hell was she doing? Trying to go over the wire? Did she want to jump? "Hey! Wait!"

I ran harder.

Fuck. She looked serious and she carried on climbing, searching out hand and foot holds.

"Are you crazy? Stop it!"

As I ran the last few yards her gaze finally turned to me. I covered the distance in moments, watching her clinging on the wire, Spiderman style.

God knows what she saw in my eyes. I could see nothing in hers except maybe fear. They were huge, and dark, staring at me like I was the weird one.

I wasn't the weird one.

My music continued playing muted sounds and air rasped into my lungs as I stopped. I lifted a hand, palm up, offering to help her down. "Come on…" My breath fogged the air around us. "Nothing's that bad…"

She held still. Her eyes had no depth. It was like looking into mirrors, reflecting back the electric light. She looked a little mad.

"Let me help you."

She was panting as hard as I was. She didn't come down.

She was only a couple of feet off the floor, I could pull her down, but I didn't want to scare her.

My fingers instinctively lifted and touched her lower back. I could feel the breath pulling into her lungs. "Look, seriously, you don't want to do anything foolish."

She didn't move.

"What's your name?" Shit. My heart was still racing like I was running. I looked along the bridge path, but there was no one else here to help.

"Honey, come on down. I can't let you do it."

She was just staring at me.

What the hell did cops say to persuade a person…? "You must be cold, you can have my hoodie. I'm not going to leave you here."

This was like some TV drama.

My hands were trembling from the blood burning in my muscles. I'd gone from running hard to standing still. A weight of responsibility fell on me suddenly. This girl's life was in my hands. I'd been running wrapped up in my own world and now… Shit. "Really. Please… Come down."

Pleading obviously touched some nerve in her, as one foot came back down onto the concrete, her cotton t-shirt catching on my glove and crumpling up, revealing the pale skin of her lower back. My gaze dropped to her plain white sneakers, as the next foot touched the ground.

Relief washed through me on a wave as I lifted my hand so her t-shirt slid back down. I looked up and met her gaze. It was still blank though, and her fingers gripped the wire.

I touched her shoulder. It lifted as air pulled into her lungs, before slipping back out. I didn't know why I was touching her, but I just… I needed to know she was okay. She didn't seem to know where she was, or what she'd been doing.

A dark smear marked her face, and whatever it was, it stained her hair too.

Every sermon I'd endured as a kid raced through my head. Help the needy; put others first; don't walk past that mugged guy in the street. I hadn't gone to church for years, not since I'd hit my teens, but religion was stitched into my DNA. No way could I walk past a person in need.

My shock dissipating, I stripped off my hoodie. The smell of my sweat permeated the cold air. She probably wouldn't want it but she needed it. "How long have you been up here? It's freezing." She could have been up here half an hour. She hadn't been here when I'd run over the bridge into Manhattan.

For a minute I didn't think she'd take it, but then her hand reached out. "I don't know?"

"You know it's twenty-one degrees Fahrenheit, right? You'll get hyperthermia." She looked at me, her eyes still dead. "I'm Jason… Were you trying to do what I thought?"

She didn't answer.

I held out my hand. "Hi."

She didn't shake my hand, just looked at it.

"Look, nothing can be that bad. You'll get over it, and be glad you didn't jump."

"Will I?" Her pitch was mocking, although maybe she was mocking her own thoughts, not my words, nothing in her eyes or her face told me though.

What now? I could hardly just run on and leave her here. Dammit. "I…" I could take her to emergency… What would they do? Check her over and spit her out. "Have you got any family locally?"

"No."

"Friends?"

"No."

Her large eyes confirmed what she'd said. She had nowhere to go. Her full lips pouted a little. Shit. What did I do?

"Where do you live then? Is there somewhere I can take you?"

She was pretty. Her face glowed in the electric light, showing a clear complexion and perfectly even features, though her skin was yellowish in this light.

"No. Nowhere."

Why was she here? What had made her life too hard to carry on?

She shivered, and pain etched its expression on her face, then tears suddenly glittered in her eyes, and the coldness in them became a lake of desolation. "I need to get away."

"From what?"

She didn't answer, but her teeth started chattering. I lifted the hood of my sweatshirt over her blonde hair.

"Look, obviously things aren't okay for you. What are you going to do?"

"I don't know."

I took a breath, looking at her and hoping some magical solution would suddenly hit me. It didn't, and I was getting cold now.

She shivered again and her arms crossed, her hands gripping the opposite elbows. She'd stopped looking at me. She was looking at the sky, like she was searching for answers too.

I sighed, my fingers running over my hair. She was nearly as tall as me, and I was six foot one. She must be at least five eight. But she was slender, like a model. My sweatshirt swamped her figure. She looked fragile.

Shit. There was nothing I could do. "What are you going to do, if I go?"

Her shoulders lifted in a shrug, but she didn't look down.

My heart was thumping to the same rhythm as the bass beat now pounding out of the earphones dangling 'round my neck

I couldn't leave her out here…

"Have you really got nowhere to go?"

She shook her head, making her blonde ponytail sweep over her back.

Shit. What option did I have? What option did she have?

"Have you got any money?"

Her head shook again. But her stillness, apart from her shaking head, made me feel like she didn't even care. I felt stupid then, of course she didn't care. She'd just tried to end her life by throwing herself off a bridge. She obviously didn't care about anything right now.

What to do with her? I could give her money… But I'd have to go back to my apartment to get my card and take her to a cash dispenser. And what would she do with it? Maybe she'd already taken something. Drugs or drink. Maybe that was why she was so dead looking. I'd be stupid to give her money.

I sighed again. I could call the cops and take her to a station. But what would they care? *I found this girl and she's got nowhere to stay.* They'd say, yeah, right, join the line of a couple of hundred other homeless people in New York.

There wasn't any choice. "I could take you home with me, if you've got nowhere to go. Just for tonight. It would give you chance to get your head straight, and get warm. If you want?"

"I…" She looked at me again then, her eyes losing their depth once more and setting up shutters, locking me out.

"What do you think?" I got another shrug, but her eyes suddenly filled with depth, letting me see into the thoughts behind her gaze. They were asking me questions.

"What are you going to do if you don't come back with me?" Another shrug. "Have you got any other options?" She shook her head, her ponytail swaying, but her gaze was clinging to mine now, like was she was considering me. Maybe she was trying to judge if she'd be safe.

This was surreal, like I'd been lifted out of real life, and placed in the middle of a fucking film. Question was; how was it going to play out? Taking her home was a risk, but sometimes risks had to be taken. Like coming to New York.

I sighed again. Sometimes taking risks didn't pay off. But I still hoped they would.

She shivered and her hands gripped her arms harder.

I lifted my hands palm outward. "I swear. I'm the nice guy. And if you've got nowhere else to go…" Lindy would go mad, but this was devil or deep-blue-sea territory. How could I leave this woman here? She'd nowhere to sleep and it was twenty-one degrees Fahrenheit.

Her shoulders shook as she shivered again.

"It's not far. I live in DUMBO."

"Down under the Manhattan Bridge Overpass…" she whispered. "It's such a cool name for a neighborhood."

I laughed. She didn't.

"Have you got any other choice?"

She shook her head.

"Then on my life, if you come, I'll not hurt you."

She said nothing just looked at me.

"My apartment's warm. You can't stay out here…" Shit, I was probably just as crazy as her, offering to take a stranger back with me.

"I…"

"I swear, you're safe with me."

She looked back at the wire, then down at the water.

"You don't want to do that. Just give it a night, you'll feel different in the morning."

She shook her head, still looking at the water.

If zombies were real, they'd look like her. My sweatshirt swamping her, she stood like a sorrowful statue, her complexion as pale as marble.

I couldn't just leave her. I rubbed her arms, gently, answering an instinct to put my arm around her, but I denied that. I didn't even know her name.

"Look, you can trust me. Honest. When we get back to my apartment you can call my Mom, or my friends, and they'll all tell you I'm the nice guy. Seriously, if you need references…" I smiled as she looked back at me, trying to convince her. "What do you say? Are you a gambler? Are you going to try trusting me?" Silence and stillness. This girl was messed up. But then I'd known that from the moment I'd seen her. She'd been standing in the freezing cold, in a tee, trying to jump off a bridge.

I held her gaze, trying to look inside her, as she looked back, trying to see inside me.

Once more there was a sudden pool of desolation and a glitter in her eyes, and she simply nodded, making the choice to put herself into the hands of a stranger—my hands.

Shit. *I was taking her home.* She could be a drug addict. I'd been so busy trying to persuade her, I'd forgotten about my own concerns. But I couldn't leave her here alone; fragility and loneliness rang from her, like she was crying out for help. And the damned Good Samaritan story I'd been brought up on wouldn't let me leave her in the street.

But what the hell was I getting myself into?

"This way." My fingers carefully closed about her upper arm, and I guided her to turn and start walking off the bridge with me, like this was a normal thing to do—like every night of the week, I took a stranger home. My guts churned. This was crazy. But my fingers wrapped right about her skinny arm, and my instincts yelled at me that she needed protecting, and she needed safety. I could let her have a haven for a few days.

She was probably a size zero, she was so skinny.

Lindy would kill to be size zero. She would hate me taking this woman home. She wasn't flooded with human kindness. She wouldn't have felt any instinct to help this woman.

"You haven't told me your name yet?" I prodded as we descended the steps onto the street.

She was moving robotically. I was a stranger to her, too, and she hadn't questioned me verbally at all. She was going home with a guy she didn't know.

Maybe she did this all the time.

Maybe her lack of concern should warn me off.

As if sensing my thoughts, she stopped and looked at me, hard, really looking into me, like she'd done on the bridge just now, maybe at last deciding she ought to check me out a little more. "It's Rachel."

"Rachel—pleased to meet you. My apartment's in a block near here, it's not far. You're sure about this, yeah? I could still take you somewhere else, if you like?"

"I've got nowhere else to go. So I haven't got any choice. You don't mind?"

I do, really, but I'm not mean enough to dump you here. "No, I don't mind."

I pressed my code in when we reached the building, feeling guilty for covering it up, showing I didn't trust her, but I didn't know her.

"My furniture's a bit sparse at the moment. I only just moved in a couple of months back. Don't expect anything fancy…" We entered the elevator and I pressed the button. "I'm on the fifth floor." That was obvious, the red light behind button five glowed, announcing it.

I turned and looked at her. What I'd thought was dirt on her face and in her hair, was dried blood. "Did you hit your head?"

Her gaze struck mine, questioning and cold, and in the white light of the elevator, I faced green eyes. They were a misty green, an unusual sort of green. I'd never seen that eye color before. She didn't answer me though. She hadn't spoken since she'd given me her name, and her fingers were curled up, hidden in the sleeves of my sweatshirt, as her arms gripped across her chest.

She looked down at my Adam's apple.

"You don't have to be worried."

Those green eyes looked up again. "I'm not scared of you. You gave me your hoodie. People who are generally mean, don't give you stuff they need themselves."

It was an odd, but reasonable, logic. "Yeah, well…." I didn't know what to say, yet all my friends in Oregon would say I was never lost for words. "Okay."

The elevator bell rang, announcing that we'd reached the fifth floor, and then the doors opened.

I looked away from her. She was a little too beautiful for comfort. She had untouchable celeb-magazine beauty, the sort you knew you'd never have, so you never wanted. Lindy was pretty, but there was a quality of perfection in this Rachel. Yet she wasn't perfect was she, or her life wasn't, she'd been trying to jump off Manhattan Bridge.

I wanted to know what led her there, but I wasn't going to make her feel like I was prying, I didn't ask.

I pulled the key from the pocket of my joggers, unlocked the door and stepped back to let her go first, flicking the lights on.

"Chivalrous to a fault…" she whispered. "Do you stand up for pregnant and elderly women on subway trains?"

Actually I did. Lindy always said I was a dying breed. Mom always took credit. "And sometimes I even carry their shopping back."

She looked at me again. "You don't come from New York do you? Are you some hillbilly?"

"I'm from Oregon, from a small town there."

"Out of college and flying the nest…"

She sounded like she was laughing at me, but there was no humor in her face or her eyes. What I saw was grief.

"Do you want some coffee, I can make a pot? It'll warm you up." I took her fingers. I could feel how cold they were even through my gloves. They were like blocks of ice. I rubbed them for a moment.

Her hands fell when I let them go.

I felt awkward, but the only thing to do now I'd brought her back here, was to act like I was completely comfortable with it.

I took off my gloves. They were damp. How'd they get damp?

There was no life in her eyes, once more, when her gaze met mine.

She turned and looked about the room. It was empty bar my TV, my Xbox and a beanbag.

I left her and went to make coffee. The kitchen was to one side of the living space.

"The bathroom's through there, if you need it?" I pointed to the door leading into my bedroom. "There's only one bed, or rather one mattress, I don't own a bed. But you can have it tonight. I'll manage on the floor in here."

Those pale green eyes turned to me again. "You're too nice, Jason…?" Her pitch asked for my surname.

"Macinlay."

"You've Irish blood?"

"Two generations ago. Dad's been back there once, kissed the Blarney Stone, driven the Ring of Kerry and stepped on the Giant's Causeway."

She smiled, but it was shallow. Yet I guessed she was doing her best to push aside the awkwardness of this too. "I have no reason to trust you, Jason Macinlay," she breathed, "but I do."

Again, I didn't know what to say. I just shrugged.

I'd left the bedroom door ajar; she pushed it wider and went through, her hand slipping off it, leaving a blood mark.

Fuck. "What did you do to your hand?" I was moving before I knew and she stopped and turned, but took a step away from me into the bedroom when I neared. "Don't tell me you had a go at your wrists, too…" I gripped her forearm.

She had nowhere to run to in my bedroom. You could barely swing a cat in it. There was about a foot of space all around the double mattress which lay on the floor.

I pulled up the sleeve of the sweatshirt I'd given her.

Her wrists were narrow. They looked so fucking breakable. But they weren't slashed. The blood had come from a jagged cut across her palm. It didn't look like it had been done by a knife, and the blood had begun congealing.

I glanced at her fingers. I'd heard people injected heroin beneath their fingernails to hide the marks. There were no marks on her arms, and there seemed to be none under her nails. It was probably safe to guess her problem wasn't heroin.

"How did you do it?" I'd been avoiding questions, I figured she wouldn't speak, but I couldn't help myself now. "What happened?"

She shrugged, letting my question slide away, as she'd been doing on the bridge. Her gaze, which had been looking at her hand too, lifted to me, but she said nothing.

I let her hand go. "Why don't you run a bath? You can talk when you want."

The cold had probably stopped her losing too much blood. "Don't get your hand in the water, though."

"What are you, a nurse?" There was that mocking pitch in her voice again.

"No, I work for a magazine."

"And from your voice, you don't like it?"

"Not at the moment, and I don't like the city either. I'm new to it."

"Well, I'm not. Maybe I can help you in return, then, seeing as you're helping me."

I didn't want to give her any expectations, we weren't friends. "You need to just get warm first."

She turned away.

Jason Macinlay wasn't like any man I'd known. He was considerate. I didn't know what to make of him. I'd met guys on the street before, but when they'd taken me back to their place, it hadn't been to get me out of the cold.

His place was minimalistic and his bedcovers were crumpled and thrown back. Yet he wasn't untidy. It just suggested he took life as he found it. Like he didn't need order.

I looked at the doors.

The first one I opened was a closet. It contained rough heaps of his clothing. The second was the bathroom.

I turned the water on and touched it with my bloody hand. A stinging pain burned in my palm. I must have left blood on the doors. I looked at the gash as blood dripped into the water. The warmth had made it bleed again. I saw the scarlet ribbons of blood spinning in the white porcelain sink back at Declan's.

I didn't want to think about how I'd cut it. I shut that out. I'd ended it. I was starting over. I had to find a job, find a life—somewhere to live.

I used the toilet as the water ran, and held the neck of Jason Macinlay's sweaty top up to my nose. The fresh male musky scent was ridiculously comforting. I breathed it in. There was something about him that made me feel safer than I'd felt in an entire year, or maybe longer. Nothing in his eyes had said he'd brought me back here because he wanted sex. He'd said he was *a nice guy*. Those words were still swimming around in my muddled head.

Was I going mad again? Had I really injured Declan? My eyes shut for a moment as images whisked through my brain and swept away. I couldn't grasp hold of them. I didn't want to. I just wanted to get away.

But I *had* got away. I'd gotten here. I had nowhere else to go.

I was suddenly very aware of the pace of my breathing. It felt too fast. I remembered seeing people breathing into paper bags when they hyperventilated and focused on breathing in the same way, trying to slow it down. I stripped off Jason Macinlay's top, then my t-shirt. Then I took off my sneakers and jeans.

I hadn't put on any underwear in my haste to get out.

I got into the water. It was really warm and the heat absorbed all my pain, physical and mental.

Pictures of the black water I'd seen beneath the bridge, swelling and rocking, played through my mind. I imagined it absorbing me, a great dark, thick, fluid weight.

It would be so much easier to slip beneath the water. I didn't have the courage or the strength to go on. How could I begin again?

A knock struck the bathroom door. Then it opened. Jason

Macinlay walked in.

"Shit, sorry… You should've shouted." His eyes skimmed over my body before he turned his back. He wasn't so saintly then.

I sat up, the water swilling around me. "It's just a body. You must've seen a hundred naked women." He was too good-looking to be inhibited, surely. He'd probably had tons of women in his bed.

"I brought your coffee."

"Yeah, I guessed."

He held it out, without turning. He felt awkward about me being here, I'd seen that the minute we'd got to his front door. I knew what it was like to sleep on the streets, though, and he was right, it was freezing. But what I'd said to him in the elevator was true. I trusted him. Probably more than I'd trusted any other guy—no one had given me their sweaty top before, when I was cold.

I took the cup from him, and put it on the lip of the tub. Blood dripped into the water. "My hand's bleeding." It was shaking too.

He looked across his shoulder, at my hand, nothing else. "I'll find something. I've got a first-aid kit. There should be a bandage in there." He went again.

The cocaine I'd taken with Declan was still spinning through my nerves and my heartbeat lifted my breasts a little as it thumped, while my damp hair brushed the skin on my back and shoulders. I had a sense of déjà-vu, though I could never have been here before. But it was like I was meant to come to this place.

I picked up the coffee with my left hand, my good hand, and sipped from it. Warmth ran into my blood. The cold had got deep inside me.

"I turned the heating up," Jason said, as he came back in. "Do you want to pull the shower curtain and just stick your hand out."

I looked up at him and met his deep brown gaze.

He had large eyes, strong features, and broad lips, and his dark brown hair was cut close to his head but it wasn't gelled.

He looked good. He'd probably broken a few girls' hearts back in Oregon.

I didn't bother with the shower curtain, I held out my hand as his gaze clung to my face, like he was trying desperately not to look down.

He needn't worry. I was used to being naked with men. My body was just flesh and bone. I knew he wanted to look down, all men wanted to look, it was in their nature. Well, unless it wasn't women they were into.

With a deep sigh his gaze fell to my hand as he gripped it. "Okay, I mixed boiled water with the antiseptic so it'll take a moment to cool."

He put the lid of the toilet down and sat on it, holding my hand and looking at the gash.

I couldn't imagine Declan ever doing anything like this. He'd have told me to fucking get on with it and stop moaning.

But I hadn't moaned had I? Jason Macinlay had seen the blood and asked about it. I shouldn't feel guilty then that he was helping. But I did. This was my own fault. *I* should be fixing it.

"It could need stitches."

"I'm not going to a hospital. I can't stand those places. I'll be fine."

I took my hand from his and he looked up, his gaze caught on my breasts then lifted.

See, a man, he couldn't help but look.

He met my gaze, and I knew he knew I'd seen him look. There was color in his cheeks. It made me want to laugh. He didn't look like he'd had that many women when he blushed, but he was gorgeous, surely he must have had a few.

His brown gaze held mine. "Okay, no hospital."

I gave him my hand again.

His touch was really gentle for a man. I bent up my knees in the tub and wrapped my other arm about them, watching him. He had some antiseptic in a cup and dunked cotton-wool pads into it, then wiped the blood from my hand, while he rested the back of it on his knee.

I couldn't remember anyone ever paying so much attention to one of my hurts. "Did your mom do this for you when you were a boy; is that how you learned to treat wounds?"

His brown eyes looked up and said he didn't appreciate the comment.

"Have you got a big family then, back in the hills?"

"The hills?" His eyebrows lifted, and then he answered in a dry tone. "Very funny… I didn't grow up in the middle of nowhere, you know. It's a small town, not a shack."

"With a small town society and small town views—"

"And moms who teach you how to clean a wound if you get injured… What's so bad about that?"

"Nothing…"

His brown eyes looked hard at me for a moment. But those eyes were easy to look at, and he had long dark, almost feminine, eyelashes.

"Right. So just let me get on with it, Rachel…" His gaze fell to my hand again, then after a moment he glanced back up. "Do you have a family somewhere?"

Yes, but not that I cared to speak of. I felt my lips compress.

His eyes hovered on mine for a moment, asking unspoken questions, before they dropped to look at my hand once more.

His touch was caring, as well as gentle.

He looked up and saw me watching, then smiled, suddenly. He had a nice smile too, a really open-hearted smile.

This was a genuine guy. Someone like Declan would eat him alive. "So you don't like your job?"

"I don't know. There's so much frigging office politics, I can't keep up with it. I think I need to be a bit more cutthroat, but I'm not that type. I can't be bothered with all the backstabbing, and I have an asshole for a boss. So I spent three years in college, and now I'm the office nobody."

Yeah, Declan would definitely eat him alive.

"Talk to me about it. I can teach you backstabbing…" I shouldn't have said that, the image and sound of the mirror splintering pierced my mind, and I felt the shard gripped in my hand as it sank into Declan's flesh.

I felt sick. I let my forehead drop onto my knees, while my hand still rested in Jason Macinlay's secure grip, and my arm hung outstretched to him. My other hugged my knees.

"Where do you come from, Rachel…?" he prodded a moment later, as though he was sweeping the previous topic under a rug and moving on.

His hesitation asked my last name, I'd give him that, but nothing more. "Shears. My name is Rachel Shears." I looked up again, as my lips compressed.

His brown eyes looked hard into mine, but he didn't push for more.

He looked down at my hand. "It's clean. I'll bandage it up."

When he let it go, I left my hand lying on his knee. His legs were parted and his sweatpants were loose, but his top was tight, it hugged his abs and the pectoral muscles of his chest as he leaned to the side and picked up a bandage from the first-aid box.

He was beautiful, but unlike Declan there seemed to be beauty inside him too, it wasn't just a surface thing. He was helping me.

I wanted to turn my hand and grip his thigh. But that would be the wrong thing to do. I knew that. But I was really good at doing wrong things.

Voices inside me encouraged me to do it. I didn't. The cocaine was still clouding my view.

He straightened and his fingers gripped the back of my hand more firmly. It sent tremors running up the nerves in my arm.

His other hand laid the bandage over my palm and his thumb pressed down on the dressing he'd used to cover my cut, securing it, then he began winding the bandage round my hand.

I shut my eyes.

His touch was doing stuff in my belly, making it clasp with need. I wanted sex. I hadn't wanted it with Declan anymore, but

I wanted it with Jason Macinlay. Sex was the best escape from the things going on in my head. It had never even really mattered who I did it with. I just liked it, and I'd always found a guy who'd give me a place to stay in return for it. They just generally weren't the right guys.

I'd never even liked Declan. And the feeling had been mutual. But we'd connected in bed. He liked things wild, and wild played to my crazy. God, had I really done that stuff with him? I needed something better now.

I opened my eyes and watched Jason Macinlay concentrating. He wound the bandage round and round, pulling it tight to stop the blood; watching what he was doing, not watching me.

I felt hot, and the tingle in my tummy slid to the point between my legs. I was sitting naked in a tub beside this guy. When had I decided to undress? I didn't know him. Really, my head was stupid.

Yes I did, he was Jason Macinlay, from Oregon, and he'd already given me more respect than Declan had done in the last year.

"How old are you?" I asked.

His brown eyes lifted and met my gaze again.

He was feeling more relaxed, I could tell, his breathing seemed more normal and his muscles less tense.

"Twenty-two. You?"

"Twenty-one."

"That's too young to want to end your life, Rachel Shears."

I shrugged, my lips compressing.

Of course he wanted to know why I'd been there, but I didn't want to talk and I couldn't remember half of it anyway. His eyes said, 'what happened?' I didn't answer.

He smiled, not his stunning smile of a few moments ago, but a closed lip smile that said, okay, so you don't wanna talk, I understand.

No one understood me. I'd learned that the hard way.

Mom would've said she did, when I was a kid. She didn't, and I hadn't even seen her in years. I didn't even know why I was thinking of her today. I hadn't thought of her in months. I hadn't spoken to her since I was fifteen.

Maybe I was thinking of her because I wished she'd been a proper mom and had taught me how to clean a wound like Jason Macinlay.

"Drink your coffee, and don't get that in the water." He stood up, letting my hand go.

I reached for the mug of coffee with my good hand. It was already lukewarm, like the water. I started to feel cold again, and shivered.

"Run some more hot water. I'll leave you to it."

He walked out then, and left me, shutting the door behind him.

I used my bandaged hand to turn the water on.

The bandage was neat and tight.

I lay back in the water, and let the heat seep into me. But it wasn't just the warmth of the water which was penetrating my body. I could fall for this guy, Jason Macinlay. That was another thing I was good at, jumping from one guy to another. It was what I did best.

~

"Hey,"

"Yeah, I know it's late. I'm sorry, I…"

I woke in bed, hearing Jason Macinlay whispering in the room next door.

He'd changed the covers on the mattress while I'd bathed. The sheet and duvet cover smelt fresh and felt crisp.

I'd rather he'd left the old sheets on, it would have felt more comforting. I'd missed his scent from his sweatshirt. He'd thrown that in the washer, too, like I'd marked it and he needed to wash me off it.

Declan must have washed all the blood off by now, mine and his. I was gone from his life. That poisonous relationship was over.

"Something happened, Lindy. I couldn't call earlier. But I'm calling now."

The door was shut between the bedroom and the living space.

"Yeah, I know."

I rolled over and listened more intently, I could even hear him breathing between the words.

He sounded defensive.

"Look…" The pitch of his voice dropped. "I found a girl on Manhattan Bridge, Lind. She was trying to jump. I couldn't just leave her."

There was silence for a moment as he breathed. I imagined this Lindy speaking at the other end.

"I brought her home."

Silence.

"Yeah, well, I didn't know what else to do."

"Lindy, leave it, she's no risk."

"I'll be fine."

"Yeah, honest, I'll take care. I can look out for myself."

"I know this is New York."

"Yeah, right."

"Look, I'm going to go. I don't want to wake her."

"She's sleeping in my bed. I'm sleeping on the floor."

"She won't."

"I won't."

"Look Lindy, I'll call you tomorrow, normal time. I'm going to go now, and don't worry."

"Yeah, I love you, too."

"Yeah, tomorrow." He sighed, like he had the weight of the world on his shoulders.

I needed a drink. I threw the covers back and got up, then knocked on the door leading back into the living space.

He didn't answer; he couldn't have heard, but I didn't like to just walk in. I knocked more loudly.

"Yeah?"

"You decent?"

He laughed. It was low and heavy. "Yeah."

I opened the door.

He was sitting on the floor, gilded by the moonlight streaming through a floor to ceiling window which lit his living room. His arms were about his knees as one hand still gripped his cell and his head was bent a little forward.

He looked defeated.

"Sorry." I didn't even know why I apologized, I just felt as if I was intruding.

"It's alright. Did I wake you? Sorry."

"I want some water." I moved to the kitchen counter and watched him as I ran it, waiting for it to run cool. He was wearing a loose t-shirt now, with boxers. His forearms and his shins were dusted with dark hair. I could see it even in the blue-black light in the room.

The clock on the TV flashed eleven-thirty. I didn't feel as though I'd get back to sleep, and my hand was hurting like hell now; it was throbbing with the beat of my heart.

"Is she your girlfriend?"

"Lindy? Yeah."

"She's back in Oregon?"

"Yeah."

"Bet she feels small town, now you've gone all big city."

"Ha. Ha." His pitch was dismissive. Life clearly wasn't all roses between them.

"I suppose you've been with her forever. What was she, the head of the cheerleaders while you captained the football team?"

"You think you know me so well, don't you..."

He *had* been captain of the football team.

I bet they were best looking girl and best looking boy in their year, and they'd gotten together because it was what everyone expected.

"I was the kid who sat in the corner and never had friends..."

I didn't know why I told him that, I just thought it might make him feel better.

"And now?"

My lips compressed.

Turning away, I opened a cupboard and found a glass. "Do you want a drink?"

"No thanks."

I filled the glass and drank, as again the images of the mirror breaking disturbed my thoughts.

I pushed the memory away. I was starting over and forgetting that.

I moved about the counter, and leaned back against it, facing him. "So what's wrong between you?"

"Tonight? You. She thinks you're going to either jump me in my sleep, or steal all my stuff, like I have anything worth stealing." His hand lifted and swept forward indicating the virtually empty room.

"She might be right, though?" I did feel like jumping him in his sleep. It would be a great way to escape the blackness which kept threatening to swamp me.

His gaze focused up at me as he scanned my face. "She could be right, yes…"

Well, he didn't know me, and I'd said nothing about myself, bar my name and my age. "She isn't. You're safe."

"Phew, thank fuck for that."

I laughed. He was a nice guy. There weren't many of those in the world. I wasn't used to them.

My eyes shifted to the white pillow on the hard floor behind him. Then I looked at him again.

"So anyway, seeing as I've promised not to jump you in your sleep, why don't you share the mattress? If you're safe, it seems silly you trying to sleep out here." I'd be good. He deserved for me to be good. He'd been kind to me.

He looked at me for a long moment. I didn't move, holding out against his assessment.

I wasn't blind. I knew he liked what he saw. I was wearing his t-shirt, my legs were bare, and I'd nothing on underneath. It would be so easy to be bad. His gaze ran up my legs and my body then came to my face. But he wasn't *that* sort of guy.

All men looked. It didn't mean all men let themselves touch.

"Yeah, okay, I won't get any sleep here anyway."

He picked up his pillow and stood, then lifted the pillow indicating for me to walk ahead.

I went into the bathroom, while he lay down on the mattress, under the covers.

When I came back in, he was watching me, one arm behind his head.

I said nothing, walked to the other side and got in.

He probably wouldn't mind if I jumped him, but he'd have a hell of a conscience the next day when he spoke to his Lindy.

I turned my back to him and felt him roll onto his stomach. My body was intensely aware of his, and all I could hear was his breathing as he drifted into sleep, while all I could smell was his shampoo, because he'd showered after I'd bathed.

This had been a weird day, I'd finally left Declan and within hours I'd acquired a stranger. My brain wasn't on the same page as where my life had gotten to. I'd walked out on the life of rich egotistical playboys, and into an opposite extreme.

An ex had once called me a parasite—maybe I was. But maybe I didn't want to be anymore.

www.ingramcontent.com/pod-product-compliance
Lightning Source LLC
Chambersburg PA
CBHW011114100726
47898CB00011B/3077